# The Fire in the Glass

# The Charismatics Series

*Explore the dark, mystical streets of Edwardian London with The Charismatics, a supernatural historical fantasy series full of deadly mystery and arcane powers.*

~

## *The Fire in the Glass*
*Book One of The Charismatics*
Books2Read.com/FireInTheGlassDigital

Lily's visions could stop a killer if she'll trust a
reclusive aristocrat with her darkest secret.

## *The Shadow of Water*
*Book Two of The Charismatics*
Books2Read.com/TheShadowOfWater

A dangerous prophecy threatens Edwardian London.
To stop it, Lily must uncover the truth behind
her mother's murder.

## *Bridge of Ash*
*Book Three of The Charismatics (Coming in 2021)*

When a ruthless man discovers their secret,
Lily and Strangford are faced with an impossible choice.

## *What the Ravens Sing*
*Book Four of The Charismatics (Coming in 2022)*

In the maelstrom of the Great War, only Lily can stop
an ancient and terrible charismatic ability from
tearing the world apart.

# *The* Fire in the Glass

THE CHARISMATICS

BOOK ONE

Jacquelyn Benson

VAUGHAN WOODS
PUBLISHING

Copyright © 2020 by Jacquelyn Benson
Cover design by Sara Argue of Sara Argue Design
Cover copyright © 2020 by Vaughan Woods Publishing
Typeset in Minion Pro and ALS Script by Cathie Plante

First edition: May 2020

Library of Congress Catalog Number: 2020901483
ISBN: 978-1-7345599-0-3

Published by Vaughan Woods Publishing
PO Box 882
Exeter, New Hampshire 03833 U.S.A.

Stay up-to-date on new book releases by subscribing to Jacquelyn's newsletter at JacquelynBenson.com.

**Content warnings for *The Fire in the Glass*:**
Contains alcohol use, drug use, absent parent, blood, graphic injuries, murder, abduction, medical procedures, needles, anti-Semitic/sexist remarks, violent fights. References to sexual assault, prostitution, eugenics, death of a parent.

*Prophecy is not an art, nor (when it is taken for prediction) a constant vocation, but an extraordinary and temporary employment from God, most often of good men, but sometimes also of the wicked.*

THOMAS HOBBES, *LEVIATHAN*

~

*Knowledge of the future is only a flowery trapping of the Tao. It is the beginning of folly.*

LAO TZU, *TAO TE CHING*
(TRANSLATION BY GIA-FU FENG AND JANE ENGLISH)

# ONE

*Hampstead Heath, London*
*February 16, 1914*

$\mathcal{L}$ILITH ALBRIGHT RATTLED ACROSS the heath on the back of her motorcycle, pushing for speed as though it were possible to outrun the inevitable.

Dark clouds scudded over the broad, open countryside, the brown fields broken by tumbled stone walls or hedges of twisted gorse. The wind was still sharp with the lingering bite of winter. It was hardly an ideal day for a ride, but Lily had not taken the green, mud-spattered Triumph out for a pleasure cruise.

It was an escape, and it was futile. What she was running from could not be outpaced. That was the trouble with the future.

~

It began early that morning with the washbasin.

She splashed the cold water over her face. Drops ran down the line of her jaw and fell into the enameled bowl, shattering the surface of the water into a thousand tiny ripples.

The ripples coursed across the shallow reflection of her features—her mother's infamous auburn hair, her father's sharp gray eyes.

Then the moving water transformed, shifting to become a whirlwind of light, spinning snow.

The blizzard obscured the uncomfortable familiarity of her face, devouring it in a veil of white that parted to reveal a new scene: the open door to her building on March Place in Bloomsbury.

Icy flakes spun around her, blowing in to dust the worn carpet.

Lily drifted inside.

Besides the snow on the floor, the hallway looked as it always did. The walls were papered in a rust-hued paisley, accented with a still life painting of a pair of oily pilchards resting next to a mug of flat ale. The air smelled vaguely of boiled nettles.

Light spilled down from the landing above, coming from the open door to the flat that sat directly beneath her own. These were the rooms where her neighbor, Estelle, lived with her companion, Miss Bard.

She rose to the landing and looked inside.

The living room was empty save for the dog on the rug. The animal was pale green and split precisely in half. It lay in a pile of ashes, looking up at Lily with sad eyes.

She moved past it, drawn toward the bedroom.

The air felt stuffy, crowded with some unseen presence. Estelle sat at her vanity, gazing into the mirror, her eyes locked on the closet behind her, the door of which sat ajar.

Inside, something moved.

It was a subtle shift of the shadows accompanied by a soft tinkling of glass like bottles dancing in a milkman's crate. The shifting gathered mass, took on speed, and rushed into the room. It swept toward them in a shape both like and unlike that of a man. It thrust forward a long silver weapon, thin and sharp as a fencer's sword. The glittering point met the skin of Estelle's arm and the mirror shattered, cracks spider-webbing from side to side.

In her seat at the vanity, Estelle tipped backwards. Her descent halted abruptly halfway to the floor. Suspended, her thin body swung from the chair and passed out of the room, heels dragging on the rug.

The snow came in, whirling with blinding intensity.

The storm passed and Lily was somewhere else, somewhere strange and wrapped in darkness.

The air smelled acrid, chemical. The walls around her were made of stacked glass, bottles and jars that caught and reflected the ghostly image of a flickering flame, then multiplied it in myriad dark, shimmering facets.

"Thief," said a voice from behind her, hoarse and thick with an unfamiliar accent.

It was Estelle. Lily turned to see her sitting on a flat wooden table, her face white and pale as death. She held a hand to her throat. Blood seeped through her fingers, staining the bright blue of her robe. Her eyes were wide, staring vacantly into the nothingness over Lily's shoulder.

Smoke curled around her feet, tendrils rising to embrace her.

"Murderer," she said, raising a long, trembling hand. She pointed into the shadows. "Alukah."

Estelle vanished, swallowed by the smoke and the darkness. The ground before Lily opened to reveal a pool of deep, dark water, its surface quaking as though disturbed by some sudden intrusion. She fell towards it, and then the dark water was at her feet, spilling across her bedroom floor from where the overturned washbasin spun slowly into stillness.

~

Lily fought a familiar cocktail of rage and grief as she opened the throttle of the Triumph, taking the motorcycle to its bone-shaking limit, her teeth clenched against the jars and jolts of the road. The brown expanse of the heath blurred into an afterthought.

For as long as she could remember, Lily had been plagued by glimpses of the future.

All manner of horrors paraded themselves across her mind. House fires promised to leave charred corpses in their wake. The bone of a neighbor's leg pointed its splintered end up through the flesh. Ships faltered in the icy waters of the North Sea.

For years, she tried to put the knowledge to use. She warned, begged, lied, and manipulated to steer events toward a different outcome. As a girl, she tripped orange sellers to keep them from stumbling into an oncoming lorry or stole travel vouchers from nightstands. She tormented dogs into taking a snap at her before they could inflict more irreversible damage on someone else.

To the rest of the world, it looked like the most rank disobedience. She went through nannies like handkerchiefs. Her mother's airy disinterest in discipline was the only thing that kept Lily from being regularly beaten.

Far worse than any punishment she did receive was the knowledge that her efforts meant nothing.

The fire she averted one day would come roaring through the next week. A bone saved from breaking would find another way to shatter. She would dash into the street to catch a cat no one else knew was about to be hit by an omnibus, only to see the same animal lying by the side of the road the next day, covered in flies.

She kept trying. She fought to win her lonely battle against fate despite the steely opposition of the nannies and the guilt, grief and gutting frustration—right up until the day her mother died.

Lily foresaw it in exquisite detail.

She used every tactic in her extensive repertoire to prevent it. For a brief moment, it looked as though she might actually succeed. Mad requests were made and acceded to. A few key personal items were successfully misplaced. Everything was in place for this future, finally, to turn out differently.

Until it didn't.

Lily finally accepted the truth. There would be no changing what she saw in her visions. It wasn't a gift or a responsibility. It was a curse, her own private torture.

Banished to a cold, gray finishing school for five withering years, she had tried to escape from that curse. Feeling a vision come over her, she attempted everything from pinches to reciting Milton or once, memorably, sticking a fork into an electrical outlet to short circuit the revelation.

None of it worked. She could not prevent the knowledge from coming to her. She could do nothing except try her damnedest to ignore it, then keep living despite the unavoidable, stabbing guilt, and the rage and frustration that threatened to burn her up from the inside out.

Most days, living was enough.

Then there were days like today.

She leaned into a turn, the motorcycle bouncing against a bump in the road. She gripped the handlebars, hands iron-tight, willing the Triumph into submission.

The profile of an old manor rose up beyond the sharp thorns of the hedge. The stone walls were stained with age, the windows fogged with years of dirt. Scaffolding ran along one long wing, tarps flapping in the icy breeze.

There were no other houses here. No cars or carriages cluttered the road. Only the dark figure of a lone horseman riding across the fields broke the isolation of the scene.

Estelle was going to die.

Estelle who made her living speaking to the dead, who loved gossip, turbans, and a particularly unctuous brand of Italian sweet vermouth. She was adept at catching Lily at the exact moment she was coming up the stairs, luring her into a glass or a chat or the whirlwind of some scandal or another.

It was not easy to make friends, living with knowledge that could never be shared. At any moment, Lily might discover that the people she had come to care for would be taken from her. Estelle had been the first one in a very long time to blow past her carefully laid defenses and find a way into her heart. Now some monster was going to make a ghost of her.

So Lily ran. She had run from the flat, grabbing her riding clothes and bolting out into the chill of the morning. She caught the tram to Highgate, on the outskirts of the sprawling expanse of London, and retrieved her Triumph from the garage. She rode it as though grief could be left behind by speed and distance.

Her tires devoured the deserted road, the chill biting at the exposed skin of her cheeks and neck. This was usually a miracle cure, a panacea for all manner of ills. The feeling of racing into the wind, of changing her course with a shift of her weight, must be the nearest thing in the world to flying. Lily could be plagued with frustrations, and an hour or two on the motorbike would leave her feeling peaceful as a monk.

Not this time.

Out in the fields, the horseman kicked into a gallop, flying across the open fields of grass and heather. Lily joined him, leaning low over the handlebars. The engine roared and shook beneath her, straining with what she demanded of it, but it couldn't push the image of Estelle's bloodstained form from her mind. It was impossible to outrun the feeling of her own powerlessness. All her reckless pace earned her were stiff muscles and a chapped nose.

Nothing changed. Nothing ever would.

Then a sharp crack splintered the stillness of the heath.

The Triumph lurched beneath her as a trail of flame blazed across her thigh. The engine skipped, squealed. Tires skidded against the dry dust of the road. The horizon shifted, rising up as the motorcycle tipped her toward the ground.

She hit the road hard and felt the bite of it tear at the thick wool covering her shoulder. The motorcycle spun, ripping from her legs and sliding across the packed earth. She rolled, finally coming to a stop on her back, arms spread, looking up at the wide gray expanse of the sky.

The clouds seemed to spin slowly above her.

Silence settled in, filling the space left behind by the roar of the Triumph's engine.

She closed her eyes, wondering vaguely just what part of her she might have broken.

A new sound rose, growing from soft to a rapid intensity. It was the pounding of hooves, falling quick and heavy enough that she could feel them through the earth at her back.

They clattered to a stop beside her.

"Hold, Beatrice," said a rich, masculine voice.

She opened her eyes.

Her unimpeded view of the sky was marred by the appearance of a man's face as he stood over her, dark eyes framed by wind-tousled hair.

There was something of the country preacher about him. It was in the sober cut of his thick black wool coat, the subtle signs of wear about his cuffs. A country preacher would have worn a collar. The man leaning over her lacked that as well as his hat and the top button of his shirt.

The neglected button left the white cloth open at the neck, revealing a triangle of pale skin dusted lightly with dark hair. Lily found it drawing more of her attention than it ought to. It did not help that he was posed against the backdrop of the windswept heath, a setting designed to make any reasonably-proportioned male look like a hero out of a Brontë novel.

"You're a woman," he exclaimed, crouching down beside her.

"Yes," Lily confirmed, wincing.

"You were riding that motorcycle."

"I was."

"What does that feel like?"

It was such an odd question that Lily glanced over at him, wondering if he was ridiculing her. His expression was open, curiosity apparently genuine.

"Rather sore at the moment," she replied flatly.

She moved to rise. A black-gloved hand pressed against her chest.

"You really ought not do that."

The accent gave him away. His rich voice was clipped into the posh tones of the upper class, sounding of Eton with a dash of Oxford. There was something else there as well, something warmer—a slight burr of the North.

A gentleman, despite his surprising lack of a hat.

Lily had little reason to like gentlemen.

"Would you please remove your hand?"

He pulled it back quickly.

"Sorry, but you might have broken something. A fall from a motorcycle cannot be much different than a fall from a horse."

"A motorcycle is much lower to the ground."

"It also moves faster. Have you any pain in your neck?"

Lily shook her head.

"Stop that," he ordered, looking alarmed. "What about the rest of you?"

"I have just crashed my motorcycle. It hurts in rather a lot of places at the moment."

"Wonderful," he announced. He seemed to mean it. "Try wiggling your fingers. Your toes?"

Lily obeyed impatiently.

"Does anything feel numb?"

"No."

"Headache?"

"Not yet."

"Move your limbs. Right arm first. Left? Now your right leg."

Lily obeyed mechanically and with barely concealed impatience.

"May I get up now?"

"You might want to take care of the bleeding before you do that."

Lily pushed herself into a seated position, feeling the ache of what would shortly be some significant bruising on her arms and chest. She looked down.

Her left thigh was covered in blood, surrounding a ragged tear in the heavy twill of her trousers.

"Blast," she swore.

She pulled at the tear for a better look.

She was aware of the man beside her, of the utter impropriety of revealing a pale sliver of her inner thigh in front of some well-bred stranger. She didn't care. His opinion of her could hardly amount to much given that he had come across her lying in the road.

The raw tear in her thigh continued to ooze blood, soaking her leg.

"It's just a scratch."

"It needs stitches," the gentleman countered.

"I'm sure that's not necessary."

"You are dripping blood onto the road."

He reached into his pocket and pulled out a bunch of black silk. He unwound the neat ball of it and Lily recognized the length of a cravat. He held out the neckcloth.

She hesitated.

"Go on," he encouraged.

"It will be stained."

"Then I have a further excuse not to wear it."

Lily gave in. She tugged off her driving gloves and took the stretch of dark fabric from him.

She circled her thigh with the silk twice, then tied it tightly, trying not to wince. She could see where the blood already soaked through the fabric, turning it a deeper shade of black.

Beside her, he stood.

"You'll need help getting up," he noted, something a bit tentative edging his tone.

"I suppose I do," Lily admitted.

There was the slightest hesitation before he extended a black-gloved hand.

The leather felt softer than she would have guessed, extraordinarily fine and well-worn. His grip was firm as he pulled, levering her to her feet.

The maneuver left them standing closer than was strictly polite. Lily noted that the stranger was of an even height with her own, his gaze meeting hers at roughly the same level, a feature that made his nearness feel even more unsettlingly intimate.

He quickly released her hand and stepped back.

"Thank you," Lily acknowledged.

He assessed the scene, his eyes moving to the great, rambling pile of the ruined manor on the hill. The canvas covering the scaffolding rippled with a gust of wind. It was the only activity to be seen. Though the place was obviously under construction of some sort, no hammer blows resounded from its walls and the drive was free of any lorry or carriage.

He glanced the other way, toward a small copse of woodland into which the road disappeared.

"There's a farmer's cottage about half a mile down the road," he noted. "You might be able to wait there while I fetch a physician."

Lily followed his gaze and could see the curl of smoke rising from the far side of the trees.

She considered her options.

The Triumph lay on its side, having slid halfway into a gorse hedge. The drive chain was snapped, which explained the wound in her thigh—it had whipped out as it broke, tearing through twill and skin. The motorcycle was useless until she could replace the part.

She knew her resistance to accepting this gentleman's assistance was entirely unfair. It was born of her reaction to that well-heeled accent.

Someone else was responsible for that prejudice, not the man in front of her. If she insisted on refusing his help, she would be left with wheeling the Triumph back to Highgate, hobbling the whole way on her wounded leg—which she was forced to admit likely did need a few stitches.

It was already mid-afternoon. She wouldn't make it to the village before dark.

"Fine," she agreed.

The gentleman whistled, the tone clear and lilting. His horse trotted over.

"Can you mount?"

"I think I can manage."

He guided the horse beside her and held the stirrup in place as she fitted it onto the boot of her good leg. She took hold of the pummel, pushed against the stirrup, and hefted herself toward the saddle.

She felt her balance shift at the last moment. The stranger's hand shot out and caught her waist, steadying her. He pulled it back as soon as she was in place.

"Are you settled?"

"Yes. Thank you," she replied.

"Slow and steady, Beatrice," he said, stroking the horse's neck as he took the reins. He lead the animal down the road at a pace sedate enough for a child on a pony.

She was aware of the incongruity of it, this well-bred gentleman parading her down the deserted road across the heath like some battered knight leading his princess home after rescuing her from the dragon.

"Isn't this a gelding?" Lily asked.

"Yes."

"Then why did you name him Beatrice?"

"I didn't."

"Then who did?"

"Virginia. My sister. She's very fond of Shakespeare."

"Why not Henry? Or Hamlet?"

"He doesn't seem like much of a Hamlet," he countered.

Lily didn't press the point. There was nothing to be gained from it. He had been courteous enough to stop and assist her. Admittedly, he didn't seem to conform to the type of his class. His curiosity was too open, his suit too unfashionable. Still, she did not need or want anything more from him.

They passed through the dark little wood, the bare branches of the trees forming a woven canopy overhead. The road turned and Lily glimpsed the farm her knight had described. It was small, just a low cottage, freshly white-washed, and a few scattered outbuildings. A muddy pony grazed in the back field, a scattering of chickens pecking in the yard.

The door opened as they approached, two small boys exploding out of it to run screeching down the drive. A stout female figure of middle age appeared after them.

"Walter, keep Reggie out of the chickens. He'll scare them up the roof again. Oh!" she exclaimed, catching sight of the strangers at her gate. "Good afternoon, then."

"Apologies for disturbing you, madam. I am Lord Strangford."

*Lord Strangford.*

The sound of the title crawled up her skin.

A nobleman. That was something even worse than a gentleman.

"My companion Miss . . ." He paused, looking up at Lily. "Miss?"

"Albright."

"Miss Albright is in need of a physician. Might she rest here while I fetch a doctor to see to her? I assume there is a someone in the village."

"That old sot?" The woman snorted. "He'll like as not be tipsy as a sailor by this time of afternoon. No, you'd best leave her to Edna Sprout. I've five lads under the age of fifteen. I've seen more wounds than a military surgeon and I've a finer hand with a stitch than any doctor. It's not as though doctors spend their evenings mending torn socks and trousers so you'd never know they had holes in them."

"Really, I should insist—"

"That will be fine," Lily cut in.

It was a petty attempt to thwart his will, which she had no indication was directed at anything other than seeing that she was properly cared for. Fairly or not, she was annoyed at him for being what he was, so any victory felt worthwhile.

"Could you help her into the kitchen, your lordship? Mr. Sprout could do it but he's been mucking the stalls. I wouldn't subject a lady to him till he's had his bath."

"Right. Yes. Of course," he bit out, a touch awkward.

"Come along, then," Mrs. Sprout ordered, heading into the house without looking back.

Lily made a quick protest.

"Is that really necessary?"

"It's possible I might be able to fit Beatrice through the door but I am not certain your physician would appreciate it."

He appeared to be seriously considering it, as though it were a possible solution to some unspoken problem.

"She said she has five boys. The horse would likely be an improvement."

A smile twitched at the corner of his lip. Her own itched to mirror it. She resisted.

He was a nobleman.

"Probably best if we just walk in."

"Let me help you down."

He set his gloved hands on her waist. Lily let herself slide forward off the saddle. He caught her, his grip steady, and guided her gently back to the ground.

He looked at her uncertainly.

"I'm not sure I can carry you."

The notion of him attempting it struck a chord of alarm through her. The last thing she needed in her day was to be carried across the heath by an aristocrat with seemingly heroic intentions and a missing top button.

"I was thinking we might hobble," Lily countered.

"Excellent suggestion."

He looked at her as though unsure where to begin.

"Perhaps if I put my arm over your shoulder to take the weight off my leg."

"Right. Of course."

He took a step closer and Lily set her arm across his shoulders.

"Shall we?" he offered.

They started forward. Lily bit back a curse. He stopped.

"You have to let me take your weight on the off-step."

"Right," Lily breathed. "Perhaps if you put your arm around my . . ."

"Your waist. Yes. That would be sensible."

His arm came around her. They took another few steps, finding a rhythm that avoided jarring Lily's leg.

"I was better at this when I was ten," he noted, a touch short of breath.

"Serving as a crutch?"

"Three-legged racing."

"What's a three-legged race?"

He stopped, surprised.

"You don't know?"

Lily shook her head.

"It's . . . this, more or less. But without the bleeding." He considered. "Perhaps that's not entirely accurate. I remember a fair bit of blood. You really never played it?"

"No," Lily replied shortly.

They reached the threshold. Lord Strangford helped her hop up into the dark interior of the house. He released her at the table, which Mrs. Sprout had cleared of everything but a basin and a pile of clean towels.

"How may I help?" he asked.

"It's only the thirteenth time I've set a needle to flesh and this one is less likely to wriggle than my usual patients. I think I can manage it just fine on my own."

"Then I'll see if Mr. Sprout will allow the use of his cart to retrieve the lady's motorcycle."

He bowed out through the low doorway.

Lily waited for Mrs. Sprout to comment on the oddity of a woman riding a motorcycle, but something far more intriguing had captured the housewife's attention.

"How lovely for you to have a lord carrying you about," Mrs. Sprout exclaimed as she took a solid black kettle from the stove and poured the steaming water into the basin on the table. "And a fair specimen of one too, if I'm any judge of it." She dipped a clean cloth in the water, wringing it out with calloused hands. "How long have you been courting?"

"We're not courting."

She winced as Mrs. Sprout pressed the hot cloth against her flesh. The wound fired in protest, pain flaring. The housewife wiped at the gash and Lily saw the blood, which was already drying and sticky, come away.

"You ought to see to that," the older woman countered. Lily knew she was not speaking about the wound.

A pair of boys came dashing into the room, whirling around like a maelstrom before zipping back out the door.

"Walter, mind the chickens. And find Reggie his trousers!" Mrs. Sprout shouted.

The evidence of family life was scattered through the cozy space around her. A wooden duck was toppled on the ground in front of the fireplace. Abandoned cups of milk were scattered here and there. A stray shoe laid in the center of the floor, laces still tied. She could hear voices from the yard, the high squeal of a child's laughter.

The noise and warmth and comfort—all of it was foreign to her, as strange as a country she had only rarely visited, never known.

The truth of that cut at her, a pain worse and more lasting than the wound on her leg.

Mrs. Sprout returned to the table with a bottle of carbolic and a well-thumbed newspaper. She handed the latter to Lily.

"Best have something to distract yourself for this part."

Lily hissed as the acid hit the wound, the burn of it shooting pain through her flesh.

The woman glanced over at her approvingly as she threaded her needle.

"Any one of my boys would have been howling." She doused the thread and instrument with more carbolic, then turned to Lily's wound. "This'll pinch," she warned.

Lily obediently lifted the paper and tried to lose herself in it, gritting her teeth as the needle was deftly applied to her wound.

It was one of the tabloids, printed on cheap, thin newsprint, covered in block-cut illustrations of all manner of horrors—arms being severed in sawmills, men crushed on docks. There were train wrecks in Afghanistan rife with bloodied heads and shattered limbs. Another story luridly described a massive, hairy beast reportedly seen in the wilderness of British Colombia.

None of that pulled Lily's attention from the prick of the needle against her flesh—until she turned the page.

*Spiritualist Vampire Claims Another Victim*, ran the headline.

The words raised the hairs on her arm.

The story was simple, an update on a case the paper had apparently been following for some time.

Three women had so far succumbed to what the paper described as "a cruel, violent demise". All of them went to sleep in the evening as usual only to be found in the morning dead in their beds.

Their bodies were drained of blood, the only mark found on them a small puncture at the throat. All the doors and windows were locked with no sign of any intrusion.

All three had made their living as mediums, speaking to the dead.

"That's a real horror, that one," Mrs. Sprout remarked, peering over the edge of the paper as she tugged at another stitch. "Right gave me chills. Of course, the police aren't saying it's a vampire. But you tell me what else could slip into a house all locked up tight and make off with a person's blood like that?"

Dead mediums. A puncture in the neck.

The images forced themselves back into Lily's mind, sharp and clear.

Snow piling against the pavement. The mirror cracking. The shadow, a blur of force and movement, rushing forward.

Estelle, pale as a ghost, with her bloodstained hand pressed to her throat.

*Thief. Murderer. Alukah.*

The coincidence was too powerful to dismiss. Lily knew in her bones that the murderer in the paper was the same monster that would come for her friend. It was not some ill chance Lily had foreseen but the act of a calculating killer, a single fiend who had done this before and would do it again.

*Unless . . .*

"There," Mrs. Sprout said, the thread in Lily's thigh tugging as she pulled tight her knot. "Just four of them. The rest of it will heal right enough as it is, or I'm not Edna Sprout."

"How is she?"

Lord Strangford stood in the doorway, the fading light of the afternoon spilling across his shoulders.

"I'm just putting on a fresh bandage," Mrs. Sprout announced.

"The motorcycle has been collected. I'm afraid it's in no condition to use. Mr. Sprout has kindly offered to take you wherever you need to go in his cart, but if you would prefer something more comfortable, I could ride back to the village and secure a carriage."

"That won't be necessary," Lily cut in quickly. "I'm sure the cart will do nicely."

"We're all settled here, unless you'd like me to try to mend these trousers," Mrs. Sprout asked.

"You needn't bother. They're quite spoiled, I'm afraid."

"What, with a bit of blood? That's no trouble. Just needs spit."

"Sorry?" Lily asked.

"Spit. Old seamstress's trick. I learned it from my godmother. Cover the whole stain with spit, then launder it in hot water with a bit of soda. Though mind, it has to be the spit of whoever did the bleeding. Won't work otherwise. Does the job like a charm, every time. Trust me, I've had plenty of reason to put it to the test."

Lily felt very aware of Lord Strangford's presence beside her, the stains of her blood marking the fine wool of his trousers thanks to their hobble up to the cottage door.

Should she offer to spit on them for him?

She stayed quiet.

"If you'll help her back out again, m'lord," Mrs. Sprout ordered.

"Of course."

"I can manage it," Lily protested.

"You will accept the gentleman's assistance," the housewife retorted. "I do not like to see my handiwork spoiled."

Lily wondered how much of the woman's intervention had to do with the stitches and how much lay in her obvious interest in playing matchmaker.

The wound throbbed.

She slid her legs from the table, feeling the tug of the thread against the skin of her thigh, and levered herself upright.

Lord Strangford placed his arm around her waist again. Lily let him take the greater part of her weight. They limped together into the yard, which was looking a bit less rough-around-the-edges thanks to the golden cast of the late afternoon light.

Mr. Sprout tipped his hat to her as they emerged. His face was kind, his rubber boots covered in manure.

"Set her in the back on the horse blankets," Mrs. Sprout ordered. "You're not to put another ounce of weight on that leg for the rest of the day. Longer if you can manage it, though lord knows my boys are up and dashing about on their stitches within the hour, however I try to keep them still."

Her rescuer stopped at the cart. He released her and Lily sat down on the open tailgate. She pushed herself back into the nest of blankets, which smelled warmly of dry straw and horse.

Mrs. Sprout leaned over the rail and patted Lily on the shoulder. "It was a pleasure to tend to a nice young miss for a change instead of a howling wee devil."

"Thank you. Most sincerely." She looked to the hatless aristocrat standing at the foot of the horse cart. "You as well, my lord."

"Beatrice and I will follow you into town and see that you're settled."

"That isn't necessary." Lily's reply was a touch quicker than was strictly polite. She saw Mrs. Sprout's eyebrow go up.

"I see," Lord Strangford replied. A guarded note had come into his tone and Lily knew that her reaction had not gone unnoticed. "If you're certain."

She acknowledged that the set-down wasn't entirely deserved. He had been nothing but helpful. It wasn't his fault he was an aristocrat.

"I'm sure Mr. Sprout is quite capable of looking after me. You have done more than enough already."

"Then I wish you good evening."

He bowed. It was elegant, without a hint of irony, the sort of bow that ladies in a ducal drawing room would find entirely acceptable. It was not a gesture a bedraggled woman in ripped trousers had any reason to expect as she reclined in the back of a farmer's cart.

It didn't matter, she reminded herself firmly.

Mr. Sprout snapped the reins and Lily's conveyance rumbled into motion.

*Spiritualist Vampire Claims Another Victim.*

Just beyond the broad, empty stretch of the heath lay the sprawling, teeming expanse of London—her home. Somewhere inside its maze of streets and alleys, a murderer waited.

One murderer. One threat. A threat that could potentially be identified, captured, and brought to justice.

There would be no other monster to rise up and take its place. Not for a crime like this. If she could eliminate the threat, she stopped the future horror from coming to pass.

The equation was unimpeachable. It also begged a desperately uncomfortable question.

Should she try?

She was not a police inspector. She had no knowledge of tracking murderers to their lairs. But if there was even the slimmest chance that she might find the killer before he got to Estelle . . .

The vision had taken place in the snow. It was more than halfway through February. Winter was nearly done. She might have months to accomplish it, the better part of a year.

Or perhaps it was only a matter of days.

Did she dare take that terrible chance again and risk all the guilt and grief that failure might entail?

The cart turned from the drive, rumbling toward the village of Highgate. Gazing back, she watched Lord Strangford swing up onto his incongruously named horse. He took the reins in his gloved hands, as natural in his seat as a centaur, then rode away.

At the gate, Edna Sprout watched both of them go, hands on her hips, and shook her head slowly.

Lily knew now what that strange emotion was, the one that started to rise as she read the article in that battered newspaper. It was a feeling far more uncomfortable than the wound in her thigh or the rage that had sent her racing out onto the heath.

Hope.

# TWO

*N*IGHT WAS FALLING.

Lights flickered on in the windows of the tall brick facades that lined March Place, the quiet, respectable little street in Bloomsbury where Lily rented rooms.

The pavement was busy with men returning home from work, dressed in sober suits and carrying briefcases. Children played in the small, tidy front gardens, the sound of their laughter ringing off the close-packed townhouses.

Lily was wearing a skirt, blouse and jacket, her hair maintaining a semblance of being pinned into place. She had accomplished the latter without a mirror in the shadows of the rented bay in Highgate where she stored her Triumph, and where the proprietor, Mr. Plunkett, would do the necessary work to make the motorcycle usable again.

There were still abrasions on her cheek and chin. She was fairly certain a large bruise was forming on her forehead. The net effect was rather less than respectable, though the denizens of March Place were too carefully polite to do more than cast her a quick, sideways glance before continuing on their way.

She was exhausted. The stitches in her thigh throbbed, burning as though someone had put a brand to her. The sensation stood out against the increasing chill of the evening. The brief warmth of the day had faded with the sun and sharp gusts of a cold, still-wintery wind cut through the tweed of her coat.

At Number 702, a lamp flared to life in the first-floor window—Estelle's window. She was home. The sight of it sparked another quick pain, a sharp stab of guilt.

She had come to her senses on the long ride back to London.

The tram from Highgate was packed. Lily was far too stubborn to admit she needed a seat, so she had stood the whole ride from the heath to the city, then limped into Bloomsbury from her stop on Tottenham Court Road. It had meant the novelty of using her walking stick—a straight staff of yew topped with a brass globe—for the purpose it was ostensibly intended.

Her usual reasons for carrying it were decidedly other than supporting a lame leg. They dated back to her sixteenth birthday, when she was cornered in a dark space by a man who thought to help himself to something she had no desire to offer him.

It was shortly after she ran away from school. She was working in a theatre, scraping a living by sweeping sawdust from the wings or sanding the paint from old set pieces. A pair of builders came by as Lily clawed and fought. Though they did nothing to intervene, the distraction they provided was sufficient to allow Lily to twist out of the rotter's grip and get away.

The next day, she approached the company's rigger, Bay. Like many riggers, Bay had once been a sailor. Like many sailors, he was also foreigner, his particular place of origin being the East Indies.

During the late hours of the night, long after the rest of the cast and crew had departed for their homes or their pubs, Lily had seen Bay on the empty stage acting out a graceful and brutal warfare against some invisible opponent.

"Will you teach me how to fight?" she asked.

His eyes flickered to the bruises on her face.

That night, as she swept the dust from the stage, Bay dropped a long, straight stick at her feet.

"Use this," he informed her. "It is better for you than a knife. Harder for you to stab yourself with it."

He called the art kali. Over the course of the next year, Lily received lessons in how to defend herself and the sailor gained an opponent to practice against. By the time he left for a better-paying job with an electrical firm, Lily was quite capable of disabling the average lecher with nothing more than four feet of stout wood.

She had chosen the yew staff from a prop box in the attic because it was both light and flexible. She could wield it more nimbly than some heavy block of oak and it was flexible enough that it did not break when it came up against an immovable object.

In the tram, the stick served to take the weight off her wounded leg as she stood crammed between bricklayers reading newspapers, a woman with a dachshund on her lap, and three unruly boys.

As the wound flared with every jolt of the car, Lily had admitted the truth. She did not know how to catch a murderer. If the police, who were trained to do this and had all the resources they could ask for at their disposal, were unable to find the monster who was killing London's mediums, how could Lily possibly presume to do better?

It didn't matter that the threat to Estelle rested in a single person. Lily was not capable of finding him. She admitted how foolish she had been to even consider it. It was another dead end, just as it had always been before—another example of how her ability to glimpse the future was only a freakish anomaly that would never be anything but painful.

Standing at the edge of a stream of evening commuters passing in front of her building, she felt the tiredness sink into her bones. She wanted to crawl into her bed, pull the blankets over her head and shut the world out.

She stepped forward, weaving through an opening in the flow of wool-clad bodies to mount the front steps.

In the hall, paisley wallpaper, faded with age, complemented her landlady Mrs. Bramble's choice of decor—the oil painting with the off-looking pilchards mounted alongside a photograph of kittens having a tea party, wearing costumes and standing in poses no live kitten would possibly submit to. The smell of Mrs. Bramble's signature nettle pudding permeated the air, leaving Lily both starving and glad that she had missed dinner. She could hear dishes clanging in the kitchen, the sound of the stout woman clearing up.

She forced her feet up the stairs. As she climbed she watched for Cat, an enormous orange beast who did not belong to anyone in the house but was impossible to eradicate. Cat had a penchant for sleeping in places designed to endanger the lives of unsuspecting passers-by. This included the more shadowy parts of the stairwell.

Her path was Cat-free but felt longer than usual. She paused on the first-floor landing outside the door to Estelle's rooms. She felt a sharp urge to slip inside, fall onto Estelle's purple jacquard settee, and let herself simply exist as Estelle buzzed about the room.

How could she, knowing what waited for Estelle around the turn of some unknown—but limited—quantity of days? She did not have the energy to pretend that all was well. It wasn't.

She moved on until, two paces up from Estelle's door, the stair beneath her foot gave off an alarming squeal.

It should not have been a surprise. There was always a stair that screamed beneath her foot as she climbed to her flat on the second floor. Yet Lily could have sworn it was usually three steps further on, or perhaps back on the floor below. Maybe it simply moved about on a whim to spite her.

The door behind her flew open. Estelle's head emerged, covered—as it generally was—in an elaborate silk turban fastened with a glittering paste brooch.

"Lily! Thank god you're here. Come in for a moment. I'm in desperate need of a fresher set of eyes."

She disappeared back into the flat without waiting for an answer, clearly expecting Lily to comply.

The only alternative was to ignore her and retreat to her room, a move sure to draw even more of Estelle's notice. The far more sensible choice was to play along for a little while until she could make a plausible excuse to escape.

Scraping together her remaining resources, Lily turned back, limped down the two steps, and entered the drawing room.

It was an eclectic space.

Every surface was augmented with decorative pieces. A stuffed cockatoo perched on the branch of a ficus. A candelabra in the shape of a three-masted schooner rested on top of the bookcase. The lamps were pink ceramic with lace-fringed shades, the curtains a forest green velvet. There were other more unusual artifacts scattered among the bric-a-brac. An enormous straw goat head stared out from beside the coat rack. The stone carving of some old god, framed with vines, was mounted on the wall between a photograph of someone's great aunt and a painting of a pig in a dress carrying a bunch of pussy willows. The goat head and the god belonged to Estelle's companion and flatmate, Miss Gwendolyn Bard. Miss Bard was a renowned scholar of folklore, publishing under the pseudonym of G.W. Bard. Only a select few knew that the illustrious Bard was not, in fact, a gray-bearded gentleman but rather a plump, pretty woman of middle years with a delightful laugh.

Miss Bard acquired pieces like the straw goat from villages across England to help her with her studies, but Estelle insisted on plucking items she deemed "less gruesome" and incorporating them into her unique sense of decor.

Estelle was just as eccentric as the drawing room. She was tall and willowy, with graceful lines of age marking her face. She wore a flowing silk caftan in a bold peacock print, and gilded bobs dangled from her ears. She held up a large green vessel, executed in Chinese style. The handles took the form of curling dragons and the lid appeared to be crafted in the shape of a crouching Shih Tzu.

"I'm looking for the right spot for my latest objet d'arte and I'm simply at a loss. I thought it might fit on the mantle next to the shepherdesses, but there are too many of them—I haven't another square inch up there. It would look marvelous on the plinth, but then where do I put the cupid?"

Lily set her stick in the stand by the door and glanced over at the plaster cherub in question, who was balanced with surprising grace on a single pudgy leg atop a fat marble column.

"Where's Miss Bard?" she asked.

"Gwen? She's at a lecture on Celtic solar deities. Or maybe it was a ladies' suffrage bake sale? I can never keep track. And anyway, she's no use for this sort of thing. She just keeps rattling on about how the dragons ought to have legs."

"What is it?" Lily asked.

"An urn, darling."

"A funerary urn? Is there anyone inside?"

Estelle plucked off the lid, peered in, and plopped the Shih Tzu back into place.

"No." She looked up at Lily and frowned. "What happened to your face?"

"It's nothing," Lily replied quickly.

Estelle popped the urn onto the seat of a worn, mustard yellow armchair. She took Lily by the arm and tugged her closer to the lace-fringed lamp.

"It looks like you took sandpaper to your chin. And that bruise! You had an accident with that contraption of yours, didn't you? How many times do I have to tell you, it's a death trap—though admittedly very exciting. Sit down. How could you let me keep rattling on about the decor when you're suffering from the aftereffects of a road accident?"

Estelle pushed Lily onto the purple settee, then lifted her feet and set them on the matching ottoman. She turned to the bar, splashing something into a crystal sherry glass. She extended it to Lily.

"Drink this."

"I'm fine, really."

"It's a restorative. Drink it."

"Is it the vermouth?"

Estelle had an inexplicable preference for a particularly vile brand of Italian vermouth, one that tasted like over-sugared cough syrup.

"No. Why? Do you want some vermouth?"

Lily sniffed the glass. It smelled like brandy.

"No, thank you. This is fine."

Estelle filled her own glass with the vermouth, then plopped down next to Lily on the settee.

"So what happened?"

"Nothing. It was an accident."

"Was anyone killed?"

"No. It wasn't a collision. The drive chain broke and I fell. That's all."

"Hmmm. You're sure there wasn't a man involved?"

Lily nearly choked on her brandy. The image of Lord Strangford rushed into her mind—the feel of dark-gloved hands on her waist as he helped her off his horse. She controlled the reaction, knowing Estelle fully capable of picking up on any sign of discomfort she might show.

"What makes you think there was a man involved?" she replied casually.

Estelle fluttered her long fingers.

"Just a little voice whispering in my ear."

Lily knew what she was implying. Estelle had a habit of casually referencing the departed in her conversations. Lily tried to view it as just another bit of charming eccentricity.

Lily had never seen any evidence that the claims of mediums like Estelle were true. On the contrary, during her theatre days she had known a stage magician with a particular dislike for spiritualism who made a point of unveiling the various tricks London's psychics used to convince those attending their séances of their legitimacy.

She couldn't believe that Estelle was a deliberate fraud, but her friend had a remarkably sharp sense of intuition and an almost preternatural talent for collecting gossip. Perhaps she took those things for something more, interpreting the insights they gave her as something otherworldly.

"The Triumph threw a chain, and I fell. That's all," Lily asserted.

"If you say so."

A silence followed. Both women sipped their liquor. Lily was left with the distinct feeling that Estelle knew perfectly well she was hiding something but allowed the matter to rest because she was entirely confident she would—eventually—wrangle the truth out of her.

It would have been a plausible confidence. Estelle was a master at getting things out of people. Lily was equally skilled at keeping secrets—like the one she currently carried inside of her, of what waited for Estelle after the next snow.

If anyone in the room was a fraud, it was Lily, she thought guiltily. Here she sat, quietly drinking her brandy, knowing full well that a horrible threat was closing in on the woman beside her . . . and doing absolutely nothing about it.

There was nothing she *could* do, she reminded herself forcefully. She had been down this road before, more times than she could count. It was always the same. The only difference here was that she usually didn't have to sit and gossip with the people she knew were about to fall victim to horrors she had foreseen.

Pretending nothing was wrong was hard. It made her miserable, far more so than the throbbing pain in her thigh or the ache in her bruised ribs.

She emptied her glass, then set it down on the table.

"Thank you for the brandy, but I really ought to be—"

She was cut off by the sound of a sharp rap on the door. She glanced over at it.

"Don't mind that. It's just Agnes," Estelle said, waving a hand dismissively.

"Are you just going to leave her out there?"

"Out where?"

"On the landing."

"There's no one on the landing."

"What about Agnes?"

"Agnes?"

"The one you said just knocked."

"Oh! Agnes isn't on the landing, darling. Agnes is dead."

Estelle reached a long arm back and plucked her vermouth bottle from the bar. She filled her glass, then set the bottle on the coffee table.

"She's been knocking about the place since last Thursday. Gwen keeps threatening to call a plumber. She thinks it's air in the pipes, if she notices it at all. You know how she gets when she has her nose in a book."

A gust of wind hit the house, rattling the panes of the windows. Of course, the knock at the door must have been the bones of the house protesting against a gusty winter evening.

Estelle went on.

"She's a bit of a nuisance, but I can't bring myself to tell her to move along. I mean, the poor thing has been through enough, being murdered in her sleep. One can hardly blame her for being a mite restless."

"Oh. She was murdered, was she?" Lily asked casually.

"Mmm-hmm," Estelle answered through her vermouth. "You might have heard about it. It's been all over the newspaper."

Lily's attention sharpened.

"Which paper is that?"

"Any of them that matter. 'Spiritualist drained of blood in her sleep.' It's been quite sensational. Really, darling, you must get out a bit more."

Dora Heller, Agnes McKenney, Sylvia Durst—those were the three victims named in the article Lily read earlier that afternoon.

*It's just Agnes.*

Estelle possessed a wild imagination. She also poured through several newspapers daily, culling gossip from the society columns. She must have read the same story as Lily and convinced herself that she was communicating with one of the victims.

"You're talking about the vampire," Lily asked carefully.

Estelle snorted.

"There's no such thing as vampires."

"I read that this killer was targeting mediums," Lily said slowly, keeping her tone casual.

"Yes, that seems to be the rub of it."

"You haven't started advertising again, have you?"

Estelle held séances twice a week, on Wednesdays and Saturdays. They were open to the public and served as the primary means by which she recruited customers for her real source of income—private sessions with individual clients. A few months ago, sheer word of mouth had made these events so busy, and Estelle's consultation schedule so full, that she had withdrawn her advertisements.

Estelle sipped her vermouth.

"Why do you ask?"

"Well, if there's a murderer out there targeting mediums, perhaps now would not be the time to put your name in the papers. You never know how he's choosing his victims."

"Or she."

"She?"

"It could be a woman, couldn't it?"

Lily was momentarily taken aback. She thought back to the vision, the shadow rushing forward from the darkness over Estelle's shoulder. It had been formless, featureless, and yet something about it had felt distinctly masculine to her, so much so that she had never even questioned it.

Not that she was about to admit any of that.

"Well, yes. I suppose it could be."

"Lord knows Agnes herself hasn't been very helpful with settling the question," Estelle complained.

"Oh?" Lily asked, picking up her empty glass and twirling it between her fingers.

Estelle sighed. "Every time I ask her about it—who was it that did you in, Agnes?—she just shows me a lamp."

"A lamp?"

"A lamp," Estelle confirmed.

"What sort of lamp?" Lily asked, mainly because she was not at all sure what else she could say.

"Built-in gas fixture," Estelle replied unhesitatingly. She picked up the vermouth bottle and tipped some into the glass Lily was still holding between her fingers. "She's dreadfully confused. It's hardly surprising, given what she's been through."

Lily looked at the brimming glass of unctuous liquor and realized she had no choice but to find a way to swallow it.

She took a sip—a large one. That got it down faster.

"I'm only saying that perhaps you ought to take some precautions," she went on, once her throat had cleared enough to speak again.

"Oh?" Estelle asked carefully.

Lily could hear the sharp interest in her tone and knew she was treading closer to dangerous waters.

She could navigate this. She would go just a touch further—hardly anything beyond what any sensible person might say, under the circumstances.

"What I mean to say is, if there's a killer out there somewhere stalking mediums, perhaps you ought to keep a low profile for a while. Check the windows are locked. Avoid hanging about the house on your own."

"I see," Estelle replied evenly.

Three sharp raps resounded through the room. They came from the ceiling, above which was Lily's empty flat.

The wind battered at the house again and the coals shifted in the hearth.

"I can't help but wonder," Estelle began, twirling the delicate stem of her glass.

"About the murders?"

"About you," she replied.

An alarm sounded in Lily's mind. She hid the tension by sipping the vermouth.

"I'm hardly anything worth wondering over," she replied, her voice just a touch hoarse from the liquor.

Estelle set down her drink.

"I think we should play a game," she announced.

Lily's sense of danger increased.

"I would love to, but it's been a terribly long day—"

"Oh, it won't take very long. It's just a little parlor amusement. You ask me a question and I tell you the truth. Then I do the same to you," Estelle went on, ignoring her protest.

There was no way out of it, short of rudely standing and saying goodnight—a maneuver sure to only increase Estelle's interest. The prudent course of action was to brush it all off as a whim, play along, and then make her escape.

"Fine. If you insist. But then I really must be off to bed before I become too stiff to move. What would you like to know?"

"No. You first. Ask me a question."

Lily searched for an idea. Her eyes stopped on the green urn, which rested on the cushion of the armchair like a particularly reticent participant in their conversation.

"How much did you pay for that?"

"Four shillings."

"You were robbed."

"My taste is my own. My turn. Are you Deirdre Albright's daughter?"

The sound of the name dropped the room into an uncanny stillness. Lily's heart thudded like a hare scenting a fox, deciding whether to blend into the landscape or bolt.

"It's the hair," Estelle explained, not waiting for her answer. "That red so dark you could almost take it for brown until the light sparked off of it. I'm old enough to remember that there was once a woman famous for hair like that, and you've got the same name. You might have come off some other branch of the family, but I've never heard you mention any relatives—not so much as an irritating great-aunt. So one could not help but wonder—"

"Yes," Lily cut in quietly.

Estelle beamed.

"I knew it! I resisted for as long as I could. You must believe that. But I had to ask. I never saw your mother perform, but I know people who did. I heard she was quite extraordinary."

Lily waited for the rest of it—for the inevitable, if sympathetic, mention of "how terribly tragic it must have been for you." Anyone who knew the name Deirdre Albright likely knew the rest of her story—how it had ended.

Estelle did not mention it. Instead, she sipped her vermouth, shifting the conversation as though she hadn't just brought up Lily's brutally-murdered mother.

"Your turn."

Lily did not like this game. She wanted it to be over. Perhaps if she could unsettle Estelle as well as she herself had just been rattled, it might bring things to an earlier close.

She knew it was not a generous impulse, particularly with a woman she cared about—a woman who was destined to die before very long—but she was too tired and shaken to resist it.

"Do you ever wonder if the spirits you talk to aren't really spirits? That perhaps they're just figments of your imagination that you take for something more?"

"Not in the least," Estelle replied easily. "My turn again. Who's your father?"

The room got smaller.

"You know who he is. That much is obvious. He's also clearly still around. It's in the little signals you don't know you're sending when Gwen talks about her dad plowing over that Iron Age ring fort in his barley field, or when I try to get your opinion about rearranging the family portraits again. And there were rumors, of course, though some were rather wild. One never can be sure quite how much stock to put in—"

"The Earl of Torrington," Lily cut in flatly. She finished the vermouth and set the glass down on the table with a sharp rap.

"Of course," Estelle replied softly. "How did I not see it before? It's in your nose, the cut of your jaw. And the eyes. That Torrington gray. So distinctive."

There was no hint of disapproval in her tone, no subtle sense of poking at someone's inferiority. Nothing indicated that Estelle thought any less of Lily, knowing that she was a bastard.

The daughter of a notorious actress and the earl who made her his mistress, who had enjoyed her company on lazy afternoons before returning home to his countess and brood of well-bred heirs.

She should have been surprised it took Estelle this long to pry it out of her. She had lived upstairs for the better part of three years and some scandals were too wicked to properly fade with age.

There was no reason for her to be angry. Her hackles were up regardless, leaving her feeling as defensive as a cornered dog. She fought not to let it show.

"I was unaware you were acquainted with Lord Torrington," she said evenly.

Estelle waved dismissively. "We're not acquainted, darling. We don't exactly move in the same circles. I've just seen him here and there. He's the sort of person one notices."

He was, indeed, the sort of person one noticed. The Earl of Torrington was one of the most powerful men in the kingdom, head of an ancient, noble house with vast holdings in Sussex. A tall man, well-built, with brilliant silver hair and a sharp, patrician nose, he was also a political player who, though he held no official position beyond that granted by his title in the House of Lords, was known to be the moving force behind a great deal of what actually got done in Parliament.

She remembered when that silver mane was peppered rather than all salt, when those elegant hands had tousled her hair or tossed sweets to her from his pockets as he passed by. She had not known him as a peer of the realm and man of influence then, but simply as an occasional, distantly affectionate presence in the house.

Until the house was empty.

"Is it my turn, then?" Lily demanded, unable to keep a slight edge from her tone.

"By all means," Estelle offered with a gracious wave of her hand. "Last round, though, so make it count."

Lily searched for a question. She knew the clever thing to do would be to simply throw one away, perhaps asking Estelle where she got the cupid or when she was going to replace those terrible curtains.

Her friend had riled her, though admittedly the questions she asked weren't entirely inappropriate. After all, how impertinent was it to ask a woman you'd known for years about her parents? Lily's reactions had been outsize, but there they were, and she found the result was an urge to engage with the stakes of the game, to find a question that would make Estelle feel as caught off-guard as Lily had been—which was no easy task.

Mentioning the Earl of Torrington had a way of doing that to her.

"If I told you that you were in danger," she asked, her voice carefully and deliberately even, "Would you believe me?"

Estelle stopped twirling her glass. She fixed Lily with that studying, penetrating look, but Lily could see that she was genuinely surprised. It gave her a small burst of satisfaction.

Then something in Estelle's expression shifted. Lily had the sense of some analysis being completed, a conclusion being drawn.

Estelle set down her glass, her movements graceful and poised.

"Tomorrow morning, I would like you to pay a call with me."

"I'm not sure that I'm—"

"Of course you're available, darling. You never have appointments before eleven o'clock. I'll arrange for a hackney at nine."

"Isn't that rather early?"

"Not where we're going." She stood and extended her hand. "I've been terribly selfish. You must be exhausted. I can't begin to imagine what sort of a day you've had, and here I am tying you up with chatter when I'm sure all you want is to climb into bed."

Lily accepted the hand and Estelle hauled her to her feet. She walked her over to the door, handing her the walking stick.

As much as she wanted to go, Lily hesitated for a moment, unable to resist her own curiosity.

"You haven't answered my question."

"We'll chat about it tomorrow."

"But you still have one more question of your own."

"Then why don't I ask it, and we'll both sleep on our answers?"

"Fine," Lily agreed. She was still rattled and the tiredness was settling more firmly in, dragging at her. She was ready to be done with this day, with every troubling minute of it.

"If I were in danger, would you tell me?" Estelle asked.

The sense of threat flared up again, the abrupt jump in her pulse as though she suddenly looked down to find she was standing on the edge of a terrifying precipice.

"Off to bed, then, before you fall over," Estelle finished cheerfully. "Watch out for Cat on the stairs. I'll see you at nine."

She slipped back into her rooms. The door slammed shut, leaving Lily alone with her ghosts in the gloom of the hall.

# THREE

*E*STELLE KNOCKED AT LILY's door promptly at nine in the morning.

Lily had been half-hoping she would sleep in. Nine was ungodly early for Estelle, who kept similar hours to the dead, yet there she was, her caftan covered with a warm wool overcoat that made her look almost ordinary.

"Come along, darling. Our carriage awaits," she announced.

Lily was ready for her. She had made sure she was up and dressed, just in case Estelle decided to follow through on the promise—or was it a threat?—of the night before. The only thing she did not have ready was an excuse plausible enough to get her out of this appointment. It was rather difficult to come up with plausible excuses when she had no idea where she was supposed to be going.

She reminded herself that whatever unusual social waters Estelle planned to sail them into, Lily was perfectly capable of navigating the current. She would almost certainly have managed odder circumstances before.

She was stiff but less sore than she had been last night. Before dressing, she had examined her stitches. They appeared to be quite neat and well-placed, the wound showing no sign of infection. The scabs on her face were also healing up well enough, though they made for a rather obvious and ugly presence in the meantime. She considered wearing a hat with a veil, but rejected the idea. She would take the occasional stare from passers-by over not being able to see where she was going.

She plucked her walking stick from its place by the door and followed Estelle down the stairs.

Miss Bard met them on the landing, pulling the door to the flat she and Estelle shared closed behind her.

"Are you coming too?" Lily asked.

"Coming where?" she asked, smiling. Miss Bard always reminded Lily of a plump brown wren.

"She's off to watch a bunch of men dance around in funny hats," Estelle explained.

"It's a mummer's dance in honor of the feast of St. John the Saxon, thank you very much. Where are you two off to?"

"Nowhere special," Estelle replied shortly.

Miss Bard raised a knowing eyebrow.

"Our hackney's waiting. Come along, Lily," the older woman ordered, hauling her down the stairs.

The carriage was an unusual indulgence for Lily. She generally viewed hackneys as an unnecessary expense. She knew this was a hangover from a time when her finances had been more severely limited. She could afford the ride now without any trouble.

"Are you going to tell me where we're going?" she asked, once they were settled in and rolling down March Place.

"I told you. To meet a friend."

Lily waited for more information. Estelle did not offer it. They rode on in silence. The carriage swayed around a turn, then came to an abrupt halt as traffic jammed the narrow street. Ahead, a pair of police constables blocked the road, waving and whistling everyone to a stop. The road beyond the policemen was broad and empty. Why weren't they moving?

Then the answer came rolling into view—the gleaming line of a royal motorcade. As annoyed as she was at being trapped in the carriage with Estelle's insatiable curiosity, Lily supposed she couldn't entirely regret the delay. It was thanks to that shining bronze motorcar that she had awoken that morning in a comfortable if modest attic flat and not a cramped room shared with a pair of chorus girls.

Lily had fled finishing school at sixteen, using her last few coins to get the train to London. Once there, she had gone to the only place she knew she stood a chance of making a living on her own—Drury Lane.

Lily was not an actress. She hated the attention of being on stage and had too much of her father in her to be considered the same sort of beauty her mother had been. "Striking" was how her appearance had been described on more than one occasion. Still, she had spent enough time exploring the maze-like world behind the stage while her mother drank sherry and gossiped with old friends that she understood the inner workings of a theatre.

It was also a world where no one judged Lily for the unusual circumstances of her birth.

Of course, it had not been strictly necessary. There were other funds at her disposal, deposited with clockwork regularity every month.

Lily never touched that account, not even when she lacked three pennies to scrape together for supper.

Five years later, when Lily's circumstances were verging on desperate, a trim, elderly solicitor had shown up at her door and informed her that—as it was her 21st birthday—she was now the sole heir of her mother's trust.

It consisted of a small fund from a starring role at the Theatre Royal which Deirdre had invested in a startup company by the name of Daimler . . . a company that later secured exclusive rights to provide automobiles to the royal family.

Deirdre Albright's little nest egg had grown to over 100 times its initial value and now paid a tidy dividend every month with occasional bonuses like the one that had purchased her Triumph. It was enough to provide Lily with a modest but entirely decent living.

It was still a lonely living. The woman beside her in the carriage was one of the only people to penetrate Lily's longstanding defenses, and now she was going to die.

The long line of shining Daimlers finally passed. The policemen waved the traffic back into motion.

"Don't think I've forgotten about him," Estelle said.

"About whom?"

"The man involved in your accident."

Lily made no reply.

Estelle smiled, leaning back comfortably. "You know I'll get it out of you eventually."

The carriage rolled around another corner, then rocked to a stop.

"We're here," Estelle announced cheerfully, hopping out.

Lily lingered for a moment behind her, surprise rooting her to the seat. Were it not for the motorcade, they wouldn't have been in the carriage more than five minutes.

The hackney was waiting. She stepped out.

"It would've been faster if we walked," she said as Estelle handed a few coins to the driver.

"I will never understand your insistence on wearing out perfectly good pairs of shoes. Besides, you're wounded."

Lily looked around as the carriage pulled away. She recognized where she was. This was Bedford Square, a posh garden park located just behind the British Museum. Though nearby, it was several steps up from the middle-class respectability of March Place.

They stopped in front of a pair of tall, fine houses built of washed limestone that stood out, pale and bright, against the red brick facades to either side. Elegant fan lights accented the doors, which were both painted a rich, deep blue, positioned between faux columns marked in bas-relief. They gave the structures a distinctly Grecian air as though the two houses were in fact a single temple to some ancient god, built with opulence and good taste, and lovingly cared for.

It looked very fine, like the sort of place where someone of Lily's social standing was unlikely to be welcome.

Estelle skipped up the steps to the door on the right. A gleaming brass plaque was mounted on the limestone beside the blue panel. It was marked with a series of characters Lily thought must be Chinese. Instead of knocking, Estelle simply turned the knob and pushed open the door.

"It's never locked," she called back over her shoulder as she went in, as though that were sufficient explanation for why she was walking unannounced into someone else's house.

The prospect of following paralyzed Lily, freezing her in place at the bottom of the steps.

The door remained open, letting the winter chill inside. Estelle clearly expected Lily to follow. What else could she do? She could hardly wait outside, nor did it make much sense for her to knock herself when the door stood half-open and her companion had already breezed inside.

With a breath, she stepped over the threshold.

She found herself in a fine, high-ceilinged entry papered in green damask. Rooms opened to either side. Ahead of her, a set of stairs rose to an open landing.

The decor was spare but tasteful, accented by items a bit stranger and more unique than usual.

A marble bust of Isaac Newton sat on a plinth by the entry to what appeared to be the drawing room. On the opposite side, on a small accent table, what Lily suspected must be a genuine Ming vase held a spray of dried blossoms. It was elegantly painted with waving blue fronds of pond weed and swirls of moving water amongst which the bright orange forms of goldfish swam. Mounted on the wall was an enormous iron shield, every inch of its round surface embossed with graceful warriors astride long-legged horses, holding spears and swords as they charged into battle.

Where were they? Was this simply the home of some acquaintance of Estelle's, or something else?

She didn't ask, still wary of why Estelle had brought her here, given the timing of when she had made the appointment—right at the end of their uncomfortable game the night before.

*If I told you that you were in danger, would you believe me?*

"Helloooo," Estelle sang.

She was answered by a heavy crash resounding from somewhere above. It sounded to Lily as though someone had been thrown into a wall. Estelle didn't seem to notice.

A figure stepped into the doorway to Lily's right.

He was tall, his advanced age clear from the deep lines on his face. His white hair was cut close as a soldier's, his mustache also trimmed with military precision. His posture displayed an unusual fitness and energy for one of his advanced years.

"Miss Deneuve."

"James!"

"To what do we owe the pleasure?"

"I've brought a friend to meet Mr. Ash. Lily, this is James Cairncross. James, Miss Lily Albright. Is the master of the house in?"

"He's training," Mr. Cairncross replied. Lily noted the Scottish burr of his accent. "But I imagine they'll be finishing up shortly."

As though to emphasize his point, another thud echoed down from upstairs, heavy enough to rattle the steel shield against the wall.

A new face appeared at the end of the hall, that of a lanky young man whose features revealed him to be of Asian descent. He wore the livery of a chauffeur, though his coat was unbuttoned and his cap set at a slightly rakish angle.

"Sam, would you let Mr. Ash know he has a visitor?" Mr. Cairncross asked.

"Sorted," the young man replied, his accent pure East End. He bounded up the stairs, taking them two at a time.

A smaller, slighter figure replaced him, clad in a dark gown and an apron.

"Mrs. Liu, could we have tea in the library please?"

The older woman nodded and then slipped away.

"If you would join me, ladies?" Mr. Cairncross made an elegant bow, gesturing them into the room behind him.

Lily glanced from the walking stick in her hand to the umbrella stand by the door, where it clearly ought to be left. She felt an odd reluctance to part from it in a place that instinctively unsettled her.

After all, she was legitimately injured. She would claim the privilege of the lame, however temporarily she might hold that position, and keep it with her.

The mention of a library had evoked visions of a glorified gentleman's study in Lily's mind, but the space she found herself in was something else entirely. It was immense, running the entire length of the house, with wide windows looking out over both the square and an expansive back garden. The ceilings were even higher than those of the hall, rising a full two stories of walls completely lined with shelves, every one of which was fully stocked. A system of wrought-iron ladders and balconies circled the room.

It was not just books that the library held. A glass case displayed a series of carvings and tablets, including one small sheet of hammered gold. Another cabinet near the front of the room consisted entirely of very slender wooden drawers, one or two of which were open, revealing what looked like yellowed parchment scrolls tucked inside.

The shelves that did hold books were clearly stocked with something other than volumes on horticulture picked up by lot for purposes of decor. The age and size of the books varied greatly. The desk in the corner, positioned next to an honest-to-goodness card catalog, made it clear that this was no showroom but a genuine working library.

More unusual artifacts decorated the space. Lily's gaze roved across a curved sword in a beautifully enameled sheath, a multi-armed idol with the face of a demon, and a ball of ivory carved into the most astonishingly intricate designs with other equally ornate spheres encased within it.

An orrery that put the earth at the center of the universe rested on a nearby table, its old brass gears carefully polished.

The room was silent save for the regular ticking of a great antique clock set in the corner. The noise was calming.

Wine-red leather armchairs with brass studs were arranged around a fireplace which clearly existed for show rather than function, heat being provided by the scrolled iron radiators set around the room.

Mr. Cairncross held a chair out for Lily before taking a seat for himself.

"How is your health, James?" Estelle asked.

"As well as can be expected. And how have you been? We haven't seen you around here in quite a while."

Estelle waved a hand dismissively. "I've less need of it than some. I'm terribly well-adjusted."

The response was strange. Well-adjusted? What did that have to do with whether or not one visited this place?

Mrs. Liu, whom Lily had deduced must be the housekeeper, came in carrying a heavily-laden tea tray. She set it down on the coffee table.

Mr. Cairncross's eyes lit up.

"Mrs. Liu, you've made lotus seed buns. You are a treasure."

"You've brought too many," Estelle announced, eyeing the pastries. "You know you needn't have put one there for me. One does not maintain a trim figure after forty by indulging in confections."

"Too thin," Mrs. Liu muttered, shaking her head as she departed.

"You must try one, Miss Albright. They are quite delectable," Mr. Cairncross insisted.

Lily picked up one of the pastries. It was very pale but felt soft and light. She took a bite, then tried not to sigh out loud. The bun was airy as a cloud, wrapped around a smooth, sweet, nutty filling.

She felt herself settle more comfortably into her chair.

Sam came in.

"They're near done upstairs." He spied the tea tray. "Lotus buns! Năinai wouldn't let me take one from the kitchen. Said they was for the house." He scooped up the remaining pastry, which disappeared into his mouth with a single bite.

As the bastard daughter of an actress, Lily had little direct experience with how fine houses treated their servants, but she was fairly certain it was completely out of line for a chauffeur to pop into rooms with house guests and steal snacks from them. Yet Cairncross showed no sign of shock or disapproval, more a grandfatherly sort of amused indulgence.

She certainly wasn't going to call any attention to the anomaly herself. In a game of social status, Lily was unlikely to come out the winner.

Another shudder of impact drifted down from upstairs, rattling the cups in their saucers.

"Let us know when Mr. Ash is available, please," Mr. Cairncross said.

"Bob's your uncle," the young man replied, then jogged from the room.

"Tea, Miss Albright?" the librarian asked.

"Thank you."

"Milk or sugar?"

"A little of both."

"I'll take mine black," Estelle cut in.

"As I know well, Miss Deneuve," he replied.

Lily sipped her tea.

"Your library houses quite an unusual collection," she noted, filling the natural lull in the conversation.

"Over 5,000 items in the catalog, spanning roughly 3,000 years and sixteen languages. Five dead, ten living. One of indeterminate status," Mr. Cairncross replied with obvious pride. "Mr. Ash has spent the greater part of his life traveling throughout the world—I was privileged to join him for a good part of it—and sent most of these home in the course of his journey. That's a Sumerian hymn to Ishtar over there," he said, pointing to one of the tablets in the glass case, then moving his teacup to indicate other items in the room. "Qing dynasty puzzle ball. Seventeenth century psalter encrusted with ten carats of emeralds and rubies. The Hindu goddess Kali—she's always given a second look."

Lily glanced at the titles on the nearest shelf. *The Lives of the Saints* sat beside a volume on the powers of Sufi ascetics. Above it were a few bindings marked with characters she couldn't read.

"There's more in the vaults downstairs, including a few goodies I have to keep locked away for health and safety reasons," Mr. Cairncross continued.

"You mean they're very fragile?" Lily asked.

"No. I mean they're fairly dangerous."

"James is The Refuge's official librarian. Get him started and you'll have trouble making him stop," Estelle warned.

"The Refuge?" Lily echoed.

The pair exchanged a look. Lily could read the subtle warning in Estelle's glance. So, it seemed, could Mr. Cairncross.

"Technically, the name is Zìzhīzhīmíng Bìfēnggǎng. You'd have seen the characters by the door. The literal translation is 'The sanctuary of coming to fully know one's self', but as that's rather a mouthful and only Ash, myself, and the Wus can manage the Mandarin, it mostly goes by The Refuge."

"You're talking about this house," Lily guessed slowly.

"Yes, darling. The house," Estelle confirmed.

"More or less," Mr. Cairncross qualified.

Another look was exchanged and Lily felt the wariness that had been banished by the warmth and comfort of the library creep back in. She was reminded that she hadn't the foggiest idea what she had walked into here. What sort of private home sported an elaborate name in a foreign language and included a librarian among its staff?

If Mr. Cairncross was indeed staff—a status that would have precluded his serving as a surrogate host, as he clearly had for the last half hour.

Estelle set down her teacup.

"Would you excuse me for a moment?" she said, rising and slipping out of the room.

The move did nothing to assuage Lily's unease.

She considered the cup in her own hands. Part of her wanted to put the half-drunk tea back on the tray, make an excuse to Mr. Cairncross, and simply walk out of the house. She could make her own way home from here, even with the stitches in her thigh.

Then it occurred to her that the room she sat in might very well hold the answer to a question that continued to haunt her, however much she tried to push it from her mind.

"Mr. Cairncross . . ."

"Yes?" he replied, sipping his tea.

"You said you speak Mandarin."

"I do."

"How many other languages do you speak?"

"Fluently? Seven. But I can get by in half a dozen more. And there are the ones I read, of course. Bit of Sanskrit, the odd hieroglyph. I've always had a knack for tongues. Useful talent for a librarian, I suppose."

"Have you ever heard the word 'alukah?'"

Cairncross frowned.

"Unusual word for a young lady to have stumbled across."

"So you know it?"

"It's Hebrew."

"What does it mean?"

"Blood drinker," he replied.

Lily felt the hairs rise on her arm.

Blood-drinker—the accusation that had rasped from between Estelle's pale lips. It was another link to the stories in the papers, to a horror that slipped into the bedrooms of sleeping women in the night and left them drained of their vital fluid.

"You mean like a vampire?" she asked.

"Yes."

"There's no such thing as vampires," she replied automatically, echoing Estelle's words from the night before.

"Tell that to the one I encountered in Trieste," Mr. Cairncross retorted. "Might I inquire where you came across the word?" His gaze was sharply curious.

Lily was saved from answering as Sam came back in.

"He's ready for her now. Said he'd see her in the reflection room."

"Interesting choice," Mr. Cairncross murmured. "Thank you, Sam. I'll show her in."

He rose, unfolding his long frame from the chair.

"If you'll follow me, Miss Albright."

She wondered if she should hold back for Estelle, but Mr. Cairncross was clearly waiting for her to join him. And why shouldn't she? There was nothing here for her to be afraid of. At worst, she was about to walk into an awkward social encounter with an obvious eccentric, a situation Lily was quite capable of navigating.

She rose and Mr. Cairncross guided her back into the hall. He stopped at the far end. A stairwell down to the ground floor echoed with the clatter of pots from the kitchen. On the opposite side, to Lily's left, was an opening veiled by a thick black curtain.

The dark fabric stood in stark contrast to the rich green of the wallpaper. A small wooden bench rested by the doorway. Under it, a mat held a single, perfectly polished pair of Oxford shoes, set neatly side-by-side.

There was no sound from the far side of the door, only a slight draft that stirred the bottom of the curtain, the cool air spilling out over Lily's ankles.

"We generally remove our shoes before going in," Mr. Cairncross said, with just a hint of apology in his tone.

Lily froze with indecision. The notion of removing her shoes made her feel oddly vulnerable. Still, if she was in for a penny . . .

She sat down on the bench and slipped off her boots, trying not to noticeably wince as the stitches tugged at her thigh.

"Best of luck," Mr. Cairncross said cheerfully, nodding at the curtain, then turning to stride back to the library.

Standing alone in her stockinged feet, walking stick in her hand, Lily faced the darkness.

The sooner she got this over with, the sooner she could go home, she reminded herself, pushing the weight of that assurance against the chill that seeped out over her toes.

She pulled back the curtain and stepped inside.

# FOUR

$\mathscr{I}$T WAS THE QUIET that struck her. It was not silence, but still-ness—a calm, contemplative hush.

The space itself was empty. White walls divided by dark exposed beams rose to a paneled ceiling. The floor itself was bare of any rug or carpet, just exposed boards polished to a sheen. The only furnishings in the space were a few simple wooden benches, lined against one wall, and a rack that contained a stack of small rugs, rolled into neat tubes. The outer wall of the building was not a wall at all, but a row of windows that rose from floor to ceiling and could be slid open on warm days to let in the air from the garden they looked over. The glass was closed today, the garden still bare, cloaked in lingering winter. The soft gray light that spilled in through the glass was the only illumination in the room, the simple oil lamps set in sconces on the walls unlit at this hour.

The most startling feature of the space was the water.

It ran from a tap in the far wall down a channel set into the middle of the floor, the shallow depth of it lined with copper. The stream, perhaps a foot wide and three inches deep, flowed across the width of the room until it disappeared under one of the windows facing the garden. The soft trickle of it was the only sound in what would otherwise have been total silence.

A man stood in the center of the room.

He was not a tall man, his build slight. He was older, his hair and beard almost entirely gray. He wore a finely tailored suit in charcoal gray, an entirely respectable ensemble save for the fact that his feet were bare.

He stood straight and still, facing the garden.

Lily coughed politely. He turned. An emotion she had not at all expected flashed in his eyes—recognition.

"It's you."

"I'm sorry. Have we met?" she asked.

"No, Miss Albright. We have not."

It was the logical answer, of course, but Lily still had the distinct impression that the man standing across the channel of water knew her.

He bowed, the movement practiced and gentlemanly.

"Robert Ash, at your service. Shall we sit?" He motioned to one of the wooden benches.

He stepped over the stream. Lily met him at the bench. She lowered herself down onto the far end of it. Mr. Ash seemed to sense her need for distance, leaving the space between them. The move offered her a touch of reassurance, lowering the instinctive wariness she had felt since she walked in.

"Are you comfortable?" he asked.

"Quite."

"This room is not normally used for conversation. It is intended as a place of silence and contemplation."

"It feels like a church," Lily noted, then wondered if that might be taken as an insult.

"It is modeled after one, in a manner of speaking. The room was inspired by a space in the South Cliff Temple in Wǔdāng, China. As that was carved out of the living rock of the mountain, however, I had to make some changes here. And of course, the view is rather different."

"You've been to China?" She knew the answer already, of course, thanks to Mr. Cairncross, but she wasn't sure how else to proceed, other than making some form of polite small talk. Not until she understood why she was here and who this Robert Ash was.

"I have."

"What brought you there? Business?"

"Grief," he replied simply.

The response was startling in its honesty, in how it so simply laid bare a vulnerability one did not normally share with new acquaintances.

It left Lily unsure how to proceed. Was the courteous thing to do to ask after the source of that grief? Express sympathy? There was nothing in Mr. Ash's tone or posture that indicated he expected either.

"How much did Miss Deneuve tell you about this place?" he asked, filling the silence before Lily could decide how to do so herself.

"Nothing," she replied, allowing her own touch of blunt honesty.

"So you do not know why you are here."

"She said she wanted me to meet a friend of hers."

"I see."

The stillness settled back in, filling the space left around the gentle song of the water.

It should have seemed oppressive. A gap in conversation with a person one hardly knew was not usually a comfortable thing. It didn't. It was as though some quality of the space itself worked to settle Lily's nerves. She didn't feel like she was paying a social call in some drawing room, but more like someone praying who had simply happened across another parishioner along the way.

"Are you a Catholic, Miss Albright?"

She was, in fact, a Catholic, a faith she had inherited from her Irish mother. Both the Irish and the Catholicism could be grounds for being looked down upon by a man of Mr. Ash's standing. There were, of course, more significant social faults Lily would be considered guilty of, but those generally didn't arise in polite conversation.

"Why do you ask?"

"I wonder if you are familiar with any of the lives of the saints."

"Some."

It was perhaps an overstatement. Lily had never paid very much attention in church.

"St. Alphonsus de Liguori?"

"I'm afraid not."

"It is said that his holiness was revealed in his ability to appear in two places at the same time. A phenomenon known as bilocation."

"How very interesting," she replied politely, thrown by what felt like a very odd and abrupt turn in the conversation.

"Then there's St. Paul of the Cross," Mr. Ash continued. "He reportedly had the ability to project sermons into the minds of people miles away and could read the inner thoughts of those souls he came into contact with."

The warning instinct flared again. She could not say why—Mr. Ash gave no indication that this was anything more than a casual exchange of information. Yet her pulse had risen, her senses sharpening to attention.

"I see."

"There are many others. Accounts of holy men and women who could project their souls across great distances, or were invulnerable to pain . . . Similar stories are peppered through faiths and cultures across the globe, from Hinduism to Santeria. In Islam, such powers are called karamat. The word parallels our own 'charisma'. Do you know what charisma is, Miss Albright?"

"It's a sort of charm," Lily replied.

In the theatre, charisma had meant everything. It was the difference between fading into obscurity and rising to stardom. She had so often heard that her mother possessed it—that unique, ineffable quality that made eyes want to linger on a form, a voice, a smile.

"There is another meaning to charisma," Mr. Ash said. "One that refers not to attractions of physique or character, but to something else entirely—a divinely-conferred extraordinary power. From the Greek khárisma—a gift of grace."

The cornered feeling rose again, that sense of something dangerous lurking in this room, something from which Lily would want to run, were she able to identify it for what it was.

She shifted her grip on the walking stick.

"There have always been charismatics. Look closely and you will see them scattered through the history of every nation, every faith. Some were exalted. Others were burned. Certainly there were more who walked quieter paths through life, leaving little if any mark in the records that are our knowledge of the past. But they have always been here."

Mr. Ash did not move. There was no change in his tone. He said the next words as calmly and simply as every other utterance he had made, since that first exclamation of surprise when she walked into the room.

"You are the possessor of such a gift. Are you not, Miss Albright?"

Panic flared, quick and urgent. How did he know?

*How could he know?*

No one knew. Since the day her mother had died, fourteen years ago, she had not told a single soul about the damnable power she possessed.

There was no possible way that the stranger who sat beside her in this dim, quiet room could have found her secret out.

*If I told you that you were in danger . . . would you believe me?*

Words Lily had uttered the night before in a burst of spite, in the middle of a game she hadn't wanted to play. They would surely have sounded like nonsense, the sort of thing any rational person would have dismissed as a leap of imagination.

Estelle was not a rational person. Estelle was intuitive—deeply, penetratingly intuitive. Had she nosed some truth from between the lines Lily had uttered?

*If I were in danger, would you tell me?*

The question Estelle had asked at the end of the night, the one Lily had firmly pushed from her mind as she collapsed into sleep.

She had been so careful for so very long. Had she made a critical slip?

She mustered her resources, holding a firm facade of calm indifference. No one could know her secret—and no one would.

"I'm afraid I don't know what you're talking about."

Mr. Ash stood. He walked to the windows, his feet soundless on the bare floor. He looked out over the stark landscape of the winter garden.

"My wife was a charismatic," he said.

Lily held herself still.

"Her power was not something so straightforward as appearing in two places at once," he went on, still gazing out the window. "I never truly understood it, not while she lived. It was only after . . . after a very long time searching across the world for answers to questions I wasn't even sure how to ask that I finally grasped what she was."

He stopped there. Silence settled in. She could not see his face. There was nothing in his voice or posture that indicated this was anything but a bare fact that he passed along. In spite of that, Lily sensed that it was pain that caused the pause in his story.

*What brought you to China?*

*Grief.*

She did not want to continue this conversation. It was dangerous—far, far too dangerous. The words spilled out of her anyway, drawn by some force more powerful than her fear.

"What was she?"

He shifted, turning back to her.

"Are you familiar with the Tao, Miss Albright?"

"No."

"That is hardly surprising. It is not, unfortunately, a concept easily explained in an hour's conversation. Suffice to say my wife had an ability to perceive the imperceptible."

"You mean spirits?" Lily asked, thinking of Estelle's purported mediumship.

"I mean purpose," Ash replied softly. "The ineffable order of all things."

"What could that possibly look like?" Lily blurted in surprise.

"Beautiful . . . and terrible."

"That's how she described it?"

"Evangeline was an artist. She did not describe anything. She illustrated it."

The notion fired her curiosity and at the same time, struck her as deeply unsettling.

This was all a distraction. If she had been exposed, somehow, in this place, she would repair the damage and move on, as quickly and efficiently as possible.

She stood, smoothing her skirts.

"I am sure her work must have been remarkable," she said politely.

Mr. Ash spoke again, the words gliding across the room before Lily could make the easy transition to some acceptable excuse for her departure.

"You are part of it."

The feeling returned, of being *seen*, like a cornered animal.

"What on earth do you mean?" she asked, keeping her tone level and cool, refusing to show the tumult raging inside of her.

"She painted you."

"I'm sorry . . . I didn't realize I had met her."

"My wife is dead, Miss Albright. She died thirty-two years ago."

Her heart beat, thuds strong and urgent, the hum of it in her ears contrasting with the constant, gentle rush of the water that ran across the room.

"That's quite impossible, then," she countered evenly.

"Yes," Mr. Ash agreed, "and also true."

"I am afraid you must be mistaken."

He showed no awareness of the sharpness in her tone, remaining quiet and resolute, as immovable as a rock.

"It is you, Miss Albright. Right down to the yew staff you carry in your hand."

Her grip on the walking stick clenched reflexively.

Nothing required her to give credence to his words. It was all a game, or some uncannily astute sort of madness.

Worse than the fear was the other emotion the madness evoked in her, something far more disturbing than quick panic.

Intrigue.

She straightened her back. It was past time she got out of here.

"I'm terribly sorry, Mr. Ash—"

"Zìzhīzhīmíng Bìfēnggǎng," he cut in, the foreign words sounding easy on his tongue. "It is a reference to the thirty-third chapter of the *Tao Te Ching*, a book of wisdom by a Chinese sage named Lao Tzu. 'To know others is intelligence. To know one's self is wisdom. Mastering others is strength. Mastering one's self is power.' I created this place to provide a safe harbor for charismatics, individuals who possessed gifts they did not fully understand, to achieve zìzhīzhīmíng— to come to know themselves. You have seen the library. The collection is extensive and covers all aspects of extraordinary human experience, both historical and contemporary. There is also a training studio, where I work with more physical techniques of cultivating focus and the balance between mastery and acceptance."

"They said you were training when I came in." The words spilled out, her curiosity getting the better of her. "The floor shook."

"A tàijíquán session. Though I teach tàijíquán primarily for its mental and spiritual benefits, it has applications as a form of self-defense," he explained. "It is one of several practices I encountered during my years abroad that have potential application when working with charismatics. Others involve less direct contact."

Her mind spun.

It was too much to absorb—that there had been others, like her, throughout history. That there existed an enormous library full of books that might be able to tell her more about who she was. That there were techniques and practices that could offer her . . . mastery. And acceptance.

Ash's words were rich with resonance.

Something inside her yearned toward the notion, deeply tempted.

No, she reminded herself forcefully. She would not go down that path. She knew what her power could do. More importantly, she knew what it could not, no matter what books she read. She could not fall into this. To explore the world that Ash revealed to her would lead her nowhere but to more pain, more suffering. More grief.

"I'm very sorry," she said, her voice steady though inside she felt she was shaking like a leaf. "I'm afraid I have to go."

"Of course."

Ash showed no hint of offense at the abruptness of her announcement. He moved closer, stopping just on the other side of the flow of water that divided the room.

"Should you wish to return, Miss Albright, the door of The Refuge will be open. It will always be open to you."

There was nothing of common courtesy in the statement. Lily knew, with clear instinct, that Ash meant every word he had uttered—that the door to this place, his home, would quite literally be open to her.

*Why?*

The urge to demand an answer was overwhelming, firing her with an energy that was part desperate curiosity, part anger. Why would he make such an offer to a total stranger? Was it the painting—the image he believed his wife had made of her, years before she had been born? Or something else? What could he possibly have to gain from this?

She would not ask it. It would only open another door and she was done with revelations today. She gave him a nod, one she recognized was barely polite, and turned to go.

She had nearly made it when another thought occurred to her, one so overwhelming in its implications it stopped her in her tracks.

Tàijíquán. A physical art of self-defense. Ash had stated that he was training when she came in and the house rattled with the impact of a body hitting the floor.

For a body to hit the floor, it needed to be thrown. Which meant there were two bodies involved.

She turned back.

"Who were you training?"

It was as much a demand as a question, the significance of how he might answer overwhelming any remaining shred of propriety she had clung to.

For the first time since she met him, a brightness came into Ash's eyes, the lines at their corners lifting.

"I have told you that charismatics may be found throughout the length and breadth of history," he replied. "Did you expect the same would not be true of the present? You are not alone, Miss Albright. You have never been alone."

The words struck with the impact of a canon.

*You are not alone.*

It was impossible. Lily had never been anything other than alone. It was who she was. It was all she ever could be.

She took a step back, then another, then turned, at last, and pushed through the black curtain into the light of the hall.

She quickly tugged on her boots, her heart thudding in her chest as though she were running a sprint—which she was, more or less. She was running away.

The wound in her leg gave a quick stab of pain at the motion, which she ignored.

She headed for the door, forcing herself to walk instead of openly dash.

As she reached the entry, she began to feel foolish.

She had just fled from a polite if strange conversation with an eccentric. That's all it had been. Ash was just a mad but well-intentioned old man with a batch of wild ideas dancing around in his head. Lily had let her imagination, and her own paranoia, get the better of her. There was nothing here to be afraid of—nor was there anything truly extraordinary about this house. It was nothing more than bricks and wood and mortar, the rambling abode of some well-off lunatic.

Estelle spotted Lily in the hall and came out of the library.

"Where are you going?"

The creak of a footfall sounded on the landing above. Lily looked up and saw someone step out into the light of the hall.

He was dressed in a loose shirt and trousers, some sort of sporting attire that revealed his well-built frame. Dark hair, a bit longer than was strictly fashionable, curled against his forehead, the tendrils of it damp with exertion.

His black-gloved hands rested on the balustrade.

He looked down at her with clear shock that mirrored the emotion flaring through her like a forest fire.

"It's you," he said, the words a cough of surprise.

"Lord Strangford," she managed to reply.

They stared at each other across the distance of the hall, the impact of seeing him robbing her of any coherent response.

"I'm terribly sorry," she blurted, speaking to Estelle, though she was unable to take her gaze off of the man on the landing. "I have to go."

"Lily . . ."

She ignored Estelle's objection and walked out the door.

Long strides carried her quickly down the length of the square. Forcibly ignoring the sharp pain in her leg, she pressed forward at something only a hair shy of a run, then turned the corner and dove into the ever-flowing chaos of Tottenham Court Road.

She wove through the stream of humanity like a needle in a tapestry until the ache in her thigh rose to a burning agony, then ducked into an alley behind a bank.

Her back fell against the bricks. She slumped down and let herself start to shake.

*You are not alone, Miss Albright.*

*You have never been alone.*

# FIVE

CHICKEN, LILY THOUGHT. NO, she reconsidered. Perhaps it was a hawk.

She lay on her back in her bed, puzzling over the shape of the smoke-stains on her ceiling.

It was more or less what she'd been doing all day. After her return from Bedford Square, she had shut the door, tossed off her gown, and proceeded to determinedly push the rest of the world out of her mind.

The chicken in the smoke failed to banish the memory of Estelle's wraith-like form, the accusing finger pointed at the threatening darkness. The awareness that death stalked her from some unknown source and that Lily could do nothing to avert it.

Nor had it done much to push Lord Strangford's shocked gaze from her mind.

Recalling it made her burn once more with curiosity.

What was he doing there? Was it simply a coincidence that he was acquainted with Ash?

She couldn't consider the alternative. To do so opened the door to believing everything Ash had told her about The Refuge and its purpose. There was too much close to madness in that, like the notion that his wife had somehow managed to paint a portrait of Lily years before she had ever been born.

It was best that she forget any of it had ever happened.

Yet no matter how she tried to distract herself, her thoughts kept going back to Lord Strangford, the tension and surprise apparent in the rigid set of his shoulders.

She sat up and glared at the only other occupant of the room as though he might be able to provide a solution. Cat merely blinked at her from his perch atop her newly-purchased scarf, upon which he had already shed a thick coating of orange fur.

A knock sounded on the door, more perfunctory than polite, and before Lily answered, her landlady, Mrs. Bramble, thumped into the room.

She was a widow of middle years, built like an English mastiff. Her footfalls defied the laws of physics, striking the floor with the impact of a person twice her size.

She carried a tray in her hands, the dish atop it covered with a dented pewter lid.

"Nettle puddling?" Lily asked, a touch apprehensively.

"Ham steak," Mrs. Bramble replied flatly. She set the tray down on a side table with an audible clatter. "Bit o' broccoli." She whipped a bundle of newsprint from under her arm with the ferocity of a fencer preparing for a bout. "Paper?"

Lily was ready to refuse, as she generally did. She paused.

"Which one is it?"

"Police News. The only one as tells any of the stories worth hearing about. The rest of 'em could know of a horde of burglars was ready to climb in through the windows and will they warn us? No. It's all politics and money, as if those ever made any real difference to anybody."

It would just be a distraction, Lily told herself. It had nothing to do with wanting to discover if there'd been any developments in the murder investigation.

"I'll take it, thank you."

The landlady dropped the paper next to the covered plate.

"Ta, then," she said and stomped out.

Lily lifted the lid, considering the ham steak, the bit of broccoli . . . and the paper.

She really shouldn't.

She picked it up and flopped back down onto the bed.

The cover story told the tragic tale of a lady somnambulist who tumbled over the rail of a ship only to be a rescued by an extraordinarily brave sailor. There was also, it seemed, an escaped orangutan who had been seen stalking the streets of Paris.

A lighter note was struck by a story of the tallest man in Leeds meeting and then falling in love with the shortest woman in Dorset.

She found what she was looking for on page five.

The article was small, only a single paragraph illustrated with a vivid question mark. It reported the result of a coroner's inquest into the latest of the "vampire killer's" medium victims, Sylvia Durst.

Her death had been ruled to be by natural causes. The paper noted that the specific nature of those causes had not been given.

Lily had no illusions about whether the police would devote any resources to investigating a death that had not been ruled a homicide.

It should not have been upsetting. A police investigation wouldn't make any difference. Lily knew that. What she had seen would happen. It always had before. It always would.

Nothing could change that.

She tossed the paper on the ground, disgusted with it and with herself. The pages separated, sliding across the floor.

She could imagine Bramble's look when she came back for the dinner tray and saw it there. The notion was unpleasant enough to give her the will to get out of her bed and pick it back up.

She paused as she gathered the last page. There, between an advertisement for a curative tonic and a new engine for polishing belts, was a calendar notice for an event. It was an opening at the Carfax Gallery, "Oils by Deceased British Masters".

Not exactly scintillating, yet the piece caught her eye thanks to a name included in the list of artists to be featured. It rested between Arthur Bardswell and Dudley Snodgrass—just five simple letters.

*E. V. Ash*

Could E.V. stand for Evangeline? That was the name Robert Ash had given for his deceased artist wife.

It was a leap. There might be dozens of English artists who had shared the name Ash. The initials on the page could refer to any one of them.

She looked at the rest of the advert.

The opening was that night, on Bury Street.

It was nonsense, really. What would she get out of it, even if the painting was by Ash's wife? But then again, staying in hadn't done anything to settle her unquiet mind. Perhaps going out wasn't the most terrible idea. Some fresh air and a change of scene might be just what she needed to banish the memory of the man on the landing and the killer in the shadows from her mind.

One could hope.

~

St. James was not a part of London Lily regularly frequented.

Sitting in her hired carriage, she rolled past the elaborate town-houses of some of the nation's finest families, a handful of embassies and elite social clubs. The granite and limestone of the buildings here seemed more resistant to London's ever-present soot. The streets were cleaner, the carriages more stately.

It was the sort of place her noble father would have felt at home, a world that perhaps Lily would have been accustomed to, had she been his legitimate daughter and not the unexpected by-blow of his indulgence with his mistress.

The Earl of Torrington was, by all accounts, a singularly serious man, which made his choice of a charming but frivolous actress for a lover all the more unexpected. Then again, perhaps it was Deirdre Albright's very frivolousness that attracted him. In addition to being one of the most influential members of the House of Lords, Lord Torrington also managed his significant estates and holdings with iron control. While many noble houses were struggling to remain solvent in the face of agricultural reforms and the loss of labor to the factories in Leeds and Manchester, the Torrington lands and enter-prises—thoughtfully diversified, of course—continued to turn a tidy profit.

For someone who spent his waking hours with account books, investment portfolios and legislative briefs, escaping to Deirdre Albright's world of silk, champagne and bright, easy laughter might have been a kind of balm.

One that his countess and their children must not have pro-vided him.

That Lily was, at most, merely a curious side effect of his pastime was made clear by what occurred once the lovely, laughing Deirdre was gone.

He disappeared.

Lily was provided for, of course. Some underling turned up at their rooms on Oxford Street to escort her to Mrs. Finch's Academy for Ladies, where her tuition was regularly paid, along with an allowance in pin money for clothing and sundries.

There had been no visits. No letters. No contact of any variety whatsoever. The man who had sired her had settled his obligation with a flourish of his checkbook, and that was the end of it.

At sixteen, Lily had as much as she could stand of table settings and French and pianoforte. Mrs. Finch's was a place for girls destined for respectable marriages or—for the unlucky few for whom marriage was not an option—life as a governess.

Marriage was out of the question for Lily. What sort of man would be willing to ally himself with the bastard daughter of an Irish actress? And on the other hand, how could she trust that any man who did make her an offer truly wanted her and not some presumed chance at a better connection with her illustrious father?

Nor had she any illusions about her suitability for a life in service.

When she escaped from Mrs. Finch's, Lord Torrington's checkbook followed her.

At her first shared room off Covent Garden, a statement arrived in her mail providing details for an account opened in her name and notice that deposits would be made monthly for her maintenance and other expenses.

Lily burned it.

She burned the statements that followed, every one of them, with coal she bought with pennies earned from stitching tears in costumes.

Eventually, she took the time to write a letter to the bank asking that they discontinue mailing the statements. They did so, presumably happy to save on the postage.

She never withdrew a dime, not even when near starvation forced her to don the sequins and paint of a chorus girl—a profession so near to her mother's "work" most men did not recognize the difference.

If all the Earl of Torrington had to offer her was his money, she would find a way to make do without it.

Nor did she have any need for his world. Her excursion to St. James's tonight, and the inevitable mingling with the *ton*—the cream of London society—that would follow, was a rare exception. She told herself the errand was only to prove that Evangeline Ash's painting was nothing more remarkable than a portrait of a banker with his beagle, or some insipid watercolor of a vase of flowers.

Her hackney stopped on Bury Street, caught in an odd little snarl of traffic. A cluster of carriages fought for space in front of a brightly-lit door on the ground floor of one of the imposing office blocks that lined the way.

As she descended the carriage steps, she analyzed the crowd.

She had chosen her gown carefully. It was one of the finest in her wardrobe, a gold silk sheath cut to the latest fashion, overlain with embroidered black gauze. From her scan of the bodies drifting from the surrounding carriages, it was entirely on par with the garments of the other ladies in attendance. She had even left the walking stick at home, knowing that it would only draw more attention to her, being rather an unusual accessory for a woman in evening dress.

This was an upper-class establishment. If the proprietors realized who she was, it was entirely possible she would be politely escorted back to the street.

The ton was generally happy to presume that a child conceived in sin carried the same loose morals in her blood like some sort of hereditary disease, one they apparently thought contagious.

Tonight, however, she looked the part of a well-bred lady. Thanks to her years of training at Mrs. Finch's, she could also act it. What she could not do was be seen arriving at the gallery alone—something no respectable woman would have done.

She paused, bending down to make some imaginary assessment of the state of her evening slipper as the queue of carriages behind her moved forward, doors opening to disgorge more passengers.

The first to come out were an elderly couple. Lily continued to fuss with her shoe as they moved by. No lady on her husband's arm would fail to notice the addition of a lovely young woman to their party.

Next was a trio of gentlemen of middling years, talking boisterously with each other. One of them stopped as they passed.

"Hullo, madam. Are you having a bit of trouble?"

His breath carried the scent of brandy. Perfect, Lily thought.

"Just my slipper. There! It's back on," she announced. "Oh, drat. Where did he get to?"

"Have you lost your escort?"

"It appears I have."

"Allow me to serve," he said, offering her his arm.

"How very kind of you," Lily replied, flashing him a smile.

She had not inherited her mother's gift for flirtation—nor would she have wanted to. While it had seen a turf-cutter's daughter rise to stardom on the London stage, it would only ensure that her bastard was all the more easily labeled a woman of equally loose morals.

Tonight, however, required an exception—just until she got through the door.

She hoped her skills were sufficient to pass muster. Likely the brandy her partner had consumed would help.

"What a curious accessory," she said, nodding toward the small brass pin her escort wore on his lapel. It appeared to be some sort of signet, marked with a symbol made up of two opposing carats melded together.

ᛉ

"Wherever did you acquire it?"

"This?" he replied, tapping the pin. "This, my dear, is the symbol of The Society for the Betterment of the British Race, a scientific association I am privileged to belong to. It is the ancient Saxon rune for 'hero'. And that is precisely what our future promises if we are bold enough to grasp it—a race of noble heroes."

"Are you a scientist, then?" Lily asked as they stepped through the door.

"A scientist? No, no. I'm in toothpicks."

"Toothpicks?"

"World's leading manufacturer of toothpicks," he confirmed with a slight slur.

An attendant swooped in at the door, plucking her cloak from her shoulders. She forced herself not to shiver as the cold winter air touched the exposed skin of her neck and shoulders. She did not often wear evening dress—she had no occasion to—so the feeling of open air on her skin was unusual. The attendant moved to pass her coat check ticket to the brandy-scented gentleman, but Lily neatly plucked it from his hand in midair, tucking it into her reticule.

"Thank you," she said.

The shedding of coats had given her an excuse to detach herself from her escort. She made sure to slip forward into the crowd before he could collect himself and wonder where she had got to.

Once away from the door, the room warmed considerably, bordering on stuffy. It was crowded with bodies. Women in silk, jewels and feathers flitted between men with neatly waxed mustaches who smelled of scotch and tobacco.

The interior of the gallery was designed to look like an elegant drawing room. It was done in tasteful hues of red and gold. Deep crimson covered the walls while antique oriental carpets warmed the floor. Potted palms and ferns offered splashes of bright green. The space was lit with electric lights, far more tastefully than usual. Instead of the typical glare, the effect was that of a warm glow, providing ample illumination for viewing the pieces covering the walls without compromising the softness of the atmosphere.

The room buzzed with conversation and the occasional tinkle of bright, artificial laughter.

She moved along the wall, studying the assortment of works carefully framed and mounted there. Most were what she had expected. There were dull landscapes and gory hunting scenes. A portrait of someone's once-scandalous grandmother reclining on a chaise in eighteenth century splendor.

She paused to accept a glass of champagne, letting the natural current of all those well-dressed bodies carry her along, until she came up short at the utterly unexpected sound of a familiar voice.

"Tell the rotters they need to circulate. Circulate!"

The point was emphasized by a quick twirl of the speaker's hand, and a name dropped from Lily's surprised lips before she could think better of it.

"Mr. Roth?"

The man in question was of middle age, his head bald save for a neatly-trimmed ring around his ears and neck. He carried a touch of extra weight, but the excellent cut of his suit did much to ameliorate any impact it might have on his appearance. He turned at the sound of her voice.

"I'm terribly sorry," Lily said, trying to think of a way to backpedal from the attention her outburst had drawn. "You likely don't remember me and are obviously busy. I won't trouble you."

"Hold on. I know that hair. And the voice! It is you, isn't it? You're Deirdre's girl."

Mordecai Roth had been a fixture of London's theatre scene when Lily was a girl, despite the fact that he neither acted, wrote nor directed. But he had, so the rumors went, once been the lover of Oscar Wilde. As the son of a powerful Jewish family with a fortune in shipping insurance and a thorough set of *ton* connections, he also had the funds to throw patronage at struggling shows he deemed worthy of the support.

Roth had been a regular guest at the salons and parties Deirdre held in her suite of rooms on Oxford Street, providing cutting commentary on the current state of British playwriting and brushing off the importunities of aspiring actors and producers. Lily had been a child at the time, but Deirdre's lackadaisical parenting style had enabled her to sit with the crowd at her soirees, so long as she could escape her nanny unnoticed—which she had always found easy enough to do.

"Of course it's Deirdre's girl," he went on, not bothering to wait for confirmation. "The resemblance is unmistakable. Though you've a fair bit of *him* in you as well—for whatever that's worth. But what brings you out to my modest little gallery?"

"This is your gallery?"

"I bought it for a song off a couple of incompetents who had managed to bring it to the brink of foreclosure. It has since been entirely turned around."

"I am sure it has. It is quite lovely."

"Thank you, dear girl. But don't tell me you've taken up collecting?"

"Heavens, no. I was just . . . curious. And looking for something to do."

"Aren't we all?" Roth sighed.

Lily realized she had inadvertently stumbled across a means of getting straight to the piece that interested her, rather than fighting her way through the crowd that continued to eddy about the room.

"Mr. Roth—your advert mentioned you were showing a piece by E.V. Ash. I recently heard of an artist by that name and am wondering if it's the same person."

"It's the Ash you're interested in, is it? Well—she is quite the popular lady this evening. Allow me to introduce you."

He took her arm and steered her expertly through the crush of bodies to a work at the far side of the gallery.

"Mrs. Ash, meet Miss Albright. Miss Albright, may I present Mrs. Ash," he announced with a flourish, waving from Lily to a portrait that hung on the wall, elegantly lit by a set of electric sconces.

"It's a self-portrait?" Lily asked quietly, the impact of the painting taking some of the breath out of her lungs.

"More or less," Roth replied.

The image was of moderate size, no more than two feet in either direction. It depicted a woman who would not have been considered conventionally lovely. Her brows were too pronounced, thick and dark, her mouth too wide. Her dark eyes and tawny skin hinted at an origin something other than entirely English.

Yet despite the unfashionable strength of her nose, there was something deeply striking about the woman on the canvas—an effect that was not purely due to the fact that she had four arms.

The oddity was depicted with subtle elegance, so that one giving the piece only a casual sweep with the eye might not even notice. The limbs in question were arranged in a manner that made them feel entirely natural, though there was still something about them that reminded Lily of the grotesque statue in Robert Ash's library—the goddess Kali, Mr. Cairncross had called her.

The woman in the painting sat in a chair before a large standing vase, its blue and white glazing done in a pattern of a thousand delicately-rendered keys. The vase itself contained a spray of long-stemmed flowers—lilies, she recognized, with a slight start of discomfort. Flame-orange calla lilies.

The artist's gown was black, a rich hue with elements of blue and purple, but it was not cut like a mourning dress. The neckline was fashionable, the sleeves—all four of them—elegantly tapered.

Her feet were bare, her toes just emerging from under the hemline of her gown.

Lily looked closer and realized there was something off about the floor as well.

It was not a floor at all but water—a dark, still surface that reflected the room above. Little ripples gathered around the legs of the chair, the bottom of the vase.

Then, of course, there were her eyes.

Instead of irises, they were filled with what appeared to be tiny, shimmering lines. The delicate network, like a spiderweb, was rendered with such skill it appeared not only on the surface, but as something with depth. Lily had the urge to ask for a magnifying glass to get a closer look and discern just how far they went.

Then again, the idea of getting that close to the woman in the painting was unsettling.

One of the artist's hands held a painter's brush and a fall of bright crimson silk. The other reached toward the edge of the painting, where, in the deep shadows, a more rugged and masculine hand could be seen extending toward it, just failing to make contact.

In her other two hands, she held a banner, a strip of parchment on which were written the words, *Méfie-toi de l'étranger dont les paroles sont douces comme le miel.* Lily's schoolgirl French was enough for her to make out the message without help: "Beware the stranger whose words are sweet as honey."

As she gazed at it, the buzz of conversation receded along with the uncomfortable warmth of the room. She felt as though she was viewing the artifact not in a crowded, brightly-lit gallery, but at the end of a long, dark hallway. Everything grew dimmer but the painting, the strange symbols woven into its fabric seeming to whisper to her from the canvas.

The understanding came to her with a clarity that defied doubt. This was not some artistic pretense. It was a language, one Lily didn't speak but was just capable of hearing.

"So that's her? That's Mrs. Ash?" The words felt strange on her tongue, as though she had to remember how to speak them.

"There are artistic liberties, of course. I mean beyond the extra appendages. She was actually much prettier in real life. Made an unexpected splash when she came out. There were several very eligible bachelors competing for her hand. It was quite the contest." He waved at the painting. "The work isn't to everyone's taste, but I've always found it engrossing. Not charming, certainly, but . . . challenging. Thankfully I am not alone in my appreciation. The show has just opened and I already have not one, but two offers on the table for her. Both highly motivated. The seller inherited the thing and could care less for it. There's barely a reserve, but my commission goes up with the price, so let the battle commence, eh?"

Roth was clearly delighted by the notion of a bidding war, but something about the prospect left Lily feeling uneasy. She pushed it aside. What did it matter to her who ended up with the painting?

"Who do you have on your line?" she asked, more to make conversation than anything else.

He took a step closer to her, scanning the room, then nodded.

"There's one. Dr. Joseph Hartwell, renowned physician, formerly of the Royal College, now in private practice. Counts among his clientele the Countess of Sussex and at least one dowager duchess."

The man Roth indicated was a tall, striking older gentleman. He had a thick head of well-kept white hair and was impeccably dressed. She imagined he must once have been quite handsome. He still cut a dashing figure.

"The good doctor is very well respected in his circle. He has apparently made some remarkable advancements in the science of hematology. There is talk of a Nobel. Pity he's such a rotter."

Lily gave him a surprised look.

"Oh, he's as gentlemanly as they come. Just thinks the likes of you and I should refrain from breeding."

"Sorry?" she nearly choked on her champagne.

"Bad blood, you see. You Irish, us Jews. The Chinese, the Africans, more or less anyone with an income of under £500 a year. He's founded a whole club on it."

"The Society for the Betterment of the British Race?" Lily offered, instinct prompting the guess.

"Don't tell me you've signed on."

"No. I met a member on the way in."

Roth sighed. "There are always a few of them buzzing about when the good doctor is in the room. He has quite the loyal following."

"They're eugenicists." Lily had heard of the notion, though it was generally not painted in such bald terms as those Roth employed. It was framed as a scientific study that expanded upon the principles of evolution and applied them to mankind. The promise was that man's rational capability for self-awareness and self-analysis, coupled with a greater understanding of the science of evolution and heredity, could empower him to take control of the destiny of his species and shape it, deliberately, in a direction that would foster growth and as-yet-unimaginable achievement.

A race of noble heroes, as the toothpick-maker at the door had promised her. One that excluded anyone who didn't look and act like the men and women who filled this stuffy room.

Roth sipped his glass. It was filled with water, Lily noted, and not champagne. It did not surprise her. He was far too canny a business-man to allow drink to muddle his brain when there were deals to be made.

"He needn't worry about it so far as I'm concerned. I've about as much interest in breeding as I do in drinking vinegar for breakfast. But he will pay for the piece."

"How can you be so sure?"

"Because he was one of those suitors I mentioned."

Lily started with surprise and was unable to conceal it. Her reaction clearly delighted Roth.

"Oh yes! And isn't that ironic? The eugenicist on his knees plead-ing for the hand of the daughter of an Indian. Her father was a major with the East India Company, but her mother was a native. The fam-ily had distant ties to a Canadian rail company, so there was a mod-erate fortune behind her, but nothing to compare with Hartwell's. It must have been impossible for him to imagine she would be any-thing but grateful for his offer. Yet she turned down the dashing, wealthy doctor for a scholar from a family nobody had ever heard of. Of course, I'm sure that the lady's choice has nothing at all to do with the good doctor's current passion for sterilizing her racial cohorts along with anyone else he believes should be tossed into the same bucket. I believe I am not taking too far a leap when I predict he will pay whatever he needs to in order to secure this painting."

Lily found herself hoping that Roth would find a way to thoroughly fleece the respected physician on this purchase.

"And your other buyer?" she asked, curious as to whom she was apparently rooting for in the contest for Evangeline Ash's portrait.

"That is the only complicating factor of this whole endeavor. He's a regular client of mine and one of those rarest of beasts: a true bohemian, though you would never know it to look at him. Very modern, extremely discerning. He appreciates works that no one else in this room would be able to wrap their tonnish heads around. I just wish he had more money to spend, but despite the title, his credit is limited. If he had an extra thousand or two a year to play around with—oh, what wonders we might work together! That's him, over there, the Byronic hero with the gloves on."

Lily followed the line of Roth's gesture, and the chaos and noise of the room focused to a point.

It was Lord Strangford.

Besides the slightly unfashionable length of his hair, there was nothing about him to support Roth's claim that he was some sort of iconoclast. His evening dress was as unremarkably sober as the black suit she had seen him in the day before, if substantially more formal. It was well-made, the cut a touch out-of-date, finished with a simple black neckcloth identical to the one she had bled all over the day before.

There were no flourishes or flash—just those black gloves wrought in fine kid leather. Lily was certain they were the same pair he had been wearing when he had pulled her up from the road. She realized that they had also covered his hands when he appeared on the landing of The Refuge.

There were other men in the room who wore gloves as part of their evening kit, though those were almost exclusively white and of a fine fabric like silk or delicate wool, not leather.

The room was warm for such a heavy material. Lily began to wonder if Lord Strangford's choice in wearing them was not a whim of fashion. Perhaps the gloves hid some scar or other disfigurement, but then, his appearance in The Refuge had been highly informal. Surely if he felt comfortable enough there to walk around in what was little better than a set of pajamas, he wouldn't have needed to hide the relics of an old injury.

But what other purpose could they serve?

Roth leaned in to give her the rest of the story.

"Both Hartwell and his lordship there offered to buy the piece sight unseen, but I insisted they come to the opening before I would accept a formal offer. With the pair of them in a room together it's far more likely the allure of the contest will get the better of them and drive up the price higher than they might otherwise allow, if they had time to think about it in the sober quiet of their drawing rooms."

Roth was right, a notion that made Lily uneasy.

"As an added bonus, my little stratagem lures Lord Strangford from his townhouse. The man is a notorious recluse. The match-making dowagers have been trying all manner of tricks—deception, guilt, a little light blackmail—to pry him out to their balls and dinner parties for years. He always turns them down. And yet now I have got him out. What a coup for me, eh?"

Lord Strangford's interest in the painting must not be for himself, but for the husband of the woman who had painted it—Mr. Ash. That Ash might choose not to come and bid for it himself was hardly shocking, given the grief she had glimpsed in him that morning when the topic of his wife had risen.

Her own sense of who ought to win the battle Roth had established was clear. Evangeline Ash's portrait ought to go to the man the artist herself had chosen.

But would it?

Roth had indicated that Lord Strangford's funds were limited, and it was clear that Hartwell was a man of substantial means. It was quite plausible he might offer more than Lord Strangford was capable of countering. As for Roth, he would not be moved by stories of lost love, no matter how poignant. He was too hard-nosed for that.

Not that it was any of her business.

Lord Strangford turned toward them. Lily looked away, pretending to study the painting.

She wasn't at all sure what she should say to him if he noticed she was there. She could not shake the image of him standing on the landing of The Refuge, a building dedicated to the education and training of . . .

*Charismatics*, Ash had called them.

People like her.

A thousand questions burned in her mind, none of which she was willing to ask, because to do so might compel her to reveal her own closely-guarded secrets.

"Good evening, Roth," Lord Strangford said, his voice rich and low behind her.

"Lovely to see you out and about, my lord."

"You did make it rather difficult to stay at home. Can we speak of my offer?"

"Oh, there will be plenty of time for that. Why don't you relax first? Have a drink, do a bit of mingling. You could start with an old friend of mine. Miss Albright, may I introduce Lord Strangford?"

There was no escaping it. Lily turned and offered Lord Strangford a polite smile.

"Good evening, my lord."

She noted the quick flash of surprise. He reined it in. There was an air of tight control about him here that she had not seen out on the heath.

"A pleasure to see you again, Miss Albright."

"You're already acquainted?" Roth asked, clearly intrigued.

"Our paths have crossed lately," Lily replied thinly.

"Then it will not be out of line for me to leave the two of you to catch up. If you'll excuse me, I need to go harangue the caterer. The canapes should have been out twenty minutes ago." He took up Lily's hand and gave it a kiss. "It has been an unexpected treat, my dear."

He slipped away into the crowd, deserting her to the awkwardness than hung suspended in the air between her and the man in front of her.

There were too many things she couldn't say. The weight of them left her scrambling for some common courtesy to fill the space left by those unasked questions.

Lord Strangford got to it first.

"How is your leg?"

"Quite well, thank you."

"I'm glad to hear it."

Another tense pause descended.

The crowd around them was growing more boisterous, the chatter amplified by the quick-flowing champagne. A particularly bright note of laughter cut through the hum of noise, as clear and resonant as a bell. Lily instinctively looked for the source of it but saw only the flash of a white gown between moving bodies by the front door.

A portly gentleman with a woman obviously not his wife on his arm moved past, a bit unevenly. Strangford took a step to the side to avoid them.

"Mr. Roth said you don't usually attend events like this."

"I'm not very fond of crowds."

There was a tension in him. It was subtle but Lily could see it in the way he avoided contact with the close-pressed bodies milling around them. He hid his discomfort well but once she was aware of it, it became tangible.

She was reminded of his strange hesitancy on the heath whenever courtesy demanded he offer her his hand or his shoulder. That, too, had been subtle.

Too many questions.

She grasped for something safe.

"I hear you are a collector."

"In as much as I can be, yes."

"What's your interest? Pastorals? Portraits?"

"Sometimes. But not exactly."

"How enlightening."

He took a deep breath.

"I am drawn to . . . anything that shows me something I did not expect to see."

"Such as?"

"A cathedral turned inside-out. The rhythm of a sunrise. A certain arch of a woman's eyebrow. It's . . . hard to for me to put words to it. The works don't fit into any box. They just . . . manage to capture some small piece of the truth."

"The truth of what?"

"Of what lies under the surface of things."

Lily considered him.

"So you really are a bohemian."

Lord Strangford lifted a dark eyebrow.

"Roth said as much," she explained. "But I found it hard to credit. Any other bohemian I have met was either far more colorful or utterly miserable."

Something twitched at the corner of his mouth, his eyes bright.

"Is that so?"

Lily felt a smile tugging at her own mouth in response.

Roth returned.

"Lord Strangford, there is someone I would like you to meet. Miss Albright, I promise I shall return him shortly."

*Dowager*, Roth mouthed to her behind him as they moved away, nodding toward a straight-backed elderly woman in an elaborate pink gown. Apparently he was ensuring that the powers-that-be were aware of his social coup in getting Lord Strangford out of the house.

That left Lily alone with Evangeline Ash. As her attention returned to the painting, she felt its influence threaten to creep over her again.

She turned the other way, letting the crowd carry her along the room. The current tossed her up against a cluster of people gathered around the tall figure of Dr. Hartwell.

Curiosity about the other bidder for Mrs. Ash's portrait—and former suitor for her hand—got the better of her. She let herself become attached to the little coterie.

Most of the bodies gathered there belonged to older, wealthy women, who were listening enrapt as a gentleman in evening tails puffed on about the greatness of Hartwell's work.

"It is quite the most remarkable development—your excellent research into the possible organization of human blood into distinct types. You must understand the potential implications, ladies," he added, addressing the crowd. "The transference of human blood from a donor to a recipient has been impossible without the risk of most terrible complications before now, but with Dr. Hartwell's discoveries—"

"You mustn't get ahead of yourself, Mr. Edwards. There is some distance yet to go before transfusion is a possibility," Hartwell cut in. The modesty seemed to play well with the ladies of the crowd.

Lily noted that a few of the men scattered around Hartwell wore the Saxon hero rune pin of the toothpick-maker who had escorted her in, the sigil of Hartwell's eugenics club.

One of them piped in.

"Of course, I am sure there are other questions you must wish to investigate. Such as whether some of these qualities of the blood constitute a superior strain, one which we might wish to encourage to propagate."

At the mention of the word "propagate", a few fans began to flutter, one woman letting out a nervous titter.

"There is quite a lot of research still to be done," Hartwell noted.

"How very remarkable!" one of the women close by murmured.

"Indeed," her companion replied, though her focus appeared to be more on the doctor's figure than on his ideas.

The heat began to get to her. She pushed away from the group, looking for more air, but there was none to be had, the crowd thick in every direction. Silk and gems shimmered, the scent of furniture polish and perfume thick and cloying.

She shouldn't have come. This was not her world. The whole endeavor had been a poorly thought-out lark.

If that weren't enough, her leg was beginning to throb. She had pushed it too far since the wreck, and it was announcing its irritation. It was well past time she went home.

She pulled her cloakroom ticket from her reticule, intending to weave her way to the door.

She turned to see Lord Strangford standing just behind her.

"Oh!"

"I didn't mean to surprise you." His gaze fell to the ticket in her hand. "Were you leaving?"

All the unasked questions flooded in, demanding answers to the mystery of his role at The Refuge. She had no intention of seeing him again, which meant this moment was likely the last where she could hope to satisfy the curiosity that burned inside of her.

"I was just . . ." she began, but the rest of her words were cut off by the high song of a female voice that cut through the hum and clatter of the crowd.

"Anthony!"

The sound had a surprising effect on Lord Strangford. Though nothing obvious changed in his posture or expression, Lily could see a stiffness infuse his frame, an air of tight control.

A woman approached them, one who did not slip through the crowd but rather parted it around her like Moses with his staff. She was small and well-rounded, clad in a striking ivory gown that contrasted with her shining dark hair. Her skin was flawless, glowing with the kind of beauty that men did not bother to conceal their admiration for. Lily realized that it was her clear laugh she had been hearing dancing above the crowd all evening, like a siren's song enchanting everyone within earshot.

"Who would have thought to find you out at something like this!" she exclaimed as she arrived. "But what a charming surprise it is. It has been ever so long since I've seen you!"

"Mrs. Boyden." Lord Strangford greeted her with a flat courtesy that contrasted starkly with the woman's chatty enthusiasm.

"You know that you may always call me Annalise—did we not grow up practically side-by-side? If that does not justify such intimacy, I do not know what would."

Lord Strangford did not answer.

Mrs. Boyden did not seem to notice the silence. Instead, she turned and called over her shoulder.

"Darling, you won't believe who I've found!"

The crowd moved again, revealing who was coming toward them.

Lily felt her own chest tighten.

She knew that face. She knew those clear gray eyes, the patrician nose. The cut of his jaw bore a neat resemblance to the features she saw every time she looked into a mirror, because both came from the same noble source.

The man standing at the side of the brunette who so unsettled Lord Strangford was Simon Carne, Viscount Deveral—eldest son of the Earl of Torrington.

And Lily's half-brother.

# SIX

$\mathcal{T}$HE FIRST TIME LILY saw her half-brother, she did so deliberately. She read a notice in the paper that an alumni match between Oxford and Cambridge veteran scullers would be taking place on the Thames. Lord Deveral's name was mentioned. Lily was unable to resist the urge to catch a glimpse of the eldest of Lord Torrington's four sons, a man who shared half her blood.

It was easy enough to spot him, even yards away on the water. He was clearly their father's son, though with the countess's light hair and a softer cut to his features.

The second time was pure accident, nearly walking into him as he exited his club with a raucous group of other young noblemen.

On neither occasion had she introduced herself. Why would she? What possible interest could he have in her? She was certainly less than nothing to him, if he even knew she existed. If he didn't, it was better it remain that way.

Faced with her father's heir in the posh, crowded gallery on Bury Street, Lily shifted her body. It was a subtle maneuver, slight enough not to attract Mrs. Boyden's attention, but it would give someone just arriving at the scene the impression that she was part of a different conversation.

Mrs. Boyden, either oblivious to or purposefully ignoring Lord

Strangford's coolness, tucked a hand under his arm, extending the other to pull Lord Deveral closer.

"Lord Deveral, Lord Strangford. There, Deveral, now you can put a face to the stories—it has taken long enough." She turned back to Lord Strangford again, flashing him a smile marked by white, even teeth. "You've become a regular hermit, haven't you? Though one wouldn't know it to look at you. You are keeping quite well."

Lily was still listening attentively, even as she pretended to be drawn into some chatter about race horses.

She recognized Mrs. Boyden—not the woman but the type.

The theatre attracted them, men and women who were beautiful and had developed expertise at manipulating that valuable resource. Mrs. Boyden wielded her beauty with an easy confidence, clearly accustomed to its power.

"Pleased to meet you," Lord Deveral replied flatly.

Lily's every fiber was aware of him beside her though he had yet to take notice of anyone but Mrs. Boyden and Lord Strangford. He appeared bored and restless.

"Lord Deveral," Lord Strangford acknowledged, bowing politely. He was clearly too much the gentleman to give anyone a snub, no matter what history lay between him and the woman beside him— and what present relation stood between that woman and the viscount.

Lily could hazard a few guesses.

She sensed the shift in Lord Strangford's body and realized with horror what he was about to do.

*Please don't*, she begged silently, but the message went unheard.

"May I present Miss Albright," he offered with exquisite formality.

It was possible the name would mean nothing to the steel-eyed man holding Mrs. Boyden's other arm. She had no notion what he knew of his father's past. He was only a few years older than herself. He would have been a child when his father's affair had been carried on, hardly of an age to be taken into confidence about such matters or even treated to gossip about them.

Lily turned from the group in which she had been hiding herself and plastered a polite smile on her face.

Any hope that he was unaware of her existence was snuffed out. His gray eyes had gone even colder, any pretense of charm dropping from his features.

"You," he hissed.

The antagonism was so strong it had substance, thickening the already close atmosphere of the gallery. It made her want to bolt, fleeing the room like the fox at a hunt.

She would not. To do anything now but play the part of graceful indifference would be to show weakness in front of this man, this stranger who was also her brother—and who clearly, unequivocally hated her.

She straightened her back, wrapping herself in cold courtesy. She curtsied, the gesture well-practiced thanks to her finishing school years. It was only as deep as was strictly necessary, an expression of pure formality.

"A pleasure to meet you, my lord."

"Do you know each other or not?" Mrs. Boyden demanded, her curiosity clearly sparked.

Lily was saved from answering, and from hearing Lord Deveral's reply, by the return of Mordecai Roth.

He addressed Lord Strangford.

"Excuse me, my lord. May I speak to you privately for a moment?"

Hesitation flickered across Lord Strangford's features. His eyes touched on Lily and she realized he must have picked up on the tension between her and the new arrival, even through his own obvious discomfort.

Thankfully, he could not possibly know the reason for it.

Lord Deveral had regained some control over himself, at least for the moment. He sniffed loudly and looked away, directing his glare over the crowd itself, fingers tapping restlessly against his leg.

She gave no response, no indication that Lord Strangford's concern was warranted. She did not need some nobleman she barely knew trying to play knight-in-armor in a battle he couldn't and shouldn't understand.

"If you'll pardon me," Lord Strangford said and allowed Roth to lead him away.

Mrs. Boyden sighed. Her disappointment reminded Lily of a cat deprived of a mouse. She applied herself to scanning the crowd for some other source of entertainment.

"Oh, there's George. I simply must congratulate him on that merger of his. Deveral?"

She moved on without bothering to confirm whether the viscount was following.

He did not follow. He remained where he was.

He made a show of glancing around.

"I don't see your escort, Miss Albright."

She tensed, never doubting that this was an attack.

"I am unescorted," she replied evenly.

"Casting your line for a new fish, eh? Odd place to go about it, but then I'm hardly the expert you must be, having learned the trade at your mother's feet."

Her ears rang as though someone had just slapped her. The shock rendered her momentarily speechless.

It was not the first time she had been so baldly insulted. There had been years of it to endure at Mrs. Finch's once her classmates learned of her origins—which had taken them very little time at all. There are few things one can keep secret from a bevy of determined schoolgirls.

This was different. There was more behind it than delight in an opportunity to set down someone who could not fight back. It was visceral, a pointed and real desire to inflict an injury, to cause her pain.

Rage rose up in her in response to being called a whore, to her face, in front of a room full of people.

Then he sniffed again.

He pulled out a handkerchief, habitually wiping at his nose. Lily noted his quick movements, the restless energy of his frame. Then there were his eyes, the pupils dilated to nearly cover his distinctive gray irises, even though the room was quite well-lit. Lily had seen those signs before. She knew what they signified.

He had taken cocaine.

Mrs. Boyden's cut-crystal laugh rang through the room, emanating from the center of a circle of well-dressed older men.

She was using it as well. They must have taken it together, perhaps in the carriage before they came in. The effect would not last much longer than an hour.

There was nothing inherently scandalous in the use of cocaine. It was a perfectly respectable remedy for all manner of ills, no different from quinine or laudanum.

However, she doubted Lord Deveral was taking the stuff for his rheumatism.

Contempt rose in her, that this arrogant man would believe himself justified in casting insults at her while making illicit indulgences of his own.

She straightened, adopting her most haughty tone and posture, both of which she knew she came by quite naturally.

"Fishing, my lord? I'm afraid I haven't any experience of the sport. And my mother landed only one catch, to my knowledge—some bony thing I expect went off before she had any enjoyment of it. If you'll excuse me."

She slipped past him into the crowd.

She would not head for the door, no matter how desperately attractive the notion of escaping back to March Place and the solitude of her room was at that moment. She would not give her brother the satisfaction of feeling that he had driven her out. She would mingle with the crowd for a while, make a point of appearing to have a marvelous time, then quietly make her exit when he wasn't paying attention.

He would not be paying attention for long, at any rate. Not with cocaine raging through his blood.

She moved without any clear direction, studying whatever paintings the current of the crowd threw her against without any real interest. Most did not justify more than a casual glance—dull, smoky landscapes, or still-life paintings of wilting flowers and glistening fruit. Amid all the drowning Pre-Raphaelite ladies and predictable portraits, however, were a scattered few pieces that did warrant a real look, works of more startling color and arrangement. She could see the mark of Roth's taste in those choices, his appreciation for something a bit more daring than most aristocrats wanted in their drawing rooms.

One in particular caught her eye. She used it as an excuse to linger and spin out more of the time that waited between her and her chance to make an escape.

The canvas was light, as though incompletely painted. The scene it depicted was one of crashing waves under a bright, cloud-streaked sky. The water was rendered in elegant splashes of pale gray-blue, accented here and there with darker tones. Negative space formed the crests and foam. The whole effect was one of startling movement and liveliness, far more true to the experience of the sea than any literal representation would have been.

"Ah, the Whistler. Roth is stretching his theme with it. The man was an American, however much he painted here in Britain. Still, excellent choice. But so is the other piece you have demonstrated an interest in this evening."

Lily turned to see Dr. Joseph Hartwell standing beside her.

She felt her guard go up, though there was nothing in the man's tone that indicated his interest in her was anything more than casual.

He glanced across the gallery at Evangeline Ash's portrait, which was just visible between the moving bodies of the crowd.

"It is not a true representation," he commented. "She exaggerated flaws I doubt anyone who knew her in life would have noticed."

"I take it you aren't referring to the extra arms."

He waved a hand dismissively. "A bit of grotesque fancy." He continued, his tone just as light, though the import of the words was clear. "You may tell Lord Strangford that I will bid as high as is necessary for the work. He may drive the price up as much as he likes, but he will not have it."

Lily was in no mood to tolerate little slights, like being assumed the errand-girl of a nobleman she barely knew—not coming on the heels of Lord Deveral's bald insults.

"I beg your pardon, but I am not Lord Strangford's page. If you have a message for him you may deliver it yourself." Her Torrington blood asserted itself in her tone, infusing it with an icy hauteur.

Hartwell bowed elegantly.

"Of course. Do accept my apology."

Her dislike of the man was visceral, as tangible as the carpet under her slippers. It struck her with surprising force. She felt an urge to goad him into shattering some part of his elegant veneer and revealing what lay beneath.

She pulled herself back from that edge, painfully conscious of her circumstances. She was an interloper in a room full of people who would be horrified to be seen with her if they knew what she was. She must tread carefully or risk exposure.

She ought to move away but a spark of curiosity made her pause. Why did he want it?

His interest in the piece could not be financial. Evangeline Ash was not so well-known an artist that her work would be seen as an investment. It also seemed a rather thin possibility that the man in front of her simply happened to be enamored beyond price with the artistic style of the woman who had passed him over for another man.

There was something else at work here, despite Hartwell's cool sophistication. Perhaps it was as simple as a sort of bitter revenge—if he could not have the woman, he would at least possess her portrait. It was a piece of her he could own, mounted on his wall like an exotic hunting trophy.

But why had he wanted to own her at all? Based on Roth's description, and what Lily herself had observed, Hartwell was a man with a healthy sense of his own worth.

Evangeline Ash hadn't possessed a fortune. She was half-native, a severe handicap in the eyes of many of Hartwell's class. She was not a conventional beauty. So what about the woman had drawn an eminent man of rising fortune to want her so badly he would still seek to possess what he could of her thirty years after her death?

Ash's words came back to her, floating across the cool, dim stillness of his reflection room.

*My wife was a charismatic.*

Fingers of unease crept up the exposed skin of Lily's arms. She was conscious of the dark gaze of the dead woman through the gaps in the glittering bodies that separated her from the canvas on the far wall.

Had Hartwell known? Had Ash? Was that what had drawn them to her like moths to the moon?

But she was jumping ahead of all sense. Robert Ash was a well-meaning eccentric. His wife was a uniquely talented artist. That was all Lily knew for certain. Hartwell's interest in the woman might very well have no logical explanation at all, unnatural or otherwise. Desire worked like that. How else could Lily's own origins be explained?

"Dr. Hartwell! A moment, if you please." A well-dressed couple sailed toward him, another pair of admirers eager to stroke his ego.

"If you will excuse me," he said with a polite nod before turning to meet the new arrivals.

A certainty arose in her, as real as it was unwelcome.

She could not let him win.

The portrait on the wall did not belong with him. It belonged at The Refuge with Robert Ash—who wasn't here. Hartwell was right to be confident. Lord Strangford would certainly come out on the wrong side of a bidding war.

Lily would simply have to ensure that this contest was not won in bidding.

But how to accomplish that? Mordecai Roth might be her mother's old friend, but that loyalty wouldn't stretch far. It likely wasn't enough to keep her from getting tossed out of the room if she caused any trouble that threatened his sales.

What she needed was a way to take Hartwell out of the equation as a potential buyer. That would leave only Lord Strangford to purchase the painting. If Roth thought one of his catches had gone off, he'd be grateful for whatever was still on his hook.

But how could she remove Hartwell from the game?

If she were her mother, she would cause a scene, manufacturing some offense or staging a violent lovers' tiff in hopes of embarrassing him out of the room. Lily dismissed that. She was not an actress and had no desire to draw any more attention to herself in this place than she had already. However she did this, she would need to do it quietly—the way her father got things done, moving his pieces with elegant strategy from behind the scenes.

Art buyers didn't walk into galleries with cash in their pocket. These purchases were negotiated on credit. If Lily could convince Roth that Hartwell was incapable of delivering whatever he promised, and then made Lord Strangford's offer contingent on being accepted that night . . .

The bright, silk-clad crowd swirled around her as the plan pulled together in her mind.

This was not something Lily could suggest herself. Roth knew that she was acquainted with Lord Strangford. Anything she told him about Hartwell would be viewed, rightfully, with canny suspicion.

She needed this message to come from another source. It needed to be someone with social clout who clearly had nothing to gain from the situation.

Her eyes danced over the jewel-bedecked bodies and stopped on the figure of Viscount Deveral.

His handkerchief was at his nose again. He tucked it haphazardly back into his pocket.

*Yes,* she thought distantly. *That could work.*

The pieces had fallen into place neatly in her mind. As the son and heir of Lord Torrington, no one would question how Lord Deveral might have access to information no one else had heard. That relationship also far outweighed any dent his lifestyle choices might have made in his reputation.

And Lily had the means to blackmail him into doing what she wanted.

The boldness of it nearly made her drop her champagne. She kept hold of the stem of the glass by sheer will, frozen in place by the audacity of what she was contemplating.

It would enrage him.

Had there ever been any chance of some rapport between Lily and her half-brother, this was sure to destroy it.

Then again, tonight's exchange had made it quite clear that a rapport had never been within the realm of possibility.

There was therefore nothing to lose. So why was her heart pounding like a steam engine inside of her chest?

He was just a man, she reminded herself forcefully. He meant nothing to her. The worst he could do to her in this crowded room was embarrass her and he couldn't accomplish that without also exposing himself to scandal.

A man still enraged about the gossip his father had brought on the family decades ago would not willingly do that.

Lily straightened her back and slipped through the crowd, coming up to where Lord Deveral stood alone next to a scene of a fox being torn to pieces by a pack of beagles.

"I'd like you to do me a favor," she announced without preamble.

"Why the devil would I agree to do anything for you?" he retorted flatly.

Lily pretended she had not heard.

"I want you to tell Roth that Dr. Joseph Hartwell's credit is not to be relied upon."

Lord Deveral turned to stare at her with obvious shock.

"Are you quite mad?"

"No," Lily replied calmly. "Nor am I currently intoxicated with cocaine."

He went still for a telling moment. Then he shrugged.

"So? It's hardly a crime."

"Would our father share that attitude, I wonder?"

His glare was like ice, cold and sharp enough to cut.

"You wouldn't dare."

"Why wouldn't I? Though perhaps he wouldn't believe me. What do you think, my lord? Would our father credit such a story, were I to ensure he heard it?"

"You're a cold little bitch."

"Just do it. Now. So I can hear you. And then I may return to ignoring you, and you to debauching yourself."

She could see the war being fought inside of him, fear battling with some other urge, likely the instinct to strike her in the middle of this room.

Even for the heir to the Earl of Torrington, that would have been beyond the pale, as he well knew.

She held herself steady, meeting the violence in his gaze without flinching. She could not show any hint of uncertainty or the game would surely be up.

He cursed. It was a particularly vile one. His glass slammed down onto the table and he stalked away.

She watched him move through the crowd, all but pushing the pearl-strung dowagers out of his path on his way to Roth.

Lily followed more carefully, slipping through the close-packed bodies until she was within earshot of the gallery owner.

"Are you quite certain?" Roth demanded.

"I have it from a reliable source," Lord Deveral replied flatly.

"And why share it with me? Out of the goodness of your heart?"

"Why does it matter?" the viscount snapped. "I shared it. Do with it what you like. I've done my part."

He cast a razor sharp glare over at Lily before turning and stalking in the opposite direction. He pushed his way through the crowd to where Annalise Boyden stood, grabbing her arm and lowering his mouth to her ear.

"Oh, fine," she replied. She flashed a charming smile at the gentleman in front of her, murmuring some excuse, and the pair turned, Lord Deveral plowing them a path to the door.

Lily's limbs wanted to tremble, unraveled by the quick catch and release of conflict. She restrained the urge. There was another move yet to make.

She singled out Lord Strangford. He had found the Whistler and stood by it alone, his attention on it complete.

"Go to Roth. Make him an offer," Lily ordered as she reached his side. "A generous one. Tell him it is contingent upon the contract being made tonight—that the portrait isn't a particularly flattering one and you're not sure Mr. Ash will be willing to pay so much for it once he's seen it himself."

"But none of that is true." He gave her a curious look.

"Let Roth believe Ash might change his mind about the purchase once he sees the work."

"What exactly have you been up to?"

"Do you want the piece or not?"

"It means a great deal."

"Then do it," she ordered.

He didn't move. He gazed at her, making some sort of assessment she couldn't guess at.

She was reminded, abruptly, of how many mysteries this man contained.

She closed her mouth against all of them.

"Very well," he agreed and set down his glass.

He pushed himself into the crowd. Through the bobbing, bejeweled heads of the ton, Lily watched her little drama play out.

Lord Strangford delivered his line and Roth's expression turned thoughtful. There was a moment's pause before he motioned for his clerk.

Then both clerk and Lord Strangford exited together, stage right—the gallery office, Lily surmised, with a quick leap of her pulse.

Roth gestured to another of his staff. There was a brief exchange before the boy was waved off.

As he went, Roth's eyes found Lily across the crowd.

He made her a subtle little bow.

He knew, she realized. And like any good player, he had accepted being outmaneuvered.

The second clerk returned and set a small white placard against the frame of Evangeline Ash's portrait.

*Sold.*

Now for Act II.

Hartwell appeared. His tall frame visibly cut through the crowd as he stalked to Roth. Lily allowed herself to drift a bit closer. His voice was low, but it carried.

"Why was I not allowed to make a counter-offer?"

"The buyer's reserve was more than met. I decided to make the sale."

"And forgo the chance of a higher commission? Since when has one of your lot passed up an opportunity for a greater profit?"

The slur was delivered so casually, it clearly came by instinct.

Roth gave no sign that it wounded him.

"There's a charming little Gainsborough yet unspoken for, if you like. The piece is quite undervalued, in my opinion. An excellent investment for a discerning collector."

"You may keep your Gainsborough," Hartwell snapped. He turned away and scanned the crowd, as though looking for some answer there to the question that was plaguing him.

His gaze stopped on Lily.

She held steady and waited as he moved toward her, though her pulse pounded with a combination of both thrill and fear.

The fear was groundless, she told herself. What could Hartwell do in the middle of a room full of London's finest, even if he guessed that she was behind this loss?

"This was your doing, wasn't it?" he demanded.

"I hope you aren't too put out. You did say the piece was rather flawed."

There was no burst of temper. Hartwell's self-control was substantial.

The painting in question, the portrait of Evangeline Ash, hung just behind him. The effect was uncanny. For a moment, it seemed as though the artist were there, in the room, peering over Hartwell's shoulder with her cobwebbed eyes—as though the dead woman could see them, watching everything that was about to unfold.

"You play well, Miss Albright."

Mrs. Boyden's bell-like laugh rang through the gallery. Lily could see her wrapped in her wool cloak at the door. Lord Deveral's arm slipped about her waist as they faded out into the darkness.

"This time, you had the element of surprise," Hartwell went on. "I am not such a fool as to be taken off-guard twice. You may find our next match a tad more challenging."

He lifted his champagne, a conscious mockery of a toast, and the pieces fell into place.

The glass in his hand blocked her view of the spill of red cloth held by Evangeline Ash. The painted silk turned the wine from gold to crimson. The black length of Hartwell's arm crossed the banner the artist held across her lap, obscuring a handful of letters from the strange French motto written across it—the end of *de*, the opening letters of *l'étranger*. The foreign text slipped away, a word in Lily's own tongue announcing itself from within the text.

*Danger.*

It was a message, the identity of its intended recipient coded into the vase of flame-hued blooms at the artist's back.

Lilies.

No. That was madness. Was she really considering that Mrs. Ash had somehow guessed where her portrait would be hanging on one particular winter's evening 30 years after her death and had designed the entire piece to send a single pointed warning to a woman who hadn't yet been born?

She must have had more champagne than she'd realized. The words, the blossoms, the dead woman's uncanny gaze—it was all just air and nothing.

"You have no idea what I find challenging," Lily replied flatly. "If you'll excuse me, I need a bit of air."

She pushed away. The room felt too close. The heat of all those bodies was oppressive, the electric candles glaring, the smells of perfume and tobacco and wine choking her. She needed to escape, to get back to her safe little garret on March Place.

The current of the crowd was against her as she fought to get to the door, but at last she made it. She handed in her ticket and waited for her cloak. It felt like an eternity. She resisted the urge to desert it and go running out into the night.

At last it arrived. She slipped into the wool, then hurried down the steps, the cold night air a welcome shock after the suffocating heat of the gallery.

A voice from behind arrested her just as her slipper touched the pavement.

"Miss Albright."

Lord Strangford stood in the doorway, framed by the gold light from the electric candles like some dark angel.

"Is something wrong?"

"No," she replied quickly. "Just unaccustomed to keeping such hours." All those questions . . .

They hung in the air between her and the man at the top of the stairs, potent with significance.

Once she left this place, it was unlikely she would ever see him again. It was now or never.

"A pleasure to see you again. Good evening, my lord."

Lily climbed into one of the waiting hackneys. The driver snapped the reins and the vehicle pulled away.

She did not look back.

# SEVEN

$\mathcal{L}$ILY WAS IN A bedroom.

It was not the one where she had lain down to sleep that night after coming home from the gallery. The room was much larger and grander than her own, dominated by an enormous four-poster bed hung with gossamer-light curtains.

Moonlight spilled in through tall windows, painting the space in shades of blue and gray. White powder hung suspended in the air like snowflakes inside a globe.

In the middle of that silent storm, two bodies moved under a tangle of sheets. Disembodied, Lily could not look away, forced to play voyeur to the intimacies of Annalise Boyden and Lord Deveral.

The scene shifted.

Lord Deveral stood by the window, clad in his trousers.

Annalise Boyden, in a pale negligee, sat at a vanity table beside him. She extended her hand and the viscount pulled a jeweled dagger from his pocket. It was a gorgeous thing, medieval in its splendor like a piece of regalia.

She waved it through the air and the white powder that still floated around them caught against the blade. She licked it clean with a neat lap of her tongue, then tossed the dagger onto the table and laughed.

Lord Deveral's expression shifted, a cruel light coming into his eyes. His mouth moved, but the shape of his lips didn't match the words that Lily heard.

*Casting your line for a new fish, eh?*

Annalise Boyden turned, her hand flashing out like the paw of an angry cat. Claws raked across his cheek, vivid red lines appearing in their wake.

A roar sounded in Lily's ears like a wind blowing through the room. Lord Deveral left, the door slamming shut of its own accord behind him.

His lover drifted over to the bed, falling gently backwards onto the sheets, her eyes closing.

The gas lamps lining the wall flickered, flames rising and falling, burning a pale blue.

A shadow detached itself from the corner and drifted into the room.

It circled the bed, making a sound like the jangling of milk bottles as it moved. Its shoulders expanded into dark wings that loomed over the sleeping woman.

The winged nightmare bent, setting its mouth to her pale neck. She sighed, her body rising as it had before when she responded to the attentions of a very different sort of lover.

The dark form dissolved, fading into the shadows of the room. Annalise Boyden sat up in the bed, her hands clasped to her throat.

She fixed Lily with a merciless glare.

"You're late," she accused and the blood began to pour from between her fingers.

—

Lily woke gasping.

She threw off the blanket, the cold air of her room crashing against her skin.

Another vision.

The moving shadow, that bottle-glass clatter, the blood spilling from the dying woman's throat—it was him. The same monster who was coming for Estelle.

But this vision was different. Lily's heart galloped, fire pulsing through her veins, moved by more than just horror.

It was urgency.

The events she'd seen weren't days or weeks away. They were imminent. The woman she met that evening in the gallery—the woman who shared some uncomfortable history with Lord Strangford, and who was currently the lover of Lily's half-brother—was about to die.

She fumbled for the matches on her nightstand, struck one and lit the candle. The glow revealed the hands of the clock on her mantle.

It was three in the morning.

The immediacy of the danger raged through her, building a pressure in her brain so great she felt like a volcano primed to explode.

She had to act, regardless of what good it would do. Even though she knew it was futile, she couldn't lie here in her bed while a woman was moments away from being slaughtered.

She threw open the wardrobe, yanking out a jacket and skirt and throwing them on over her nightgown. She shrugged into her overcoat and grabbed her boots, tucking them under her arm with her walking stick as she raced out the door.

She ran down the stairs, her stockinged feet quick and quiet against the boards.

On the ground floor, she pulled the boots on, tugged open the door and dashed outside.

She stopped for a moment to consider her options. Unsurprisingly, there was no sign of a hackney on March Place in the middle of the night. She might have better luck on Tottenham Court Road, but it would almost certainly be faster to get where she needed to go on her own two feet.

She ran.

The stitches in her leg pulled in protest. She ignored them, bolting past the rows of dark, silent houses.

She didn't slow until she had reached the well-kept garden of Bedford Square and the wide granite steps of The Refuge.

She paused to stare up at the door, her leg burning with pain.

What was she doing? Did she really propose to knock at the door of a virtual stranger at three in the morning?

More frightening than the impropriety of that was the notion of what would happen if her knock was actually answered.

She couldn't hope to get what she needed from those inside that building without opening herself up to questions she had no desire to answer—questions that might expose her for what she really was.

The urgency firing through her did not care about any of that. It screamed in her ears, deafening. She thought of the blood pouring through Annalise Boyden's fingers and mounted the steps.

She grasped the knocker and pounded it against the door.

A moment later, it swung open, revealing the figure of Sam Wu, his nightshirt hastily tucked into a pair of trousers.

She caught the quick, sharp suspicion in his look and knew that his own instincts were telling him to slam the door in her face.

Instead, he stepped back, making way for her to come into the hall.

"I realize this is quite irregular, but I need Lord Strangford's address."

The desperation in her own voice surprised her, urgency stripping it raw.

"What do you need it for?" Sam demanded.

"Please—there's no time. I must speak to him."

"He's right here."

The reply came from behind her. Lily turned to see Lord Strangford standing in the doorway to the library.

He was still in his evening clothes, though his tie was gone. Behind him, Mr. Ash set down his teacup and rose from a chair by the fire.

He looked tired and older than he had that morning.

It was the painting, she realized. Lord Strangford must have left the gallery with his purchase that evening and brought it straight here. The two men had not yet gone to bed.

It was understandable. Seeing the face of one's dead wife for the first time in decades was bound to be unsettling. Lily couldn't know if Lord Strangford's purchase had been welcome or something that stirred up a great deal of old pain. Perhaps both.

"I need you to tell me where I can find Mrs. Boyden."

"Annalise?" Lord Strangford said, surprised into using the more intimate name. "Why?"

The question demanded an answer. She could not possibly expect him to give her what she wanted otherwise.

But that answer . . .

Other figures emerged from various parts of the house. Cairncross was on the landing, wrapped in a dressing gown and pajamas. Mrs. Liu stepped into the hall.

They would all hear it. The notion terrified her but she had no choice. A woman's life was a stake.

Lily forced the words past the lump in her throat.

"Because she's going to die."

A perfect silence followed, clear and sharp as crystal.

She watched a quick tumult of emotion flash through Lord Strangford's dark eyes—surprise and concern chased by others she wasn't entirely sure how to name. They moved too quickly, mingled too intimately to distinguish.

"How did you get here, Miss Albright?" Mr. Ash asked.

"I ran."

"With a row of stitches in your leg?" Lord Strangford cut in.

"There's no time," she countered sharply.

"Sam, what's the state of the Rolls?" Mr. Ash demanded.

"I have the carburetor out for cleaning. The engine is in pieces all over the garage floor. It would take me at least an hour to put it back together."

"Which is faster—readying the carriage, or running for a hackney?"

"Hackney," the younger man replied without hesitation.

"Go."

Sam turned and bolted nimbly down the steps, out into the night.

Lord Strangford moved around her, plucking his coat from the hook and shrugging it on. Lily realized what that signaled and felt a quick jolt of alarm.

"I just need the address," she protested.

"No, you need me," he countered, picking up his hat. "She won't admit or listen to you otherwise."

She wanted to object, but he was right. Annalise Boyden would undoubtedly think Lily was insane if she showed up at her house in the small hours of the morning shrieking about murder and death.

The hall was silent as they waited for Sam to return, the tension thick enough to suffocate her.

Every person there must be filled with questions. Given the circumstances, they had every right to ask them. No one did.

She remembered her conversation with Ash earlier that day in the still, quiet room at the end of the hall.

Perhaps he wasn't asking because she had simply confirmed what he had already known to be true.

The thought left her raw, as though someone had peeled back her skin.

Ash was the first one to speak.

"Could this situation be unsafe for you and Lord Strangford?"

Her thoughts turned to the shadow stalking Annalise Boyden's room. She had to fight not to shudder.

She adjusted her grip on her walking stick.

"We'll manage," Lord Strangford replied quietly, meeting Ash's gaze.

Sam leapt back up the steps. Lily heard the rattle of carriage wheels behind him.

"It's an old brougham," he said, barely short of breath. "That's all I could find."

The closed carriage would have only two seats. That settled the matter.

"Let's go," Lily ordered.

She did not give Mr. Ash an opportunity to protest. There was no time. She turned and hurried down the steps.

Lord Strangford followed, catching up to her in time to pull open the door to the carriage.

He gave the driver an address in Belgravia, promising him double fare for speed.

He climbed in beside her and the brougham leapt into motion.

They bounced along the deserted streets. In the close confines of the cab, Lord Strangford was uncomfortably near. Unspoken things lingered in the narrow space between them, filling it with tension.

She could let the ride pass in silence and force him to take her at her word. He would do it. His very presence there was evidence of that. It would be easier, and unfair.

She swallowed thickly, pushing past the fluttering terror inside of her.

"Sometimes I know things before they happen," she said quietly, the words falling into the silence of the carriage.

She waited for his answer—for the scoffing disbelief or the cool derision that would indicate he thought her a liar.

"How does it work?"

Her heart pounded, nerves fraying with the awareness of how much she had just revealed.

"Different ways. Sometimes like a dream while I'm sleeping. Sometimes when I'm awake. It's not something I can control like a carnival fortune teller. It just . . . comes." Her mouth was dry. "I know how it must sound."

"I believe you."

The words were clear and weighted with intention.

*I believe you.*

They had impact. She felt the solid warmth of it shaking something deep inside of her.

"Thank you." There was a sharp prickling at the corners of her eyes. She blinked it back, straightening her spine.

The houses with their dark windows spun past, the night air biting at her cheeks.

This errand had a different meaning for the man beside her. There was history between him and Annalise Boyden. She didn't know what that history was, or what Mrs. Boyden meant to him now, but if she meant anything at all—and Lily knew she must—then she owed him another very important piece of information.

"They have never been wrong," she announced quietly.

"Never?"

"Never."

He was silent for a moment.

"I see," he said at last, and she could hear in his voice that he did.

The cold air poured over them, seeping into the carriage through the cracks between the window panes, turning her breath to fog as the brougham rattled on through the empty streets.

The urgency still snapped at her. The carriage swung around another corner. True to his word, the driver was going faster than was prudent. The pounding in her veins told her it was still not fast enough. She had to fight the impulse to wrench open the door and leap into the street, sprinting to Belgravia instead. It would not be any quicker than they were going now, but at least she would feel like she was doing something instead of sitting there uselessly.

The clocks struck four as they passed the Wellington Arch and entered the well-kept streets of one of London's finest neighborhoods.

It was quiet. They passed a milkman on his rounds and a gasworks man with his case, headed back from some midnight call.

The carriage stopped at a pristine brick town house with freshly-painted black shutters and a wrought-iron gate. The windows were uniformly dark, giving no sign of a glimmer of life inside.

What if she was wrong?

One did not go knocking on people's doors at four in the morning.

If it had been nothing more than a dream, some particularly vivid nightmare, then she was dragging Lord Strangford into a situation certain to cause him a great deal of embarrassment.

Except it hadn't been a dream. Lily was as sure of that as she was of her presence in the carriage and the paving stones under its wheels. The difference between dream and vision was visceral, clear as dropping her hand in boiling water or a bucket of ice.

She was less certain of the timing. Her visions had never been generous with the details of when the events they foretold would come to pass. It was always a wretched game, guessing at the possible time frame. More often than not, she got it wrong.

The sense that the threat here was immediate was overwhelming, but Lily had a moment of doubt as she looked at the clean-swept steps of Annalise Boyden's home. Shouldn't they turn around and come back at a more reasonable hour instead of rousing the entire household for what might very well be a false alarm?

She found herself hoping that Lord Strangford would pause to ask her if she were quite sure about this.

He didn't.

He climbed out of the carriage and stood waiting for her on the pavement.

They shouldn't have come. Whatever they did here wouldn't matter. It never did, whether the events she foresaw were to play out in a matter of minutes or months. Trying to change things didn't work.

She lifted her skirts and stepped down beside him.

They climbed the stairs to the dark, still house. Lord Strangford knocked firmly on the front door.

After what seemed like an age, a housekeeper appeared. She

looked as though she were trying to decide whether to be worried or cross.

"I'm sorry to disturb the household, but there is an urgent matter I must discuss with your mistress," Lord Strangford announced.

"And you are?"

"Lord Strangford."

The title seemed to mollify her a bit.

"Please. It is a matter of life and death."

"I shall see if she will receive you," she said and opened the door.

She lit a lamp on the table in the entry. It gave off a feeble light, casting the fashionable appointments of the hallway in an unfriendly gloom.

The housekeeper took her candle and mounted the stair, her footfalls practiced and light.

Lily's skin crawled. Every shadow cast by the flickering flame seemed to jump at her.

She gripped her walking stick and cast a glance over at Lord Strangford, measuring whether he looked capable of handling the monster if it should appear. He was not a large man, but there was no fear in his expression, just concern, serious and attentive.

Then the housekeeper screamed.

Lily heard the thud of her candle hitting the floor overhead.

Lord Strangford was on the steps, mounting them two at a time. Lily snatched up the lamp and followed, pushing past the burning pain in her leg.

She reached the landing and saw the housekeeper framed in a doorway, wax splattered across the carpet at her feet. Lord Strangford plunged past her into the darkness. Lily hurried up behind him, the fickle light of her lamp spilling into the room.

It revealed the shape of the grand four-poster bed, its pale white curtains splattered with dark stains—the blood of the woman who sprawled half-naked across the sheets with her throat sliced.

The voice of a ghost in a vision echoed in her ears.

*You're late.*

Lord Strangford dropped slowly to his knees. Lily pushed back the wave of horror, guilt and rage that threatened to overwhelm her. Her attention shot to the details of the room. A porcelain vase lay smashed on the floor by the window. The hand mirror on the vanity table was dusted with something like snow. A clean white tangle of sheets wrapped itself around the dead woman's legs.

On the floor by the bed lay a bloodstained knife.

Doors snapped open behind her, footsteps pounding up stairs and down hallways. The household gathered at the door, the silence breaking in a wave of gasps, the sharp intake of a sob.

"Is there a footman here?" she asked. She did it without turning, unable to take her eyes away from the bloodstains on the bed curtains.

"Aye, ma'am."

"Run to Gerald Road station. Find the inspector. Tell him there's been a murder."

—

Two hours later, Lily sat on the edge of the divan in Annalise Boyden's elegantly appointed drawing room, watching the blue-uniformed bodies of B Division constables pass back and forth across the hall.

Minutes. That's as much time as could have passed between Lily's vision and the moment the events it foretold came to be.

It was uncommon and unsettling.

The image of Annalise Boyden's pale, bloodstained corpse refused to leave her. In addition to the familiar, impotent guilt, it clouded her with confusion.

It had felt so clear in the vision, so obvious that the shadow that took Annalise Boyden was the same threat that stalked Estelle. But last night's victim was a fast society widow, not a medium, and her throat had been cut from ear to ear.

This murder looked nothing like the others.

Was Lily wrong? Could she have misinterpreted the signs? The content of her premonitions wasn't literal. It was all wrapped up in symbols, as though her brain had to patch together ways to anchor the quantities of the vision in things Lily already knew or had experienced.

There was always a degree of interpretation—a bit of a guesswork. Perhaps this time she had guessed wrong.

No—the connection to the other murders was real. Every cell of her screamed that it was so. She just couldn't see how yet.

Lord Strangford stood by the cold fireplace, staring down at the empty grate. He had barely spoken since they discovered Mrs. Boyden.

She didn't press him. It was not her place and this was certainly not the time.

A crowd gathered in the street below, illuminated now by the rosy light of early dawn. Lily could hear the susurration of it through the windowpanes. It would be the usual assortment of the curious and the ghoulish, a handful of reporters and perhaps an itinerant preacher or two.

Even in posh Belgravia the punters loved a bit of slaughter.

The inspector was whip-thin and small with a neatly trimmed mustache, but he carried himself with the presence of a much more substantial man.

"Inspector Gregg. Sorry to keep you waiting," he said as he came in, followed by a tall constable of that awkward age where limbs seem made too long for one's body. The inspector gestured and the boy flipped open a notepad, pulling a pencil from his pocket.

"Miss Albright. Your lordship." He nodded acknowledgment to Lord Strangford, who did not seem to hear him. "I have been told it was the pair of you who discovered the body."

"I believe the housekeeper preceded us," Lily corrected.

"You must understand that I find it rather curious that you were here in the first place. According to the housekeeper your call was made at an unusual hour. May I inquire as to the cause of your visit?"

Lily had been waiting for this. Of course, it was impossible to give the true reason for their presence in Annalise Boyden's home. But what plausible alternative could she offer?

None, of course. Which left only one option—to brazen it out.

Channeling both her mother and the woman they had tried to train her into becoming at finishing school, she straightened her back, lifted her chin, and flattened her accent.

"I hope you do not mean to imply that we are under any sort of suspicion."

She felt rather than saw Lord Strangford glance over at her. Her own attention remained on the inspector. Being stationed in Westminster, he would likely be experienced in dealing with the nobility. He would know what the unspoken rules were when his class happened to collide with theirs. However disheveled Lily herself might appear, the weight of those four letters—*Lord*—attached to the man behind her could not be ignored.

His expression revealed nothing of the dissatisfaction he must have felt with her answer. The young constable was less smooth, his glance moving quickly from her face to that of his superior, his pencil hovering expectantly over the notebook.

"No," he replied shortly. "As you only arrived at the scene after the crime had already taken place, and were observed for the entirety of that visit, you are not."

"Then I imagine it will suffice for me to say our call here related to a private matter."

There was a pause, a silence just long enough to make clear that the inspector found it anything but sufficient.

"If you would do me the courtesy of giving your addresses to the constable here, I should greatly appreciate it. In case further questions arise during the course of my inquiries."

"Of course," Lily agreed. She let her gaze drift away, an unmistakable sign of dismissal.

It was a gamble, but one did not rise to the rank of inspector in B Division without learning how to behave tactfully with the ton.

He left.

The constable cleared his throat, clearly out of his element.

"Your address, miss?"

"702 March Place."

"And my lord?"

"Sussex Court, Bayswater," Lord Strangford said quietly.

"Thank you. You've been most helpful." The words were rote and the young man seemed almost embarrassed by them. He turned to go. Lily called out to stop him.

"Constable . . . can you tell me if there is any notion as to who was responsible for this?"

She felt rather than saw the shift in Lord Strangford's attention, hearing the rustle of his coat as he turned from the fireplace.

"I'm afraid I really ought not say." The policeman looked nervous.

"Please. You must understand that we are both deeply concerned that the murderer be brought to justice. If I were to leave at least knowing there was some hope that the devil might be found . . . "

Lily let her voice trail off.

The constable shifted uncomfortably, but was compelled to fill the space left at the end of her words.

"The inspector's fair certain he's got the man. He's the one brought her home last night. Had a right terrible row with her then stormed out. No one saw her alive after that. It'd be open and shut, except he's a toff. Begging your pardon," he added quickly, with a nervous glance over Lily's shoulder at Lord Strangford. "It was his knife cut her throat."

"How do you know?"

"Has his initials carved into it." He flipped open his notebook, turning back a few pages. "S.J.C."

He seemed to realize he had given away more than he should have, color rising into his cheeks.

"Ought to get back to it. You're free to go." He added a quick bob of his head, then ducked back into the hall.

Lily didn't move, shocked to stillness by what the young constable had said.

*The man who brought her home . . . had a terrible row . . . his initials carved into the murder weapon . . .*

She remembered Annalise Boyden's bright, bell-clear laugh, and the dashing figure on her arm as she flitted around the gallery the evening before.

She recalled the image of the same figure standing in the moonlit intimacy of the bedroom, turning from the sharp blow of a woman's hand across his cheek.

*S.J.C.*

Simon James Carne, Viscount Deveral.

Her brother.

# EIGHT

$\mathcal{L}$ILY SAT IN THE vast, dark interior of the carriage on a seat worn to little more than board wrapped in tattered leather.

It was a four-seater, likely grand when it was made seventy years ago but since reduced to squeaking hinges and shreds of silk lining. An old crest on the door had largely peeled away, only flakes of color remaining, stained gray with soot.

Lily knew every eye of the crowd gathered on the street at the front of the house was waiting to see who would emerge from inside. The gossip of it would pass like wildfire across the city.

She had led Lord Strangford to the back of the house, knowing there would be a service entrance in a place this grand. Lily found it in the kitchen and took him out into the narrow mews that ran behind the buildings.

There were still gawkers there, but they were fewer in number. For a sixpence one of them agreed to fetch her a hackney.

The conveyance he brought could not have been the nobleman's typical class of vehicle, but he seemed oblivious to it as he sat across from her, gazing distantly out the filthy window.

Lily tried to suggest the entirely sensible notion that they drop him in Bayswater first before driving on to Bloomsbury, but when she started to give the address to the driver, Lord Strangford broke his silence to firmly insist he would see her home.

The morning traffic had emerged, clogging London's streets and slowing them to a crawl.

Silence blanketed the interior of the carriage. It was not comfortable.

Lily knew she had to break it, though she doubted her words would make things any less tense.

"It wasn't Lord Deveral."

"Did you see who it was?"

"No," Lily admitted.

"Then how can you be sure?"

"Deveral was there. They fought, like the inspector said, but then he left. It was someone else who killed her. There was someone else in the room."

"Do you know who it was?"

She thought of Dr. Joseph Hartwell—of the moment in the gallery when Evangeline Ash's dark, sad eyes had gazed at her over the physician's shoulder while the banner in her hands spelled out a warning.

Dr. Hartwell had a particular interest in blood, the substance the killer had drained from his victims. But by the same logic, every hematologist in England must be a suspect.

Lily admitted it was not hematology that made her think of him, but the experience of seemingly receiving a warning about him from an artist thirty years dead. She knew it could be nothing more an uncanny coincidence. To believe otherwise stretched Lily's credulity to a point that felt akin to madness, even for a woman of her own unusual experience.

And even if she were to believe it was something more, there was no indication it related to the murders. It seemed more likely that Hartwell might be threat to Lily herself thanks to her interference in his attempt to purchase Evangline Ash's portrait.

"I do not," she admitted. "But I know he has done it before." She forced the next words out past a block in her throat. "And I know that he will do it again."

They crept past the broad expanse of Hyde Park, the carriage rocking to a halt in the river of vehicles. Pedestrians wove past, slipping between the close-packed traffic. Their voices mingled with the snorting of nearby horses and the occasional beep of a motorcar horn.

"Why?"

Lord Strangford's question was simple, just a single word, but it was raw with feeling, a desperate and unanswerable need for a reason for the horror they had both been confronted by in that blood-stained bedroom.

Her reply felt wholly inadequate.

"I don't know."

The carriage inched forward. The giggles of a row of girls in pinafores, slipping past them on their way into the park, penetrated into the dark interior, along with the shout of a paperboy. There would be a different headline by evening when it came out that the heir to one of the most powerful peers in the realm was suspected of murder.

She was certain Lord Deveral was innocent. He was spoiled, cruel and forthright in his hate of her . . . but he had not been the one to kill Annalise Boyden.

It wouldn't matter. The case the constable had described looked very bad for him, even given that he was a nobleman and as such would not be tried in the common court but by his peers in the House of Lords. It was a body unlikely to convict one of its own for a capital crime, a body over which her father exerted a great deal of influence.

Enough influence to bury a murder charge?

Certainly not without losing his own role and standing in the nation. No matter how one approached it, the case would be an immense blow against the family, one from which they might never recover.

Not that she cared. They weren't her family.

Still, she was left with the nagging matter of knowing that a despicable but innocent man might hang for this.

What could she possibly do about it?

And yet to do nothing . . .

A horn blared beside her, shouts breaking out as a motorist raged against a cart that would not remove itself from his desired path.

In that moment, Lily wanted nothing more than to get out of this coach—to open the door, step down, and simply walk back to Bloomsbury. It couldn't possibly be any slower.

Then Lord Strangford spoke.

"I was engaged to marry her."

His gaze was directed safely out the window at the jumble of slow-moving vehicles. He had taken off his hat and set it on the seat beside him. The shadow of day's beard darkened his jaw, his eyes tired.

"Her people were the other family of means in our village in Northumberland. Our parents were quite close. The arrangement suggested itself."

Northumberland. That was the source of the slight burr she heard in his accent, that bit of warmth underlying the aristocratic polish.

Though his voice was steady, Lily could sense the tension beneath his words. This story was not easy for him to tell, but something was driving him to get it out. Right now she was the only one available to listen.

The silence lingering after his words begged for her to push the conversation forward.

"Were you amenable to it?"

"You met her in the gallery. You saw what she was like."

"Captivating."

"Captivating," he agreed tonelessly. "She had always been captivating."

He closed his eyes. She could see the old pain in him rising to mingle with the new.

"You loved her."

"It would have been impossible not to."

"What happened?"

Silence lingered in place of an answer. He looked down at his fingers, wrapped in black leather, spread over his knees.

"My hands." He swallowed thickly. "You might have noticed . . ."

His voice faltered.

"The gloves." Her heart quickened, pulse pounding in her ears. "You're always wearing them."

Steeling himself, he tugged the fine well-worn kidskin free.

The skin beneath was beautiful, unmarked by any scar or disfigurement.

The atmosphere of the carriage felt charged like the moment before a lightning storm. The clatter of the world outside receded, becoming nothing more than a tense hum in the background. All of Lily's attention sharpened, focused on the man sitting across from her holding his two perfect hands up like weapons he was prepared to brandish.

"I wear them because I'm like you, Miss Albright," he said quietly. "I can't see the future. But I can touch the past."

The tension exploded as Lily's world was shattered.

*You are not alone. You have never been alone.*

Years flashed past, years in which there had never been any hint or sign that Lily was not unique her power. Years of holding the secret close against her chest lest she be taken for a lunatic or a liar.

She had carried this burden in isolation and silence all of her life.

"How?" Her throat felt like sandpaper.

"I touch something. It . . . opens to me. I can feel everywhere it's ever been. All that it ever experienced."

"When you say 'all' . . ."

"I mean everything."

Lily tried to comprehend that and found she could not.

"How far back can you go?"

"As far as there is. To the beginning. There was a Greek vase . . . Three thousand years old. I could smell the straw on the floor of the potter's studio. Feel the texture of the wet clay." He ran a finger along the leather of the gloves where they sat on the seat beside him. "I can't just buy these off a rack at Harrods. I picked the tailor—very dull fellow but kind. Doesn't shout at his wife or beat his apprentices. The tanner plays in a fife-and-drum band. He drinks but he's a jolly drunk. I have him source the kidskin specially from a Muslim butcher out of Brick Lane. Do you know they are required by their faith to kill an animal in a manner that imposes the least possible suffering?"

Her gaze flickered to the exposed skin at his wrist, the pale triangle at his collarbone.

"Is it just your hands?"

"No."

Her head spun as it unfolded the implications. She looked at the black lapel of his evening dress where it emerged from beneath the wool of his overcoat.

"Your suit . . ." she began, the words drying up.

"I can't wear cotton. Most of it is American and there's too much pain in it. Wool is best. It feels like open skies, dogs barking, heather. I can usually manage linen. With silk it depends on where it comes from."

There was no doubt. She dismissed the notion of trying to convince herself that perhaps it was all a twisted joke. Every atom of her knew that this stranger was speaking the truth, that the man sharing the shadowed interior of this once-grand carriage was exactly what he said he was.

Someone like her.

Another charismatic.

The next words spilled out of her before she could think better of them.

"Would you show me?"

He stiffened. She could feel him withdraw, as though the bench a few inches across from her own had pushed back a yard.

"I apologize. I shouldn't have asked that."

"It's reasonable for you to be skeptical."

"It isn't that. Please don't think it's that. I just . . ." She struggled for the words to frame her motivation. It wasn't doubt that drove her, or curiosity, but something else—something that needed what this man had said to be made entirely and irrevocably real. "I wasn't thinking," she finished at last.

He was quiet for a moment. One hand rested against the gloves on the seat. He held the other close to his lap. She could see how carefully he moved, avoiding any accidental brush of his fingers against the leather of the carriage seat or the threadbare silk on the walls.

He had always been like that, she realized. The caution had been there in the moment he came across her in the road on Hampstead Heath. She knew now why there had been a hesitation before he offered her his hand to get up or helped her from the horse and into that farmer's kitchen. Avoiding contact with any unfamiliar object must be ground into him, a habit drilled so deep he carried it like a constant shield.

"Give me something," he said, surprising Lily out of her reverie. "Nothing too personal. I can't filter what I see. It comes whether I want it or not, no matter how . . ."

"Unpleasant?" Lily offered into the silence hanging at the end of his words.

"Intimate." He met her gaze, making the import of his words unimpeachably clear.

Lily had dashed out of the house with nothing more than her staff and whatever happened to be in her coat. The staff was out. It was too close to her, something with far too much history.

She put her hand into her pocket, brushed her fingers over the few things that had been forgotten there. She stopped on a small, round tin, its surface smooth and cool.

She pulled it out.

It was a powder compact.

She hardly ever used powder. The tin had been purchased back in her theatre days, but she had dropped it into her coat the evening before in case she needed to touch up at the gallery.

It was a cheap little thing, simple and impersonal.

She offered it to him.

He hesitated.

"Are you sure you're willing to share this?"

She could hear the warning in his tone.

"It's nothing."

He extended his hand. Lily set the compact against his palm and his fingers curled around the tin.

He breathed in deeply, sharply, and his gaze shifted, the focus leaving his eyes, turning them strange and distant.

"Sawdust," he said. His voice was clear, steady. "I can smell it. Something else—grease. Machine oil. Not unpleasant. Familiar. Small spaces, cluttered. Bright lights set around a mirror. Lots of little spaces like that, but they all feel the same. You're in the glass, powdering your face, and it's cold. Legs are bare. Won't let you wear anything else. It's . . . sequins and feathers, too small, makes you feel like . . . alone. So alone, even as the other girls move through the glass. Even in the other places, where the men are drinking and it stinks of their cigars. They put their hands on your—"

Lily's hand flashed out, snatching the compact from his grasp.

She'd spent a year as a chorus girl. She had resisted it for as long as she could, but she was near to starving and facing a hike in her rent that would put her on the street. The pay was so much more than she could make on odd jobs backstage.

She hated it. The tight, glittering costume felt like a cage around her guts. The spotlights glared. There was never enough heat, and the men—the way they looked at her. How they whistled, tossed coins at her. Then the producer informed her that her presence was required at certain off-stage events, where in the same paint and sequins she fetched glasses of brandy and lit cigars for his friends and patrons.

They treated her body like an amenity, patting or grabbing it with an air of propriety as though they had a right to it. She saw how the other girls let themselves be drawn off to the rooms that lined the hall, knew full well they were supplementing their pay with another sort of work. Lily managed to dance around those expectations, but it was noticed. She was near to a rather desperate choice when her mother's solicitor arrived with her salvation.

It made for a tawdry picture—her powdered cheeks, pale skin on display, the men with their coarse laughter and their entitled hands.

She thrust the compact into the deepest corner of her pocket.

The silence of the coach was uncomfortable, dancing with tension.

He was the first to break it.

"I'm sorry. I told you that I—"

"It's fine," Lily interrupted sharply.

He picked up his gloves, tugging them back on.

"How long have you been able to do it?" she asked. The words came out steady, a bit of her mother's acting talent exerting itself.

"As long as I can remember."

"Who else knows?"

"Ash. The others at The Refuge."

"Your family?"

"No."

His answer surprised her—yet why should it? She had never had a family. How could she presume to know what secrets were shared within the bounds of those relationships?

"That wasn't what you expected to hear." He rubbed at the stubble darkening his cheek. Lily was conscious that it must have been nearly twenty-four hours since the man had last slept. He gathered some reserve of strength in himself, though she could hear the effort in it.

"Ash believes that we . . ." He stumbled, challenged by the words. "That we are something like saints."

"Yes. He mentioned that. When I spoke to him."

She could almost see the fit of it with the pale light of dawn filtering in through the soot-grimed glass, illuminating the weary lines of his face, the worn edges of his collar. He reminded her of one of those portraits hanging in the museum, baroque depictions of black-robed ascetics finding ecstasy among the rocks.

"It did not go very well for them," he noted quietly.

"But we aren't claiming to speak for God."

"Neither were witches. They still burned for it. We aren't lighting up the countryside with pyres or pinning people to crosses in 1914, but what you and I do is still dangerous. People are as likely to fear it now as they were then. They just have different weapons at their disposal."

The words resonated. Lily knew that fear. It had lingered at the back of her mind for as long as she could remember. Humanity was not kind to difference.

"But surely you wouldn't expect that from your family." The notion shouldn't shock her, but it did.

"No. Not like that. But it would . . . complicate things."

Yes, she thought. It was complicated to know more than one ought to in a way that couldn't possibly be explained. It risked being cast as a madwoman or a manipulator. Even if you were believed, it raised expectations that couldn't or shouldn't be met.

Secrets also grew exponentially more difficult to keep each time they were shared.

It was so much easier to stay hidden, to stay safe.

"What about Mrs. Boyden?"

"Annalise . . ." The name sounded halfway between a prayer and a curse. "The mistake was mine. I knew her. I had always known her. We grew up together marauding across the moor—how could I not? She was clever and ambitious, unbound by anyone's rules or expectations. I knew she was a liar, but the lies were always on my side—until I went away to school and came back to find her grown into a woman. She could have had me even then, if I had been anybody else. She was a consummate performer when pursuing what she wanted, and she wanted me."

"But not the way you thought," Lily put in quietly.

"No. Not the way I thought."

"How did you learn?"

"A kiss. I begged it of her a month before our wedding. I was—well. A young man, in love. Impatient. And I learned she found me dull but attractive enough to be tolerable and weak enough to manipulate. She liked the notion of a title. She had also been engaging in intimacies with her father's stable master, a married man with four children at home."

"It isn't just objects," Lily blurted, shock releasing words which otherwise she might have tactfully kept to herself.

"No," he replied. "It isn't."

The implication of that shook her into silence.

Every touch, a window into someone else's history. Their secrets, their lies. Everything they'd thought or done laid open like a book he was forced to devour. There could never be anything as simple as a kiss for him, or a handshake, or a friendly embrace.

She thought of the warm, soft texture of Estelle's cheek under her lips. The calloused grip of a stagehand giving a hearty congratulations after a sold-out performance.

The long fingers of the Earl of Torrington, ruffling her hair as he passed by on his way to her mother's bedroom.

To be deprived of the simplicity of contact, closed off from it forever . . .

The loneliness of it floored her.

"But is it always like that? Doesn't it come and go?"

"It was more spontaneous when I was younger, something that happened here or there. I could even choose to do it, when I was in the right frame of mind. But now it's . . . consistent."

"You mean that it's always there."

He nodded, the gesture tight.

"And it always works the same?"

"There are occasional anomalies."

"What does that mean—anomalies?"

He shrugged, clearly unwilling to elaborate.

"Can't you exert any control over it?"

"Ash has been trying to teach me."

"That technique you were practicing in The Refuge."

"The tàijíquán. Yes."

"Does it work?"

He looked away from her, out through the soot-darkened glass.

"Ash says it will take time."

"And the gloves?"

"They block it, at least so far as my hands are concerned."

"Do you ever take them off?"

"Rarely."

Of course. Why would he? When that carefully-sourced kid leather kept him safe from unwelcome revelations about the people he hoped to become close to, or from being ambushed by every stranger's tawdry secrets.

It was his armor. If Lily had been able to devise some shield that protected her from the pointless knowledge of unavoidable horrors, she would have wrapped herself in it as tightly as she could.

It struck her then that the man sitting across from her in that wreck of a coach was perhaps the only one in the world who would understand that desire. He knew exactly what it felt like.

In the course of a single night, he had come to know more about her than any living soul.

It was not a notion she felt very comfortable with.

She reminded herself why they were there. A woman was dead, her killer still little more than a shadow across Lily's mind.

"Did Mrs. Boyden have any enemies?"

"I am certain that she did, but I don't know who they are." He turned to face her, his eyes dark with sadness and weighted with intent. "Will you tell me whatever else you know?"

She pushed past her own discomfort with that question, knowing he deserved it.

"I know that he has been targeting mediums."

"Annalise wasn't a spiritualist."

"No. The other victims were found in their beds, drained of blood without any visible wound." She hesitated, then plunged on awkwardly. "I know it doesn't sound at all like the same thing, but I could . . . feel it."

Strangford was quiet. Lily forced herself to wait despite the urge to demand to know whether he believed her.

"There was not enough blood on the bed," he said at last. His gloved fingers flexed against his knees. "Given the extent of her wound, one would have expected . . ."

"Yes," Lily cut in, her own heart pounding. "You're right. The sheets were practically unmarked. There was just a splash of it against the bed curtains, the pillowcase . . ."

It was thin as evidence went, certainly not enough to convince a cynical police inspector that there was a connection, but it offered Lily some slender reassurance that the truth she sensed from her vision was not just some sliver of madness.

"You said that he will try it again."

She thought of Estelle's pale face, the accusation in her glare. She nodded, unable to voice it, torn with guilt.

"Then we shall have to stop him," he replied.

One word, one syllable . . . *We.*

It hit her with the force of a hurricane.

Outside the shadowy confines of the carriage, London continued to wake, echoing with the cries of street hawkers and the ringing of church bells.

Inside, Lily stared across the darkness to the stranger leaning against the weathered silk.

*We shall have to stop him.*

Was it possible?

It would never work, she reminded herself fiercely. It had always led to failure, every time.

And yet, there was Lord Deveral. Her brother.

If she could not hope to find the killer before he struck again, there was still a life she might save by ensuring that the monster who had done this was brought to justice.

It was madness. It was almost certainly doomed to failure . . . and yet the truth settled into her, as uncomfortable as the battered coach seat she sat upon.

She was going to try.

She would not be doing so alone.

"I don't even know where to begin," she admitted.

"We should start with the witness."

"Witness?"

"If Lord Deveral didn't do it, then he's our best chance of learning more about what happened in that room last night."

Lily's heart sank.

He was right, of course. Interviewing Lord Deveral was the obvious course of action.

It was also the last thing she wanted to do.

The carriage lurched to a halt. Lily glanced out through the dirty glass and saw they had arrived at March Place. Strangford climbed out, then turned back to her.

"Do you require a hand to step down?" he asked quietly.

"No," Lily replied, now fully aware of the import of the question. She lifted her skirts and climbed out of the carriage. She stopped next to him.

"Should I assume time is limited?" he asked.

She thought of the snow, the white flakes spinning through the air, and felt the chill of the early morning against her skin. "I don't know," she admitted.

"Then we must proceed as though it is. We should call on Lord Deveral this afternoon. When should I collect you? Is three o'clock too early?"

"No," Lily replied, steeling herself. "I'll be ready."

He hesitated, as though there were more he wanted to say. Lily felt the same impulse twist inside of her, the utter inadequacy of polite conversation to respond to what had just passed between them in the dark confines of that run-down coach.

"Good day, then," Strangford said at last. He bowed.

He climbed back into the coach as a window clunked open from above. The battered conveyance swung around and rattled back off the way it had come as Estelle, clad in a bright pink silk dressing gown, thrust her head out into the cold morning air.

She looked down at Lily, then raised an eloquent eyebrow.

"Well?" she demanded.

"I'm sorry. I really ought to get some sleep. I've had a long night."

She glanced at the departing carriage.

"Have you, now?"

Lily felt a wave of tired frustration.

"It wasn't . . ." She stopped. She was too tired to argue and any denial would only add fuel to Estelle's fire. "I'm going to bed," she announced with finality.

"Pleasant dreams," Estelle countered as Lily trudged through the door.

# NINE

$\mathcal{W}$HAT DOES ONE WEAR to visit the brother who called you a whore?

Lily did not have much time to fuss over the decision. When she arrived back at March Place that morning, putting off Estelle's blatant curiosity, she had thought it would be impossible to sleep.

Her eyes shut the moment she collapsed into her bed, still wearing her tweed skirt and boots, and did not open again until nearly half past two.

She wriggled into her corset, using the bedpost to help her tug the strings extra tight. The forest green silk she had chosen to wear featured waterfalls of fabric from a wide sash-belted waist, accented by velvet trim and embroidered lace. The fit was unforgiving but perfectly balanced high fashion with respectability.

Dress buttoned, she twisted her hair into an elegant chignon and topped it with a green velvet hat.

*Casting your line for another fish, eh?*

Her hand, preparing to jab a pin into place, faltered. The pin went awry, scratching her scalp. She cursed, pulling it out.

This was a fool's errand. Lord Deveral would not admit her. No green silk would be enough to overcome his vicious dislike. Even if by some slim miracle he did let her in the door, he would hardly be inclined to tell her and Strangford anything useful about the death of his mistress. Why would he? Just because they claimed their interest lay in his welfare and not prurient gossip?

They certainly couldn't tell him the truth.

She considered whether Strangford ought to make this excursion on his own. Lord Deveral's opinion of her was clear and would certainly bias him even further against answering their questions. If she weren't there, Strangford might stand a better chance of getting him to cooperate.

Of course, explaining that to Strangford would mean sharing the reason why Deveral despised her.

*It's because my mother was a whore, you see . . .*

A knock resounded from the front door. Lily glanced at the clock. Strangford was precisely on time.

She finished lacing her boots, picked up her yew stick and headed down the stairs.

Mrs. Sprout's handiwork had held up nobly against the rigors she'd put it through, but her leg was aching. She would be using the stick for more than show today.

She turned onto the landing by Estelle's door. Below, Mrs. Bramble reached the front entrance and threw it open.

"Good afternoon, madam," Strangford said politely. "Is Miss Albright in?"

Bramble took his measure, her gaze flicking from the just-too-long hair under his hat to the sober cut of his black suit.

"Hmph," she said, her assessment clearly high enough to prevent him having the door slammed in his face, though perhaps not much more than that. "We don't allow gentleman callers in this house."

"He's not calling. I'm going out," Lily announced.

His gaze rose to where she stood. It locked there for a moment. "Miss Albright."

"My lord," she replied, keeping her tone distantly polite. She was aware of Mrs. Bramble's pointed curiosity as the woman glanced from her to the dark-haired nobleman on the threshold.

She finished descending and moved past the landlady. "Thank you, Mrs. Bramble."

There was a hired hackney waiting at the curb. It was in better condition than the ride they had taken the night before.

Lily did not wait for Strangford to offer her his hand again. Instead, she put the staff to use as she climbed into the carriage, trying not to strain her protesting leg.

Strangford followed, settling himself beside her.

She directed her attention out the window as the carriage rolled into motion, not yet sure how to speak to the man beside her.

Someone on the street beyond the glass caught her eye, odd enough to register amid the blur of other passing figures. He was a tall man, whip-thin, dressed nattily in a green paisley waistcoat and a black bowler hat. He leaned against the house across the street from her own, looking quintessentially the part of the Oxford Street loafer—only March Place was not Oxford Street.

Lily had just enough time to register his presence before the carriage turned and he slipped from view.

"Your leg is bothering you," Strangford noted.

"It's nothing."

They continued in silence. The intimacy of the morning had passed, replaced with what at first glance might look like polite distance.

It wasn't.

Lily had never thought she would find another person who lived in the world of being ambushed by things one didn't want to know and could never share.

Now here he was and she hadn't the foggiest notion what to say to him.

"You don't keep a carriage," she noted, a lame attempt to fill the space of their silence.

"No. The coachman stays with my mother in Northumberland. She has more need of him than I do."

"I thought maintaining a carriage was de rigueur for a nobleman."

"So is going into debt. Neither are trends I'm particularly moved by. Besides, I like walking. Though it is hardly as exciting as your chosen mode of transportation."

The Triumph. She had almost forgotten that he knew about her motorcycle.

"What about your horse?"

"Beatrice? I keep him stabled in Highgate. I have been told he dislikes the city."

Lily wondered how precisely someone was told what a horse was feeling.

"I assume you know where we're going?"

"Yes. Thanks to Mrs. Jutson."

"Mrs. Jutson?"

"My housekeeper."

"Does she know Lord Deveral?"

"Not at all." He seemed to realize she was waiting for a bit more explanation. "I might have looked it up in Debrett's, but the only copy in the house belonged to my grandfather. Lord Deveral obviously wasn't in there. Thankfully, Mrs. Jutson is a fervent monarchist and keeps up on that sort of thing. Lord Deveral resides in one of his father's houses. In Bayswater, on the park."

One of *their* father's properties, Lily silently corrected. It would not be the family townhouse. As Parliament was in session, the earl would likely be residing there himself. Lily knew where that was, in St. James's, but had never seen it. She had gone out of her way once to avoid the street. What good would it have done her to look at a place she would never be welcome to enter?

The house they approached now would be one of who-knew-how-many properties that were part of the Torrington holdings. Had her father lived there himself when he was younger and the old earl, her grandfather, still held the family seat? She didn't know.

"Your neighbor?" she asked, recalling that Strangford's own home lay somewhere in Bayswater.

"More or less."

They rode along for another minute.

"Did I ask you about your leg?"

"You did."

An awkward silence settled back in. Lily could not think of how to break it. She wasn't sure she should.

They reached the eerily clean streets of Bayswater. The carriage stopped in front of an elegant townhouse set just across the road from the green, manicured expanse of Kensington Gardens. The house was Georgian, the limestone free of soot and ornamented with the sort of balconies that spilled flowers in the summer and evergreens over the holiday season.

"We're here," Strangford announced.

Lily hesitated only a moment before climbing out of the confines of the hackney into the cold gray light of the afternoon.

It was easily twice the size of the house that Lily shared with Estelle, Miss Bard, and Mrs. Bramble. Lily knew the rent on this place would top £1,000 a year, should her father have opted to turn it to making income instead of offering it for the use of his heir.

The door was polished ebony, the brass gleaming. Perfectly trimmed laurel hedges lined the steps.

The carriage rolled away behind them as Lily faced the front door.

She was aware of the people moving through the park behind her. A pair of well-dressed older women passed arm-in-arm, dangling parasols. A nurse minded a horde of aristocratic children who ran in screaming circles. A man in tweed leaned against the wrought-iron fence. Lily was quite certain the latter was a plainclothes policeman watching the front door. He was surely making a note of who came and went from the home of a lead murder suspect, and whether they were admitted.

She knew other eyes marked their presence as well. Word of scandal traveled faster than a telegraph wire in this world. The news that Lord Deveral was entangled in the murder of Annalise Boyden would have spread far by now. The morbid and the curious would be attending closely to what happened at this address.

She mounted the front steps, Strangford at her side.

The women stopped, ostensibly to chat about a pocketbook. The policeman looked up. She felt other eyes on her—a fellow reading a newspaper on a bench in the park, a passing street sweeper.

She held her back straight, her carriage as perfect as Mrs. Finch at the academy could ever have wished it.

Strangford clapped the brass knocker.

Footsteps were audible inside.

There was a pause, just long enough to start feeling unnatural, and then the door opened.

The man who stood in the entry was clearly the butler but could just as easily have been making a living breaking knees in the East End. He was enormous, his arms like ham-hocks under the well-tailored black of his suit. His head was bald and as well-polished as the brass knocker.

Strangford plucked a card from his pocket.

"Lord Strangford and Miss Lily Albright to see Lord Deveral."

"I'm afraid Lord Deveral is not in."

Lily highly doubted her half-brother would have braved his club today. "Not in" was also what well-trained servants said when their master or mistress was not up to receiving callers.

Lily could hardly blame Lord Deveral for closing up the house. Any visitors he received today would almost certainly be intent on collecting gossip, which would then be mercilessly distributed around the ton.

They needed a way to get past that blanket prohibition, to surprise the butler into at least informing Lord Deveral that they were there.

Lily knew one way to do that.

She had only a moment to consider it. The notion sent a bolt of fear and shame through her, but so much was at stake. Could she really let their efforts dead-end on this step simply to preserve some illusion of her own respectability?

It wouldn't matter. Every eye that currently tracked her movements would have sussed out the truth by suppertime regardless of what she did or didn't say now.

She lifted her chin, channeling all the hauteur she carried in her half-blue blood.

"Please inform Lord Deveral that his sister would like to speak with him."

The butler did not show his surprise, but Lily sensed it in his silence. She watched his eyes flash from the suitably fine quality of her gown to her finishing school carriage. They stopped at her eyes, with their distinctive steel gray that undeniably matched that of his employer.

"If you'll excuse me for a moment."

He did not invite them in, but he did not close the door. She watched as he walked down the checkered marble tiles, then disappeared around the corner.

"Sister?" Strangford asked quietly from beside her.

"Half-sister," she corrected.

"Lord Deveral is the Earl of Torrington's son."

Lily was tense as a bowstring.

"You are correct."

"I was not aware that the countess had been married before."

"I am not related to the countess."

"You're Lord Torrington's daughter."

"I'm Lord Torrington's bastard," Lily corrected him.

"Ah."

Lily felt the shame rage through her. She sensed every one of those eyes from the park at her back, measuring her, assessing her. Once they knew who she was, they would find her wanting. They always had.

She might be able to act the part, but she was not a lady. She never would be. She did not belong here and in that moment, she was certain that everyone around her knew it.

The silence stretched for an eternity. Then, at last, the looming form of the butler appeared at the end of the hall. He approached them, his steps maddeningly regular, until his enormous frame filled the doorway once more.

"I am afraid that Lord Deveral is not in."

The phrase was delivered with precisely the same inflection as before—a cool and impersonal courtesy.

It was nothing more than she had expected, Lily told herself.

"Very well," she said evenly.

The butler deliberately cleared his throat, halting her before she could turn to go.

"Yes?"

"I should inform you that I am instructed to offer a more forcible response if you call here again."

The words struck with all the impact of a slap to the face.

"I see."

"M'lord," the butler said, bowing politely to Strangford. Then he closed the door.

The sound of the latch falling into place reverberated through her.

"Well," she said, forcing a false cheer into her tone. "That was a waste of time."

She turned and descended the stairs, focusing every scrap of her energy on keeping her back straight, her hands from shaking.

Strangford lengthened his stride to catch her. A black gloved hand slipped under her arm. She stopped in surprise at that unexpected touch.

"Let's take a turn."

His tone was neutral, but the pressure of his hand was steady as he steered her toward the gates of the park.

The urge to run was overwhelming. She could not give in to it, not with those eyes still watching them, more openly and attentively now that they had been turned away from Lord Deveral's door. Instead, she walked beside Strangford like some courting couple out for an afternoon stroll as he led her across the rolling green lawns to the flat, gray expanse of the lake.

The day was cold, the air biting. The raw wind tugged at her hat. It meant the park was less crowded than usual, only a scattered few making their way along the paved pathways.

He stopped at the edge of the lake in the middle of a broad, open space, releasing her arm but staying close by her side. It would have been impossible for anyone to approach them or come within hearing distance without being observed. They stood in plain sight, but Lily knew the situation was as private as her own drawing room might have been.

The water reflected the dull steel hue of the sky. The winter wind stirred little waves on its surface.

"Why didn't you tell me?"

"Because it wasn't important," Lily replied flatly. "I don't know him. You can see what good it did."

The wind whipped at her skirts, chilling her. She ignored it.

She didn't want to ask the next question, but it refused to be pushed back, spilling from her lips.

"Does it matter?" she demanded.

"That you're Lord Deveral's sister?"

"That I'm a bastard."

She waited for some sign of what she knew must be there. He was a nobleman. His type was trained to judge people by the circumstances of their birth. The circumstances of hers put her utterly beyond the pale for someone of his class. He might pretend otherwise out of courtesy, but that was the truth of it.

The dark-haired man beside her in his sober black suit bent down and after careful consideration, selected a pebble from the ground by the shore. He stood, eyeing the wide expanse of the lake. With a sharp flick of his wrist, he sent the stone skimming across the water.

"I was less cautious of it when I was young—what I could do," he clarified without looking at her. "It was a game. Shaking hands and delving into everybody's secrets, uncovering scandals from a forgotten set of spectacles or a handkerchief." He hesitated. Lily felt certain he was thinking of the time where his power had ceased to be a game and had instead become a vulnerability.

He plucked another stone from the ground and weighed it in his hand, testing.

"I learned very quickly that the circumstances of someone's birth are a poor indicator of their quality."

He threw the stone. Lily counted the number of times it bounced— six, seven, eight—before succumbing to gravity.

She remembered how Mordecai Roth had described him back in the gallery.

*One of those rarest of beasts, despite appearances: a true bohemian.*

"I should have told you to go alone," she concluded.

"I doubt it would have made any difference. I'm not exactly a person of influence. We'll try something else."

"We," she echoed, unable to keep a hint of skepticism from her tone.

He skipped another stone.

"You don't have to. If it seems like too much. I wouldn't blame you for it."

"That isn't what I meant." The words stumbled out, pushed by her surprise at how he had misinterpreted her.

He paused, looking over at her.

"I told you that I would support you in this."

"That was when you thought I was respectable."

There was a twitch at the corner of his mouth.

"Miss Albright. I found you sprawled across the road in trousers. I was never in danger of assuming you to be something so mundane as respectable."

Another gust whipped at her, snapping her green silk skirts and tossing the dark curls of Strangford's hair.

It pulled against her velvet hat again. She reached up, grasping the brim, and deliberately yanked out her pins.

She felt the wind tug at the tendrils of her hair, liberating them to dance around her face.

She plucked her own stone from the lake shore, snapping it at the water.

It sank.

"It's all in the wrist. You're teaching it to fly, not pitching it like a cricket ball."

"I don't see what our options are," she retorted, her frustration rising. "The obvious course of action would be to find people who knew the other victims. Learn more about what they were doing, who they were seeing, before they died. Look for themes or commonalities."

"That sounds quite sensible."

"Except that the police must have already done the same and with far more experience and greater resources than we have. I am not an investigator. Are you?"

"I am afraid that line is not part of my curriculum vitae."

"We don't have any time. We can't muddle about speaking to people who may or may not know anything about the murders. We need to cut right to the heart of it."

Then it came to her, a notion so audacious and yet so plausible that it stopped her flat. She turned to the man beside her, wide-eyed.

"But we can cut to the heart of it. Can't we?"

Something shifted in his expression, becoming guarded.

"What do you mean?"

It was terrible. It was beyond horrific.

And it would work.

"You could read one of the victims."

He went still. The impact of it was greater than a shout of protest or outrage would have been. Lily's instincts flared, warning her that something had gone awry.

The wind gusted across the lake, stirring dark ripples on its surface.

"I don't mean Annalise Boyden. It would have to be Mrs. Durst, the second-most-recent victim. They've only just buried her, in Abney Park."

"I'm not sure you understand what you're asking of me."

"We would be breaking the law. I know that. The penalties for grave robbing can be severe."

"That's not what I mean."

Tension snapped in his voice, finally cutting through the rushing excitement of the idea.

"What is it?" she asked quietly.

"What I do—it isn't like standing back and looking at a bunch of actors on a stage. It's . . . immersive. Smells, textures, emotions—I'm there inside of it. I feel the experiences as though they were my own. What do you imagine I would feel if I put my hands on a corpse?"

Horror rose in her, filling in the details he left out of his words—the suffocating cold and the darkness, the slow descent into rot. The feeling of flesh bloating and then crumbling in on itself.

And before that, violence. Terror and pain.

It was a nightmare, and she had just suggested he walk into it.

Of all people, she should have understood that.

She felt the hot shame of it as a few drops of water pinged against her neck, harbingers of a raw winter rain.

"I'm sorry. Forget I suggested it."

Silence stretched as the rain turned to drizzle, obscuring the gray surface of the lake.

"Shall I walk you back to the road?" he said at last.

"Thank you," Lily replied. She replaced her hat, pinning it back into place.

He did not offer his arm again. She didn't ask for it.

He led them down a different path out of the park, away from Lord Deveral's pristine residence. When they reached the street, he flagged down a passing hackney.

It rolled to a stop. He opened the door for Lily. She moved to climb inside.

His hand flash out, stopping her, black-gloved fingers gripping her arm.

She held there, halfway up the step, as scattered drops pinged against the pavement around them.

His eyes were darker, more hollow.

"I'll do it."

"You can't possibly be serious."

"If it works, we will discover the identity of the killer in a single move."

"But what you would be putting yourself through . . ."

"You said there were other lives at stake. Was that an exaggeration?"

She searched for some argument that would convince him there was a better option.

She found nothing.

"No," she replied. "It was not."

"It will have to be tonight," he muttered. "Before things have . . . progressed . . ."

*Progressed.* The word sent a shudder through her.

"I'm coming with you."

His attention returned, sharpened.

"No."

"It was my idea."

"There are others who can assist me."

She stepped down, coming even with him, and put steel into her words.

"I am coming with you."

She met his stare, daring him to find any fracture in her resolve.

"We'll collect you at one." He released his grip on her arm and tossed a coin neatly to the driver perched atop the hackney. "March Place, Bloomsbury," he ordered, then stepped back.

"You aren't riding?"

"I need to walk. Good afternoon, Miss Albright."

Lily watched him go, rooted to the pavement, until a cough from the driver reminded her of his presence.

She climbed into the hackney and closed the door.

It jolted into motion, bouncing over a pothole. Her heart lurched into her throat.

She forced it back into place as the park slipped by outside the window and fat drops of rain began to pelt against the carriage roof. She pressed against the glass, looking back, but Strangford's form was already lost around a bend.

Something else caught her eye.

It was the tall figure of a thin man with a fair mustache, dressed in a black bowler hat and a green paisley waistcoat.

He strolled along the pavement. She was close enough to have reached out through the cold drizzle to touch him, close enough to note the unusual symbol on the brass pin on his lapel.

It was the hero rune, the sigil of The Society for the Betterment of the British Race . . . Dr. Joseph Hartwell's eugenics club.

Was it the same man she had seen on March Place? She struggled to be sure but could not. If it was, then it seemed a far coincidence that he would appear both outside her flat and at the very corner of the park where she had been talking with Strangford.

The rain fell as the carriage turned and the figure in green paisley disappeared from view.

# TEN

*S*HE HOVERED IN THE shadows of the stairwell, clad in a second-hand tweed skirt and jacket, relics of her theatre days that ought to have found their way to the rag man but had instead been stashed in the back of her wardrobe. They were covered with a dark cloak. The light but sturdy boots she usually wore for motorcycling completed the ensemble.

She had been listening to the sounds of Estelle's séance. They echoed up through her parlor floor, gasps and sobs and the occasional scream. It reminded her of the noises of the crowd at an illusionist's show, when rabbits emerged from hats and smiling girls were sawn in two. It was likely because Estelle put on a similar performance.

The noise was different now, the rumble of low and steady conversation as Estelle's guests prepared to depart.

The door opened. Lily waited. The crowd began to filter out, an assortment of men and women of all ages and classes, from washerwomen in threadbare calico to a prosperous banker with a diamond ring on his finger.

Lily descended the stairs and slipped in among them. No one paid her any notice.

The séance-goers spilled out the front door, some milling on the step, the rest dividing to meander toward either Bloomsbury Street or Tottenham Court Road. Lily moved with them, hanging just behind a group of girls whose high voices rattled off the bricks of the surrounding houses.

Halfway down the lane, she took a quick step to the side, slipping into the narrow space between two houses and ducking back into the darkness.

She waited.

The last of Estelle's guests turned the corner, the echoes of their voices fading. March Place was silent and still.

There was no sign of the man in the green waistcoat, nor anyone else for that matter. She felt a bit foolish. The escapade she had engaged in so that she might slip out of the house without being noticed had apparently been for naught. Joseph Hartwell hadn't sent some minion to watch her. Lily might just as well have been waiting in the comfort of her room for a civilized knock at the door. Instead, she stood in the chill darkness of the alley, her breath fogging in the air.

The street smelled of rain, fresh and crisp.

It would be fresher still in Abney Park, where paving stones were replaced by lush grass growing over the graves of the dead.

This was madness. She was dragging Strangford out into a cemetery in the middle of the night to dig up the grave of a murdered woman. It was a move that would subject him to unimaginable horror and could easily get both of them tossed into Newgate, not to mention the others he said would be joining them.

She wondered who they were and what Strangford had told them to convince them to lend their assistance.

A street over, someone slammed a door. The sharp rapport of it echoed down March Place, resounding off the dark, silent buildings.

It would all be worth it, she reminded herself, if tonight's errand gave them a glimpse of the murderer, the monster who was draining these women of blood in their beds. And it could. Strangford had admitted that himself.

The thought did not make her feel any more easy about what they were about to do.

She scratched at her leg through her heavy skirt, then stopped herself. The wound had begun itching earlier that afternoon, a sensation that had only grown worse through the evening. It nagged at the back of her awareness, making it difficult to concentrate.

It made her nervous. She thought of what she'd put the injury through over the last two days. It would serve her right if it was infected. She tried to recall what the symptoms of such a turn were. Her memory refused to cough it up.

The clatter of an approaching carriage bounced off the darkened windows, sounding loud enough to wake the dead. Lily hovered at the mouth of the alley as a plain but well-kept black coach turned onto the road.

It was too fine for a hackney. It must be private conveyance, one designed more for function than show.

She was unsure of the identity of one of the two figures perched on the box. His features were covered by a thick wool muffler.

The other she recognized. Sam Wu, Mr. Ash's chauffeur, held the reins easily in one hand, leg braced against the bar, a flat cap turned at an insolent angle on his head.

As the carriage moved past, Lily stepped from the alley, jogging alongside the vehicle. She tucked her walking stick under her arm, hopped up onto the step and turned the handle of the door. She slipped inside before it had begun to slow.

"Good evening," the occupant of the interior said evenly.

He was a large man, well over six feet, and of perhaps 45 or 50 years. His thick hair and beard were touched with gray. He had the build of a boxer, an effect amplified by the size and strength of his hands. His nose also had the sort of bend that spoke clearly of a past break.

The front window slid open, Sam leaning down to glare through the gap.

"It's quite alright, Mr. Wu," the man across from her said. "Miss Albright just joined us."

The younger man leaned over and spat down onto the pavement. "You startled the horses."

The glass slammed shut and the carriage resumed its quick pace.

"Was there any particular reason for the unorthodox entrance?" her companion asked. He spoke with a thick Ulster brogue.

"No," Lily replied.

The carriage rolled past a broader alley than the one Lily had concealed herself in. She spotted the brief orange flare of a cigarette against the darkness. She reminded herself it was almost certainly just some clerk sneaking out for a late night smoke, but felt a bit less foolish about her precautions.

"Dr. Harold Gardner, at your service," the stranger said.

Lily wondered how Strangford knew the doctor, whom he clearly trusted enough to call to assist with a grave-robbing.

"Is Lord Strangford meeting us there?"

"His lordship's up on the box with Sam."

Lily recalled the wool-wrapped figure she had seen before jumping in to the carriage and felt a guilty start that she had not recognized him. That he chose to ride on the box, exposed to the chill of the night, instead of sitting inside the carriage was telling.

"He's a bit off tonight. Can't say I blame him. It's an odd business we're about. Have you much experience with corpses, Miss Albright?"

"Some."

If the doctor was surprised at her answer, he was polite enough not to show it.

"There's none here would think less of you if you decided you'd rather return home to your bed."

"We are here tonight at my suggestion. I intend to see the matter through."

"Fair enough," he concluded.

Lily fought the urge to itch her leg.

"Are you a medical doctor?"

"Do I look like a philosopher?"

"You don't look much like a physician," she admitted frankly.

He let out a hearty bark of laughter.

"You're direct. I like that. I might not look the part but I've the papers to prove it. A fully vetted assistant physician at St. Bartholomew's Hospital, at your service."

"Are you here to examine Mrs. Durst?"

"The deceased lady whose final rest we are violating this fine evening? Aye, for whatever good it will do. I'm no pathologist. I work on the living."

Was he simply a friend that Strangford had pulled in for this unsavory errand? Or was he was here because he, too, was associated with Robert Ash and The Refuge?

She didn't ask. That was none of her business, nor did she want it to be.

They left London proper, passing into the quieter suburban streets of Stoke Newington. The carriage stopped on a pretty little lane lined with a tidy row of houses, the sort of place where everyone had a back garden for hosting birthday parties and Sunday tea.

A broader intersection lay at the end of the road. On the far side of it stretched a tall fence of black wrought iron punctuated by white stone columns that looked as though they had been lifted from an Egyptian temple.

It was the gate of Abney Park, the final resting place of London's iconoclasts and dissenters. Beyond it was a wilderness of dark, leafless trees and crumbling stone.

Dr. Gardner climbed out of the carriage, crouching to fit his massive frame through the door. He turned and offered her his hand. His grip was strong but gentle.

The itch flared again. Lily shifted, grimacing, but kept her hand on her walking stick.

"Something wrong?"

"A twinge in my leg," she replied shortly.

"It's just the wound healing."

Lily's attention sharpened. She looked to the big man beside her as Sam hopped down and moved to tend to the horses.

"How do you know that?"

"Cuts like that always itch like the devil."

"That isn't what I meant."

"No," he replied evenly. "I don't suppose it was."

The figure on the driver's box stepped down, tugging aside the muffler to reveal the poetic lines of Strangford's face.

"Miss Albright."

"Lord Strangford."

"You have met Dr. Gardner?"

"She has," the doctor replied.

Strangford said nothing more. An uncomfortable silence settled in.

Ahead of them, Sam stood beside the bay mare that made up the left side of his team. He leaned in close to her, murmuring in her ear. The horse snorted in reply, her breath fogging in the cool night air.

The chestnut beside her whickered, harness jangling as it shook its head.

Sam stepped back from the animals.

"I suppose you want me to see if I can manage the lock?" he asked.

"If it isn't too much trouble," Dr. Gardner replied.

"If trouble was stopping us, we'd all be home in our beds," Sam retorted with a quick but unmistakable glare at Lily.

He walked to the end of the lane, shoulders slouched, hands tucked into his pockets. He crossed the thoroughfare, then stopped at the wrought-iron fence. He leaned against it and pulled something from his pocket.

Lily caught the flare of a match and realized the driver had lit himself a cigarette.

She felt a flash of irritation that he would take a break for a smoke while they all stood in the cold, waiting to get on with what was sure to be a time-consuming and unpleasant task.

She glanced over at Strangford. She could see the tension in the line of his mouth, the iron set of his jaw. It was there because of her.

Then she heard the sound of laughter.

A couple turned the corner, walking arm-in-arm and a touch unsteadily. They strolled past Sam, casting only a cursory glance at where he stood taking a draw.

They passed. He tossed the cigarette down, ground it under his boot, and moved to the door of the squat little lodge at the end of the gate.

He worked quickly. Within a minute, she saw him push the door open. He peered inside, then pulled it closed and jogged back their way.

"He picked the lock," Lily said with surprise. "How does he know how to do that?"

"Our Mr. Wu has a wee bit of a checkered past," Dr. Gardner replied.

"That's it, then," Sam announced as he returned.

"We need some sort of watch," the doctor pointed out, looking to Strangford. "That place is a jungle. We'll have no way of knowing otherwise whether someone is coming."

Dr. Gardner was right. Abney Park was spread over acres of heavily wooded wilderness—good cover for what they had planned, but also a situation that would make it hard to know if a threat was approaching.

"Sam?" Strangford asked after a moment, a note of apology in his voice.

It wouldn't be enough, Lily thought. Even if she and Sam watched from opposite directions, there would be more angles than two sets of eyes could possibly cover. The cemetery was a jungle run through with crisscrossing paths.

Sam rubbed his hand over his face, looking tired.

"Suppose it'll have to be rats, then," he said.

"Couldn't you make do with birds?" Dr. Gardener asked.

"There aren't many out at this time of night and they're less organized." He nodded toward Lily, eyes narrow. "Is she going to start screaming?"

"No, she is not," Lily retorted flatly. She met his gaze evenly, daring him to contradict her, though inside she felt far less steady. Rats? What did any of this have to do with rats?

He shrugged.

"Fair enough. You lot wait here."

He walked across the lane, stopping at the dark, narrow gap of a sewer grate.

Then he whistled.

It was a strange sound, low in tone. Lily felt an involuntary shiver tickle across her skin. A long minute passed.

Then the rat appeared. He peered out of the sewer grate, black eyes like tiny stones in his face. A long tail whipped back and forth.

Sam crouched down and started speaking. His voice was far too low for Lily to make out any words, just the murmur of some unsettling conversation—one that the rat appeared to be listening to.

Sam stood and the animal slipped away, darting into some bushes at the edge of a tidy little front garden.

He pulled his driver's gloves from his pocket, tugging them on.

"The next move up will be the alpha," Dr. Gardner explained. He had come to stand near her, enormous frame looming at her back. He spoke like he would to a startled horse, tones even and soothing, and Lily wondered why, exactly, he expected she might be about to bolt.

A new rat emerged from the sewer.

It was a large creature, big enough to have to squeeze to make it through the bars of the grate. It saw Sam standing at the curb and hissed, baring vicious teeth.

Lily was not generally afraid of rodents, but this creature was unsettling, even when viewed from the far side of the road.

There was a moment's pause as the combatants took measure of each other. Then Sam took a quick half-step forward.

The rat darted at him, aiming for his ankle, and Sam's hand flashed down, pinning the animal to the ground.

It screeched in rage and fear, scratching and nipping at his fingers.

Lily realized there were other rats present at this scene. Black pebble eyes shone from all around them—under the neatly trimmed hedges, atop the freshly-painted fence posts. They were watching the drama unfolding by the sewer grate with rapt attention.

The rat under Sam's hand whipped its tail back and forth furiously, hissing with rage.

Sam leaned in, increasing the pressure of his grip, and hissed in return.

Lily felt an uncomfortable urge to run across the street and break it up. She forced herself to stay still.

The tail continued to whip, lashing at Sam's wrist. Then it went still. The rat lay limp under his hand, black eyes staring up at the driver, unblinking.

Another long moment passed before Sam opened his hand and stood up.

The large rat flipped to its feet and scurried away, disappearing into the sewer.

The others—the owners of those myriad eyes shining in the darkness of this quiet suburban street—remained where they were.

"This is likely to get a mite unpleasant," Dr. Gardner warned quietly.

"You mean more unpleasant than it has been already?"

Strangford stepped up beside them, his profile highlighted by the glow of the street lamp at the top of the lane. His voice was low.

"They have to touch him to accept him as king."

The shadows around her began to shift. Sleek brown bodies darted from the cracks in foundations, from bins and barrels. Lily saw them racing to and fro, writhing through the grate into the sewer and back out again. Behind her, a bay laurel rustled. She stiffened as a trio of rodents darted out across the street.

Others followed, coming from every direction, dozens upon dozens pouring into the tidy street of this quiet, sleeping neighborhood. They converged on Sam and, to her horror, began to climb up his body.

Claws dug into the wool covering his legs, hauling their thick bodies up the length of his coat. He held out his arms and rats scurried along them, clinging to his shoulders, dislodging his cap. The man was barely visible under the mass of writhing animals.

The mass thinned, more of the beasts gathering at his feet. Sam looked down, rats still clinging to his shoulders, and spoke, the words too low for her to hear.

But not for the rats.

They stared at him enrapt, their focus complete and unblinking except when they turned and focused their gaze on her and the others.

Their eyes glinted.

They heard him, she realized with a rush of horror and wonder. He spoke, and the rats listened.

Waves of them surged across the road, up the Egyptian columns and over into the cemetery. Others skirted the fence, scurrying up onto rooftops or branches.

Sam bent down to retrieve his cap. He placed it back on his head and walked over.

"They'll watch," he reported. "One of the blighters tugs at your leg, make scarce."

"Thank you," Strangford replied.

The younger man nodded, then cast a quick glare at Lily before moving back to the horses.

He clearly knew who was responsible for bringing them there that night.

What had she just witnessed?

She had heard of snake charmers before and carnival types who claimed to be able to hypnotize bears or lions, but she had never known of a rat charmer.

Was that all it had been? Some sort of carnival trick?

She looked over to where Sam stood by the horses. The bay was nuzzling his neck, threatening to dislodge his cap again. Sam stroked her neck. He whispered something to her and the animal snorted in reply.

Was it only rats?

She thought of Ash's words in the quiet gloom of the reflection room.

*You are not alone, Miss Albright.*

She had been struck before by how Sam failed to act as one would expect of a household servant. Perhaps that was because he was, in fact, something more.

Another member of Ash's menagerie.

She glanced over at Strangford, wrapped in shadows and silence, then to Gardner, the doctor who had so easily guessed at the presence of a wound on her leg that was currently buried beneath layers of tweed and linen.

Were all of them charismatics?

"We'll need the light," the doctor said.

Sam unhooked one of the carriage lamps. He snapped a shutter into place. Only the faintest glow leaked through the seam in the tin.

"Keep it closed until you need it. The glare'll give you away right sharp, rats or no rats."

"We defer to your expertise in the matter," Dr. Gardner replied, taking it.

"Let's get to it," Strangford cut in, his tone uncharacteristically short. He turned and started across the road.

Lily and Dr. Gardner followed him along the gates of the cemetery. Pale tombstones were just visible through the gaps in the wrought-iron fence, wrapped in the cloak of a night-dark forest. It was as though this stretch of suburban sprawl had cracked open, revealing a sliver of the world of fairy-tales. Not the pretty ones, but the sort where the witch eats the lost children.

"Hold," Dr. Gardner warned. Lily stopped, following his lead by stepping back out of the light. The racket of carriage wheels echoed off the silent houses and a moment later the vehicle itself came into view—a tired hackney pulled by a saddle-backed old mare.

It passed near enough that Lily could make out the holes in the driver's gloves from where she stood close by Strangford and the doctor, veiled in the shadows from an overhanging oak.

When the last resonant clatter faded, Strangford stepped out of the darkness and led them the rest of the way to the lodge.

It was built in the same pseudo-Egyptian style as the columns of the fence, though the effect was compromised by the broadsheets pasted to the exterior. An advertisement for skin cream half-covered a polemic about the end of the world.

It was another paper that caught Lily's eye, a notice of a lecture on "The Glorious Future of Mankind", sponsored by The Society for the Betterment of the British Race.

Before she had a chance to think better of it, Lily's hand flashed out, grasped the peeling corner of the broadsheet, and tore it from the wall. She crumpled it into a ball.

"I take it you aren't a supporter of eugenics," the doctor commented from beside her.

"Are you?" Lily asked.

"I believe it to be one of the most dangerous ideas I have ever heard," he replied simply.

Strangford put his hand to the knob and the door opened.

It was a small space and cluttered, a desk and chair run up against several heavy file cabinets, walls covered in papers set into them with pins. There were muddy footprints on the floor and a pair of work gloves, stained with earth, on a shelf by the door.

Lily tossed the crumpled broadsheet into an overflowing wastebasket.

Dr. Gardner opened the shutter of the lantern, releasing a thin beam of light.

"What's the name of the woman we're unearthing this evening?"

"Sylvia Durst," Lily replied. "She would have been interred here three or four days ago, at the most, based on when the coroner's report on her death was in the newspapers."

"Four days, eh? Good thing we've had cold weather," he replied blandly.

Strangford went to the file cabinet, yanking open the drawers and searching through them. Dr. Gardner ran a finger across one of the few inches of the desk not covered in papers. It left a line in the grime and he made a noise of disgust.

Abney Park was immense, covering dozens of acres and including the graves of countless dead. If they couldn't find some sort of record for Durst's burial, they'd have no way to know where to find her grave. They couldn't possibly hope to locate it by chance.

It was clear to Lily that the cemetery caretaker was not a stickler for cleanliness or organization. Durst's burial had been recent. She could hazard a guess where she stood the best chance of finding those records and it wasn't the file cabinet.

Lily sat down at the desk itself.

She found what she was looking for in the middle of the mountain of grimy papers piled on its surface.

"It says she's ten yards north of something called 'Path K'," she reported before snapping the file closed and shoving it back into the pile.

Dr. Gardner flashed the lantern around the cramped interior, stopping at a map mounted on the wall. It was yellowed, crumbling at the corners and half-covered in notices.

"Here. Toward the north end."

Strangford pushed shut the file drawer. It closed with an abrupt clang.

He flipped the bolt on a door at the back of the lodge and stepped through it, Dr. Gardner and Lily following.

They emerged under a sprawling oak tree, looking out over a wilderness. Graves rose like ghosts from the darkness, pale forms whispering into view from behind overgrown shrubs and slender trees, wrapped in shrouds of ivy.

The doctor selected two shovels from a pile leaning against the back of the building and set them over his shoulder. He paused, then plucked a crowbar up as well.

"Which way?" Strangford demanded.

"Over there."

Dr. Gardner led them onto a tree-lined avenue that would have looked lovely in a city park were it not for the dead that lined the way. Lily moved past stone lions, their flowing manes mingling with dry grass. Stern angels dripping with moss watched their passage.

The silence was complete. It far surpassed the quiet of a Bloomsbury night, absent even the vaguest echo of wagon wheels or the hoot of a distant train. There was only the scratch of the tree branches and the rustle of dry leaves.

She thought of the illustrations in the tabloid press of a fanged monster looming over the supine form of a sleeping woman.

Lily did not think the killer they sought was some supernatural being. Men were far more plausible and certainly capable of acting like monsters.

However, in the night-shrouded atmosphere of Abney Park, on her way to remove a woman from her grave, the implausible became a bit harder to dismiss.

She shifted her grip on her staff and continued walking.

The avenue led to a clearing where an immense Gothic chapel towered unexpectedly, complete with spire and buttresses. The white tombstones surrounded it like worshipers at the feet of an ancient god.

Strangford walked through the center of the open ground. The doctor followed him, the shovels clinking softly as they bounced against his shoulder.

Lily paused, her instincts urging her to keep to the forested verge where she could conceal herself in the darkness. After all, how could they know there wasn't some caretaker strolling the grounds or a constable set to watch the place and guard against exactly the sort of crime she and the others were here to commit?

There was a sound of scratching against stone. Lily whipped around and saw a fat brown rat haul itself up over the edge of a nearby mausoleum. It stared at her, whiskers twitching.

She looked out over the clearing around the chapel and realized she could see more of them, the movement standing out here in the stronger glow of the unimpeded moonlight. Dark, greasy bodies scurried between the graves, finding perches on top of headstones.

Their watchmen, charged with raising the alarm if danger approached.

She quickened her stride, hurrying across the clearing in Strangford and Dr. Gardner's wake.

Beyond the chapel, the park grew wilder. Trees met and tangled overhead, casting the narrow paths into such deep shadows Lily could barely tell if she had wandered off the way.

The world was wrapped in a coat of ivy and moss, save here and there where the odd vigilant family member kept the resting place of some still-loved one clear. The rest of the grounds felt abandoned like the ruin of a lost civilization.

The shovels rattled as the doctor shifted his grip. He nodded toward an opening in the forest that grew around them. It was barely more than a darker gap between the trees.

"This ought to be Path K," he announced.

It was thickly overgrown. Lily moved along the gravel-lined walk slowly, using her stick to avoid tripping over some unseen tombstone. The doctor kept the lantern shuttered. Lily could see the wisdom in that. They couldn't afford more than a narrow beam without risking detection and the light would only make it harder for their eyes to adjust to the darkness. Seeing their way along the path was less important than spotting a fresh grave amid the riotous growth around them and that required a broader field of vision.

Without speaking, they split up, stepping off the path into the deeper verge. Lily felt her way around thick gray tree trunks and tilted mausoleums. Something cracked under her foot. She hoped it was only a tree branch.

"Here," Dr. Gardner called softly, swinging the shovels and crowbar down off of his shoulder and planting them in the earth.

Lily moved to where he stood. There was a path cut through the brush and ivy, the ground churned up and muddy, showing where heavy foot traffic had recently passed through. At the end of it, under a thin alder tree, was a tumbled rectangle of fresh earth.

"There's no tombstone," she pointed out. "How can we be certain it's Sylvia Durst?"

"We can't."

"So what do we do if we're wrong?" she demanded as he yanked free one of the shovels.

"More digging," he replied and thrust the blade into the earth.

# ELEVEN

$\mathcal{L}$ILY STOOD AT THE edge of the path, watching the dig.

Strangford had shrugged out of his coat, tossing it over a tomb nearby before he picked up the other shovel. He and the doctor had already moved several feet of earth from the grave. It was mounded up beside them, illuminated by the narrow band of light from the lantern.

She felt useless. She wasn't the medical expert who might be able to glimpse some new clue as to how the murder victim they were exhuming had died. Nor was she the one who could read the past with her hands. She couldn't even say she was keeping watch, not as the rats continued to dart back and forth through the brush around them. She could see them in the branches of the trees, dark eyes glinting like wet pebbles.

She had nothing to offer but a vague and pointless sense of guilt.

Dr. Gardner grunted, his brow glistening with sweat in the occasional bands of moonlight that found their way through the twisted branches overhead.

Strangford dug with a grim determination, moving earth with the relentlessness and silence of an automaton.

She wondered just what they would find at the bottom of the hole they were opening in the ground.

Answers, perhaps, that would save Lord Deveral from hanging for a crime he hadn't committed.

Maybe even the knowledge they needed to save Estelle's life.

No, she thought firmly. She would not go down that path. To allow that hope a space inside of her would only lead to more heartache.

Or it could all turn out to be just a big, humorless mistake.

Strangford's shovel struck wood with a dull, hollow thud.

"I think you've got something there," the doctor commented.

They cleared the remaining earth away until the top of the coffin was fully exposed.

The doctor wedged the crowbar into the edge of the lid. He worked it, struggling a bit for leverage in the narrow confines of the open grave.

Lily moved closer.

There was a horrible crack, a scream of protesting metal, and the nails holding the coffin closed wrenched loose.

"I'll require a bit of assistance."

Beside Dr. Gardener, Strangford wedged his gloved hands under the lid. He hauled at it, his muscles straining under the soiled linen of his shirt.

It popped free.

The smell rose up like a cloud, reminding her of meat left too long in the icebox.

The worst of it dispersed, leaving a lingering foulness.

"Where's the lantern?" Dr. Gardner asked.

Lily collected it and brought it over. Strangford climbed up to intercept her, putting his body between her and the dark hole in the ground.

She stopped. It was not because she had any fear of what she would see if she looked down into that grave. She was sure she had been confronted with worse. One did not try—and repeatedly fail—to avert all manner of disasters without coming across a fair share of corpses. Those had almost always been in a fresher state but also likely more brutalized than Sylvia Durst, who had died in her bed without a mark on her body.

It was for Strangford's sake. If it gave him some kind of comfort to think she'd been protected from the worst of this endeavor, it was the least she could do after being the one to drag him out here in the first place. Her eyes weren't going to tell them what they needed to know, anyway. It was Strangford's hands they depended upon for that.

Strangford passed the lantern to the doctor, who opened the shutter. Light brightened the hole in the ground, spilling out across the surrounding cherubs and memento mori.

Rats scurried for darker spaces to hide in, eyes glinting.

Strangford moved to the edge, looking down. Lily took the opportunity of his distraction to slip a bit closer.

The body of a middle aged woman lay in the opened coffin. A bit of dirt had crumbled onto her cheek, which was colored a mottled purple. Her skin looked like wax but was otherwise unmarked.

"I can't be sure if it's her," she admitted. "The newspapers never published a picture."

"Right sex, anyway. Age?" the doctor asked.

"She was said to have been around fifty."

He prodded her arm.

"Hard to tell if there was any exsanguination. She's been fully embalmed and they would've drained her for that anyway. Pardon, madam," he murmured as he opened the buttons of her black funeral gown, exposing her neck and chest. "There was an autopsy, at any rate. That's promising."

"It is?" Lily asked.

"Aye. They wouldn't have bothered if she'd died of pneumonia. Ah, here we are."

He ran his hands over her neck, turning her head to the side.

"What do you see?" Strangford asked. His tone was flat, a mask of calm firmly set in place, but Lily could see the tight set of his jaw.

"There's a needle site right over the jugular artery."

"The papers mentioned a puncture wound in her throat," Lily recalled.

"This was a physician's needle. Something was injected or withdrawn. Probably the latter—it's a larger bore. Fresh. Must have happened right as she died. Needle sites heal very quickly and this is still open."

"You're certain?"

"I'm a doctor, my dear. I have rather a lot to do with needles. I'm quite certain."

A physician's needle, right at the jugular. It made a perfect and terrible sense.

Despite the sensational assertions of the papers, there had never been a supernatural power at play here. The killer had exsanguinated his victim by simple, practical means—a needle in the neck, a length of rubber tube. She thought of the vision of Annalise's death, the sound that had echoed through the room as the dark shadow of the murderer moved closer.

Clanging glass, like the rattle of a milkman's crate.

Bottles.

That's why there was no blood in the room. The murderer had drained it into bottles and carried it out with him.

The knowledge raised as many questions as it answered. Chief among them was why—what possible reason could any man have for stealing a woman's entire store of blood?

Dr. Gardner moved the lantern, adjusting the angle of the light. The focus of his examination had shifted to Sylvia Durst's face.

He tapped at a series of angry red marks that surrounded her nose and mouth.

"There's something about these burns."

"Burns?" Lily had thought the marks just another form of the discoloration that mottled her skin after death.

"Aye, they're burns." The doctor opened the dead woman's mouth and looked at her tongue. "It's something I've seen before, but where is escaping me." He frowned at the body a moment longer, then shook his head. "I'm afraid that's all I can give you. It's possible I might be able to say more if I reopen that autopsy incision, but in this light, without any instruments . . ."

"Thank you, Doctor. That won't be necessary," Strangford cut in.

The physician narrowed the shutter of the lantern, then hauled himself back onto level ground.

Strangford stared down into the open grave, his face pale in the moonlight. He tugged off his gloves, tucking them carefully into his pocket.

The trees shifted overhead, branches rattling in a wind that tasted of winter. Lily pulled her coat closer.

He dropped down into the grave. The dirt crumbled under his boots, rattling hollowly against the coffin. He looked at the dead woman at his feet.

"It is possible that I might start screaming."

Lily fought against the impulse to intervene. Instead, she stood sentinel-still at the edge of the grave, watching. If she couldn't stop this, she could at least bear witness to it.

The nobleman knelt down in the loose earth.

He closed his eyes, taking in a deep, uneven breath. The moment dragged. Lily began to wonder if perhaps he would lose his nerve.

Then he placed his bare hands against the exposed skin of the dead woman's chest.

Lily saw his shoulders stiffen. He gasped as though someone had just struck him. Every instinct ordered her to dive into the grave and haul him out.

She didn't move.

The trees swayed overhead, skeletal arms dancing against the night sky. Rats darted through the tall grass behind her, the scrape of their claws whispering in the darkness.

Finally he started to speak.

"They gave him a christening. He was already dead but the vicar was a friend and agreed to it. He feels cold in her arms. She hates how it feels—like a bundle of cold rags—but she can't bring herself to put him down because she remembers how he felt when he was still breathing. Warm. Present. So much grief . . ."

His voice was raw with it, the pain of a mother holding what was left of her child.

He turned his head, as though forcing himself to look away.

"The tables. Rough wood under her fingers. Holding the hands of strangers. Warm hands, cold hands. Hands like sandpaper. The dead are fickle. Refuse to come half the time but you put on a bit of a show. It keeps coins in one's pocket. A widow has to do what she can to get by. Gives them comfort, believing there's something after, but it's just wisps of memory, bones and dust. Bones and dust."

He was meandering, she realized, pulled into the dead woman's experiences—her sharpest grief, the endless routine of her work. He needed help to focus on what mattered—on the reason they were all here.

She moved closer, dropping to her knees at the edge of the crumbling soil.

"Enough of that. Find the night she died," she ordered.

Dr. Gardner looked over at her from across the grave, where he sat on the edge of a lichen-encrusted tomb.

"Sleeping," Strangford said after a moment. His voice was thick. "Not sleeping. Something else. She wants to wake but she can't."

"Is anyone there?"

"Yes."

Lily's pulse pounded.

"Who?"

Strangford shook his head.

"She doesn't know. Can't wake up. It hurts."

"What hurts?"

"Her neck. Aches."

"We need to know who else is in the room."

Strangford's shoulders were bunched, muscles knotted with tension.

"Just a shadow. She can't see. Lights . . . The gas is broken."

The words triggered an unexpected memory.

*Every time I ask her . . . she just shows me a lamp.*

Estelle's words, the story she claimed to have gotten from the ghost of Agnes McKenney.

It was an uncanny connection but far from helpful. Gas lamps didn't murder people and carry off their blood.

"If she can't see, can she feel? Hear? There must be something," she demanded, frustration edging her tone.

"There's a smell," Strangford said. "Overpowering. She's drowning in it. Can't get enough air."

"What kind of smell?"

"Sweet. Acrid. Burning sugar and lamp oil."

On the far side of the grave, Dr. Gardner straightened.

"Chloroform," he announced.

"The anesthetic?" Lily asked.

"Those marks on her face . . . some patients react to the stuff when it touches their skin. I haven't seen it in ages, but I remember well enough what it looks like. The odor's distinctive but it disperses. Outside half an hour, no one would've caught more than a whiff of it."

"So this is some sort of surgery she's recalling?"

"Surgeons don't use chloroform anymore. Not at any hospital in London. It's all ether. Has been for over a decade."

Her mind whirled, putting together the details.

"Can chloroform be applied when a patient is already asleep?"

"It works through inhalation. Patients are still breathing even when they're dreaming."

The pieces fell together. A killer waiting until his victim was already lost in sleep. Drugging them into a deeper and less volatile unconsciousness, then inserting a needle and siphoning blood into bottles.

But how did he get inside? There had been no signs of a break-in at any of the murders and a man carrying a case full of bottles of blood would hardly have been inconspicuous.

None of which even started to answer the question of *why*.

"Chloroform is tricky stuff," the doctor continued pointedly. "Hard to administer without killing your patient by way of overdose or having him wake up in the middle of surgery. The dosage is precise and you've got to do it continuously. There's little margin for error."

"You're saying the murderer is a medical man."

"I'm saying he certainly must have trained as one."

She thought of Joseph Hartwell, a doctor with an interest in blood. Of course, by that logic every hematologist in England must be a suspect, and yet Lily still could not shake the skin-crawling intensity of Evangeline Ash's seeming warning about the man.

A background in blood science and a mystical revelation from a dead artist were hardly enough evidence to accuse someone of murder. That eerie moment in the gallery had undue influence on her judgment, making her fixate on Hartwell instead of seeing the whole picture.

She needed more.

She leaned forward, getting as close to Strangford as she could without falling into the hole in the ground.

"There must be something else you can tell us about the man in the room with her. Please, Strangford."

He looked pale and his breath was labored like a man in the midst of a sprint.

"She doesn't deserve it," he rasped.

"Of course she didn't. But we must know more if we're going to find the man who did this to her," Lily urged.

"The power," Strangford ground out in retort. "She doesn't deserve it."

Lily's pulse quickened. Her fingers clenched against the loose earth at the edge of the grave. Strangford wasn't sensing Sylvia Durst anymore. He was connecting with the thoughts of the last man who'd touched her, the monster who had taken her life. Their imprint was marked into the dead woman's flesh just as Lily's memories had lingered in the cold tin of her powder compact.

"Just a fat, stupid housewife. Someone better . . . stronger . . . could do more with it. Great things . . . sweet Christ," he swore, his voice shaking. "The rot. The stinking rot."

"Miss Albright," Dr. Gardner began. Lily cut him off before he could say what she knew was coming.

"You must keep going," she ordered Strangford. "You're so close."

She felt it then—a sharp tug on her skirts. Lily grabbed at them and pulled back absentmindedly, assuming she must have snagged them on some rotten old branch.

The branch yanked back.

She whirled, looking down to see the flat black eyes of a rat staring up at her, her garment caught in its teeth.

It released the fabric and hissed, a sharp and urgent sound.

Then it dashed away into the grass.

*One of the blighters tugs at your leg, make scarce.*

A warning.

She whirled to face the doctor.

"Hide!" she hissed.

He read the urgency on her face and glanced to the grave.

"Go! I'll get him," she ordered.

The doctor's massive frame disappeared behind an obelisk, lost in the shadows.

"Strangford!" she whispered. "Come!"

"Feel them digging. Under the skin. Too blasted cold," he muttered in reply. He shuddered, the movement coming from deep in his core.

He couldn't hear her—or if he could, he was incapable of responding.

Behind her, she heard the crunch of boots on gravel.

Should she try to pull him out?

A flicker of light appeared between the tangled branches, moving along the path.

They were out of time.

Lily whipped off her cloak. She tossed the dark spread of fabric over the grave, covering it and blocking the glimmer of the near-shuttered lantern. She threw a scattering of dry leaves across it for good measure. Then she dove behind the nearest tombstone, crouching in the weeds and the dirt, cold seeping through the now-exposed fabric of her shirt.

The footsteps drew closer, the light bobbing past the slender trees.

Her thoughts shot back to the hole in the ground that lay a few feet in front of her.

What was happening in there?

The frustration and worry gnawed at her as the light swept across tangled branches.

There was a soft moan from Strangford, little more than a gasp, half-choked.

The lamp stopped.

Lily risked a peek from between the vines that spilled over her hiding place.

The watchman stood on the path, just a few yards away. He held his lamp aloft, looking around the jumbled graves.

She held her breath, praying for Strangford to stay silent.

The light shifted and the footsteps continued, moving away along the path.

Lily waited in an agony of stillness until the glow of the watchman's lamp had receded.

Silence descended. She counted off the seconds until she could bear it no longer and scrambled out of her hiding place.

"Doctor!" she hissed, moving to the grave and yanking her cloak out of the way. She climbed inside, her boots sending little stones rattling off the coffin. She wrapped her arms around Strangford's solid torso, bracing her feet against the edges of the wooden box and hauling him back.

He fell away from the dead woman, landing against the dirt beside her. He groaned, his breathing ragged.

The physician's face appeared above them.

"Get him out of here!" Lily ordered.

Dr. Gardner leaned down and slipped his hands under Strangford's arms. He pulled the smaller man up onto the surface again.

Lily cast a glance back at the tumbled corpse of Sylvia Durst.

She had told them so much . . . and yet nowhere near enough.

She grabbed the side of the grave and scrambled back up onto the ground beside Strangford, who remained on his back, staring up at the dark branches overhead.

"Can you stand, man?" Dr. Gardner asked.

Strangford rolled over, bracing himself on his forearms.

"I don't need you," he snapped, his voice raw. He crawled to his knees. One of his pale hands fell against the earth, and he snatched it away as though burned.

"In your pocket," the physician offered.

Moving like an old man, Strangford pulled the gloves from his pocket and tugged them back onto his hands. He tucked them under his arms, keeping them close.

"My lord . . ." Lily began.

"I'm fine." He cut her off quickly, turning away.

Lily saw the physician give him a sharp look. Then Dr. Gardner shook his head, turning to the grave. He jumped down, grabbed the lid of the coffin and set it back into place.

The seal was far from perfect, jagged ends of nails keeping it somewhat askew. The doctor tried to shift it, then stood back.

"Well, it's all for dust now, anyway."

He climbed out, bringing the shuttered lantern with him. He crossed to the heap of earth and pulled one of the shovels free.

The clods of dirt bounced hollowly off the coffin as he tossed them back into the grave.

Lily looked back at Strangford. He stood at a distance, hands still tucked protectively under his arms, his shoulders hunched under his earth-stained shirt.

To the east, the sky was kissed with a rosier light than the ambient glow of the city's gas lamps. Dawn was coming.

She needed to help clean up the mess she had made.

Lily trudged over and picked up the other shovel.

~

She was exhausted by the time she tipped the last mound of earth onto the grave. The sky had brightened noticeably overhead. The air was still cold but Dr. Gardner wiped sweat from his brow with his handkerchief.

Lily looked down at her boots. They were caked with grave dirt, streaks of filth staining her skirt.

Dr. Gardner extended a hand for her shovel. Lily let him take it. He swung the pair of them over his shoulder with the crowbar, then picked up the lantern.

"My lord?" he asked.

It was a moment before Strangford responded. He looked back slowly, as though locked in a dream.

"Yes. Of course." His voice was flat. He turned, moving like man twice his age.

He set off down the path, not looking back to see if the others would follow.

"Come along, then," Gardner said at last. He moved after the nobleman, leaving Lily to trail along in their wake.

The graves that lined the narrow path were more visible now in the early morning light. They passed through the clearing with the chapel, its ornate windows still darkly shadowed.

The rats followed, skipping along the stones at the corners of her vision.

At the lodge, Gardner set the shovels down and pushed open the door.

Once inside, Lily reset the bolt. Their muddy footprints blended with the dirt already covering the floor.

"Wait," the doctor said, crouching to look out the small window. He held the lantern against the glass, flicking the shutter open and shut three times in quick succession.

A few moments later, she heard the clatter of carriage wheels.

Sam stopped the coach just outside. The doctor waved Lily through first, Strangford trailing behind her.

"Make it sharp," Sam ordered as he jumped down from the box. He ran over to the door of the lodge, pulling his picks from his pocket. He was resetting the lock, Lily realized, so that no alarm would be raised when the caretaker arrived later that morning. It was something he would have to do quickly before their presence here drew notice.

She opened the door to the coach to climb in, then paused, some instinct calling for her to look back.

Behind her, Strangford stared into the dark, close interior of the carriage with an expression of naked horror on his face.

The big physician took his arm and pushed him toward the front of the vehicle.

"Get on the box, m'lord," he ordered.

Strangford snapped into motion, climbing up onto the driver's perch. The wool muffler was pulled back up over his face and he slumped down, looking like a man half-drunk.

Sam moved past her to join him, mounting to the high seat with practiced ease.

"Miss Albright?"

Dr. Gardner stood at the door of the carriage and Lily realized that she was the one now lingering on the pavement, risking their discovery.

"Of course," she said automatically and hurried inside.

She had barely taken her seat when the carriage lurched into motion.

Across from her, the doctor leaned back, stretching his long legs out in front of him.

Lily's mind spun, trying to pull together some coherent picture from the splintered facts they had uncovered.

A man with medical training slipping into houses to steal blood from sleeping women. Carrying it off in bottles . . . for what? What good could it possibly do him to make collecting it worth such extremes?

"Doctor?"

"Yes?" he muttered from under the low-tipped brim of his hat.

"What could someone do with human blood?"

He pushed the hat up an inch, glancing over at her. He considered it.

"In theory, human blood could do a great many things. It could save the lives of patients undergoing surgery or suffering from a violent accident. Do you know how many pregnant women hemorrhage during labor? If there was a safe way to transfer blood from one person into another, a great many lives we currently lose could potentially be saved."

"But you can't," Lily surmised.

"No. There were experiments done nearly two hundred years ago. The results were . . . unpleasant. There is something in human blood that very often reacts poorly to being transferred into another body. It is almost always fatal."

"Almost always?"

"There are times where the procedure works. The trouble is that no one has discovered a way to reliably determine the difference. Nor does it look likely they will anytime soon, since the experiments themselves are likely to kill the research subjects."

"Does this have anything to do with Dr. Joseph Hartwell's work?"

"Dr. Hartwell is a brilliant man. His theories on blood typing are intriguing. But they are still very much just theories. I'll grant Hartwell more credit when I can apply them in an operating theatre."

"I see."

There were other questions she burned to ask. They were questions about Gardner himself and his role in all of this, about Sam Wu and The Refuge.

She did not ask them.

Silence settled back over the interior of the carriage. Gardner closed his eyes. Lily's thoughts turned to Strangford, hunched above her on the driver's box.

He would be fine, she assured herself. His current state was likely due to the lingering memory of what he had experienced inside Sylvia Durst's corpse, coupled with the exhaustion of a sleepless night. A bath, a nap—a stiff glass of brandy—and he would be right as rain again. He simply needed to be left alone in the meantime, she told herself firmly.

And then . . . ?

It was a question Lily could not answer, one that brought her own exhaustion weighing down on her like a cloak of lead.

The city had come to life by the time the coach passed onto the familiar streets of Bloomsbury, rocking to a halt in front of her flat on March Place.

Lily rose.

"Miss Albright," Gardner said courteously, though his eyes were still closed.

"Doctor," she replied.

Sam opened the carriage door.

"Thank you," Lily said to him as she stepped down.

The chauffeur slammed it shut behind her in answer.

"Miss," he said with bare courtesy, then climbed back onto the box and snapped the reins.

She watched as the carriage rolled away, her eyes on the hunched figure beside Sam on the box.

Then she was alone.

Doors were opening around her, early morning commuters emerging to begin the day. Some fine private carriage was parked at the end of the lane, the horses stamping restlessly, their breath fogging in the cool air.

Lily's clothes were stained with grave dirt, her boots caked with mud. She must look like a character out of a Dickens novel, wretchedly out of place on this respectable street. If she lingered here any longer, someone was likely to call a constable.

She forced her feet to mount the steps and pushed inside, closing the door quietly behind her.

She had never been so tired in her life.

Her shoulders ached, her wound itching like the devil. She desperately wanted a bath but couldn't imagine staying awake long enough to fill it.

Mrs. Bramble emerged from the far end of the hall, hands firmly planted on her hips.

"You've a caller," she barked. "I settled him in your parlor."

"Him?" Lily echoed thickly.

Mrs. Bramble's attitude toward men in the house was unambiguous and yet this one had been brought up to Lily's flat—even though Lily herself was not in attendance. What sort of man would possibly impress her landlady enough to be granted those privileges?

And why would such a person be calling for her at the near-ungodly hour of half-past seven in the morning?

"I'll have the tea ready in a moment," Mrs. Bramble announced, then turned to march back into the kitchen.

Lily faced the staircase.

She didn't want to deal with a caller. She wanted to crawl into bed and close the door on the world.

Whoever had come, he would not be there long enough for tea.

She mounted the steps, her leg protesting with each move. It felt like an eternity before she reached her landing and pushed open the door.

He rose from her secondhand armchair next to a cozy fire that Bramble must have set for him. Lily could see the light flickering across his familiar profile—the sharp-cut jaw and patrician nose. It was a face made to be carved in marble and labeled with the name of a long-dead emperor.

It was a face she saw echoed every time she looked in a mirror—the face of the 12th Earl of Torrington.

"Good morning, Lilith," her father said.

# TWELVE

⁂

$\mathscr{S}$HE HAD LAST SEEN him at her mother's funeral.

The day was beautiful, sunny and clear in a way one rarely saw over London. The breeze was warm with a lightness that made you feel as though it could lift away your skin and carry off your soul.

The little chapel was packed, bodies crammed into every bit of open pew. They lined the walls, spilled out the door onto the path. Many were people Lily knew. There were former stage managers and directors along with the better part of an orchestra. A slew of chorus girls sobbed noisily in the back. Actors both famous and obscure peppered the crowd between ardent fans and onlookers who had never seen Deirdre Albright perform but simply wanted the chance to gawp at the others in attendance.

There were men in mourning gowns and women in trousers and formal coats. There were boas and parrots and hats that defied gravity.

It was a theatrical event as spectacular as any Deirdre Albright had starred in before, though this time she played her part from within a shining ebony box.

Lily knelt in the front row beside her nurse, a thin-faced girl who had been hired only a few weeks before. Lily had heard her audibly grumbling before the service about how she had only been paid through the end of the week.

"I hope no one expects me to stay on with some actress's brat without wages," she had announced.

The men and women who shared her row were strangers. There were no family here, no distant relatives from Deirdre's homeland. They were all dead or emigrated, or had long ago disowned any connection to her.

Lily felt as though she, too, were on a stage, playing a part in a show that had been written for someone else.

The crowd was surely bigger and more demonstrative than it would have been had Deirdre Albright merely died in her sleep. To have anyone of fame, even a slightly tarnished and faded fame, stabbed in the chest by a common thief was bound to bring every sensation-seeker out of the woodwork.

The image of it was branded into Lily's brain.

She had seen it from the rocking chair in her room, the vision washing over her with more brightness and intensity than life.

Of course, she had done everything she could to prevent it. For once, it had seemed as though events were conspiring in her favor. Her mother always was an indulgent woman and had breezily agreed to the conditions Lily had desperately set, conditions carefully designed to make it impossible for her to end up as Lily had foreseen—clad in a bright red gown, alone, gazing sightless up into the night sky while jewels glittered in the pool of blood that surrounded her.

It hadn't mattered.

After all, a white gown could easily turn to the red Lily insisted she leave at home when it was stained with blood. And a necklace of paste and glass, borrowed from a costumer friend, looked even finer in the darkness of Covent Garden as the true jewels she had agreed to forgo for the evening.

She had kept her promise not to go alone, so the costumer had died with her.

Every precaution Lily took turned to dust. Every warning heeded, every circumstance carefully avoided, had instead all conspired to bring about the very horror Lily sought to prevent.

She felt as though she was the one who held the knife. Her guilt was just as real, just as substantial. She had known for two full weeks that her mother's life was in danger and still she had failed to save her.

The cold, quick thrust of it threatened to swallow her whole.

Around her, London's players and dancers wept luxuriant tears into black handkerchiefs or bombazine-clad shoulders. Lily remained still and silent, her eyes dry as the pallbearers hefted the black coffin onto their shoulders and carried it down the aisle.

"I'd just like to know what's going to become of me," the nurse muttered to the weeping stage dresser beside her as Lily rose to follow the dark box out into the churchyard.

The words rang with a terrible significance, one that put the slightest hitch in her forcefully even step.

*I'd just like to know what's going to become of me.*

Deirdre Albright had been as bright and heedless of practicalities as a butterfly. There would be no plan for the future, no contingency to determine what became of her daughter should the unimaginable come to pass.

At the end of this service, the crowd of wailing mourners around her would trudge off to drink or sleep or kick up their skirts on the music hall stages.

There would be no one left.

The cold fear rose up, elbowing its way into a space already tight with guilt and grief, and then they arrived at the dark hole in the ground where her mother would be lain.

The grass of the churchyard was lush and green, the soft-leaved trees whispering overhead in that perfect breeze.

"As for mortals, their days are like grass; they flourish like a flower of the field," the priest intoned. "For the wind passes over it, and it is gone, and its place knows it no more."

Sunlight dappled down through the dancing branches, glittering on the white marble of the graves. Lily fought the urge to scream.

A hand settled onto her shoulder.

It was warm, steady and solid.

She looked up and he was there—the man who was constantly moving through her life, passing on his way to or from, familiar but always a little distant.

He stood straight-backed, the light moving over the Roman profile and salt-and-pepper hair she knew so well, but something different was carved into the lines of his face, something strange and yet shockingly familiar.

Grief.

He looked down at her as the priest droned out the rest of his psalm, the weight of his hand like an anchor in a storm.

"I know," he said and she realized that he did—that of all the myriad, wailing mourners pressed around that dark, waiting hole in the ground, there was one who shared her pain, who understood what she had lost because he had lost it too.

His hand remained through all the effusive eulogies, the throwing of roses, the wails and the rattle of earth on the coffin lid. When it was done and the crowd dispersed, he knelt down before her, his steel gray eyes meeting her own.

"All will be well."

The words had the weight of a vow made as he held the slender bones of her shoulders in his hands.

He stood, murmuring something to the nurse, who had become all sweetness and obedience the moment he appeared. She bobbed her head.

"Yes, m'lord."

He turned back and smiled at Lily. It was a smile that carried a promise Lily read as clear as if he had spoken it aloud.

She would not be alone in this. Someone would be there—someone who understood.

Then he was gone.

And he did not return.

Three days later, it was not the Earl of Torrington who appeared at the door of the rooms on Oxford Street, but an elderly solicitor. He paid the nurse a generous severance and waited with barely concealed impatience while Lily packed her belongings into a trunk. She was delivered to Mrs. Finch's, where she spent the next five years of her life without hearing so much as a single word from the man who had been the source of her strength at that terrible moment—the man who had made her a promise she had been foolish enough to believe and which had been thoroughly betrayed.

Unless one counted the bank statements.

～

The parlor was not a room designed for entertaining. Lily did not have guests. There were two chairs but only one of them was ever used. The other had been purchased on a whim at a flea market and even Cat disdained it, preferring to find some new jacket or Lily's bedroom slippers to sleep on and leave coated in orange fur. The cushion was stiff, taut enough to bounce a penny near to the ceiling.

A pile of newspapers and a few motorcycle magazines lay in an untidy pile by the fireplace. A handful of exceptionally hardy house-plants, capable of withstanding perennial neglect, crowded the top of the bookshelf. The walls were decorated with just enough art to keep them from being conspicuously bare, and those were mediocre land-scape paintings, the sort one never noticed unless the nail broke and they came tumbling to the ground.

There was only a single photograph, set inconspicuously on the mantle—an image of her mother, which Lily kept half-hidden by a brass clock. In it, she was dressed as Cleopatra and her face was a little blurred as she had clearly broken out into a smile at some point during the exposure.

To a man like the Earl of Torrington, it must seem like a tawdry little garret.

Not that it mattered to Lily. She was beyond being judged by him.

Fourteen years.

He had changed and yet he was the same. Those carved-from-mar-ble features were as she remembered them, though the lines around his mouth and eyes were heavier now. His hair had turned more salt than pepper, but his back was still straight, his gray eyes just as sharp.

Why was he here? What possible reason could there be for him to break fourteen years of silence and turn up in her parlor?

Deveral.

Lily's visit to his townhouse must not have gone unnoticed.

It still didn't make sense. If Torrington wished to warn her away from his family, he certainly didn't have to do it in person. A letter would have done just as well or he might have trudged out another solicitor. The one who brought her to Mrs. Finch's was almost cer-tainly dead by now, but she was sure he must have several on his payroll.

She wondered what consequences he would threaten were she to refuse to comply. Revoking the allowance she refused to accept?

She owed him nothing. He could do nothing to her.

She dropped her walking stick into the holder by the door, collected her filthy, earth-stained skirts, and made an elegant and entirely formal curtsy.

"My lord."

There was a flicker of response in his familiar gray eyes. It was not the irritation she had expected to elicit but something else. Something sadder.

"Is this your chair?" he asked, indicating the plush, comfortable piece he stood before.

"No," she lied and lowered herself onto the seat of the flea-market acquisition—slowly, so that it did not promptly bounce her back out. The springs dug into her thighs.

He took his seat opposite her.

"I apologize for the hour. I know it is unsociably early, but I am expected at Parliament by nine and the matter is of some urgency. Your housekeeper told me you had just stepped out and would be back in a moment."

Lily was sharply aware of the filth staining her second-hand skirts and the mud caked onto her boots, flaking from them onto the carpet.

"My landlady."

"Sorry?"

"Mrs. Bramble is my landlady. Not my housekeeper."

"I see."

Silence descended. She could hear the brass clock ticking on the mantle. She offered him nothing. If that left him feeling awkward or unwelcome, so be it.

Traffic rumbled along outside the window, the sound muffled by the glass.

"Lilith . . ." he began at last, but stopped at the sound of heavy footsteps on the stairs.

There was a knock at the door.

"Come in," Lily said without taking her gaze from the man in the more comfortable of her two chairs.

Mrs. Bramble entered, carrying a laden tea tray. It was the silver one, an item which had never found its way to Lily's flat before, laden with a fine porcelain teapot and biscuits glazed with chocolate.

She set it down on the table by the fire with uncharacteristic grace, the cups barely rattling against the saucers.

She stepped back.

"Anything else I can fetch you?"

Lily wondered what rabbit hole she had fallen into. Then again, it probably wasn't often that Mrs. Bramble had a peer of the realm in the house. She felt quite certain that the fib about Lily's imminent arrival had been designed simply to get Lord Torrington upstairs so that Bramble could brag for the rest of her life that she had served tea to an earl.

"That will be all, thank you," Lily replied flatly.

Mrs. Bramble curtsied and then slipped out of the room, closing the door gently behind her.

Lily let the service sit there. She did not offer to pour.

Let him think her rude.

How dare he turn up in her parlor? How dare he invade her life? And for what? Simply to tell her to stay entirely out of his?

He would not have to ask her twice. She would do it and gladly.

"Perhaps you had best get to it," she said, once Bramble's footsteps indicated she was safely out of earshot. "It is nearly eight."

He leaned forward and took a biscuit.

"You called on Lord Deveral yesterday."

"I did."

"May I inquire what prompted the visit?"

She considered how to answer. She quickly dismissed the notion of presenting a falsehood. There was simply no plausible reason she would suddenly try to visit the half-brother who hated her on the day he was accused of murder and she felt rather certain her father was extraordinarily good at spotting a lie.

Movement flickered in the corner of her vision. She glanced over and saw Cat slowly creeping toward the earl's chair. Lily found herself visualizing a stone's weight in orange tabby leaping onto his lordship's noble lap. Why not? The morning could hardly get any worse.

"I wished to speak to him about the events of last evening."

"You refer to the death of Mrs. Boyden."

"Yes."

"Why?"

She shrugged. "I wanted to know if he had seen or heard anything unusual when he was there."

She could see his sharp mind working behind those familiar gray eyes.

"You speak of him as though he were a witness. You do not believe he was Mrs. Boyden's killer?"

"No," Lily admitted, since there was little alternative. "I do not."

He leaned forward, picking up the teapot and pouring a cup.

"Tea?"

"No, thank you," Lily replied.

He took it black.

"How well do you know Simon?" he asked.

"Not very."

"So your belief in his innocence is not based on your faith in the quality of his character. Have you some sort of evidence that indicates another was responsible for Mrs. Boyden's death?"

"No."

"Which leaves . . . what, exactly?"

The clock ticked on the mantle. Her leg itched. Cat had made it across the room and now sat at the foot of the earl's chair, gazing up at him with rapt attention.

She was weary to the bone, frustrated and angry and half-starving. She wanted to climb into her bed, not sit here and be interrogated by the father who had deserted her over a decade ago.

"Call it a hunch," she snapped dismissively.

Cat leapt. He landed on Lord Torrington's lap. Lily waited for him to swat the animal away. Instead, her father's hand went to the back of Cat's thick neck. He scratched at it absentmindedly.

Cat began to purr.

Cat never purred.

Lily heard a coal fall in the fire, the crackle of the flames.

"So you still have them, then. Those hunches."

Her senses snapped into alertness. She could hear the motor engine rumble from Cat's throat. She could smell her father. It was a familiar smell, like cedar and bergamot. How could it be familiar?

Her thoughts flew back to the flat on Oxford Street. Burying her nose in the wool of his coat where he'd tossed it over a chair before going into her mother's room. The lingering scent on the pillows when she curled up with her mother the next morning.

She had forgotten that smell.

"I don't know what you mean," she replied evenly.

He stroked the animal on his lap, hand moving absentmindedly along its sleek orange fur.

"I didn't always know when I would make it to Oxford Street. Sessions might end early or some obligation be canceled . . . but no matter how unexpected I was, you always managed to be playing on the floor in the drawing room when I arrived."

Her pulse thudded and the memory came flooding back.

How she would know. That simple, unquestionable awareness that he was coming would announce itself and she would connive a way to escape her nurse and be in his path when he turned up at the door.

The memory was shocking, hitting her with all the force of a train. There had been more—what was coming in the post. That a night's performance would be canceled. That rain would ruin plans for a picnic. She had known it the way astronomers know a star is about to rise or seafarers that the tide will turn.

It hadn't always been visions, waking nightmares she knew were destined to become truth. It had been something else once, an easy awareness of what was around the bend that she had been surprised those around her did not share.

It shook her to the bone. She reached for the teapot to cover it up, pouring herself a cup. It clattered only slightly against the saucer as she lifted it.

"Of course. Children always like to play where they are most underfoot, I imagine," she said easily.

"Indeed. Though from the reaction of your minders when they discovered you there, it was not a place you were generally permitted to loiter. So it is quite a remarkable coincidence that you always managed to be there just when I made an appearance."

Lily sipped her tea.

"Indeed. Quite remarkable."

"Your mother certainly thought so."

Lily's teacup rang against the saucer. She forced her hands to steady.

"Pardon?"

"She called you her little telegraph. Bragged about how you always knew before the rest of the house when a package would be delivered, or that an acquaintance would be dropping by. I remember one time I brought a little bauble for her—not for any occasion, just something I knew would brighten her eyes. 'Lily told me you had something for me,' she said. You quite ruined my surprise."

His tone was light, but his gaze was fixed on her, pinning her like a butterfly to a board. She summoned every ounce of her self-control to keep her face and form steady, to revealing nothing of the tumult his words were opening up inside of her.

"The nurses always said I was rather difficult," she replied easily.

"You come by it honestly."

She felt a quick flash of anger. She latched on to it—it was safer than the other emotions that were threatening.

"You refer to my mother?"

"No. I do not."

She looked at him, sitting in her chair by her fire, stroking the clearly rapturous Cat. This man with her nose and her eyes who had no right to be anything other than a stranger to her had showed up here in her sanctuary and threatened to blow the walls apart with his casual recollections.

"Not so honestly, then," she remarked.

His fingers were the tell—the slightest hitch in the rhythm of their attentions to Cat's neck. It was a subtle indicator that her words had hit their mark.

It did not leave her feeling very victorious.

Cat jumped down and her father stood. He moved over to the gable that housed the window, looking down at the street.

"Simon is difficult." His words were bald in their honestly. "He always has been. I have tried to teach him to manage it, but he is not inclined to learn. There is only so much a father can do, even one with the resources I have at my disposal. Yet I do know him—your brother—and he would not murder a woman in her bed."

His figure was straight, stiff, every inch the proper aristocrat even in her cramped little parlor. But Lily could see there was more than aristocratic training in that stiffness right now. There was tension and something else—fear. And perhaps a little guilt.

He turned to face her, arms folded neatly behind his back.

"I take it your interest in this matter does not lie in Lord Deveral's welfare?"

"No," Lily replied.

*Or in mine?*

He might have asked it. He did not.

Lily stared down at her hands. They were clenched into fists in her lap.

"I do not like to see an injustice done," she ground out. "No matter how unsympathetic the victim."

The little brass clock chimed the hour. It drew his gaze to the fireplace and he moved closer, stopping at the small, ebony-framed image of Deirdre Albright. He brushed one long finger along the side of her blurry smile, then returned his hand to his side.

"I will instruct Simon to receive you and to answer any questions you wish to put to him."

"He won't do it," Lily blurted, surprised into honesty by his announcement.

"Yes," the Earl of Torrington replied. "He will."

There was no threat in his tone, no anger, but it carried with it a weight of iron, something that reminded Lily that this man routinely bent the most powerful names in the realm to his will.

He turned from the photograph.

"I have taken up enough of your morning. I apologize again for disturbing you unannounced. If there is anything more I can do to aid your efforts, please inform me."

"Should I write through your solicitors?"

The retort slipped out before she could stop it, laced with bitterness. It galled her, as she would far rather have kept that emotion hidden. Bitterness implied hurt. Hurt implied that he still retained some capacity to wound her.

He stopped, his hand brushing the wool of his coat where it hung on the stand.

She sat frozen in her chair, waiting for his response, wondering what form it would take. Courteous indifference, perhaps? Or would she finally have broken through his calm to unleash some ill-will or resentment?

His hand withdrew, falling back to his side. Something came into his posture, a weight she had not seen there before. It made him look more the age she knew he must be, the lines seeming to deepen on his face.

"I wish you knew . . ." he said, his voice rough with something that sounded very like grief.

He went no further. He stood lost on her threshold as the clock continued to tick on the mantle.

The words struck her, leaving a terribly vulnerable opening in her carefully-wrought defenses.

*I wish you knew . . .*

She remained silent, holding herself forcefully still.

He straightened, repairing himself, the decades of aristocratic training coming back into his bearing.

He turned back to her and bowed.

"I apologize for disturbing your morning."

She remained perched on the unforgiving cushion of her terrible chair long after the sound of his footsteps had finished echoing down the stairwell.

# THIRTEEN

$\mathcal{L}$ILY WOKE TO THE sound of the clock in the parlor chiming three.

Three in the morning? She wondered why she was awake. The weight in her bones told her she was still exhausted.

She rolled over to go back to sleep, her face settling into a pile of orange fur.

Lily sneezed and pushed herself up out of Cat, who opened a single green eye to glare at her before settling back into a fat feline puddle.

The sun was filtering in through her bedroom window. It was not three in the morning. It was three in the afternoon.

Which afternoon?

Memory flooded back to her. She was wearing her chemise, lying on top of the blankets. She had been too tired to change or bathe, managing only to strip off her filthy clothes and toss them onto the floor before collapsing into bed.

That had been after her father left.

Her father.

*I wish you knew . . .*

She needed to focus. She had to consider what came next. Lord Deveral—Torrington had said he would admit her next time she called and answer any questions she asked.

She could imagine how happily her half-brother would comply.

Her best hope of moderating his viciousness lay in having respectable company with her when she called.

Lily could think of only one such person who would be willing to join her on the errand.

Strangford had demonstrated his level of commitment to their cause clearly enough last night.

He had been so uncomfortably quiet as they left Abney Park.

It felt like a scene out of a dream—the midnight graveyard, white tombs rising up out of the tangled darkness, the dead woman in her coffin. It had smelled worse than any dream had a right to.

Lily sniffed. It still smelled.

What she truly needed was a proper bath—the enameled tub filled all the way to the top with steaming hot water in which she would soak until someone booted her out.

It was already three o'clock in the afternoon. If she was to take advantage of her father's intervention with Lord Deveral, she had better do it sooner than later, when her half-brother might have mustered the courage to turn her away and damn the consequences.

An hour later, after an unsatisfactory wash at her basin, Lily was ensconced in another hackney, rattling toward Bayswater.

She gazed out the soot-fogged window at the elegant townhouses. The white Georgian facades looked the same. They were all unremarkably fine, accented with perfectly trimmed bay laurel hedges and washed granite stairs.

The carriage stopped to wait for a turn to pass a newsman's wagon. Lily spotted a cast iron pug crouching incongruously on the steps of one of the houses just ahead of them. It was an absurd piece of decor, quite out of place in the midst of all that clean-swept, fresh-painted respectability.

The carriage stopped directly opposite the fat metal animal, the driver informing her they had reached their destination.

Strangford had mentioned a sister, she recalled, one who possessed a sense of humor whimsical enough to result in a gelding named Beatrice. She sensed the woman's influence. It at least reassured her that she might very well be at the correct address.

She climbed out.

"Shall I hold for you, miss?"

She hesitated. Perhaps Strangford's silence the night before hadn't been the lingering after-effect of a nightmarish experience. It was possible he had withdrawn because of a new resentment toward the woman who had suggested the business in the first place. If the latter, her call here today might be much briefer than planned.

She would chance it. There were other cabs in Bayswater.

"That won't be necessary, thank you." She paid the fare and the hackney departed.

She contemplated the steps. The pug looked back at her, iron tongue lolling stupidly out of its mouth. It was singularly unhelpful.

Lily mounted the stairs and knocked briskly at the door.

She heard the sound of footsteps, then a pause. Quick, whispering voices filtered through to her.

Nothing happened.

Lily waited. Uncertainty rapidly replaced by irritation, she knocked again.

After another rush of whispers—which now sounded more distinctly like an argument—the door opened.

A young man in footman's livery stood in front of her. Lily guessed he was about eighteen, with dark hair and freckles and a touch more softness about the middle than most footmen she had seen. The ton tended to like them trim and pretty.

"Yes?" he asked. Lily's ear picked up a hint of country in his accent.

Behind him, a housemaid of about the same age darted her head out of one of the rooms lining the hall.

"Miss Lily Albright for Lord Strangford."

He looked at her without answering. He glanced back at the maid, clearly uncertain how to proceed.

It would not surprise Lily to learn that Strangford received few callers, but his footman should still have had some notion of how to handle an unannounced guest at the door.

Something was off.

It was not simply that Strangford was out or unavailable. There were simple procedures for handling that. Even a boy fresh from the country would have learned them quickly enough upon taking up his position in the household. The confusion she sensed here went beyond that. It was clearly shared by the housemaid, who ought not to have even been within view of a guest.

The scowling girl made an urgent gesture then disappeared into the bowels of the house. The footman awkwardly cleared his throat.

"I'm afraid that his lordship is . . . er . . . not receiving."

He glanced back over his shoulder nervously.

"I see," Lily replied evenly.

"Would you care to leave a card?" he asked, as though just remembering the more basic aspects of his duty.

"I do not have one with me. If you would let him know that I called?"

"Oh! Yes. Most certainly. Just as soon as . . ." He trailed off, at a loss for how to continue. "As soon as he asks. Who has called," he finally finished, lamely.

He looked back down the hallway again.

"I see. Thank you."

She turned and began walking down the steps.

The door slammed shut behind her before she had even reached the pavement.

She was so startled by it, she turned back to look. It was as though the footman had flung the thing closed and run from the threat that Lily posed.

What would make a casual caller such a terrifying prospect?

Only a situation so unusual a footman's training didn't even begin to touch upon it.

An empty hackney clattered down the lane. Lily did not hail it. Instead, she walked to the end of the street, turned the corner, and stepped into the mews that lead to the carriage houses behind the grand buildings.

She picked her way around a pile of horse droppings. They were fresh and the mews were otherwise clear of them. In posh Bayswater, even the alleys were routinely swept.

She counted the gates as she passed, then stopped when she reached the one which led into Strangford's garden.

A pair of stablemen called to each other from somewhere nearby.

Lily tried the door. The latch did not budge.

The gate looked as though it had not been maintained in some time, the iron of the hinges rusting, the boards gray and weathered.

She heard a door close at the far end of the narrow way, followed by the clatter of carriage wheels.

There was only a moment to make her decision.

If her instinct was right and there was something amiss in Strangford's house—well, it was likely related to their visit to Abney Park last night.

That meant Lily might very well be responsible.

She felt the conflict of it pull at her, that sharp feeling of unease fighting against the utter impropriety of the act she was considering.

She remembered the moment the watchman had moved past them, the long minutes where she had deserted Strangford in Sylvia Durst's grave.

A healthy dose of guilt settled the matter.

She leaned her walking stick against the brick wall, lifted up the purple skirts of her afternoon dress and kicked sharply at the door with her good leg.

It popped open with a crack.

The remains of the latch hung from the frame, bits of rotted wood still clinging to the exposed ends of the screws that had held it in place.

Lily stepped inside, closing it behind her.

She stood next to a carriage house and stable, clearly unused. A tall yew hedge blocked her view of the house.

She followed the narrow path around it and entered the garden. It was little more than a square of lawn framed by tall brick walls covered in ivy. A riot of untrimmed shrubs and perennial beds would lend color in the summer, but the space looked brown and leafless now, bedded down for winter.

A white wrought-iron table stood on the flagstone patio, along with two chairs. It was the sort of spot she could imagine a gentleman sitting with his lady wife on a warmer day, enjoying breakfast al-fresco.

One of the chairs was crossed with a large cobweb.

She walked across the dying grass toward the house. There

was little point in trying to appear inconspicuous when clad in eggplant-hued satin.

The windows of the first floor were just low enough for her to see over the ledge. She peered into the room on the left. It was a dining room. The maid stepped inside and Lily slipped out of her view.

She moved to the room on the right. There was a bit of frost on the windowpane. Lily rubbed it away to look inside.

It was a gentleman's study. Through the fogged glass she could make out the dark expanse of a bookshelf, the uncluttered surface of a desk. Bolder splashes of color were visible on the wall. Her attention was quickly drawn to the fireplace, where she could see that someone sat in one of the two chairs that faced the cold hearth.

He was so still, she nearly overlooked him.

Lily moved to the other window for a better angle.

Strangford was a mess.

He slumped in the chair, still wearing the clothes he'd had on in the cemetery. They were stained with filth. His coat and neckcloth were gone, his shirt open at the throat. He still wore his boots, which were caked with grave dirt. She could see the trail of mud they had left on the floor—one trail, leading from the door to the chair and nowhere else.

He was not asleep. He stared into the cold ashes of the fire, eyes darkly ringed with exhaustion.

She heard the sound of a door closing, voices speaking somewhere deeper in the house. Seizing the moment before she could think better of the idea, she strode to the back door and tried the knob.

It opened. She let herself in.

The hall was sparely furnished. A carpet ran along the floor, tending towards threadbare. The paper on the walls had likely been the height of fashion seventy or so years ago, but was now faded. The dated furnishings were still well-polished and a spray of fresh flowers brightened the entryway.

She heard a creak of footsteps on the stairs and quickly slipped through the door into the study.

The sight of the room stopped her in her tracks.

It was not simply some glorified gentleman's smoking room. It was a gallery. Art covered the walls from waist-level all the way to the high ceiling. These were not the dull scenes and portraits one might expect in a typical aristocratic home. The paintings were remarkable, canvases splashed with vibrant colors, conflagrations of brilliant line and shape.

Mordecai Roth's assessment of Strangford's taste in art had not been exaggerated.

They called for Lily to delve into them, to explore Strangford's unique selections with rapt attention, but this was not the time.

She closed the door quietly behind her. It clicked softly.

Strangford spoke from the chair, his back to her.

"I told you not to disturb me."

The words were ground out with uncharacteristic sharpness.

"If you did, I'm afraid I missed your message."

He didn't rise.

"Miss Albright."

"My lord."

She came into the room, moving around the chair to face him.

He looked worse up close. His skin was pale, drained like that of a man in the midst of a long illness. He was sweating despite the chill of the room. She could see the damp of it on his brow and around his neck. He didn't meet her eyes.

"I am discomposed. Roderick should have said . . . I am not receiving visitors."

"He did. I broke in."

His response came slowly, the words seeming to move through mud.

"Am I in need of a new window?"

His slow-motion attempt at humor gave her a palpable flutter of relief, which in itself revealed how concerned she was about his current state.

"Perhaps a replacement latch," she replied. She knelt down before him, forcing him to meet her eyes. "Tell me what is wrong."

"I feel unwell. I would prefer to do so in private."

"You're ill?"

"I am trying to ask you to leave."

Lily stood. She studied him, her gaze moving over the earth staining his sleeves, the pallor of his skin.

This wasn't some sudden fever. Something else was the matter, something far more serious.

A piece fell into place—his hands, clenching the arms of the chair, fingers digging into the wood.

They were bare.

She wasn't family. She could barely call herself a friend. He had asked her to go and every social rule said she should respect that—that she never should have come inside in the first place.

Well, she and social norms had never had more than a passing acquaintance.

There was danger here. She could feel it.

"Perhaps I should go," she agreed. "Perhaps I should proceed directly to Bedford Square, where I should inform Mr. Ash and Sam Wu and Cairncross and Dr. Gardner and anyone else within earshot that you are sitting here in front of a cold fire in clothes covered in grave dirt. Which is exactly what I will do if you do not tell me precisely what is the matter."

He laid his head back, closing his eyes. She could see the pulse throbbing at his throat and felt a stab of deeper alarm. It was too fast, too shallow. She wondered for a moment if this standoff was only a waste of time better spent running for a physician.

"The reading stuck."

The room was silent save for the regular ticking of the clock in the corner, the muffled hum of the city outside the walls.

"Last night's reading?" she asked.

"Yes," he confirmed with some effort.

Lily sank into the chair across from him.

She thought back to the carriage ride when he had first told her of his power.

*There are occasional anomalies . . .*

"Tell me what that means."

His hands clenched against the arms of the chair.

"I'm still there."

"Still where?"

"With Sylvia Durst."

The implication came clear with a wave of horror.

Strangford's reading of Sylvia Durst's corpse had not ended in Abney Park. Somehow, he had become trapped in it—trapped inside the experience of a dead woman rotting in the ground.

She remembered the sensations he had described as he crouched in the grave—the suffocating darkness, the rot and the cold.

He had told her before that his readings weren't just observations, something happening at a safe distance. They were completely immersive, enveloping every sense—his taste, his touch.

He had spent the last several hours buried alive in someone else's corpse.

"It's been like this since last night?"

He nodded. She could see the tension in his jaw, his shoulders.

"Why didn't it stop when you let go of her?"

"It's like that. Sometimes."

"It's happened before?"

"Yes."

"How did you break it then?"

"Read another object. Something potent."

"Have you tried that here?"

"Yes."

Her thoughts spun. How long could a man's mind withstand being consumed by a slow and stinking decay? How much of this could he take?

She had to stay calm, no matter how much his state alarmed her.

"It didn't work."

"No."

"So you need something more potent."

"The inkwell. The paintings. I keep things here . . . in case something like this recurs. Things with powerful histories."

*Things.* The word struck her oddly. She looked around the room, her eyes dancing over the art on the walls, a brass letter opener, a battered pewter inkwell.

Objects. Inanimate, lifeless.

"Have you tried something living?"

"I don't read the living."

The words were delivered with iron finality, clearly intended to close the door on that line of inquiry. Lily ignored them.

"Wouldn't living beings be more potent than objects?"

He bristled.

"That is not an option."

"You're stuck on a reading of something dead. If your pipe or china teacup won't shift it, perhaps you need a subject that still has a beating heart."

"You don't understand," he snapped.

"Then explain it to me," she shot back, her own frustration rising. She met his stare steadily, though the tumult in his dark eyes unsettled her more than she would have liked to admit.

"I can't control what I see. Whoever I read might as well be stripped naked in front of me. Who should I use like that?"

The harshness of his words hit her like a blow, shaking her growing resolve. She forced herself to hold firm.

"What about an animal?"

"I don't keep pets."

"Your horse?"

"Stabled on the heath."

He was pale as a ghost, bare hands gripping the scarred wood of the arms of the chair like a line to a lifeboat. The wood would not save him. She could see how precariously he was hanging on, willing Sylvia Durst's death not to swallow him.

There was no time to debate options. Something had to be done now.

The solution was as obvious as it was fitting.

She tugged off her gloves, setting them on the table.

"Then it will have to be me."

He stood. The movement was sudden enough to startle her. His hands were clenched and shaking at his sides.

"You need to go."

She rose as well, a quick anger at his stubbornness flaring through her.

"It was my suggestion that brought you to this. It's only fair I be the one to set it right."

"I said no."

"This will drive you mad," she snapped back, stepping closer to confront him. "Do you expect me to accept that, knowing it was my notion that brought it about? Set your blasted principles aside for a moment and take what I am offering you."

He stared back at her, his dark eyes hollow.

"I will learn truths about you that you wouldn't share with your closest friend. And I am a man you barely know. Is that what you want?"

The words gave her pause.

Her past was far from spotless. It would be particularly so in the eyes of someone who had been raised as a nobleman, whose standards for female behavior had been set by dowager aunts and society matrons.

She thought of what he had nearly discovered about her simply from touching her powder compact.

It didn't matter. The stakes were greater than his opinion of her. She needed to conceal any hint of fear or unease and convince him to do this before the darkness he was trapped in swallowed him whole.

"As you say, you are a man I barely know. Why should I care what you think of me?"

She met his gaze steadily. Through the horror and pain, something else became visible to her—a shattering vulnerability.

This wasn't just about her. It was about Annalise Boyden, about the secrets he had pulled from countless others who didn't matter until he learned the truth about those that did. How many times had a brush of the fingers lead to disappointment, to the crumbling of trust or respect? There was a reason he had turned to the gloves, smothering his talent in something he could control, something safe.

How long had it been since he had touched another human being?

The notion made what she was doing even more terrifying. It didn't matter. She owed this to him, whatever it cost them both. The knowledge made her next words something more than a request. They were a vow.

"Let me help you."

He closed his eyes and let out a long, shuddering breath. When he opened them again, that bristling defensiveness was gone, leaving the fear even more obvious than before.

He lifted his hands. They were shaking. He stopped, holding them just shy of her skin.

"Are you certain?" His voice was hoarse.

Fear fluttered at her. She refused it admittance and met his gaze evenly.

"Yes."

His touch was light—first tentative, then delicate. His fingertips grazed over her cheek, dancing along the line of her hair, his palms just brushing against her jaw.

It electrified her senses, sent goosebumps shivering down her arms, her spine. The slightest movement of his hands on her skin was a nexus of feeling magnified far out of any just proportion.

His breath caught. His eyes lost their focus, going distant. He took a deep, even breath. When he exhaled again, she could see the change—how the stiffness fell from his shoulders, the color slowly blooming back into his face.

His hands began to move, subtle changes in pressure and texture. The slide of his thumb across her cheek, fingers drifting into her hair. It was a slow, elegant dance playing out across her skin. She felt it on a level that went beyond nerve and tissue into a deeper sense she possessed, the same one that opened unwelcome doors into knowledge she had tried for years to wish away. It responded to Strangford's touch, waking up inside of her and humming in sudden, alert response as though sensing the presence of a kindred energy.

Time hung suspended like the space between breaths. Seconds, minutes, an hour—she couldn't know how long it lasted.

His expression changed, flashing through emotions like a shuffle of cards. A line of grief formed, then quickly faded, from between his brow. Confusion tugged at the corners of his eyes and then a laugh spilled out of him, a sound of pure delight.

It was her memories that were doing that, evoking those quick, intense reactions. They were a reflection of his shared experience of her own history, playing out across his face.

It should have been uncanny, but in that moment, with his electric touch dancing across her skin, nothing in the world felt more natural.

Then came another change, accompanied by a sharp intake of breath, a subtle tremor in his fingers on her skin. His lips parted, more color rising into his face.

She was suddenly, overwhelmingly aware of him.

The closeness of his body. The shape of it, lines of bone and muscle and skin. His scent. His heat. How perfectly he fit her, eye to eye, shoulder to shoulder. The sensation crashed over her with the power of a tidal wave, a desire unlike anything she'd experienced in her life.

Less than half a step and she would be pressed against him, molded to his form. Her hands tangling in that dark hair, tasting him.

He shifted, raising his head. His gazed sharpened, gaining focus.

He was looking at her—here, in the present—and Lily was entirely certain that he knew exactly what she had just been feeling.

The moment suspended, balanced on a pin.

Then he pulled his hands away and stepped back.

He turned to the window, his back to her. She saw his grip tighten on the sash, knuckles white.

Her body burned, surprised by unexpected need.

She snapped to awareness. This was madness. A step from disaster.

He was a baron. She was a bastard. She could never be anything to him but his lover. Another mistress, like her mother, left waiting like some doll on a shelf. A thing to be taken down and played with at his leisure until he had to return to other obligations—like a legitimate family.

No. Never. She would not be the source of another woman's betrayal, would not allow herself to love a man who could never be completely hers.

She would never leave herself open to the pain of the inevitable day he was forced to choose between two lives.

She brushed at some invisible dust on her skirt.

"Did it work?"

She was glad her voice came out with more steadiness than she could rightfully have expected.

"Yes. It worked."

He moved to the desk. His coat hung from the back of the chair. He reached into the pocket and pulled out his gloves, slipping them back on.

He had not looked at her.

Her heart lurched. She thought of everything he might have seen. Working on her knees like a charwoman, a scrub brush in her chapped hands. Her face painted like a whore's, body wrapped in a chorus girl's sequins, serving cocktails to men who helped themselves to parts of her she had no desire to offer.

Perhaps he had experienced the lives she had failed to save, over and over again.

She would not ask. What she told him before was true. She barely knew him. He was nothing more than a convenient partner in this endeavor she was entangled in.

That, and the only human being in the world who might understand what it was like to be inside her skin.

She picked up her own gloves.

"I should leave you to recover. I'm sure you need rest."

He turned back from the window, facing her.

"Why did you come?"

Did he want to know what brought her to Bayswater? Or what had driven her to kick through his garden gate and invade his study?

She chose the simpler question to answer.

"I had a visit from my father this morning."

"From Lord Torrington."

"Yes," she replied shortly. "He informed me that Lord Deveral will receive us whenever we wish to call upon him again."

Strangford picked up his coat.

"We'll go now."

"But you must be exhausted." She couldn't keep the shock from her voice.

"You told me this killer will strike again. That means we are trying to stop a murder. Do we have time for rest?"

"I don't know," she answered honestly.

"I would rather not give the viscount time to decide to defy your father."

"You at least need a bath." The point brought an unwelcome blush to her cheeks, but it had to be made.

He paused, looking down at himself.

"I suppose I do."

He rang the bell.

"I'll collect you . . ." He glanced at the clock, frowned. "It will have to be around seven thirty."

"That's a rather unfashionable hour for paying a call."

"We're not calling. We're interrogating. And I doubt he has any other engagements."

"Isn't his residence in Bayswater, not Bloomsbury? Why don't I just meet you here?"

"Because despite appearances, I am still a gentleman. And gentlemen do not ask ladies to travel unaccompanied for their own convenience."

The awkward footman entered. His eyes widened at the sight of his master's disarray, his jaw dropping in concert when he noticed Lily standing in the room.

"Roderick, fetch us a carriage, please. I need to see Miss Albright back to Bloomsbury."

"You will not," Lily retorted. "I will see myself."

"I just told you—"

"That gentlemen do not ask ladies to travel unaccompanied, I know. But you've better things to do than ride around London for no good reason." Like sleeping, she thought, looking at the dark circles under his eyes. "If you must insist on it, then send your footman with me."

She saw him waver and turned to the wide-eyed young man beside her.

"Roderick, would you be so kind as to escort me back to Bloomsbury?"

"Of course, m'lady. I mean miss," he corrected himself quickly, cheeks flushing. "Of course."

Strangford rubbed at his eyes. His exhaustion was clear in every line of his body.

"Fine," he agreed. "Go on, then, Roddie."

The footman bowed, then hurried away.

Strangford gestured for her to proceed him into the hall, then accompanied her to the front door.

There was an awkward pause as they waited.

He was still utterly disheveled, standing in his shirtsleeves, his hair awry, covered in filth, but he looked alive again. Dreadfully wrung-out, but alive.

"So," he said at last. "Where might I need that latch?"

She felt a laugh tickle up her throat. It was harder to contain than it ought to have been.

"Perhaps you should check your garden gate," she replied evenly.

She caught the flash of lightness in his eyes, the twitch at the corner of his mouth.

"What state, precisely, might I find it in?"

"It was hardly in fine fettle to begin with," Lily countered neatly.

A carriage rolled to a stop at the curb. Roderick jumped down from the back.

"Miss Albright?" he called.

She turned to the man beside her and tried not to wonder whether the events of that afternoon had too deeply changed his opinion of her.

"Good afternoon, my lord."

Strangford bowed, an incongruously formal gesture given his current state, but one he pulled off with aplomb.

"Miss Albright." He rose, meeting her eyes. His expression deepened, becoming serious. His gaze lingered on her face.

That hitch in her chest announced itself again. Lily nodded, then turned and made her way as gracefully as possible to the carriage.

She climbed in, sinking back against the seat and closing her eyes.

Seven thirty.

She wondered if she had time for that bath.

# FOURTEEN

$\mathcal{L}$ILY'S HANDS FUMBLED WITH the delicate fasteners of her dress. The small hooks along the silvery fabric of the bodice always gave her trouble, clearly designed for someone with nimbler fingers. She closed the last of them, then pulled on the matching jacket. It was lighter than her winter overcoat but suited the dress far better.

Given what she knew she was walking into, it felt important to look polished tonight. The armor of a respectable ensemble comforted her more than an extra layer against the chill in the air.

The knock on the door came at precisely 7:30, as Lily had known it would.

It took Mrs. Bramble a moment to reach it, enough time for Lily to descend to the landing outside Estelle's flat. Strangford's rich tenor rose up to her, speaking to her forbidding landlady with perfect courtesy.

"Good evening, madam. I am calling for Miss Albright."

"I'm here," Lily called.

His dress was neat and sober, absent any sign of the disarray in which she had found him earlier that afternoon. His dark hair was covered by a top hat, a black necktie neatly knotted at his throat. At the sound of her voice, his gaze rose to where she stood and locked there.

He seemed to catch himself, offering her a bow.

"Miss Albright. You look very fine this evening."

A blush rose in response, as did an abrupt recollection of the feelings he had provoked in her when they stood together in his study earlier that afternoon. She forced both of them back, acknowledging the compliment with a curt nod.

He motioned her out. She moved past him down the steps, the cold air biting through the fabric of her jacket. He caught up to her at the bottom in time to open the door to the hackney. As she moved to climb inside, his gloved hand touched her arm.

She looked to him, surprised. There was something both awkward and solemn in his expression.

"You don't have to do this."

The realization struck like a blow.

He knew.

He knew how much reason she had to dread this errand. How she felt about Deveral, about her father. How deeply it had hurt when he deserted her to schools and solicitors, managing her as he would any other bothersome obligation. Things no other living soul knew—things she would not have admitted even to herself. All of it had been laid open to him, read like a book, along with more she couldn't even guess at.

"I could go alone. I would report all of it back to you."

"It was me Torrington told him to admit. Not you."

"Deveral must understand it amounts to the same thing."

"No," she countered evenly. "I am not at all sure he would choose to understand that."

She did not wait for him to respond. She climbed into the carriage and sat down on the narrow bench. He followed, shutting the door behind him and closing them in together.

The sun had set, the darkness making the narrow confines of the carriage seem more close. Strangford smelled like soap and shaving oil mingling with something more raw and masculine.

Lily put down the window. The cool night air flooded in.

"Did you sleep?" she asked.

"I'm rested enough."

She caught a glimpse of his face in the light of a passing street lamp. He looked far better than he had that afternoon, but there was still a deeper darkness than usual around his eyes. She chose not to challenge him, though she felt quite certain that his afternoon had been something other than restful.

"When we get there—assuming he actually lets us inside—what do we ask him?"

"He'll let us in."

"You can't know that."

"Your father is not a man lightly crossed."

Lily had no response to that. She turned her gaze back to the window, letting the silence stretch. It was Strangford who broke it.

"I'm no more experienced with this sort of thing than you are, but I suppose we ask him to recount the events of the night of Mrs. Boyden's death. Anything and everything he can recall. We won't know what might be significant until we hear it."

"If we aren't just wasting our time," Lily retorted.

"You're worried you're wrong."

"Mrs. Boyden's death looks nothing like the other murders. Her throat was cut, not pricked and drained of blood. And she wasn't a medium. All the rest of the victims claimed to speak to the dead."

There was a silence. A motor car rumbled past them, engine deafening.

"Ash would tell you to trust it." Strangford's voice seemed closer in the darkness. "Your gift. Even if it appears to contradict the facts."

She did not want to know what Robert Ash would say. It made her next words sharper than she intended.

"If I am wrong, Lord Deveral looks like a very strong suspect. And that would mean that we are about to interview a man who might have murdered someone you once cared very deeply for. Have you considered that?"

She felt him shift beside her. Every movement was amplified.

"I have."

"And?"

"I know better than most that things are rarely as simple as they seem on the surface."

That quiet reply silenced her. She understood enough of how he had come by that knowledge not to challenge it.

The carriage slowed, waiting for an omnibus to spill passengers onto the curb.

A crowd was gathered in front of one of the buildings that lined Tottenham Court Road. Toffs in silk hats mingled with working men in flat caps and patched sleeves. Lily's attention was drawn to a pair of men approaching the place, her gaze falling onto the brass pins that decorated their lapels.

She recognized the symbol—the interlocked carats of Joseph Hartwell's eugenics club.

There were more of them scattered through the crowd. She glimpsed the headline of a poster by the door announcing the evening's attraction.

*A Lecture Presented by The Society for the Betterment of the British Race*

Aware of how incongruous her actions would look to the man who sat behind her in the carriage, Lily called out to the two gentlemen, pushed by a curiosity bordering on impulse.

"Excuse me, but is Dr. Joseph Hartwell speaking here tonight?"

The pair stopped, surprised. The surprise shifted to charm as they realized it was a well-dressed young woman who had called to them.

"Hartwell? Oh no. There'd be twice the crowd as this if himself was coming out," one of them replied, tilting his hat back to a more rakish angle. "It's Mr. Caymus tonight, one of his colleagues. Speaking on the virtues of marriage restriction."

"Marriage restriction? What does that mean?"

"Nothing a fine lady like you need worry yourself about," the younger of the two men replied, flashing her a grin.

The omnibus rumbled forward and Lily's opportunity for further questions was cut short as their hackney trundled in its wake.

She sat back down.

Strangford shifted uncomfortably beside her.

"They want Parliament to outlaw marriage between people they deem deficient," he said. "That's what it means. I've heard talk about it in the Lords."

"What exactly does that mean—deficient?"

"Whatever they like it to."

There was a rare ferocity to the words. It surprised her.

"I take it you disapprove."

"It is not the place of government to tell anyone whom they may love."

Lily thought of many couples she had met during her time in the theater, of men like Mordecai Roth. Of Miss Bard and Estelle.

"But it does already."

"That doesn't make it right."

—

They drove into Bayswater. A gust of wind pushed against the carriage, blowing a current of dry leaves across the road, illuminated by the gas lamps that lined the way. A couple in evening dress hurried past, coats pulled tight about their shoulders.

The carriage stopped in front of Lord Deveral's house. It appeared dark, but Lily could see light seeping through the cracks in the curtains that covered the windows.

She waited for Strangford to descend and hold the door. The air had grown both heavier and more sharply cold, biting through her jacket.

Lily looked up at the sky, but one could rarely tell the difference between a clear night and a brewing storm in the middle of London.

"Should I have the driver wait?" Strangford asked.

"We have no idea how long we'll be. We can have a hackney sent for when we're through."

As the carriage rolled away behind them, Lily could hear snatches of music from a string quartet playing in some neighboring townhouse. A coach rolled by, freshly painted with a crest on the door. She heard a burst of laughter from inside as it passed.

The street was otherwise deserted. There was no sign of a lingering constable. If anyone was monitoring Lord Deveral's movements, they were doing it from a more discreet distance. She would not have wondered to learn that her father had something to do with that.

The house was still and silent, only that sliver of light through the curtain betraying that it hadn't been closed up and abandoned.

Strangford stood quietly at her side as she stared up at the dark steps.

He was waiting. Lily knew that his quiet patience came from his knowledge of why exactly she might hesitate to approach that door.

It was too much. She didn't want to be known like that—not by someone she didn't understand herself.

"Let's not linger in the street," she muttered and mounted the steps.

She knocked with all the firmness she hoped to project.

Silence lingered just long enough for Lily to wonder if perhaps she'd been wrong about that light in the window.

Finally the door opened, revealing the butler who had dismissed them the day before. His face was the same mask of bored respectability.

Lily looked for some subtle marker of irritation or disapproval but couldn't even find a flash of recognition. The man could act. She wondered if she should suggest a second career on the stage.

"Lord Strangford and Miss Lily Albright for Lord Deveral," Strangford said. There was no hint in his voice that the man in the doorway had all but tossed them out the last time they'd met. It seemed Strangford could play a part as well.

"Please step in and I will see where his lordship would like to receive you."

They waited in the hall. It was elegantly appointed. The marble floors were warmed by thick carpets, a few tasteful antiques breaking up the texture of a rich blue Morris print wallpaper. She wondered how much of the decor reflected Lord Deveral's taste and how much bore the stamp of her father.

The butler returned.

"I will show you to the drawing room. May I take your coat, my lord?"

"Thank you," Strangford replied, slipping out of the overcoat.

He handed the garment to a footman who materialized, silently, then faded away again.

"This way, please."

The butler led them down the hall past a fine Chinese accent table and an enormous painting of some suitably dramatic seascape. He stopped at an open doorway.

"Lord Strangford and Miss Lily Albright, my lord," he announced, then stepped aside to let them through.

The butler's perfect formality had almost tricked her into thinking this would play out like any ordinary social call, all sherry and small talk.

One glance into the drawing room shattered that tidy illusion.

The space was dark, lit by little more than the glow of the fire raging in the hearth. Her brother was slumped across an elegant settee, dressed in pajamas and a black silk dressing gown. There was a bottle of wine on the table beside him, another—already empty—on the floor. The smell of cigarettes suffused the room, emanating from a packed ashtray on a brass stand beside him.

"Strangford. Dear sister. Forgive my admitting you while en déshabillé. But then, this is a family call, isn't it? So we needn't stand on ceremony."

Lily straightened her back.

"No. Of course we needn't."

She lowered herself into the chair across from her brother with all the demure grace drilled into her at finishing school.

Strangford remained standing. She saw his eyes flicker from her brother's attire to the empty bottle. His jaw tightened. He turned and walked to the far side of the room, making a seeming study of the art on the walls.

"I suppose you are aware of the reason for this call?" Lily prompted.

"You mean your ghoulish curiosity? Yes. Father informed me. That's 'his lordship the Earl of Torrington' to you, I believe," he added as though in afterthought.

Every word was intended as a blow. Lily felt the impact of them like tiny stones. She met it with a smile. It was deliberately thin, an expression she had learned from her classmates at Mrs. Finch's, girls who would likely have offered their left foot to be in the same room as the eminently eligible Viscount Deveral, heir to an earldom.

She would rather have been anywhere else, but she needed to understand how Annalise Boyden fit into this puzzle. Learning why the killer had chosen her, and why her death looked so different from the rest of the victims, could be key to uncovering his motive and identity.

Assuming, of course, that Lily was right about Mrs. Boyden being a sister in death to Dora Heller, Agnes McKenney and Sylvia Durst.

If the man sitting across from her hadn't simply slit her throat himself.

"Could we get on with it?" Lord Deveral asked. "As you can see, I'm about to retire for the evening. We don't all keep chorus girl hours."

It was another blow, one that revealed knowledge he could not possibly have acquired in the last two days. There was little difficulty following the activities of the members of Britain's upper classes—an entire industry was devoted to gossip columns and society news. Lily could hardly avoid hearing about the Torrington clan. Tracking her own history would not have been so simple a matter. It would have required deliberate effort.

That meant Lord Deveral's dislike of her was far from casual. It was old and root-deep, and had existed since long before she crossed him at the Carfax Gallery.

This time, however, the shot had not been intended to strike her directly. Her brother's eyes darted immediately to Strangford, watching for his reaction to what he had revealed.

There was none.

If Lord Deveral hoped to use Lily's past to drive a wedge between her and her apparent defender, he would be sorely disappointed. There was nothing he could throw at her that night that would come as a surprise to her companion.

She supposed the notion should have been comforting.

Her brother plucked a cigarette from the case on the table and lit it, the match flaring orange light across his face. The glow illuminated a set of vivid red lines scratched across his cheek.

"Your face . . ." Lily gasped, the words slipping out of her before she could stop them.

Her mind flew back to the vision. The cruel twist to Lord Deveral's lips, his bitter words slicing through the air. A woman's hand flashing out, raking claws across his skin as white powder sparkled, suspended, through the air.

"Oh, this? Yes, that particularly delighted the inspector. Apparently they found blood under Annalise's nails. It quite makes his case, I imagine."

He exhaled, blowing a plume of smoke up toward the darkened chandelier.

It was undeniable. He had been the last one to see the victim alive and had been overheard having a vicious row with her. His initials were engraved into the murder weapon. Now blood evidence proved that he and Annalise Boyden had engaged in a physical struggle on the night of her death.

No jury would doubt such a case, not even one made up of Lord Deveral's illustrious peers.

He would hang for this unless an equally compelling case could be made that he had not, in fact, slit the woman's throat.

Unless the true killer could be found.

They would not even bother looking, Lily realized. Inspector Gregg and his comrades would surely assume, with ample justification, that they had found the murderer. Why waste resources continuing the investigation? The case was undoubtedly considered closed.

Which left only her to stand between the bitter man sprawled across the settee and the noose.

She took a breath, mustering her strength, her patience. He would undoubtedly seek every opportunity he could to antagonize her.

She could do this. She would do this. Because there was no one else.

"I need to ask you some questions."

"So I was forewarned," Lord Deveral replied.

"You and Mrs. Boyden were lovers."

"A brilliant deduction."

"For how long?"

He shrugged.

"I don't know. It wasn't a formal arrangement. You'd know all about those, of course."

She ignored the jab.

"A year? Two?"

"More or less," he snapped.

"Tell me what happened the night she died."

He took a long drag on his cigarette.

"We went to an opening. I had the most charming run-in with my dear half-sister. We returned to Mayfair. There was a quarrel. I left. Then someone came in and cut her throat."

"A touch more detail would be helpful."

"What sort of detail would you like? What we ate for dinner? How I had her over the bench of the carriage on our way to the gallery? She was a randy little minx, our Annalise. Wasn't she, Strangford?"

"I wouldn't know," Strangford replied. His tone was carefully controlled, flattened into a pretense of indifference. He appeared to be studying a portrait of a blond, blue-eyed woman in a voluminous gown. Her features were a touch too soft to be called striking. There was also something familiar about her.

Lily glanced at Lord Deveral and realized why. There were echoes of those soft features in his own visage, layered between the more familiar elements she knew belonged to their father.

The countess, his mother. That was her on the wall—the woman her father had betrayed every time he'd come to Oxford Street.

Lily looked away.

"What a pity for you," Lord Deveral drawled.

Lily pushed on.

"Tell me what happened after you got back to Mayfair."

"I told you. We went upstairs. We had a row. I left."

"Who else was in the house?"

His replies grew shorter, his irritation at failing to rile either her or Strangford showing.

"Her staff."

"List them."

"Housekeeper. Two footmen. Her lady's maid. A chambermaid or three—I don't know. They all look the same."

"No one else?"

"Not that I was aware."

"What did you fight about?"

"Nothing in particular."

"It doesn't look like nothing." Lily nodded toward the wounds on his cheek.

"She was like that at times. It was one of her less charming characteristics."

"Had it anything to do with the cocaine?"

He shrugged.

"Anything is possible."

"She took more of it after you returned to the house?"

His eyes narrowed.

"Yes."

She thought of the vision. The white powder on the blade of Lord Deveral's dagger, the storm of it suspended in the air of the room.

All this did was confirm what she already knew. It wasn't enough. She needed something more, something useful. Something that could prove to her that Annalise Boyden had died at the same hand that had drained the life from Sylvia Durst and the others. The same hand that threatened Estelle . . . and not the hands of the man who sat in front of her, calmly smoking his cigarette.

There was the blood, she reminded herself. The splatters of it on the gauzy white fabric of the bed hangings did not seem like enough, given the violence of the injury. The lack of gore soaking the sheets could mean that Annalise Boyden had been drained of it before her throat was cut . . . or it might merely indicate that Lily and Strangford were not physicians and therefore hadn't the slightest notion of how such a wound would bleed.

She needed an undeniable link between Annalise Boyden to the other victims. The appropriate inquiry to settle that was as obvious as it was absurd.

"Was Mrs. Boyden a medium?" she asked.

Lord Deveral's head snapped up.

"How the devil did you know about that?"

Her heart skipped, her senses sharpening. She could feel a similar shift in Strangford's attention. He moved closer, coming to stand directly behind her chair.

"You mean to say she was?" he asked, his voice a low rumble.

"Yes," Lord Deveral confirmed warily. "Or at least, she pretended to be. It was something she would do for friends—a bit of a show she put on at parties."

"Was it a convincing show?" Lily asked.

He shrugged.

"People seemed taken in by it."

"But that's all it was—noise and illusions?"

"What else would it be? Unless you're one of those fools who believes in the spirits of the dead flitting about fat housewives' drawing rooms."

She glanced up at Strangford. He met her gaze, his eyes communicating clearly that he had not missed the significance of this revelation.

"Who knew?" she demanded.

Lord Deveral rubbed his eyes. He could not have slept much since the death of his mistress. Another emotion was visible through the cracks his exhaustion wore in his facade—grief. The sting of it deepened the circles under his eyes and sharpened his words.

"That she purported to speak to the dead? Like I said, she trotted it out at parties. Her friends would all have known, so likely half of the ton did as well. There are no real secrets."

That was not a narrow list of suspects. Nor did it explain the most gruesome and obvious difference in the crimes. Why had her throat been cut where the rest of the women had been quietly and delicately exsanguinated?

The cocaine, Lily thought . . . there was something about the drug she was missing, something that tickled at the back of her memory.

"What are the effects of cocaine?" she asked.

"It's a stimulant," Lord Deveral replied, plucking another cigarette from the case. He lit it off the remains of the last. "Provokes sensations of euphoria."

"For how long?"

He shrugged. "An hour or two."

"Does it interfere with sleep?"

"Not if one downs a sufficient load of brandy."

Lily looked back at Strangford.

"How would such a drug interact with chloroform?"

"We would have to ask Dr. Gardner," he replied.

"But presumably it could compromise the effects of an anesthetic?"

"It's a bloody shot of lightning," her brother interrupted flatly.

Lily stood, moving closer to Strangford as the pieces fell into place, sparking her to urgency.

"What if she woke up?"

"While he was administering the chloroform," Strangford filled in.

"He would have had to find a way to silence her before she could alert the staff. And there was the knife on the vanity."

"How do you know that?" Lord Deveral snapped, swinging his legs to the floor. "How do you know so much about what went on in that room?"

Lily ignored him, pressing on, carried by the force of this revelation.

"This one doesn't look like the others because it didn't go as planned. But if she hadn't taken cocaine just a few hours before . . ."

"What's your interest in this, anyway?" her brother cut in, surging to his feet. "Why do you care about Annalise? Is it because of him?" He turned to Strangford. "You know she's a bastard, don't you? Unfortunate result of my father's dalliance with a music hall whore? You've always been an odd duck, but I would have thought it beyond the pale to associate with something like that, even for you. Unless, of course, you're engaging in a dalliance yourself. One would think the fact she's lifted her skirts for most of Drury Lane might put you off. Picturing her spreading her legs for every heaving stagehand . . ."

The shock of it silenced her, the sheer, vicious vulgarity of his words robbing her of the ability to reply.

"That's quite enough."

Strangford's voice was soft and deceptively even, but Lily could hear an element of threat in it she had never sensed in him before. She was conscious of his presence beside her, the stillness that felt like the moment before a storm breaks.

Lord Deveral threw his cigarette in the fire, then stepped closer, pointing an accusing finger at her. "You come in here like you have any right . . . You use our father to force me to go along with your little game. You think you've won? I won. I won fourteen years ago when Father wanted to foist you off on us like some lost puppy—the bastard he'd sired on that thick Irish slut when he should have been home with his wife."

The words struck like bullets, tearing her armor to shreds.

*Fourteen years ago . . . when Father wanted to foist you off on us . . .*
Could it be true?
*I wish you knew . . .*

"Mother would've done it," he went on, musing, the firelight casting cruel shadows across his aristocratic visage. "She was that desperate to make him happy, as if making him happy would've kept him home when it was always perfectly obvious he'd keep taking his pleasure wherever he bloody wanted to. *I'm the one who made her refuse*," he snarled. "I told her if he brought you home, I'd walk out the door and never speak to any of them again. Better that than stay in a home I had to share with the living, breathing embodiment of our humiliation. My family's humiliation."

She felt them hit, every dagger-pointed line. They cut her with their truth, their horrible and undeniable veracity.

"Do you know how I heard them speak of it when they thought I was too young to know better? All the gossip, the women with their pitying looks for the poor countess who couldn't keep her lord at home. The men who'd all seen him parading his whore around town. And he dared ask us to accept you?"

He moved closer. He was tall, like their father. He loomed over her, his long shadow blackening the silk-papered wall, the scent of tobacco and stale claret thick on his breath.

*"It will never happen."*

It was a killing blow, his final cut, and Lily knew that she was done. She held herself together, impossibly, like a vase that had already shattered, some delicate thing suspended in the moment before it hit the floor.

She didn't want any of them. She never had, she told herself, grasping at the notion like a lifeline that dissolved under her desperate hands.

The anger radiated off of him, a palpable force in the room, searching for another way to strike its target.

She could not take another hit. Not without falling apart and exposing all her terrible vulnerability in front of this man who hated her.

She summoned her last fleeting reserves of strength, mustered them to steady her tone.

"Thank you, m'lord," she said evenly. "You have been most helpful."

Then she turned and walked out of the room.

# FIFTEEN

$\mathcal{L}$ILY'S PACE WAS CALM and even as she walked down her half-brother's hall. Her hand remained steady as she turned the knob of the front door and revealed a street soaked with bitter sleet.

On any other night, on any other call, she would have waited in the warmth of the drawing room while some poor footman bundled up against the foulness found her a hackney. They might have joked over another glass of brandy about how quickly the weather could turn this time of year.

This wasn't any other call. It was a battlefield. Lily needed to retreat before her defenses crumbled and her vulnerability spilled out across Deveral's plush oriental carpets, where her brother would surely see her and know that he had won.

She stepped out into the storm.

The streets were deserted. The only carriage in sight was some nobleman's coach-and-four which raced past her with a hiss as the wheels cut through a puddle of standing water.

Ice drenched her, plastering her hair to her scalp. The wind gusted, whipping her damp skirts against her legs.

She walked on in spite of it, putting a tenacious distance between herself and the pain that threatened to overtake her.

Footsteps splashed along the pavement.

"Lily!" Strangford called.

She stopped.

He stood within arm's reach, still in his coat and shirt, his hat and overcoat deserted back at the house.

"I'm fine," she told him before he could ask. "None of it matters."

Her voice hitched on the last word.

She realized, with horror, that she was going to break.

She fought to hold herself together, to at least spare herself the indignity of shattering into a mess in front of him.

"None of it matters," she repeated, more forcefully this time as the rain pounded down against her like tiny daggers of ice.

He didn't answer. He didn't have to. Even through the storm, she could see that he knew perfectly well she was lying.

"We need to get inside," he said, the sleet flattening his hair, soaking the pale fabric of his shirt.

The cold was bone-chilling. If they stood out in this weather much longer, it would turn dangerous.

She considered their options, grasping at that welcome distraction from the tumult of emotion raging inside of her—feelings that were far less comfortable than the sleet.

The road they stood on lined the park. At this time of night on any other evening, it would have been busy with carriages.

It was deserted. She and Strangford were utterly alone. Which left what option?

The great fine houses marched up and down the street, their windows either dark or thoroughly curtained, closed off against the black expanse of the park. The gaslights of the distant carriageway were wavering and uncertain through the curtains of the downpour.

Deveral's house was just down the road behind them.

No. She would not go back. She would rather freeze.

A carriage turned the corner, the rattle of wheels on the pavement cutting through the hiss of the storm. Lily turned to see a lone hansom cab hurrying down the empty thoroughfare.

Strangford raised his hand to flag it.

It didn't slow.

"He must already have a fare." Lily stuttered over the words, embarrassed to realize her teeth were chattering.

"It's empty," Strangford countered as the vehicle approached.

The driver continued as though blind to them, hunched resolutely over the reins—at least until Strangford stepped into the road in front of him.

The horses clattered to an abrupt halt, the driver raising his head.

"Oy! Watch it, mate. I'm off for the night. Not taking any fares."

"Make an exception," Strangford countered, still in the middle of the road. "Please. I need to see this lady home. I'll happily double your fare. Just one more run, as far as Bloomsbury."

Lily could see the man readying his refusal, but Strangford's last word gave him pause.

The sleet continued to rattle down around them, bouncing off the pavement at her feet. Her jacket was soaked, the icy damp seeping into her shoulders and crawling in rivulets down her neck.

They would find another way, she told herself firmly as the ice stung at her skin. She would not go back. Not if she had to walk to Bloomsbury.

"Come along, then," the cabbie agreed ungraciously. "I'll take you. But only as I'm headed to Clerkenwell myself."

Strangford didn't hesitate. He strode to the door and opened it for Lily.

She climbed quickly inside. He pressed in beside her. The carriage immediately rocked into motion.

A hansom was a tiny space when enclosed, something Lily had not really appreciated before. The front panels were perhaps six inches from her legs, the glass of the enclosing window near enough she could fog it with her breath. The sleet tapped against it as they moved, the cold still penetrating through to where they sat.

She glanced at the empty streets outside the window and felt a flash of recognition.

"We have to stop," she burst out.

"No, we don't," Strangford countered evenly.

"But that was your road."

"I'm seeing you home."

"How will you get back to Bayswater if you do that? The driver said he isn't accepting any other fares tonight. He won't take you."

"I'll find another cab."

It was a senseless sort of chivalry. Lily found she had little patience for it.

"You are aware that I spent years walking far worse streets than Bloomsbury by myself."

"Yes."

"So why do you think it necessary to accompany me here, in the comfort of a carriage?"

"I don't want you to be alone right now."

It was not the answer she expected and rattled her more deeply than the uneven road.

Deveral's words came flooding back with all their deliberate rage, their focused intent to cause her pain. They were an earthquake shifting the ground beneath her feet, the comfortable rock of isolation she had carefully built for herself after learning, long ago, that she could never depend on anyone else.

But if her father had wanted her . . .

It wouldn't matter, she reminded herself fiercely. In the end, he had not done it. She had not been brought into his home, made a part of his family. What did intention matter when measured against action?

Except that it did matter.

Habit told her to retort that she was fine, that she didn't need anyone. She never had, and nothing had changed.

She hesitated. With her long-held pretense stripped away by the cold, Lily admitted to herself that she was not fine.

"Thank you," she replied.

The silence of the dark, close space was broken only by the song of the sleet against the glass. Lily found herself exquisitely aware of Strangford's presence beside her, quietly studying the world through the ice-streaked window. She wasn't sure if she wanted to close the narrow space that separated them or move as far away as she could.

"I should have called him out," he said at last.

"Pardon?"

"Deveral. For what he said to you."

"Are you talking about a duel?"

"What else?" he replied with all apparent seriousness.

She was at a loss for a response, picturing Strangford in his sober vicar's suit standing in some forgotten corner of the heath, plucking an awkward eighteenth century flintlock from a case and then marching his twenty paces from her arrogant half-brother. Turning at the mark, drawing, and putting a bullet into the center of Deveral's cold black heart—which he would clasp dramatically as he tipped backward onto the lawn.

"Pistols?" she suggested.

"If I make the challenge, he chooses the weapon."

"Deveral would pick swords. He's too much of a coward for pistols. Can you handle a sword?"

"That depends."

"On what?"

"On which end I'm handling," he replied.

Lily burst out laughing. It was wrong that she should be laughing after everything she had been through that evening—after all they had experienced over the last few days—but it felt good. It felt very good, and she knew that had been exactly the intent of it.

She was grateful and a touch uncomfortable. This man beside her wasn't supposed to know her that well.

He smiled with her, then grew more serious.

"I'm only half joking," he admitted.

"About fencing?"

"About what I should have done to your brother. I should never have let him say as much as he did. I should have . . ."

"But you didn't," Lily cut in quietly.

"No."

"Why not?" Her curiosity was genuine.

"Because in amongst all that bile coming out of him, I knew there were pieces of truth you deserved the choice to hear."

Tension stretched between them, both aware of how Strangford came by that knowledge.

Standing in that smoky drawing room, hearing all the viciousness pouring from her brother's mouth, the man beside her had known exactly how important it was. He knew her pain and her confusion, the whole of her history. He knew it because she had given it to him when she told him to touch her. This was the consequence—a stranger who knew more about her deepest hurt, her unspoken and long-abandoned wishes, than any living soul on earth.

"It wasn't my place to decide where that had to stop."

She understood it then. This man whose gentlemanly instincts wouldn't let him see her take a hackney on her own had swallowed his own outrage and ceded control to her.

It was something a shade braver than challenging her brother to pistols at dawn.

He turned from the window to face her, his face drawn and earnest.

"I just hope that you understand . . ."

"I do," she cut in before he could go any further.

There was more to say, but she let it fall into the silence. She could still feel the damp chill of her soaked jacket leaching through to her skin, her toes numb inside her boots, but something warmer had risen up inside of her. She felt dangerously close to the edge of a precipice that dropped into a place she was very afraid to go. She pulled back from it as the carriage swayed along the ice-slick streets, the deserted night flickering past the windows.

The hansom swung around a familiar bend, and she found herself looking at the drenched facade of March Place.

The vehicle rocked to a stop. Conscious of the wet, tired driver on the seat above her, Lily wasted no time getting out of the cab. She fumbled for her purse, but Strangford was quicker, passing what she recognized was an exorbitant amount of money up to the driver.

The man acknowledged it with a curt tip of his hat—a fair enough gesture, given that they had all but extorted the ride out of him. Then he snapped his reins and clattered down the empty street.

The sleet continued to drill down, stinging against her scalp. The unheated interior of the now-departed carriage felt balmy by comparison.

Beside her, Strangford had something of the look of a drowned cat, his dark hair plastered to his head, dripping rivulets of icy water down his face.

"And now you are safely delivered," he announced, nodding toward her front steps.

"It appears I am."

"Then I will bid you good evening," he replied. The tone almost made her expect him to offer her a gallant bow, like some beau dropping her at home after an night out courting.

"Where are you going?" she demanded as he turned down the road.

He considered. "I thought I might have better luck finding another cab on Tottenham Court Road."

She took in the deserted street around them, empty even for quiet March Place. It was well after one in the morning. In this storm, even Tottenham Court Road would be as barren as the heath. He could be waiting for hours before someone came by.

The solution to that problem was obvious. She found she had less hesitation than she might have expected in accepting it.

"Come on," she said, mounting the steps. "You can wait inside till it stops."

He did not follow, lingering uncomfortably on the pavement behind her.

"I'm not quite sure that's . . ." he began, then trailed off, not quite knowing how to finish.

She felt her cheeks burn, recognizing the apparent implications of her offer. She held her head high against them, refusing to give in to it. Someone had tried very hard to shame her for what she was that night, for history both her own and inherited. She was not having any more of that, at least not before dawn broke a new day.

"I'm not asking you to go to bed with me," she replied neatly. "I'm offering you tea."

"Well. When you put it like that . . ."

She fought back the urge to smile.

He joined her on the steps as she unlocked the door. She turned the knob, then paused, glancing back to where he stood just behind her.

"My landlady disapproves of gentlemen. In the house."

"I gathered as much."

"So we will need to be quiet."

He raised an eyebrow. "Have you any idea how many sugar cubes I removed from the pantry of my childhood home?"

"No," she replied.

"Neither did the cook."

Lily stifled a laugh. It came out something like a cough. The sleet picked up, coming down in heavy sheets.

"Come on," she ordered and pushed inside.

He followed her into the darkened hallway. Lily did not typically keep late hours and so had never seen it like this, cloaked in thick gloom so that even the oily pilchards in the still life on the wall were barely visible. She carefully closed the door, then considered what to do next, acutely aware of Strangford's presence in the shadows beside her.

She glanced from the stairs to the hallway that lay before them. The stairs were the obvious option, but she had been out for hours. She had no idea what the state of her little parlor stove might be. Her attic flat was likely freezing. It would still be better than standing in the sleet waiting for a cab that may or may not come, but . . . at the end of the hall lay the kitchen. Mrs. Bramble banked down her stove for the night but would only have done so a few hours before. It would have been a roaring fire up until then. The blaze could be brought back up without any trouble at all.

It also felt a bit safer to bring her illicit male guest into Bramble's kitchen, where the landlady herself might walk at any moment, than to sneak him up to the isolation of her rooms.

"This way," she whispered and led him down the hall.

She paused at the entrance to the kitchen, glancing past it to the door leading to Mrs. Bramble's rooms. It was closed, no light shining through the crack underneath it. The house was silent save for the sound of the storm pattering distantly against the windows.

She stepped inside.

Immediately upon entering the room, she was enveloped in warmth, a sensation so delicious she had to bite back the urge to sigh out loud.

It was a generous space, dominated by a large, scarred wooden table. A scattering of chairs surrounded it, but the surface was meant for work, not dining. It was clear now save for a single porcelain biscuit jar in the center of it.

She moved past the table to the enameled kitchen stove and opened the door. The low, glowing bed of embers inside flared up hungrily in response to the influx of air. She reached for the coal bucket.

"Don't," Strangford said, stopping her. "I'll do it."

"My dress could hardly be the worse for a bit of coal dust at this point," Lily countered, trying to be firm while keeping to a whisper.

She read his response in his face.

"Fine."

She stepped back. Strangford shrugged out of his wet coat, laying it on the table. He loosened his necktie, tucking it into his pocket, then tugged off his gloves and rolled up the sleeves of his shirt. The fabric of it was damp at the cuffs and collar.

He worked quietly, rolling coals from the scuttle onto the shovel and sliding them neatly into the stove. When he finished, he moved to the basin and rinsed his hands.

There was already a rocker by the fire. While Strangford washed up, Lily carried over another chair before picking up his coat and hanging it on the rack by the stove.

She considered her own jacket. It was palpably cold and wet. The idea of shedding it was deeply attractive.

Strangford returned, stopping as he contemplated the two chairs—one softened with a cushion and blanket, obviously built for relaxing by the fire, the other stiff-backed and practical.

"Take the rocker," Lily ordered.

"I really shouldn't."

"You had a longer night than I did," she countered pointedly.

He wavered, then sank down into the more comfortable chair. He leaned back in it, closing his eyes gratefully, and every line of him seemed to relax.

It looked very natural—Strangford in his shirtsleeves, coal stains on the cuffs, bare hands resting on the age-polished wood of the rocker. She had seen him in a superficially similar state before, of course, that morning after Abney Park. This was different. Then, it had been a sign of distress. Now it was something else, a guard dropping. The caution she so often sensed in him was gone, revealing in full what lay beneath it—an openness that reminded her of the windswept expanse of the heath, of chill air and rippling grass. She recalled the wild art she had glimpsed on the walls of his study and thought of Mordecai Roth's characterization of the man as a bohemian. It was clear to her now. His sober dress and the restraint of his manner were a disguise, a thin veneer he had built around himself to keep the truth hidden from casual view. Yet it had always been there for anyone who paused to look more closely.

She understood that duality. She lived it herself. It was imbued into every stitch of her respectable wardrobe, of her own unimpeachable behavior since leaving Drury Lane. She shed it when she went to the heath with her Triumph. The motorcycle was about more than just speed. It was the freedom to be what she was without worrying about the eyes of society, of being exposed to them as an object of curiosity.

Strangford knew that fear. It was gone from him here, wrung out by exhaustion and the sheer quiet comfort of this space with its lingering scent of cinnamon and roast chicken. The pretense fled, and something else rose into view in the lean lines of his body, something she realized she rather envied.

The icy damp slowly dripped through the soaked fabric of her jacket.

*Toss it.*

She worked free the finicky fasteners and shrugged the blasted thing off. She dropped it over the rack next to Strangford's coat

She felt his eyes on her. Though nothing changed in his posture, she could sense the strict focus of his attention. Something in her body responded, her skin tingling with awareness—the slide of damp silk against her shoulders, the penetrating warmth of the stove.

The rising desire was matched by a quick and powerful fear.

*No.*

Without looking at him, she sat down in the other chair, stretching out her legs towards the fire. The sleet softened against the windows, gentling to a subtle chorus at the edges of the room.

She studied the response even as her heart still pounded with it. She was skirting up against something dangerous, something that set her to flight. She pushed it back, that unnamed thing, and grasped for a distraction.

"I just wish . . ."

"For what?" Strangford asked, his voice a low murmur from the darkness beside her.

Something in his tone set her heart pounding again. She forcibly ignored it.

"I wish that it hadn't been for nothing. Deveral," she added in explanation.

"We learned what we needed to about Annalise. We know it was the same killer. That isn't nothing."

"But we have no idea who that killer is."

He was quiet after that, gazing into the flames.

"It shouldn't have been necessary at all. If I had done more with Mrs. Durst . . ."

"You can't possibly mean that," Lily blurted.

"I might have spared you Deveral if I had been able to read more details about the killer."

"You put yourself at incredible risk to learn what you did."

He did not seem to hear her. He was looking down at his ungloved hands.

"I have this power. This . . . *gift*, Ash calls it. This charisma. And I am constantly afraid to use it. What could I have learned in Deveral's house if I had the wherewithal to take my gloves off? In Annalise's room?"

The last suggestion filled her with horror.

"You couldn't possibly ask that of yourself."

"If I were stronger—"

"Stronger?" Lily cut in. "I watched you walk straight into death itself and back out again without so much as flinching, and you ask yourself to be stronger?"

It was a moment before he answered. The pause was filled with the tap of the sleet on the windowpanes and a subtle shift of the coals.

"Well," he admitted quietly. "One must admit there was a flinch or two along the way."

"Don't you dare underestimate yourself. You are extraordinary in a way that has nothing to do with your hands."

The words snapped out of her before she could think better of them, compelled by the need to correct him on what seemed to her so obvious a misconception. Yet once out, they rattled her to a quick silence.

The intimacy of this room, the comfortable silence of the fire, the focused attention of the man beside her—there was a threat in it, something with the potential to undermine all her carefully-wrought defenses.

She needed to back away from this place, to steer them to some safer ground.

Before she could think of how to do so, Strangford spoke, and she could hear from his tone that he was taking them in exactly the opposite direction.

"Lily . . ."

She was saved by the creaking of a door.

"Bramble," she hissed, sitting upright in her chair.

The name shattered the tension building between them, replacing it with a different sort of urgency.

Strangford rose.

"The table," he ordered.

She dove beneath it and he grasped her chair, turning it neatly around to face the way it had been when they came in. He managed to do so without so much as a tap when the legs touched the floor again. Then he was sliding in beside her.

They crouched together under the great oak plank of Bramble's work surface and waited.

Footsteps sounded in the hall. Lily was painfully aware of Strangford's presence beside her, the warmth of his body palpable. The sensation threatened to reignite the tension she had felt so intensely a moment before.

Then it occurred to her that she was currently hiding under a kitchen table with a peer of the realm, as fearful of getting caught as any schoolgirl.

The urge to giggle rose up. Her efforts to stifle it had an inverse reaction, making the impulse overwhelming. She felt it stiffen her shoulders and had to exert herself to stay still.

Some sign of her distress must have communicated itself to Strangford.

"Don't start." His voice was low from beside her, barely more than a breath. "Or you will set me off as well."

Bramble thumped into the room.

She was dressed in an enormous flannel nightgown. Despite its volume, the garment had clearly been in use for a decade or more and was worn thin as silk in places, offering her a rather more intimate glimpse of her landlady than Lily might have preferred.

Behind her, Lily realized that the door of the stove was still cracked. A warm orange light emanated from it, the glow of their resurrected blaze. She thought of their coats hung in the shadows beside it.

She waited for Bramble to notice but the landlady's course was unfaltering, as though it were a path she was very accustomed to walking in near-darkness in the middle of the night.

Even steps took her to a cupboard. She opened it and plucked out a tin cup.

Her next stop was the icebox. She removed a bottle of milk and poured herself a cup.

Beside Strangford, Lily watched the routine in silence, praying it did not involve lighting a lamp.

Then Bramble turned for the table.

She stopped with her bare feet just a few inches from where Lily hid.

Strangford was still as a statue beside her, his tension matching her own. She found herself wondering what exactly would occur when Bramble looked down and realized that her tenant was huddled beneath the table with a baron in his shirtsleeves. She held her breath, waiting for that explosion.

The silence of the room broke with a clatter of porcelain. It was the sound of the biscuit jar.

There followed a stretch of quiet crunching.

Bramble did like her biscuits rather dry.

The laughter asserted itself more overwhelmingly this time. She fought against it, perfectly aware of the consequences, but the force of that effort made her shake.

She glanced over at Strangford, hoping perhaps that his seriousness would guilt away her hysteria. He had covered his mouth with his arm, head bowed, and his shoulders were shaking violently.

Lily began to resign herself to losing her lease.

Then the cookie jar lid clanged back into place.

Her hand flashed out, gripping Strangford's arm through his shirt and willing him into silence for a moment longer as Bramble's bare feet retreated. Her steps echoed back from the hallway, punctuated by the creak and snap of her bedroom door.

Lily waited for the space of a breath, making certain Bramble did not suddenly recall something else she wanted from the kitchen. Then she released her grip on Strangford's arm.

"You have no idea," he whispered softly from beside her, "how badly I wanted to reach out and pinch her toes."

It broke her. The laughter spilled out, and she could only be grateful it was fierce enough to take the form of breathless gasps rather than a roar that Bramble would surely have heard from down the hall.

"Stop," she ordered, when she had the air for it. "If you get me booted out of here . . ."

"I would have to offer you my rooms and move into the carriage house with Roderick, which would be terribly inconvenient."

That threatened another wave of hysteria. She wrestled it into submission, though she could see by the watering of his eyes that she was not alone in the struggle.

Finally, they both caught their breath, facing each other across the darkness.

"Perhaps we should get out from under the table," Lily offered.

"An entirely sensible suggestion," Strangford returned.

He climbed out, then turned to offer her his hand—and stopped, flinching.

The gloves, she realized. He had recalled that he was stripped of them.

"It's fine," Lily hurriedly assured him, making her own slightly awkward way out.

She straightened beside him and that abrupt, exquisite awareness returned. She knew exactly what it demanded. The possibility of realizing it felt precariously close.

They were alone in the dark, her rooms just a short climb up the stairs.

She teetered at the edge of that desire then felt it shift beneath her, the ground she was clinging to dissolving into quicksand.

She was falling for him.

The truth of it washed over her as hot and real as the flames roaring in the kitchen stove, shattering through the defenses she had carefully, unconsciously built against it. In a matter of days, the man beside her had threaded his way past her shield and into her life.

*It must not be.*

He was a lord. She was a bastard. There was only one possible form such a relationship could take, the form that was her own origin story—a man and his mistress. The bit on the side. He would be hers at his own convenience and then return to another family, another life that she could never be a part of.

And if it came down to the choice, what would win? Obligation or affection?

She had learned the answer to that question fourteen years ago.

Silence slipped into the room, licking at the edges of the crackling flames as the tension danced between them.

She stepped back.

"I think the rain has stopped."

"Yes," he confirmed. "I suppose that means I shouldn't risk your lease any longer."

*Risk it,* she wanted to urge him. She bit back the words.

He reached for her. She realized she was standing in the way of his coat. He slipped it back on, pulling the gloves over his elegant hands. She winced inwardly, knowing the black wool must still be damp from the storm. She could not afford to let him wait until it was dry. Even now, she felt her resolve shifting, threatening to crack.

"Is there anything else you need? Before I go."

She fought against her response to him, clinging to what she knew she needed to do.

"No. No, thank you. You've done more than enough already."

"If you're sure."

"I am," she replied. "I'll show you out."

She turned and led him to the chill darkness of the hall.

They stopped at the front door, still wrapped in the long shadows of the night. She opened it. He stepped through, then paused and looked back at her across the darkness.

*Danger.* It was written into every line of him. She was exquisitely aware of it now, could hear it in each word that fell from his lips.

The only way for Lily to save herself from the inevitable pain he entailed was to walk away. As fast and far as she could.

"Good night, Miss Albright."

The words were formal, but the warmth of his voice flooded through her.

"To you as well, my lord," she replied.

He left.

She closed the door behind him, then leaned against it, her hands shaking.

Distance. That was what she needed. Distance would make it safe again.

She clung to that, ignoring the soft voice inside of her that shivered for something entirely different.

# SIXTEEN

*S*HE WOKE TO COLD. It penetrated her room, creeping in around the feeble warmth of the dying fire in her stove.

Frost glittered on the windowpanes, etching elegant fractals across the glass. Beyond it, the street itself was glazed with sharp, lingering winter, from the icy pavement to the shimmering tips of the wrought-iron fences.

She remembered the spinning white flakes of her vision of Estelle's death, the snow acting as harbinger to the threat that stalked her.

The cold air took on a greater significance, one Lily didn't want to acknowledge.

Why couldn't spring arrive? If the weather warmed, then perhaps she could be assured that the danger to Estelle wouldn't strike for another year. She would have months to try to find the killer.

She would need them. She had exhausted her ideas of how to seek the murderer. She had forced Strangford to thrust his consciousness into a corpse, had faced her half-brother in all his viciousness. All she had earned for those efforts were more questions.

If this cold were a precursor to snow . . . If the danger to Estelle loomed closer . . .

Lily tried to push the thought from her mind. This had never been about saving Estelle, she reminded herself. She knew better than that. The best she could hope for was justice.

It felt like a slim hope.

She rose, pulling on her slippers and dressing gown, then crossed to the stove to build back up the fire.

Through the bare floorboards under her knees, she heard a resounding crash. A muffled, extended outburst followed from downstairs. Lily's was fairly certain it would have turned her ears pink if she were capable of making out the words.

She closed the stove, sighing, then headed down the stairs.

Estelle's door was cracked open, as usual. Lily still knocked before stepping inside.

"Something wrong?" she called in greeting.

"In here, darling," her neighbor sang out, the words tinged with irritation.

Lily followed the sound to a doorway at the far end of Estelle's parlor.

It opened into a room Lily knew of but had never seen before. It was the flat's second bedroom, a space Estelle had converted to use for her weekly séances.

It was not a large room. A massive round table dominated the space, circled by twelve chairs. The table had a thick central pillar and a round base. There was just enough room outside of it for someone to walk around and take their seat.

The wallpaper, which was probably another dull floral print like the stuff that covered Lily's walls upstairs, was hidden here, covered with curtains of a rich, dark purple. Tapestries billowed from the ceiling, draped to hang along the corners. A few fake potted palms added to the vaguely Eastern theme. The only other furnishing was a plain wooden cabinet, as tall as Lily, built into the far wall.

In near-darkness or candlelight, the space would look exotic and mysterious. In the full glare of the gaslights, it felt a little tawdry.

Estelle was under the table.

"It's these blasted wires," she grumbled, her derriere shifting as she worked. "Something has gotten crossed."

She was wearing silk trousers and a kimono. Lily wasn't entirely sure whether they were day wear or some form of nightgown. It was often difficult to tell the difference with Estelle's wardrobe.

Estelle climbed out from under the table and went to the cabinet. She threw open the door, then, with a soft click, triggered a hidden latch. The back wall of the wardrobe—which any casual observer would have assumed lay flat against the wall of the room itself—opened to reveal a hidden alcove. A series of bells and a tambourine were mounted inside. Lily could see wires running from the instruments into holes in the floor.

She had seen such tricks before. Freshly escaped from Mrs. Finch's, Lily had watched the magicians set up their tricks while she swept or scrubbed backstage. Their shows had involved all manner of wires, used to replicate the exact tricks used by spiritualist mediums.

She felt a sharp, and unexpected, pang of disappointment.

There was no reason for it, of course. Lily had never given much credence to Estelle's claims to communicate with spirits. Why should she be surprised that the medium engaged in a bit of deliberate fraud, a few spectacles aimed at pulling wool over the eyes of her spectators?

Estelle returned to the table. Lily could now see an open panel in its base. A series of metal rings were mounted there. As she watched, Estelle pulled each one. Back in the cabinet, bells rang and the tambourine jangled, delicate noises that would certainly have a ghostly impact when heard in a dark, atmospheric chamber.

She pulled the last ring, peering over at the window, which was covered by a heavier black curtain.

Nothing happened.

"Stupid, useless . . ."

"What's the matter?"

"It's the damned billows." Estelle stalked over to the curtain and pulled it back. Mounted on the wall behind it was an ordinary fireplace billows. This, like the instruments in the cabinet, was attached to a wire that ran down the wall and then disappeared into another hole in the floor. "When I pull the wire, it's supposed to compress, like this." She demonstrated. "Except then it needs to billow again, so I can keep puffing. It's not billowing."

"Why do you need it to billow?"

"Aha!" Estelle said proudly. "My new toy. Allow me to demonstrate."

She closed the curtain, then turned down the gas lights. The room sank into moody gloom, the oriental tapestries glittering softly in the near-darkness.

Estelle reached under the lip of the table. Lily heard a click. Suddenly a ghostly, glowing figure appeared on the surface of the black curtain.

The effect was startling.

"Isn't she magnificent?"

"What on earth is it?"

"A magic lantern!" Estelle announced proudly.

Lily bent down for a better look at the device.

"It uses an electric bulb, powered by a battery. The light only lasts for a few minutes, but that's really all I need. Any longer and she might start to look a bit cheap."

Estelle flipped a switch and the device powered off. She turned on the gaslights, then pulled a thin piece of glass from the mounting over the lens and handed it to Lily.

"I call her Desdemona. I picked her up at a pawn shop in Notting Hill. I painted out the background in black so it wouldn't show—she was in the most dreadful approximation of some sultan's harem. I've been considering adding a little rouge to her cheeks, but then, she's supposed to be dead."

She plucked the plate from Lily's hand and slipped it back into the lantern.

"The problem is, she's utterly lifeless if she's just hanging there on the curtain. The zing factor is ever so much bigger if there's movement. A little rustle of the curtain—that's all it would take and she'd be undulating her hips like any proper inhabitant of a seraglio ought to be." She stalked over to the curtain, ripping it back again and pointing accusingly. "Yet my billows stubbornly refuses to billow."

Lily considered the arrangement.

"That's because you've got it hooked up backwards."

"I do not," Estelle countered pertly. "The wire has to run through the floor. There isn't any other way it can go."

Lily walked over to the device. "What you need is some sort of hook—or preferably a ring, so you don't have to worry about the wire slipping out—right here. That way, the wire actually runs up, rather than down. And then you add a counter-weight to the bottom of the billows, and—"

"Brilliant! Magnificent, darling! Who knew you had such hidden talents?"

"I have some experience with illusions," Lily replied, keeping her tone even.

Some note of disapproval must have slipped into it in spite of her efforts. Estelle regarded Lily steadily, her tone shifting. "You're wondering if it's all just tricks."

Lily felt a quick pang of guilt.

"I never said that."

"Well, I gave up trying to convince people a long time ago. So you can either believe it or not. I don't care one way or another."

"If you're not trying to convince people, what's all this for?"

Estelle dropped down into one of the chairs, stretching her legs out in front of her.

"A show, darling. A performance. What else could it be?" She leaned forward. "Do you think most people really come here to contact the dead? They don't want to hear what the dead have to say. I tell them anyway, of course. It's the least I can do for the poor departed things. But the living are far more likely to listen if you warm them up first with a few spectacles. It's the spectacles that turn them into private clients, which is the real bread-and-butter in this enterprise. It's also what they tell their friends about, which is how the new clients keep coming. Now . . . why don't you tell me who you snuck in here at one in the morning last night? Don't bother trying to deny it. I could hear you both chattering in the hall."

"I was out with a friend when we got caught in that storm. This was the sensible place to take shelter until it was possible to find a hackney."

"Was this friend a certain broodingly handsome baron of our mutual acquaintance?"

Lily forced herself not to show any reaction.

"I'm not sure I know what you mean."

"Not that I disapprove. I don't know the fellow particularly well, but if Robert likes him, he must be decent. And it can't be anything but good for you to get out and stretch your legs a little."

"Stretch my legs?" Lily echoed in shock.

"Oh." Estelle's eyes widened. "I see. You haven't done any leg stretching as of yet. After bringing him home with you in the middle of the night? Hmmm. I hope that doesn't imply that he's . . . well, you were in theatre. You know what I mean."

Lily was speechless.

"No. I don't believe that's the issue here . . ." Estelle continued, musing. "But there's certainly something the matter . . ."

"Perhaps he's simply a gentleman," she managed to choke out.

"Yes, I suppose that could be it. How dreadfully inconvenient."

Lily's thoughts flashed back to the night before, to that racing flush of desire she had felt when standing with Strangford in the kitchen.

It had been far too narrow an escape, and not because of any lack of gentlemanly consideration on Strangford's part. It was Lily who had nearly lost control.

She must never forget the unalterable truth: she was a bastard. She would always be an outsider in his world, her father's world. At best, she might be tolerated or ignored. At worst . . .

Deveral's words the night before came flooding back to her, all his vile insults designed to inflict the maximum pain on someone he believed could not strike back.

That memory lead to another, one far more shattering than any of Deveral's deliberate verbal blows.

*He dared ask us to accept you.*

What might her life have been if her father had gotten his way? If she had been brought into his house, raised as his acknowledged daughter? How would the world view her then? An alliance with an illegitimate daughter might not seem so beyond the pale, if it meant a closer connection with one of England's most powerful men.

Yet it was something else that put a vise grip around Lily's heart when she thought of Deveral's revelation, something that struck at the core of her vulnerability: the vision of being part of a family.

Sitting down together for dinner every night. Opening presents on Christmas morning. Racing around the house with an army of wild brothers, bickering over borrowed toys.

To have had a home. A father.

She reminded herself, fiercely, that it could never have been like that. Even if her father had chosen to exercise his authority, that home would still have been filled with people who hated her. Nothing the earl did could change that, nor could his influence ever completely stop the whispers, the quiet set-downs, the reminders from the aristocratic circles in which he mingled that she was there on tolerance. That she didn't belong. That she never would.

"Is something the matter?" Estelle asked.

"No. Not at all." Lily smiled forcefully. "Have you any hardware? Perhaps I can rig up that billows for you."

Estelle plucked a toolbox out from under the table and presented it to her.

Lily picked out the pieces she needed and moved over to the window, setting to work with the screwdriver. Behind her, Estelle reclined in the chair, her feet up on the table.

"Where is Miss Bard today?" Lily asked to fill the air.

"Oh, she's flitted off to an auction out in some twee place with 'shire tacked onto its name. She's hoping to secure a folkloric what-not she has her eye on. I suppose you heard about the murder?"

Lily paused only a moment, then continued turning the screwdriver.

"Which murder would that be?"

"The one they're accusing your brother of having committed. I know you pretend to disdain the newspapers, but you can't tell me you weren't aware of *that* story."

"Half-brother," Lily replied. "And I can't say I've been following it."

"It's remarkable, really. They're actually bringing him up on charges. It could be the first time a peer is indicted since Lord Cardigan, and that was in my grandmother's day."

An indictment, one where the evidence against Lord Deveral would be listed before a grand jury—evidence that made for what looked like an ironclad case.

How could she possibly hope to counter that and convince anyone of his innocence?

Her thoughts shot back to Dr. Joseph Hartwell as they had so often since that night in the gallery.

Her gut told her that the renowned physician was somehow involved in this, but she had no evidence to connect him to the crimes—nothing but the coincidence of his line of work and her own deep dislike of the man. She could follow that, digging into Hartwell's activities, but in doing so she might let the evidence pointing to the true killer slip through her hands.

She had to stay focused on the murders, but what options for investigation did she have left?

Frost crawled up Estelle's windowpane. It didn't care that Lily was out of ideas. The events she had foreseen were wending toward her, regardless of her efforts.

She felt a hot burst of frustration and an equal burden of guilt.

"It's none of my business," she lied. With a tug, she loosened the wire that held Estelle's trick together.

"So it has nothing to do with your father calling here yesterday morning."

"No."

"Or why you were in Abney Park on Thursday night."

Lily dropped the screwdriver.

"What did you say?"

"I had it from Agnes," Estelle explained breezily. "It's one of the easier things to pick up, you see—places, if it's someplace you've both been before. I don't know who Agnes has there, but my great-aunt was a famous Dissenter. I have to pop by on occasion to keep the ivy from completely overgrowing her grave or she starts turning up in my dreams. And I have much better things to dream about than Great-Aunt Prudence."

"I see," Lily replied carefully, retrieving the tool from the floor.

"Agnes says you went there to talk to someone, though I can't quite settle on who. She just keeps showing me those gas lamps. So of course, I'm dying of curiosity."

Estelle settled back in her chair, smiling patiently.

Lily's head spun.

Was it luck? Some bold streak of intuition? Estelle could certainly have discovered that Lily had been out on Thursday, but how could she have guessed where Lily had gone?

She might have learned it from Sam or Dr. Gardner . . . but Lily found it almost as hard to believe either of those two would spill their story of casual grave-robbing with one of London's most notorious gossips.

The only explanation left was that Estelle was, in fact, communicating with the spirit of a murdered medium.

Lily waited for the familiar skepticism to return.

It did not. Instead, she found herself wrestling with an unfamiliar and far less comfortable sense that Estelle was telling the truth. Despite the bells and whistles of her evening performances—the evidence of which Lily held in her hands—Estelle's ability was as genuine as Lily's.

She set down the screwdriver and turned.

"How does it work?" she demanded.

Estelle did not need to ask what she meant.

"Well, it's not exactly like sitting down for a chat over sherry."

"Then what it is like?"

"Like . . . daydreaming, I suppose. As much as it's like anything."

"Daydreaming?"

"The dead don't speak in words. They communicate in ideas. So you have to open your mind. Put it out there that you're here, and that you'll listen, and then be absolutely open to anything that comes into your head, no matter how absurd."

"Then how do you tell the difference between something you get from the dead and something you just dream up yourself?"

Estelle shrugged. "You just do. The hard part is having enough faith in yourself to make sense of it. An impression of a rose can mean love, or a flower shop, or a name. It's all in the sense of it . . . whether it feels like a flower shop or a name."

"What did Agnes show you about me?"

"I saw the cemetery where my peevish great-aunt is buried. A telephone ringing in an empty room. And a single orange calla lily—that was you."

The calla lily. She thought of the blooms that had decorated Evangeline Ash's portrait, elegant blossoms tumbling over the sides of an antique vase.

"Oh. And the gas lamps, of course. They were part of it as well. Funny, isn't that? The image Agnes gives me any time I try to ask her who it was that murdered her, and it shows up when she's telling me about your little excursion."

Lily could hear the nuance in Estelle's tone.

She knew.

She knew that Lily was interested in the murders. That Lily was keeping something from her.

The urge rose in her again, wild and fierce, to warn her—to try to tell her what was coming.

Should she? Was there a chance it might actually make a difference?

Lily knew from hard experience how unlikely that was. If she gave into the urge and let herself warn Estelle, she would fill the woman's last days with fear and worry as she struggled to escape the horror destined to overtake her.

If there was any hope, even the slimmest chance, of changing what Lily had foreseen, it would not lay in another fruitless warning.

It required action. And all Lily's actions so far had led her to a hopelessly dead end.

She twisted the last bit of wire, fastening the weight into place, then tugged on the shining filament that ran from the floor up to the ring she had just mounted on the wall. The billows collapsed, the puff of air stirring Lily's hair, then fell open again as the weight did its work.

Estelle applauded.

"Wonderful!"

"You'll want to cover the weight in felt so it doesn't make an audible scrape against the wall as it moves."

"Felt. Yes. Certainly. How convenient to be neighbors with a woman of such diverse and useful skills. Where would I be without you?"

"Short one undulating Desdemona," Lily replied automatically, but her thoughts had skipped ahead.

*Such diverse skills . . .*

Estelle didn't need a wire rigger nearly as badly as she needed someone who could discover the identity of the man who stalked her, who could solve a crime that hadn't yet been committed.

Someone with the power to know the future.

Lily had that power. It came and went as it pleased, with no discernible pattern other than some inexplicable whim.

But . . . what if that could change? What if it could answer to her whim?

That had been Ash's promise. It was why he said he had founded The Refuge, as a place of both acceptance and mastery. Was it possible that there might be knowledge there that could empower Lily to take control of her ability, to learn to direct it to serve her purpose?

Her gut shied away from the idea. Acknowledging what she was, what she could do, risked the return of that dreadful responsibility— the burden of guilt for her failure to avert the tragedies she knew were coming. It meant the risk of engaging in a battle she was destined to lose, over and over again. She couldn't bear that again. It was hell.

Yet there were lives on the line. Estelle's life. Deveral's life. Four women had already died and the one responsible still walked free while the law comfortably pinned at least one of the crimes on an innocent man.

It was wrong, all of it—terribly wrong. If there was even a chance that Lily could change that, that her power might make it possible for her to identify the true monster responsible for these crimes and bring him to justice . . . could she really walk away from that without even trying?

It was Strangford's face that appeared in her mind in answer. She thought of how he had responded when she made the awful suggestion that he use the power in his hands to read the history of Sylvia Durst's corpse.

And yet he had done it, knowing the pain and horror it would entail. He had done it because it was right, because it was worth putting himself on the line for the slim chance of saving a life or two. How could she refuse to take the same chance herself?

She couldn't.

"I'm sorry," she said, handing Estelle her tools. "I'm afraid I must run. I have a call to make."

# SEVENTEEN

$\mathcal{L}$ILY HESITATED AT THE door of The Refuge. Her gaze moved from the polished brass knocker to the doorknob. Ash's words rang through her memory.

*It will always be open to you.*

A place of sanctuary for charismatics—for people who, like Lily, carried the burden of knowledge they shouldn't have. Ash had invited her to consider herself a part of it after nothing more than a few minutes conversation. It was an exceptionally generous offer . . . one that Lily had no intention of accepting.

She knocked.

The door opened, revealing Sam Wu dressed in tweed coat and dark wool trousers.

"Oh. It's you," he said. It was a singularly unenthusiastic greeting. Lily refused to let it throw her off.

"Is Mr. Ash receiving?"

Instead of answering, Sam whistled.

A small brown sparrow fluttered down, settling onto the rail beside her. It cocked its head, hopping closer to the door, then flew up on to his shoulder.

Sam whispered to it. The bird took off, whizzing past Lily's hat.

He opened the door, stepping back. It wasn't much of an invitation, but Lily moved inside. She pulled off her gloves.

He was silent for an uncomfortable minute, then finally spoke, his tones bland.

"May I take your coat?"

"Thank you," Lily replied coolly.

He came behind her, helping slide the jacket off her shoulders. He held out his hand for her gloves and hat, then disappeared, presumably to place them in the closet.

Lily waited beside the bust of Isaac Newton in the silence of the hall, refusing to appear awkward. She devoted herself to studying the intricate battle playing out on the antique shield mounted on the wall until Sam finally returned.

"This way, if you please," he said, motioning her into the drawing room.

The space was elegant but comfortable, the couches and chairs showing just the right amount of wear. A fire burned in the hearth and another assortment of unique artifacts were scattered about the room. An ancient sword rested beside the iron poker and shovel for the fireplace. A glass-fronted case held an assortment of tiny turquoise figurines covered in hieroglyphs, along with what she was fairly certain was a mummified lizard.

Sam leaned against the door frame, his arms crossed over his chest.

"Where is Mr. Ash?" Lily asked.

"He's meditating."

A clock ticked on the wall, punctuating the silence.

"As soon as he's finished, I'll let him know that you're waiting," he finally added.

"How will you know that he's finished, if you're in here?"

He didn't answer. Nor did he leave, or offer her tea, or do any of the things a servant might normally be expected to do.

It was a subtle but effective means of intimidation. Lily respected the audacity of it, even though she had no intention of letting it put her off her purpose. What she had come for was too important.

Important and terrifying. She was here to ask Robert Ash how she could provoke a vision, using her power to demand that the future reveal its secrets to her—not just any secrets, but the ones she needed to see.

If he provided her with that knowledge, she would be faced with a choice. Should she use it and open a door to a part of herself she had spent the last fourteen years trying to bury, or refuse, and do nothing while a man was hung for a crime he hadn't committed and a murderer drained the life from innocent women in their beds?

It had been hard enough to walk through the door. She would not be driven out now by Sam Wu's antagonism. And yet, could she entirely blame him? She was a stranger, an interloper in what was very obviously a realm he considered his own. He didn't know her motives or her place, what she wanted or whether she posed a threat to the people he loved.

She strolled slowly around the room, examining the curios.

She stopped at a small painting. It was no bigger than a piece of writing paper, done in oils on a very old block of wood. It depicted a brown-robed saint, recognizable as such by the halo of delicate gold leaf crowning his head. He stood in a field against a dark blue sky, his hands held out as though gesturing in the middle of a sentence.

The audience he spoke to consisted of a flock of birds that hovered before him as though transfixed.

"St. Francis of Assisi," Sam said. "They say he was so holy, God granted him the power to speak with animals."

"You mean that he was like you."

Lily felt the boldness of her words. To acknowledge what she had seen with the rats outside Abney Park aloud felt shocking, even dangerous.

"I'm not Catholic," he replied.

The laugh slipped out before she could help herself. It was answered, to her surprise, by a quirk of Sam's own mouth, one that had clearly been involuntary. It was rapidly drawn back into hiding.

Still, she had seen it, a little sign of a crack in his bristling armor. Curiosity tugged at her.

"It's the sparrow, isn't it? You asked it to watch Mr. Ash for you."

"Maybe I did," he replied coolly.

"Does it work with every animal like that? Do they all do what you say?"

"You mean, can I command them like a lord? Not hardly." Sam left his post by the door and dropped himself into a plump armchair as though he belonged there. It was another indicator of his ambiguous status in the house. Servants didn't typically make themselves comfortable in the drawing room.

"So how does it work?"

He shrugged. "Some you can ask for a favor, and they might grant it. They're usually not the clever ones, though. The clever ones you can do more with, but they'll want something for it."

"You mean like a payment." She thought back to Abney Park. "Were the rats like that? Did you have to pay them for what they did at the cemetery?"

"No. They ain't very bright. Show up their king, they'll follow you around for a while, do what you like, long as it's not anything too complicated."

She thought back to his confrontation with the monstrous rat that had emerged alone from the Stoke Newington sewers, how the whip-thin young man in front of her had bodily forced the animal into submission while it hissed and nipped at his fingers.

"What's the cleverest animal, then?"

"Ravens," he replied without hesitation.

"What do you have to pay them?"

"More than you'd want to give."

Something in his voice gave her a chill. She returned her attention to the painted icon on the wall.

"When I was here before, Mr. Ash mentioned something about the stories of miracles and saints."

"He thinks they were like us."

She did not miss the significance of the slight emphasis he placed on "us". With her questions about the birds and rats, she had called out her knowledge of his difference. He was returning the favor.

"That they could . . . do things that others can't. Just naturally. Not as some kind of act of divine intervention," she clarified.

"Don't get him started on divine intervention or you'll be here all night."

He rose abruptly from the chair, as though catching himself and pulling back from the ease he'd let slip into his manner. His expression closed again and his tone sharpened.

"What are you here for, anyway?"

236

Lily knew the question wasn't about the purpose of that afternoon's visit. It was a demand to know why she had invaded his world, threatened to upset its balance with the introduction of some foreign element.

Her immediate instinct was to put him off . . . but this man had already been pulled into her affairs, whether or not either of them liked the idea. She remembered the sight of him standing stiff and still as the rats crawled over his body—something he had endured because of her, in the name of a cause he didn't even know.

"I'm trying to prevent an injustice. And perhaps . . ." she stumbled over the words, her mouth feeling dry as she forced them out. "Perhaps to stop a threat to someone I care about."

"That's all?"

"That's all."

Sam absorbed this.

"What about after?"

Lily didn't know how to answer that. It should have been simple. She would go back to her life and forget any of this ever happened. Somehow, that promise wouldn't quite come out.

Instead, she seized on something else, a line of inquiry that would almost certainly make Sam forget he'd ever asked that more difficult question.

"Were you a thief?"

Sam's posture immediately turned defensive.

"What's it any of your business?"

"I saw you pick that lock on the lodge at Abney Park."

"So what if I did?"

"Could you get into a locked house and then make it look locked again after you'd left?" she pressed.

"I've got nothing to do with that anymore. And even if I did, what makes you think I'd do it for the likes of you?"

"I'm not asking you to do it. I'm asking if it would be possible."

He crossed his arms, still wary. "A bloke might do it, if he knew what he was about. 'Course, the best thing is not to break in at all. Just make sure you're inside before everything is locked."

Lily was suddenly very attentive.

"Before it's locked?"

"It's easy enough, if you know what you're about. Then you find someplace to hole up till night. Make your way out through a door with a latch, not a bolt. A latch, you can set behind you. If you're lucky, nobody notices anyone was there, or that anything was nicked, till it's well out of your hands."

"It's that simple?"

"Well—not anybody can pull it off. Takes a dab hand. Why? You looking to pinch something?"

"The something has already been pinched."

"What was it?"

"Blood."

Sam considered this. His defenses had lowered, overcome by his curiosity.

"Odd thing to nab. Can't sell it, save maybe to a butcher and he wouldn't give you much for it."

"I don't think he intended to sell it." Lily considered the problem, then realized the man in front of her might be able to offer a more informed answer. "What else would someone steal a thing for? Besides selling."

"Could be he just likes it. Knew a bloke in Limehouse used to jack ladies' hats. He'd pluck 'em right off their skulls. Didn't sell them. Just kept them all lined up in his room. That's right rare, though. Most like, if it ain't something you can turn into dosh, you'd take it because you needed it. Nippers lifting bread because they're hungry or drunks pinching spirits."

"But what could you possibly need another person's blood for?"

Sam shrugged.

"Search me."

A bird swept into the room. It was the sparrow, brown and delicate.

Lily had seen wild birds in a house before. They were generally panicked, careening about in circles and bouncing into the walls.

This bird looked as comfortable in the space as Cat was on her pillow. It made one easy circle of the room, then settled down on the mantle beside Sam. It chirped.

"Cheers, mate," Sam replied.

The bird ruffled its feathers, then darted away.

He stood.

"The old man's done meditating now."

"He has been, ever since someone's little helper pecked him in the ankle."

Ash stepped into the doorway. He was dressed in a well-tailored suit, his feet clad in polished leather shoes, every inch the respectable English gentleman.

"You sit so still, she probably wanted to make sure you weren't a topiary," Sam replied easily.

Ash smiled, briefly, before his expression turned more sober.

"Your father is asking for you."

Sam stiffened. Lily could see his posture grow formal, more what one expected of a chauffeur speaking to his employer.

"Shì, Lǎoshī," he replied.

The strange sound of the words jarred her. She had become so accustomed to hearing that rough East End patter come out of him, she had ceased to wonder if Sam was a native of some other tongue.

"Miss Albright for you, sir," he announced, his tone faultlessly proper.

"Thank you, Sam," Ash replied.

He gave Ash a bow. To Lily's deeper surprise, he followed it up with one to her as well. Then he left.

"His father?"

"He manages the gardens."

"And Mrs. Liu?" She recalled the older Asian woman who had served her tea in the library, the maker of the divine lotus seed buns.

"His grandmother."

Lily had a hundred questions. Where had the Wu family come from? Why were they in England? How long had they been here and how had they ended up working for Ash?

"Would you mind terribly if we stepped out?" Ash asked, pre-empting her questions. "I find I am rather in need of a walk."

"Not at all," Lily agreed.

~

They strolled along the square. The trees were bare, the web of their dark branches obscuring the view of the houses on the far side. In a few months, a thick cover of green leaves would conceal those brick facades entirely, giving the place the illusion of rural privacy.

Lily considered how to broach the subject that had brought her there. In the end, it seemed there was nothing for it but to dive in.

"Can you teach me how to make a vision come when I want it to?" Lily asked.

The question nearly stuck in her teeth. It acknowledged that she was what Ash had claimed she was—a charismatic. Then again, the time to deny that had passed the night of Annalise Boyden's death, when she had turned up on his doorstep demanding help to respond to a murder that hadn't happened yet.

Ash didn't ask any of the questions he had every right to ask. He merely answered her.

"Yes."

"How?"

"There are several ways. The one I would prefer you learn is the long path. Study and practice, building a solid relationship with your power."

Lily tried not to visibly frown. She didn't have time for study and practice. She needed answers now.

"What about the others?"

"It depends on what you're looking for."

"I just need something that will let me see what I want to, when I want to see it."

"That, I'm afraid, is impossible."

She stopped walking. They were on one of the quiet residential streets that bordered Bedford Square.

"You just said there were ways."

He looked not the least bit perturbed by her tone, something that only increased her own irritation.

"To provoke a vision when you wanted to, yes. What I can't teach you is how to dictate what that vision will—or will not—show you."

She felt that familiar frustration rise up in her again. What good was bringing on a vision if she couldn't control it? She could end up seeing more disasters she couldn't hope to prevent instead of the information she needed to deal with the one she already knew was coming.

"There must be some way."

He turned, walking again. Lily was forced to move to keep up with him or give up the conversation and go home.

"You have met some of the others associated with The Refuge."

"Yes," she replied shortly, thinking of Sam casually thanking a lit-tle brown bird in the middle of Ash's well-appointed drawing room.

"Your power differs from theirs. Can you tell me how?"

The question irritated her. She didn't have time to be lead down some philosophical path. She needed answers, but clearly she was going to have to play along for a while in order to get them.

"Your driver talks to animals," she answered bluntly. "Miss Deneuve communicates with the dead." She didn't mention Dr. Gardner, though she felt certain there was something going on with the big Ulsterman as well.

"And Lord Strangford?"

Ash glanced over at her, his pale blue eyes giving no sign that the question was anything more than casual.

"He touches things," Lily replied evenly, trying not to think of the electric brush of his fingers on her skin.

"What do those powers have in common? Something that your ability does not share."

Lily felt her patience thin.

"You might as well just tell me. I've never been any good at tests."

"I doubt that."

"You may inquire for my records at Mrs. Finch's Academy for Young Ladies, if you think I'm lying."

"The assessments you received there weren't tests. They were hoops you were instructed to jump through."

Lily felt a smirk tug at the corner of her mouth, despite herself. It was a cuttingly accurate statement.

"What do Sam and Lord Strangford and Miss Deneuve all have in common that makes them different from you?"

Lily suppressed a sigh and blurted the first answer that came to mind.

"They're always on."

"On?"

"Their . . . gifts. Sam seems to be able to communicate with all manner of creatures anytime he likes. If the dead are around, Estelle can receive messages from them. And Lord Strangford . . ." She hated the brief tightness in her throat when she said his name. She forced herself to speak past it. "Lord Strangford's ability manifests itself anytime he touches something."

"And you?"

"I never know when I'm going to see something. The visions come, or not, as they like. There's no rhyme or reason to it."

"You do not control when your visions occur. What, then, do you presume does?"

"I don't presume anything. I've never thought about it."

Ash stopped. They had reached the end of the lane.

"You have had this power all your life and you have never once stopped to ask yourself what it is that determines whether you have a vision, or do not?"

"I was generally too busy trying to stop people from getting hurt or dying to worry about philosophy."

"Or you were wishing it would stop."

Ash's words, delivered with bald simplicity, cut like a blade. Lily stepped back as though he had in fact struck her, her chest tight.

"How would you know that?"

"Who could live in the grip of a power like yours and not, at some point in time, wish it was gone?" He reached out, his hand lightly touching her arm. "I have called it a gift, Miss Albright. And it is a gift. But that does not mean it must always be a welcome one."

He moved his hand away and motioned forward, the gesture practiced and gentlemanly. They stepped from the lane out into the current of men and horses and engines that flowed up and down Tottenham Court Road.

It was one of the city's busiest thoroughfares, a chaotic and ever-moving river of life. The flow of bodies reshaped itself around them like water passing around stone. It was an unnatural feeling for Lily, who as a born Londoner had always plunged into such flows, melding herself into it as smoothly as possible. To deliberately neglect to do so—to become, instead, an obstacle that the moving bodies were forced to avoid—was an uncanny sensation.

Ash seemed unperturbed.

"You may not have asked the question of the cause of your visions in the past, but I have put it to you now. How would you answer it?"

It was a line of inquiry she had no desire to pursue. Something in her rebelled against it, pushed her to abandon this conversation and lose herself in the anonymous safety of the crowd that continued to move around them.

She forced herself to stay. She would play along for a while longer. There was no time for her to find another source for the knowledge she needed.

"I would say it was like a reflex. A cough or a sneeze," she replied, unable to keep all of the impatience from her tone.

"Reflex implies an initial cause. You cough to expel matter from your lungs. A sneeze is triggered by dust in the air or a feather to the nose. What's the feather for your vision?"

"I don't know. It could be anything."

"Come, now. Surely you've looked for patterns in the past. It would have been the sensible way to try to rid yourself of the thing—determine what triggered it and avoid such stimuli in the future. And you are a sensible woman."

Lily felt that quick, defensive anger return again. He was trying to walk her into a box, like a child tugging another through the family hedge maze. She didn't have time for this.

"Why don't you just tell me whatever it is you're trying to get at?"

He showed no sign of being offended or taken aback by her directness.

"I believe I know what your feather is, Miss Albright."

"And?"

"I don't believe it will be an easy concept for you to grasp. Simpler minds adopt it readily, but your mind is anything but simple."

"Try me."

"God."

An omnibus clattered by. An oyster girl brushed past, calling her wares, her path crossing with that of a pair of dandies bent over with laughter at some unheard joke.

"God," Lily echoed numbly.

"Or dharma. Logos. The Egyptians called it ma'at. In China, I encountered it as the Tao. In nearly every system of belief across this world, there is a principle of acausal causality—a connection between events that has no basis in the commonly understood laws of physics, but is no less real. An organizing principle of the universe as fundamental as gravity, but based on meaning. On heart. Call it fate, if you like. The Parliament of Stars."

A gull cried overhead. A carriage jolted to a halt nearby, releasing a line of finely-dressed ladies who wove their way to a milliners. Somewhere nearby, a motorcar honked, adding another note to the symphony of noise and movement that surrounded them.

"You're saying you believe my visions are triggered by . . . fate."

"Miss Albright, we are speaking about the realm of miracles. Your visions. Sam's chatter with the birds. Lord Strangford's touch. These are impossibilities by every physical law we know. Yet here you are. Here men and women like you have always been, since the beginning of human history. We have always had miracles, and miracle-workers. If you are not bound by the linear nature of time, the regular rules of space, then what principle does move you? It must be some greater force, and the Tao is as great as they come."

Her head was spinning. Was it because of this wildly unexpected turn of the conversation, or simply the disorientation of being the only still point in a sea of moving bodies, carriages and apple carts?

"I just want to know how to make it work."

Ash smiled. There was patience in it and a hint of sadness.

"Miss Albright. If fate is your feather, then your visions are already working. They are not sneezes. They are emanations from the source of all meaning in this universe, and as such, they are infused with purpose."

The quick, old anger returned again, hotter than ever.

"If they have a purpose, I'm either a terrible failure, or your fate has a twisted sense of humor."

"Why do you say that?"

"Because every time I try to change something I foresee, it happens anyway. Every time. So what am I supposed to conclude? That I'm inept? Or that this is all just some rotten joke?"

She couldn't keep the sneer from her tone. This side of her was uglier than anything she usually let out, but something in Ash's calm as he tore open the fabric of her reality made it impossible to care about social niceties.

"What if changing it was never the point?" he replied.

The ground beneath her feet seemed to shift. Lily's anger shivered away.

The shoppers and clerks and loafers and dog-walkers continued to weave around her, but for the first time since they had started this conversation, Lily felt the world go still.

"What exactly does that mean?"

Ash laughed.

"Oh, my dear girl . . . I suppose there are few better places for tackling the problem of suffering than the middle of Tottenham Court Road, but I fear I've thrown far more at you already than you asked for, or expected. There will be ample time to discuss all of this—with, I hope, more leisure, and more space for the necessary contemplation—when you are ready. As I told you before, the door has always been open. You may walk through it any time you choose."

"Why?" Lily demanded. "Why would you offer that to me? You don't know me. You don't know anything about me."

"I know enough."

"You mean that painting, don't you? The one you told me about before. It isn't me. Your wife couldn't possibly have painted me. She died before I was born."

"Says the young lady who sees the future."

There was a brightness in his eyes that made Lily rather certain he was laughing at her. It infuriated her.

She needed more than this. She needed an answer, now, not months or years down the road when Deveral had been hung and Estelle murdered.

"You said there was more than one way to bring a vision about. Something faster than study and practice."

"Yes. There are ways. You could try scrying. And there is the Wine of Jurema, which for other charismatics has acted as a shortcut to a greater sense of their potential power. But there are often . . . unintended consequences. You must know, however, that none of these techniques will allow you to see only what you choose. Fate is your feather, Miss Albright. No matter how a vision comes about, whether it simply happens or you drive it by your own will, something quite outside of you will determine what you see. As for what you are meant to do with that knowledge . . . perhaps you are the herald who warns people of what is to come, granting them time to set their affairs in order. Perhaps the struggle itself is the rub of it—the very effort to change things, even though it appears to fail, could have an impact on the world you couldn't possibly discern. Or perhaps, now and again, you may be meant to succeed."

Could that really be true? Had the point of her visions never been to try to stop the events she foresaw from coming to pass? Were they meant to serve some other purpose? The notion was revolutionary. It also begged a vital question.

"How would I know the difference?" she demanded.

Ash smiled.

"You won't."

His answer left her speechless.

"I'm afraid I must hurry to another engagement," Ash apologized. "May we continue this conversation another time?"

"Right. Another time," Lily replied automatically, as her mind spun with unanswered and perhaps unanswerable questions.

He bowed.

"Good afternoon, Miss Albright. I do hope you will call again soon."

He stepped into the crowd and was gone, swallowed into the rolling mass of people as though he had simply blinked out of existence.

# EIGHTEEN

$\mathcal{L}$ILY KNEW ONE PLACE where she would certainly be able to learn more about scrying and the Wine of Jurema, the two methods of provoking a vision that Robert Ash had mentioned during their talk.

The enormous library at The Refuge.

She would not go.

She knew what Ash wanted of her. Though he had not pushed the issue, Lily had no doubt that his goal was to lure her to join Strangford and Sam and who-knew-what others under his tutelage, where she would be guided along a years-long path of discipline and study that would eventually see her reaching some mystical state of perfect acceptance of who and what she was.

That wasn't going to happen.

Lily would never be at peace with what she could do. How could she? What sort of person could make peace with a power that showed them the worst the future had in store without granting them the ability to change it?

Perhaps it did have another purpose, as Ash had suggested. But if whatever higher power was pulling the strings didn't stoop to share the plan with Lily, she felt under no obligation to play along.

No, she wouldn't be going back to The Refuge, not if it could possibly be avoided. She was certain there was somewhere else in London she could come by the knowledge she needed.

After Ash had deserted her on Tottenham Court Road, she headed directly to Guildhall Library, a space she was certain had been designed to intimidate the less-than-scholarly. The massive collection was housed in a building modeled after a cathedral, complete with soaring, buttressed ceiling and naves lined with shelves instead of saints.

The catalog had no entry for the Wine of Jurema, nor did it offer a lead on scrying. She had better luck when she pressed a flustered librarian directly.

"If we had anything on that, it would be filed under folklore," he said. "But we don't. Perhaps if you made an application to one of the learned societies . . . presuming, of course, that your project is of sufficient scholarly value," he added, with a skeptical look at her fashionable walking dress.

Lily was quite certain no learned society would find her current project sufficiently scholarly. Thankfully, she knew of a folklore archive that did not require a letter of introduction for her to access.

She need only knock on the door.

—

A crisp, clear evening had fallen over the city as Lily climbed the steps of her building on March Place. The bite in the air tasted far more of winter than spring.

The chill cutting through the fabric of her gown lent a greater urgency to her task.

She quickly climbed to the first landing and rapped at the door.

"Who's there?"

Estelle's tone was uncharacteristically sharp.

"It's me," Lily called in reply.

The door flew open. Estelle was wrapped in her dressing gown. Her ubiquitous turban was missing, revealing a cap of thin brown hair cut as short as a boy's, streaked with gray. She had applied a bit of cosmetics to one of her eyes but not the other.

"In, quickly."

Lily darted through the door, which Estelle slammed shut behind her. Lily envisioned Mrs. Bramble glaring up at them through the floor.

"Sorry, darling. I thought you were one of *them*," Estelle explained, striding across the drawing room to the hall, leaving Lily to follow in her wake.

"One of who?"

"The guests! They're not supposed to be here for at least another hour, but it wouldn't be the first time one took it in his head to pop in early. I'm usually dressed by now, but that bother with the billows this morning put me behind."

Of course—the séance. Lily had nearly forgotten that Estelle was hosting one of her events that evening.

"So you see, darling, I'd love nothing more than to visit over a little vermouth, but I'm afraid I'm in rather a rush at the moment."

"Actually, I came to call on Miss Bard. But if it's a bad time . . ."

"Gwendolyn? Oh, no—she's just holed up in the study, playing with those gruesome little dolls of hers. I don't know how I could find a place for them out here that won't have house guests shrieking and dropping their glasses."

"They are meant for study, not decor. As I have told you several times before." Miss Bard's voice rang out cheerfully from the room at the far end of the hall.

"You could at least study something less macabre," Estelle retorted.

"Says the woman who speaks to the dead for a living."

"The dead aren't macabre. They're mostly just confused, the poor dears."

Miss Bard appeared in the doorway.

"Do come in, Miss Albright. Let us leave Miss Deneuve to prepare for her performance."

The folklorist's study was a tiny space, little bigger than a dressing room. The dimensions were made more narrow by the bookshelves which lined every wall from floor to ceiling. A single window let in the last of the evening light, but the gaslights mounted on the walls banished the rest of the gloom.

The shelves were heavy with volumes packed together with stacks of journals, bound papers, and sturdy cardboard boxes. Several such boxes were scattered about the table that served as Miss Bard's desk. Tucked inside, resting in nests of tissue paper, were the "gruesome little dolls" Estelle had mentioned.

"Isn't that Punch?" Lily asked, surprised, recognizing the puppet's characteristic hooked red nose and peaked cap.

"It is indeed. A complete set of the characters. I had it off an estate sale in Buckinghamshire—the gentleman's father was a Professor who performed the show as far off as Glasgow. The figures must date to the late 18th century. They are in remarkably good shape, except for our friend Jack Ketch. He's nearly lost his arm. Can't have a one-armed hangman, can we?"

"Are you starting a puppet theatre?"

"Oh, no!" Miss Bard chuckled.

"Then what will you do with them?"

"Not set them out in the drawing room, apparently. Though I certainly never intended to. None of my collections are intended for display, though Miss Deneuve does insist on reviewing them in case she finds something to liven up the mantle. I'm relieved she decided these weren't to her taste. They really ought to be kept out of direct sunlight as much as possible."

"So you are studying Punch and Judy?"

"Indeed I am."

"But what do Punch and Judy have to do with folklore?"

"Goodness!" Miss Bard exclaimed, smiling. She put another stitch into the black-cloaked hangman, tugging the thread tight. "The narrative is simply packed with Old Britain. I mean, there are still clear connections to the Italian source material, but that couldn't have remained intact for very long. Now it's all trickster archetypes and ritual sacrifice. Anyone who doesn't peg Crocodile for the dragon of the medieval mystery plays clearly hasn't read their York Cycle. Never mind all that death and resurrection . . . they might as well just make the figures out of corn and call them the harvest gods."

"I see," Lily replied, her own lack of familiarity with mystery plays and harvest gods leaving her unqualified to make any further comment on the matter.

Miss Bard didn't seem to mind. She snipped her thread, then set Jack Ketch down in his box, popping the lid on over his masked face.

"I rather doubt you stopped by just to have your ear chewed off about the syncretism of traditional English entertainments. So tell me, how can I help you?"

Lily crossed her legs, adopting a casual tone.

"Are you by any chance familiar with the term 'scrying'?"

"Of course I'm familiar with it," Miss Bard exclaimed. "It's hardly obscure. How could it be? It's still practiced by nearly every adolescent female in Britain at some point or another."

"It is?" Lily didn't bother to hide her surprise. "But they didn't have an entry for it at Guildhall."

"Oh? A prestigious collection curated by eminent men did not cover a practice that largely belongs to women and young girls? How very surprising." Miss Bard's tone was droll. "When you were a girl, were you ever told that if you lit a candle in front of a glass on Halloween night and gazed at your reflection, you'd see the man you were going to marry?"

Lily hadn't been told that, but she had overheard similar tales being passed between other girls at Miss Finch's. Presumably, they hadn't thought Lily would have any need for it, as she couldn't possibly marry anyone worth the trouble.

"That's scrying. Watered down, of course, and narrowed in scope to the question of marriage—the only thing young women are permitted to find of importance in today's society. But still very much a survival of the more ancient practice."

"Which I assume had to do with more than husband-hunting?"

"Oh yes. Most certainly. Scrying means, quite literally, to gaze. That's more or less all it is—gazing. It can be done in any reflective surface. An oiled plate of brass. A crystal ball. A still pond. A mirror. A bowl full of water."

"A bowl of water?" she blurted.

The morning she had seen Estelle's death . . . Lily had been standing at her washbasin. She had been about to wash her face, but something about the shimmer of the early morning light on the water caught her eye, making her pause for a moment, and then . . .

Then she had slipped into a vision.

"Certainly," Miss Bard replied. "That would have been very common in ancient times. Bowls were likely made specially for that purpose out of precious metals, to make the liquid within even more reflective."

Scrying. She had been doing it without even knowing. But she had washed at that basin hundreds of times before. What made it different this time?

*They are not sneezes. They are emanations from the source of all meaning in this universe, and as such, they are infused with purpose.*

Lily pushed Ash's words from her mind. She couldn't afford to wait for an emanation.

"How do you get it started?"

"There's not much of a trick to it. Oh, some of the old stories had you climbing backwards up the stairs before you begin, or waving a candle in front of a mirror and chanting 'Bloody Mary'. But that's really another thing entirely—a summoning. No . . . for scrying, it's simply a matter of entering the right state of mind. Sometimes a candle or some other source of light serves as a focal. You watch it, in silence, until some other fire appears in the glass and the truth opens up to you."

*A fire in the glass . . .*

Lily tried to hide her disappointment. This didn't sound like a reliable method for achieving her goal. To simply sit in front of a mirror . . . she'd done that a thousand times in her life and almost never had it resulted in an incident of foresight. There was nothing in what Miss Bard was describing that promised more control of what a vision might show her. Too much was still left to . . . what had Ash called it? The Parliament of Stars.

Lily wasn't feeling well inclined toward the stars at the moment.

"So that's it, then? Just sitting in front of a mirror and . . . looking."

"Precisely." Miss Bard smiled. "You're not trying to figure out what your future husband will look like, are you?"

"No," Lily replied quickly. "I most certainly am not."

"Has it anything to do with why you're worried about Miss Deneuve?"

Miss Bard's tone was casual, but Lily's senses sharpened.

The older woman smiled. Her smile was always rather pretty, plump and full. Lily could now see how it was also threaded through with tension, worry tugging at the fine lines around her bright brown eyes.

"You must know that Miss Deneuve is . . ." Her voice hitched for a note. "That she is the most important person in the world to me. You are a fair actress, Miss Albright, but I am particularly sensitive to any indication of a threat to her. I can hear it in your voice when you speak of her. I suppose I must assume that you have good reason to keep the nature of this threat to yourself?"

Lily swallowed thickly.

"I'm . . . sorry."

"I see."

The folklorist cleared her throat. She picked the box with the hangman up from the table and slid it into its place on her shelves.

"I hope it is understood that if there is any other way in which I might be of assistance, you need only ask."

Lily stood.

There were so many things she wanted to say, promises that ached to pour from her lips, offering some kind of explanation or solace.

She kept her mouth shut.

There was only one vow she could make. *I will do everything in my power to stop it.* But was that true? Would she really do all that she was capable of in order to save Estelle?

Or would the fear, all the years of guilt and grief, get the better of her?

"Thank you for your time," she said, the words flat and rote.

Miss Bard reached out. She clasped Lily's hand, squeezing it firmly.

"Of course," she replied.

Lily left.

She walked down the hall, forcing herself not to dash. She told herself that she was not afraid to run into Estelle, that she would be perfectly capable of concealing the tumult of emotion rioting through her.

She was halfway there when a knock sounded at the front door.

"Drat," Estelle swore, popping her head out of the bedroom. Her turban was back in place, and her eyes symmetrically lined, but she was still shrugging into an elaborate robe. "Darling, could you do me the enormous favor of playing hostess for a moment? Roger is running late."

"The paperboy?" Lily asked in surprise, thinking of the plump adolescent who routinely shouted the headlines outside their windows.

"I know. I had the most marvelously dour young man—looked like a funeral director. But he's gone and twisted his ankle. Please?"

"Certainly."

Estelle disappeared into the bedroom again. Lily made her way through the parlor.

There had been no further knocking. She wondered if perhaps the one they'd heard had been a mistake and that she would find herself facing an empty hallway.

She opened the door.

A man waited patiently on the threshold. He was not what Lily would have expected at a séance. There was no black armband, no weeping widow at his side. He looked perfectly ordinary and well-groomed, with carefully combed brown hair, a clear complexion and a waxed mustache. Something about him made her feel as though she had seen him before—but then again, he had the sort of face one seemed to see a dozen times a day on any London street.

"Good evening," he said. "I hope I am not too early."

"I haven't the foggiest idea," Lily admitted impatiently, "but do come in."

He was contemplating the straw goat head by the coat rack when Roger dashed into the room.

"I'm late, aren't I?" he gasped, bending over. "That's a dashed lot of stairs. Had to go back for a second round of papers tonight. The headline was a real corker. They're bringing some toff up on a murder charge. They put him up on the box just like our lot. The punters are wild for it."

Lily felt the floor sink from under her feet.

"Do you mean Lord Deveral?"

"That's him. They held his indictment today. They're moving on with it right sharpish—set his arraignment for less than a fortnight."

"What date?" Lily demanded. She glanced over at the mustachioed séance-goer, afraid the sharpness of her tone might have caught his ear, but he continued to look engrossed in the goat head.

"March 8th," Roger replied, unperturbed. "I'll have an extra shilling or two in my pocket over it. There's a bit of luck!"

March 8th. Ten days.

It was just the arraignment, Lily reminded herself. A full trial in the House of Lords would still follow, and perhaps even a round of appeals before her half-brother's neck met the noose.

The notion brought little comfort.

She was running out of time.

"See to the guests," Lily snapped in reply. She hurried into the hall, pushing past a pair of gossiping widows and quickly climbing the stairs.

~

Lily set her twenty-pound vanity mirror down on the floor, trying not to make too much of a thud.

The ground seemed a safer place to attempt this than a chair. Her parlor, where she had dragged the mirror, was also further from Estelle's séance room, which made it less likely Lily would be disturbed by gasps and clatter of the orchestra in the wardrobe.

She leaned the big looking-glass against the wall.

The room was dark. Once she had made certain that Cat was not hiding somewhere nearby, she had killed the gas lights and drawn the curtains, leaving only a single candle for illumination. It burned in a holder on the windowsill, casting flickering shadows over the familiar shapes of the room—the bookcase, the umbrella stand. The chair where her father had sat the morning before.

She collected the candle and set it down on the ground in front of the glass, then knelt behind it.

Was this really it? It didn't seem like enough. A more elaborate ritual would have given her greater confidence. A methodology that seemed to rely entirely on Lily's capacity for sitting quietly and concentrating stood on shaky ground.

Perhaps she should try chanting "Bloody Mary".

She stared at the reflected flame and waited.

There was a murmur of voices from the hall downstairs. A door closed, the sound muffled by distance.

In the mirror, Lily's face looked pale, lost in an enshrouding darkness.

The candle burned steadily. She felt a cramp start in her foot. She shifted, trying to get more comfortable.

Nothing continued to happen.

This was madness. What was she doing? Spending her evening sitting on the floor, staring at her vanity mirror. It was a colossal waste of time—time she didn't have.

What was worse—wasting time? Or risking that this endeavor might actually succeed?

She was asking for a vision—asking for one, after spending most of the years since her mother's death fighting tooth and nail to push the blasted things away. What if she got what she came for?

There was no way for her to direct her precognition. She couldn't ensure that she saw only what she wanted, a clue that would point her to the true identity of the killer. Instead, she might open herself up to a vision of some new disaster, another tragedy she would be powerless to avert—more grief and guilt and helplessness to be heaped on her plate.

She should forget all of this and walk away right now. Ignite the lights, put on a phonograph and pretend she'd never heard of any of it.

The cold seeped up through the floor, crawling through the thin carpet and the fabric of her skirts to settle in her knees.

Before her, the flame danced, the light echoed in the dark glass.

She closed her eyes.

Strangford. Abney Park. Lily's thoughts went back to the sight of him crouching in Sylvia Durst's grave, his pale hands, so terribly vulnerable, resting on her corpse. He had risked so much on the chance it might reveal some sliver of useful information, some way of determining who was at the center of this.

Avoiding more guilt was a poor reason to refuse to take a lesser chance herself.

She would do this. She owed it to him, no matter what it cost her.

Lily opened her eyes to see that the fire in the glass had moved.

It was set against the wall behind her and burned more brightly, framed by the glass of a gas fixture. A shadow passed across it, and Lily glanced up, pausing in the act of brushing her hair. Her nightgown was open at the throat, exposing the skin of her collarbone.

She resumed, the bristles sliding through long waves of unbound auburn.

Strangford stepped into view.

He was naked to the waist, all dark hair and lean muscle—beautiful, as she had known he would be, when stripped of even more of his armor.

His bare fingers brushed her neck. They slid down the column of pale flesh, grazed along her shoulder. His touch was electric, the fire of it tingling across her skin, casting sparks down into her core.

Lily tilted her head back, letting herself fall against him as his hands roamed down her body, tangling her in a hot embrace. Desire rose in her, fierce and urgent.

*No,* she thought, summoning the will to fight against it. This couldn't happen. It would end in hurt, in heartbreak.

This wasn't what she wanted. She was here for another reason. She framed that need into a demand, clutched at it against the tumult of emotion raised by the feeling of Strangford's hands dancing over her body.

*Show me who will hurt Estelle.*

She felt the chill seeping back into her knees. It tugged her out of the trance and back into herself. She focused her gaze on the flicker of the candle, ignoring the two figures entwined behind it.

The flame guttered, hissing against some impurity in the wax. It rose up again, illuminating crimson wallpaper and the edge of a gilded frame.

The city's finest, in their silks and tails, drifted around the room like debris stirring in some unseen current. Conversation burbled. Waiters carried trays of champagne and the art on the walls favored dull landscapes by dull dead men, with the occasional interspersing of something more daring.

She had been here before. It was the Carfax Gallery. A vision or a memory? The future or the past?

*You play well, Miss Albright.*

Dr. Joseph Hartwell—eminent physician, eugenicist, and spurned fiancé—stood before her, polished in his coat and tails. He held a crystal glass in his hand.

The noise of the crowd battered at her, making it hard to think. She reached for an anchor, something that would help her root herself in the midst of the whirling bodies.

*Strangford . . .*

He wasn't there. He had just walked away, following the curator to his office to sign the paperwork for the purchase of Evangeline Ash's portrait.

A feminine laugh sounded behind her—familiar, bell-like in its clarity.

Her skin crawled.

Annalise Boyden. She was here—and in a few hours, she would be dead.

Lily turned, searching the crowd frantically. If she could find her, warn her . . .

Flashes of a shocking white gown teased her from the corners of her vision, then danced away again.

The patrons of the gallery shifted, turning. Lily realized their movements weren't random, but regular, like the clicking progression of gears in an automata. Where faces should have been, there was nothing but paint and plaster, tawdry theatre masks chipping paint onto the plush carpeting.

They were false, every one of them, from the railroad baron to the caterer with his plate of canapes, all except the man who stood at the far side of the room, as still as stone in the middle of the eddying bodies. His gaze cut through the crowd to find her, carrying enough hostility to take her breath away.

Her brother.

*It will never happen.*

The words took form in the air, crossing the room to pierce her like daggers.

She turned away from the blow and there was Evangeline Ash.

The dead woman looked down at her from her portrait, serene, locked behind oil and pigment, but this wasn't the painting Lily had seen before. Something had changed.

It was the lilies. The bright blooms that had burst from the vase at the artist's side before were crushed now, blooms battered as though torn apart by vicious hands. Bruised petals covered the ground, bent stems hanging over the sides of the elegant porcelain.

Letters had fallen from the banner she held in her hands, the black characters drifting down to the bottom of the frame. Only a handful remained, the message they spelled made that much more stark.

*Danger.*

Hartwell lifted his glass. His face cracked, bits of flesh flaking like old paint.

*You may find our next match more challenging.*

The flute was no longer full of champagne. It brimmed crimson, thick, warm enough to fog the rim. The doctor drank, pouring rich, fresh blood into his mouth . . . drank and drank as the glass refused to go empty. All the painted faces in the room turned to watch, then stepped forward, their flat black eyes fixing on Lily.

*Go. Now.*

The thought was desperate, as clear as Annalise Boyden's laugh.

The word in Evangeline Ash's hands vibrated with intensity. Lily fought for escape as the masked horde pressed closer.

*Get out of here. Now. NOW.*

She was gone.

The air around her was cold, sharp with a London winter. The acrid scent it carried burned her nose, harsh with smoke.

She stood on a deserted street under a starless sky, the city sprawled and sleeping around her.

The building in front of her was long, taking up the full length of the block. It lay silent, windows dark, with the feel of a place closed for more than just the night. The limestone blocks were stained with soot.

It could have been any of a hundred such buildings in the city. An accounting firm, or an insurer—a place so nondescript, it almost seemed to fade as she looked at it, slipping out of focus.

Where was she? Why had she come here?

Something moved.

Her attention locked on the source, a glow in one of the windows. The glass was cracked and stained but behind it, something flickered, a dancing orange light.

Flame.

The building was on fire.

She could almost feel it, the blast of sudden heat, but the air was still cold, still winter crisp, and there was none of the roar and crackle of flames. No smoke poured from the roof, no onlookers crowding onto the curb to watch the show, as they would with any proper London fire.

Yet the flames still flickered in the glass. They glowed in not just one window, but all of them, the same hungry glare dancing before her, mirrored a dozen times over.

Mirrored . . .

Reflections. It wasn't this building that was burning. It was somewhere else, someplace close by, the conflagration echoed in all those panes of glass.

A clatter of hooves broke her concentration, pulling her gaze from the building to the deserted street.

Not entirely deserted.

A single sheep trotted toward her down the empty road. It shone in the darkness, its wool gleaming like spun gold.

"Bitter," it bleated as it hurried past her. "Bitter. Bitter."

Bells rang out, shattering the silence. Their clear sound sparkled through the winter air.

Lily knew that sound. The tones were familiar. If she could just place it . . .

Something rustled overhead.

A raven sat at the pinnacle of the roof. It looked down at her, tilting its head, black eyes glittering with dark intelligence.

It ruffled its feathers again, then burst into flight—not one raven, but five. Ten. Dozens, a wave of ravens, rising from the roof to obscure the sky. They arrowed south, moving with fierce purpose.

What was the collective name for ravens?

The thought was vague, inconsequential, but it tugged at her, refusing to be set aside.

Then the answer clicked into place.

Murder. It was called a murder.

The murder dove, consuming her in a whirlwind of sharp beaks and black feathers. Lily threw up her hands to protect herself and felt the burn of hot wax as the candle clattered to the ground.

The flame guttered, then blinked out, leaving her in darkness.

A soft chorus of gasps rose up through the floorboards, Estelle's séance-goers reacting to some manufactured wonder. The smell of dust mingled with the mineral scent of snuffed candle.

Lily crawled to the window. She rose and pushed back the curtains, letting the soft blue moonlight filter down into the room, making it once again the familiar space she knew.

For good measure, she lowered the surface of the looking-glass down onto the rug.

Hartwell.

Why had the vision taken her back to her encounter with him? It might be because he was the killer she sought . . . or it might have been warning her of some other impending horror he would be involved with. Another disaster she would be incapable of preventing.

The flames in the windows and the bleating sheep were inscrutable signs, offering her nothing concrete that she could grasp onto.

Her visions had always been like that, full of useless vagaries and dream-like distortions that offered any number of interpretations. They were useless. They had always been useless.

The frustration burned hotter than the wax on her hand. How could she have ever believed it might be different? Once again she was left with nothing but a pile of symbols and guesses that made her feel like she was moving blindly through darkness.

No, she protested. There had to be something here, a lead she could grasp on to even if she was taking the chance of being pulled in the wrong direction. She had run out of other options.

She forced herself to concentrate on that bland building, on the ravens and the sheep with its shining coat. The bells . . .

Of course.

Lily knew those bells. They could be heard echoing across the river from the tower of Southwark Cathedral, which Lily, like many other Londoners, still knew by its old name of St. Saviour's.

The building from her vision was across the Thames in Southwark. Would it grant her answers or only more unwelcome questions?

There was only one way to find out.

# NINETEEN

*T*HE PUNGENT SCENT OF the Thames at low tide rose up to meet her as the omnibus clattered over London Bridge, crossing into Southwark.

The jolting movement felt too slow. Lily longed for her Triumph and the quick, nimble way it might weave through the traffic that crowded the city's streets. She had never brought it into London before, preferring the fresh air and open roads of the heath for her rides, but it seemed to her now that the motorcycle might serve a more practical function—at least if she would be spending much more time crisscrossing the city chasing rumors and shadows.

Southwark Cathedral loomed before her over a sprawl of low buildings, its bells hanging still and silent.

She left the omnibus at the Borough Market. The street bustled with shoppers and vendors, the air rich with the moist, yeasty aroma of the neighboring brewery. Further back, the iron girders of the gasometer rose over the buildings like an elegant modern sculpture punctuated by tall smokestacks. Coal smoke mingled with aromas of grilling sausages, old onions, and fresh haddock.

The noise was a rich blanket, woven with brash laughter, factory whistles and the clang of machinery. It was very different from the bourgeois quiet of Bloomsbury, all polite murmurs and subdued footfalls.

She threaded her way through the crowd, walking stick tapping on the pavement and offering a touch of support against the lingering soreness in her leg. She moved past stalls selling oysters and sacks of flour, racks of hanging ducks and vats of writhing eels. Apple cores crunched under her feet.

Which way should she go?

It was cold. The chill of the previous evening had carried over into the day and frost glittered on the rooftops. Winter lingered. Even if it hadn't—even if a sudden thaw promised there was more time before the killer reached Estelle, she had another reason for urgency now.

Lord Deveral's arraignment was only nine days away.

She thought back to the vision. The building she saw had not been on the river, but further back. There were no stalls or shops crowding against it. It had to be on one of Southwark's quieter streets, somewhere within range of the cathedral's bells.

It was too broad an area. It could take her days to cover all those lanes and byways. There had to be something more that she could use, some other clue she could draw on to narrow her search.

Then it came to her. In the vision, old soot stained the tops of the windows, relics of a past conflagration.

Fires were an event in London, both a danger and a terrible thrill. If the place had burned within the last few years, the natives of Southwark would remember it.

She stopped an elderly man with a loaf of bread tucked under his arm.

"Excuse me. Could you tell me if there's a building nearby that suffered a fire?"

He considered, chewing on a wad of tobacco.

"Which sort of building are you looking for? Church?"

"No."

"Warehouse?"

"No. Just an ordinary sort of building."

"House?"

"Bigger than a house."

"Hmph." He spat. "Don't know of any ordinary buildings 'as been burnt of late."

Lily fought not to show her frustration.

"I see. Thank you for your time."

"Unless you mean the hospital," he added as she turned to walk away.

Lily stopped.

"Hospital?"

"The ladies' clinic, by the Golden Fleece." The word *ladies* rang slightly off. Something had also shifted in the way he looked at her, as though Lily had offended him but he was too polite to say.

Lily thought of the gleaming sheep she had seen in her vision.

"The Golden Fleece?"

"Aye. The public house."

*Bitter.*

That was the word the gilded animal in her vision had called as it trotted past. Not an adjective, but a pint.

The Golden Fleece was a pub.

—

The old man's directions took her past the market and down Borough High Street, a busy thoroughfare where pipe-makers and cheese shops stood cheek-by-jowl with coffee houses and linen drapers. She paused for a moment in front of a confectionery, its window glittering with frosted delicacies. Behind her, carts rumbled past, punctuated by the hiss of the odd steam wagon.

The noise and bustle drifted into the background as she turned down a quieter street. She was close to the old Liberty of the Mint. Not long past, this had been a notorious slum, the sort of place respectable folk told tales of in order to frighten disobedient children. It had been mostly cleared, the tenements razed, but remnants of the old aura of the place remained.

The Golden Fleece announced itself to potential gin-guzzlers with wooden sign depicting a strapping young man in Greek armor holding what looked like a fuzzy gilded afghan. Past it, Lily found herself looking at the unremarkable facade of the building from her vision.

It sat across from the parochial school. At some point in its recent history, it had been thoroughly burnt. Soot stained the limestone above each window, the path of the smoke tapering like a Medieval banner. The windows of the upper floors were cracked or shattered while those of the lower level had been nailed over with boards. The front door hadn't opened in a very long time, judging by the weathering of the advertisements for hair pomade plastered over its surface.

Lily approached. She could see holes in the stone by the door where a plaque might once have hung, but there was nothing else to indicate what the building had once been, or why her vision would have drawn her here. It was just a shell, boarded up and abandoned, at the edge of a district once known for its pickpockets and cutthroats.

She felt the bite of frustration. How much energy should she devote to uncovering whatever secrets the building might hold, when she had no way of knowing that it was a genuine lead and not a useless distraction?

"If you've got yourself into a bit of trouble, you'll not find a way out in there."

The voice came from beside her. Lily turned to see a woman of middle years, plump as a baker's wife. Her cheeks were rosy in a way that required no powder, her ample figure squeezed into a corset that pushed some of her more substantial assets into prominence.

Lily took in the bright striped pink of her bodice, the skirt cut high over her ankles, and knew she was talking to a woman who made her living on her back.

"It's been closed six months now, ever since the blaze. But you'd not have wanted their help, even if it was to be had. Take my word on that."

The woman assessed the cut of her coat and the well-heeled quality of her boots.

"You from one of them fine houses? I thought they had quacks as came in to take care of any girls who got themselves up the spout."

Lily had spent enough time in the world of theatre—a realm heavily populated by women formerly of her interlocutor's occupation—to know what the lady meant. She had taken Lily for a denizen of some higher-end brothel who had been unfortunate enough to find herself pregnant and was seeking a way to end it.

Inside that building.

She made a quick decision.

"What's your name?"

"Berta," the whore replied. "After His Majesty."

"Berta, could I treat you to a gin?"

"What would you do that for?"

"I'd like to know what else you can tell me about this place."

Berta's gaze flickered from Lily to the burned-out shell they stood before.

"What's to know? There ain't nothing left of it now."

"I could pay you," Lily offered quietly. "Please. It's important."

Berta shrugged.

"Shilling for an hour."

—

The interior of the Golden Fleece was much as Lily might have anticipated—dark, low, and wreathed in tobacco smoke. She and Bertha were the only women inside, but the handful of men who lounged at the scattered tables gave them only a cursory glance before turning back to their ale. A lady in a public house would raise eyebrows, but a whore on the publican's bench was a common enough occurrence, particularly one frequented by types as rough as the men who lingered at the scratched wooden surface of the bar.

Berta led her unhesitatingly to a snug at the back, settling herself onto the bench. The coal stove nearby gave off a welcome heat. Lily tucked her walking stick against the seat, then unwound her scarf and unbuttoned her coat.

"You're not showing yet," Berta noted. "That's good. It goes easier if you take care of it early."

"How often have you had it done?" Lily asked.

"Just the once. But one hears about it from the other nuns, of course."

"And you had the procedure over there?" Lily nodded toward the far side of the street, where the boarded-up facade of the hospital was just visible through the glass of the pub's small window.

Berta nodded.

It was surprising. Lily had heard about abortions being performed before. Occasionally, an actress might find herself in that sort of trouble. But the procedures she knew of had taken place quietly, in private homes or even more out-of-the-way places. The clever or lucky found a midwife willing to do the deed. Those less fortunate resorted to barbers or persons even more poorly qualified. She knew of women who lost their lives as a result.

None of them reported having an abortion in a regular hospital. Ending a pregnancy carried with it a penalty of life in prison. What respectable physician would take such a risk?

Yet it was clear that, before it had burned, the building across the street had been a substantial and well-funded establishment.

It didn't make any sense.

The publican came over. He was an older man built as solid as a keg, his hair cut close around a balding pate.

"Berta," he said flatly.

"Hello, Art."

"I'll not have you working my room."

"We ain't here for tricks. Just two girls after a pint."

His sharp eyes moved from Berta to Lily, flickering over the fine cut of her dress.

"What'll it be?"

"Stout for me. And a sausage roll," Berta replied promptly.

"Lager, please," Lily said, handing him a few coins. She had no intention of drinking it but felt fairly certain that neglecting to order would render her even more suspicious in the publican's eyes.

"Right, then," he said after a brief but noticeable pause. Then he returned to the bar, where he picked up his conversation with a thin man in a brash gold waistcoat and bowler cap. The thin man noticed Lily's attention and flashed her a grin marked by a slight gap between his front teeth.

"Don't try to pick him up. That's Frank the Spiv. He ain't worth the dosh, trust me on that," Berta warned.

"I haven't the least inclination to do so," Lily replied honestly. She leaned back as their pints were set down on the table along with a greasy lump of sausage and pastry. Berta tore into it happily.

"Were there many girls who got help with that sort of trouble over there?" Lily nodded toward the hospital.

"It weren't like they advertised it, but word got round that a real doctor was doing the thing for charity, like."

"For charity? You mean you didn't have to pay?"

"That's right," Berta replied. "And if it sounds too good to be true, you can be sure it was."

The publican moved past as Berta spoke. He cast them a sharp glance. Lily lowered her own voice and waited until he had returned to Frank the Spiv at the bar before she continued.

"What do you mean? Did they not do as they'd promised, then?"

"Oh, no. They did it, right enough. Though for a while I did wonder."

"Why?"

"Well, there was a fair bit of bleeding . . . after, you know. Then I kept waiting for my monthlies to return. I started to think perhaps it had all been a lark and maybe I was still carrying that babe around after all. But I never felt it quicken and there weren't no swelling in my belly."

Lily frowned. This was not a symptom of the procedure she was familiar with. Then again, her knowledge of ridding oneself of a pregnancy was entirely composed of overheard snippets of conversation.

"So your cycles just . . . stopped? How long did that last for?"

"I'll let you know when I find out."

"You mean they still haven't resumed?"

"I know—sounds a right treat, don't it? Took me an age to convince my house that I could work right through the month. That's put an extra few quid in my pocket. But I mightn't have been so pleased if I thought I'd actually want a babe of my own someday."

Lily wondered if what Berta described was unusual. By some accounts, ending a pregnancy was neither safe nor easy—but then, she had heard others say the thing could be accomplished in less time than it took to pull a tooth.

She did not recall the ladies whispering backstage reporting an end to their female cycles as a result of the procedure. Something in Berta's account left her feeling uneasy, especially since the women treated at the wreck across the road would never have been able to appeal to the authorities if they felt they had been mistreated.

Who would the enforcers of the law have believed? The proprietors of a well-funded charity hospital or a batch of whores?

None of this went any way toward answering the more pressing question of whether the burnt-out building had some connection to the killer she sought.

"So you were inside the place, then," she pressed.

"Well, they hardly would've done it on the pavement, would they?"

"Can you tell me what it was like in there?"

Berta shrugged, looking a touch more uncomfortable.

"It was clean and all. Each patient in her own bed and the blankets fresh laundered. Everything very orderly."

"But outside you told me I'd not have wanted their help. What you're describing doesn't sound so terrible."

"Well—it weren't how they treated us that were up the spout. It was them others."

"Others?"

"The girls they put up in the East Wing."

"What happened in the East Wing?"

"I couldn't tell you. They kept it locked up tight as a drum. All the time I was there, I never saw a body come out of it. Just the orderlies, carrying bottles or linens and such. They said it was the ward for them as had the French disease, but it looked like a regular prison. I had it from an oyster girl who'd been in for a month—consumptive, she was. She told me any girls as were put in that part of the place never came out again. Not unless they was being carried to the bone yard." Berta lowered her voice. "She said you could hear screams sometimes, during the wee hours of the night. She didn't sleep well, you see. Once there was a great clatter at the door and she saw a girl pounding on the glass like she'd break through it with her bare hands if she could. Had sores on her face, she did, and burns all over her arms."

It made for a horrible tale, but the mention of the French disease gave Lily reason to pause.

Syphilis was a terrible illness. She knew something about its progression. There had been an old stage mistress during her theatre years who had been in the late stages of the disease. She'd been prone to irrational fits of rage or would make explicit and forceful sexual advances on horrified members of the crew. She'd been no use for her job but the owners kept her on regardless. It had been a pension of sorts, Lily realized, a way to keep her from rotting in the street while the rest of the crew simply worked around her.

The disease could also cause lesions. If the East Wing had indeed been a ward for patients with advanced syphilis, it was possible that

Berta's 'burns' were sores and that the locked door was justified for the safety of the other patients.

There was also no cure for it. If the hospital were only accepting women with the most dire or advanced cases, it was entirely plausible the patients were only discharged when dead.

To a frightened woman in pain in a hospital bed, it might have looked like a nightmarish conspiracy, but to undertake to treat such lost causes at all—and on charity—may have in fact been an act of great mercy.

"What about the fire?" Lily asked.

"It started there."

"In the East Wing?"

Berta lowered her voice.

"I heard it was a witch that done it. That they tried to lock her in so she turned herself into a witch-fire and burned the whole place up with her."

It was a fantastical story, clearly a new myth the denizens of the old Mint had cooked together from bits of rumors and third-hand story. It unsettled her nonetheless.

She remembered her vision, the flames flickering eerily in the smoke-stained glass of the windows. Those belonged to another fire, she knew, not the one that had ravaged the place. Her sight was directed forward, not back in time. And yet she found herself wondering about the locked doors Berta described. If the fire had, in fact, started in that wing of the building, what had happened to the patients kept inside? Had they been rescued . . . or forgotten, trapped and left to burn to cinders?

None of this told her why the place had shown up so prominently in her dark glass. All Berta's revelations pointed to past pain and suffering, not an imminent threat, and nothing in this linked the building to the dead mediums.

She thought of the scale of the building, how well-kept and well-funded it must have been.

"Berta . . . can you tell me anything about the doctor who treated you?"

"The lieutenant, you mean?"

"He was an officer?" Lily's surprise raised her voice a notch and earned her quick looks from Art the publican and Frank the Spiv at the bar.

"Well, 'lieutenant' ain't a Christian name, is it?"

"Were they all carrying rank?"

"No. Just him."

"Describe him for me," Lily demanded.

"I don't know . . . he was an ordinary looking sort of bloke. Brown-haired with a mustache."

Those were features that might apply to half the city's bankers or grocers.

"You never caught his name?"

"He weren't of much mind for chatter," Berta retorted. "Just did what needed to be done. But . . ."

"Yes?" Lily prompted, after her voice unexpectedly trailed off. "What is it?"

"Nothing, really. Except . . . There was something off about him. You know how it is. You don't make it long in our line of work unless you get a sense for it—those punters you'd best pass over even if there ain't nothing off about the look of them. Something about them makes your skin go all cold. You ever feel that, you tell 'em you're booked through the next fortnight, no matter what dosh they offer."

Lily understood exactly what the whore meant. The thought of it put in a chill in her even as she sat a few feet from the piping heat of the coal stove.

"He was like that, then? The lieutenant."

"He was," Berta answered. She took another draught from her glass. She had nearly finished her stout. "You see now why I told you, you didn't want none of their help? Better ask a cure of a butcher than that lot. It was God's own work that burned the place down, you ask me. God's own work."

"What about the supervising physician?" Lily asked quickly as Berta tossed back the last of her pint. "Surely someone must have mentioned him while you were there."

"You mean the toff who ran the place? Sure, he had his name in brass by the front door, like they all do."

"What was it?"

"Hartwell," Bertha replied, setting down her empty glass. "Bloke's name was Hartwell."

⁓

Hartwell. The eminent physician and eugenicist had been running a charity clinic for whores in the shadow of the old Mint. Lily considered it as she strode through Southwark after taking her leave of Berta, her walking stick rapping against the pavement.

The eugenicists considered women like Berta degenerates, a condition they believed hereditary. They had advocated that such women be refused the right to breed. So why would Hartwell, their leader, offer his services to the very people he believed should be weeded out of the future of the human race?

There was one obvious possibility, of course. Hartwell's clinic had been offering abortions. Lily found it hard to believe that the doctor did so out of sympathy for the plight of unfortunate women who lacked the means to support a child.

It fit too neatly into his scheme for that.

The thought made her sick.

But what about the syphilis patients? Providing free services to whores with an incurable illness didn't fit so neatly into Hartwell's philosophy.

She searched for a way to connect what she'd learned to the murders. Did any of the activities Berta had described at the clinic explain why a prominent physician would go about stealing the blood of mediums?

The answer was no.

Her suspicion of Hartwell was deepening but there were still too many missing pieces. None of it made any sense.

Lily was still struggling with that when she became aware that someone was about to walk around the corner.

The knowledge was something more than an instinct, a spark of insight that rang with the same urgent tone as one of her visions.

The shock of it made her halt mid-step. Then she watched as a tall, thin figure emerged at the end of the lane and turned toward her.

It was the flash dresser from the bar, the one Berta had called Frank the Spiv, his gold waistcoat framed by a bright blue jacket.

It might have been a coincidence. Anyone leaving the Golden

Fleece and heading for the market or the bridge would have walked the same way. Still, living as a single woman in London for years had ingrained a habit of caution in such matters.

Lily turned away from the busy traffic of Borough High Street, moving down one of Southwark's quieter byway.

She walked past the long brick facades of warehouses to an empty lot ringed by a high iron fence. A few bright rags tied to the iron bars gave the place away. Lily had found her way to the old burying ground, the patch of earth that had served, for a century, as the unconsecrated grave of Southwark's prostitutes, thieves and suicides.

There were no carriages here, no shoppers with baskets full of fish and bread. The street was broad but deserted.

Perfect.

Lily stopped in the center of the lane and waited.

A moment later, Frank the Spiv turned the corner.

Sunlight reflected off his polished brogues. One could almost make the mistake of assuming that a man with such well shined shoes would be hesitant to get his hands dirty.

Lily knew better.

"You're a curious thing, aren't you?" he said. He took a toothpick from his pocket and set it between his teeth. "Asking all sorts of questions."

She felt her senses sharpen, her pulse kicking up. Her muscles wanted to tense. She didn't let them.

It had been some time since she'd had to do this. The streets of Bloomsbury weren't exactly rife with thugs looking to take advantage of a woman walking alone.

She hoped she still remembered how.

"What's your interest in it?" she demanded.

"I've been asked to see that you're discouraged from making further inquiries about goings-on in our little corner. Now that's a simple enough thing, isn't it?"

Was it simply a rote response to nosy newcomers in this corner of London? Lily dismissed the notion. This close to the market and the shops on Borough High Street, there would be new faces coming in and out of the area all the time.

This was something else.

Her thoughts flew back to the way the publican had glanced at her when he passed their table as Berta shared her tales of the hospital.

He had gone directly from there to the bar, where the man in front of her had been sitting . . . sitting without any glass in front of him, Lily realized as she recalled the scene. That meant he wasn't at the pub as a patron but for some other business.

It had to be about the hospital. There were secrets there still worth protecting, even though there was nothing left of the place but a burnt-out shell.

*I've been asked to see you're discouraged.*

It begged the question of who had done the asking.

Lily didn't imagine Frank the Spiv would be forthcoming with that information.

"It's rude to eavesdrop," she retorted, shifting the brass knob of her walking stick from her right hand to her left.

"Pity. I hoped you'd be a quicker study. It would have made this a more pleasant exchange."

"Is it to become unpleasant, then?"

"I need to give you a little scare, is all. Nothing too harsh. Just to be sure I've made my point."

He moved in. He was quick, as Lily had expected he would be.

She flipped up the walking stick, catching the center of the solid length of it in her right hand. Then she snapped the wood at the arms reaching for her throat.

She felt the yew vibrate with the energy of the impact.

Her attacker pulled back, cursing, rubbing his forearm. A more violent light came into his eye.

Next would come a grab for her stick. She made a quick mental rehearsal.

*Push with the right, pull with the left . . .*

He snatched at it, hands closing around the far end, which Lily deliberately left closer to him. Before he could yank it from her grasp, she twisted the staff, forcing his arms into a cross, then levered it down until he released it.

Now, to put a point on the matter.

She snapped the end the staff against his nose.

Blood splattered across the shimmering gold of his waistcoat. He clutched at his face, spinning back. His gaze was murderous above his hands.

She saw the war in him, the ferocious desire to hurt her battling against the knowledge that for the moment, he was outmatched.

He had come alone and unarmed, expecting her to be an easy mark.

He lowered his hands. She could see the new bend to his nose and knew that she had broken it.

"You should take care of that," Lily noted politely, the stick still posed and ready in her hands.

She waited for his answer, heart thudding.

He spat a mouthful of blood onto the pavement at her feet, following it with a curse vile enough to make a sailor blush.

Then he walked away.

# TWENTY

$\mathcal{T}$HE OMNIBUS SWAYED AROUND a corner, Lily shifting her weight to keep from falling into the lap of a portly vicar.

The traffic was thicker than it ought to be at this time of day, the vehicle inching along through a snarl of restless horses and motorcars. It made the trip back from Southwark far longer than it should have been. And for what?

Nothing but more questions.

Those questions left her trapped in a different sort of snarl, a limbo of indecision. Should she keep pursuing the truth about Hartwell's activities at the hospital, knowing there was a very real possibility it was only a distraction from her more urgent purpose? What other course of action could she take, with no real leads on the table?

She still hadn't settled on an answer when she exited the bus on Tottenham Court Road and made her way back to March Place.

The front hall smelled of beans. Lily had missed lunch. She didn't mind that terribly. Frustration and exhaustion had sapped her appetite.

There was a card on the table by the door.

*Lord Strangford, 14 Sussex Court*

The top right corner had been turned down, indicating he had called in person.

Lily felt a quick jab of guilt. She had not contacted him since the night of their visit to Lord Deveral's house—the night they had been caught in the rain and had ended up alone together in the warm darkness of Bramble's kitchen.

Perhaps she should have called to update him on her progress. Then again, what progress had she made? It was all trial and conjecture, nothing of substance. Surely it was better that she didn't disturb him if she had nothing of substance to report.

It was a fair enough excuse, though Lily knew she was really avoiding a visit to Bayswater for other reasons.

She was falling for him, and she knew it would lead to disaster.

Staying away was her only line of defense.

She plucked the card from the tray and buried it in her pocket.

In her distracted state as she climbed the stairs, she failed to think of the betraying creak of the boards outside Estelle's door.

They squealed under her weight, announcing her presence to anyone within a quarter-mile.

The house remained silent, even though Estelle's door hung slightly ajar.

That was odd.

The empty flat upstairs could wait, she supposed. Lily turned and pushed open the door.

"Estelle?" she called.

The drawing room was empty, the lamps unlit. The soft gray light through the windows made everything seem exceptionally still. The straw goat head and the ugly green urn with its squatting Shi Tzu—which Estelle had placed on an accent table by the hall—had the air of artifacts in some long-sealed tomb.

Lily felt a quick panic, an irrational fear that something terrible had happened. She knew it was not so. Though the day was sharply cold, it wasn't snowing. The danger she horribly anticipated could not have come to pass—not yet—but Lily couldn't resist the urge to check.

She stepped inside.

On the far side of the room, she could now see that a low but warmer light seeped through the crack under the door to Estelle's séance chamber.

Lily walked over and knocked.

"Come in."

Estelle sounded tired but very much alive.

"Shut the door again, would you?" the older woman asked as Lily entered the room.

Lily obeyed, then turned to find herself enveloped in another world.

The room was dark save for the flickering of a single candle on the great wooden table. Shadows lingered in the corners while threads of gold in the hangings that draped the walls and ceiling picked up the fragile light and shimmered, making Lily feel a bit as though she were enveloped in stars. It smelled of hot wax and just a hint of machine oil.

Estelle sat at the table. Her fine brown hair was uncovered, her eyes scrubbed free of cosmetics. She wore a simple pale blue robe, a garment far less exotic than her usual attire. It made her seem uncharacteristically ordinary, but in her unadorned state, the fine structure of her cheekbones and the elegant length of her neck were more apparent.

"Desdemona needs to be recalibrated," she announced.

She flipped a switch under the table and the projection of the odalisque flared to life against the curtains. Then the dark fabric began to move, the veiled figure shimmering along its surface. Lily could hear the subtle hiss of the bellows and knew that Estelle must be working the wire under the table with her foot.

"Did the séance not go well last night?" she asked.

"Oh, it went well enough. There were several delightful shrieks when she made her appearance. It just seemed to me she was jiggling like a bowl of gelatin when she should be undulating. Of course, that bit of espionage might have thrown me off."

"Espionage?"

"I had a competitor at my table last night." Estelle's tone dripped with disapproval.

"Someone you knew?"

"No. I had never met the fellow before."

"So he just told you that he was a rival?"

"He wasn't as brazen as that."

"Then how did you know?"

"Darling, I'm well aware when I'm in the presence of another person who can see the dead."

In the still, dark atmosphere of the séance room, Estelle's words evoked more of a chill than they would over vermouth in the parlor. Lily told herself it was a testament to the effectiveness of the decor.

"His powers weren't exceptionally strong," Estelle continued. "He was aware of some of the spirits in the room. I specifically saw him react to one lady's departed husband. But he seemed utterly oblivious to the ghost that was following him around all evening."

"How do you know it was following him?"

"Because she was hovering at his left shoulder," Estelle replied. "I could see her as clear as I'm looking at you now."

Lily felt uncomfortably aware of the presence of the veiled figure projected onto the now-still curtains behind her.

She tried to recall what Estelle had told her before about her methods of communicating with the dead. It had sounded much more abstract than what she was describing.

"Is that normal, then? For you to see them."

"No. It's quite unusual. Hers was just a particularly strong presence."

"It was a woman?"

"Oh, most definitely. A foreigner. She was muttering all through the séance in some incomprehensible language. And that, before you ask, is also very rare."

"Foreigners?"

"Language," Estelle replied. "The dead don't generally speak with words. It's all symbol and suggestion, like reading smoke signals. But I could hear this one and yet that fellow just sat there the whole time as if she wasn't hissing at his ear."

The image was a disturbing one.

A knock resounded, echoing solidly through the wood of the table.

"Quiet, Agnes," Estelle ordered.

"This competitor of yours. Who was he?"

"He gave me a name when he made the booking but I'm sure it was false. I'm fairly certain I'd never seen him before, though he did have a forgettable sort of face."

Something about Estelle's description of the man as 'forgettable' nagged at her.

"Dark eyes, brown hair, and a neat mustache?" she asked, taking a chance.

"There were two or three gentlemen there last night who could match that description," Estelle replied wryly.

"Arrived before everybody else?"

"That's the one."

Lily remembered the man she had let into the drawing room the night before. Yes, his was a forgettable face, yet something about him stuck in her memory. Maybe it was how engrossed he had seemed in Miss Bard's straw goat head.

*Something about them just makes your skin go cold . . .*

That was how Berta had described the sort of clients that a whore with hopes for longevity quickly learned to pass over. It was a characteristic she said had been true of the physician who treated her at Hartwell's clinic.

There had been something about the man in Estelle's parlor that put him in that same category. He was inexplicably unsettling.

"Do you think he'll be back?" Lily asked.

"I don't know. Any time another medium has turned up at one of my events before, she was usually trying to puzzle out how I pull off my little tricks. This fellow didn't seem particularly interested in them. Perhaps he was trying to gauge the quality of the competition before he set up his own shop."

The odalisque flickered. The effect startled Lily more than the moving curtain had, coming more unexpectedly.

Estelle reached under the table and flicked the switch for the magic lantern. The figure vanished. She rose, then moved to the curtains and threw them open. The magic of the room fled, the shimmering hangings and dark corners exposed to the harsh light of the day.

"Would you like to stay for a vermouth?"

"Another time, perhaps. I really ought to be going." Lily rose and moved toward the door.

"I'm not afraid to die, you know," Estelle said lightly.

Lily stopped. She turned toward the older woman, who stood by the edge of the window, the naked light falling across her unadorned features.

"Why do you say that?" she asked carefully.

"Because I know you've seen something. I make my living reading people, darling, both living and deceased. You are hardly a cipher."

Estelle's tone rang with certainty, leaving Lily sharply aware of how thin any attempt to deny it would sound.

That left her with nothing to offer but a stunned silence.

Estelle didn't seem to mind.

"I assume you've been trying to do something about it," she went on. "That has to be why you've been in and out at all hours of the day and night, when a week ago it was just the odd ride on the heath or jaunt to the theatre. And you've been keeping some very interesting company."

The glimmer in Estelle's eye made it clear she was talking about Lord Strangford. Lily thought guiltily of the card in her pocket.

"I'm not sure that I . . ."

"No. Don't," Estelle cut in, raising her hand. "I know you must have good reasons for not telling me the details. I didn't bring this up to press you. I just wanted you to know—in case it doesn't go so well—that . . . it's fine."

"Your dying," Lily clarified flatly.

"Yes."

"How can you say that?" She blurted, her anger quickening. "How can you say it would be fine?"

"Because I've been surrounded by it my entire life," Estelle replied simply. "It is not the least bit strange to me. It's only the unfamiliarity that gets us so riled up. That, and the people left behind. Death is much harder on the living."

Her anger rose. It was a palpable thing, one with a mind of its own, pushing her to be far bolder than she would otherwise choose. It searched for a target and settled on Estelle herself, however unfairly.

"So that's it, then."

"I thought it would serve as something of a comfort," Estelle replied wryly.

"No," Lily retorted. "It does not."

A tense silence stretched across the room.

There was so much more she should say. The words that had come out of her mouth felt unpleasant and insufficient, but a more eloquent and compassionate response refused to come. She was painfully aware that her opportunities to speak to the woman in front of her were almost certainly limited. She should at least apologize for the harshness of her tone.

"I'm afraid I must be going," she forced out.

"Of course," Estelle replied graciously, unperturbed.

"If you'll excuse me?"

She turned and left. She stalked through the drawing room and out onto Estelle's landing, shutting the door behind her.

Her hands were shaking. Was it anger, or regret, or something else? She felt torn, unsure of which way to turn. Part of her pulled to the right, wanting nothing more than to storm through her empty flat and collapse into bed.

The rest of her, the part quivering with outrage—it wanted to *do something.*

She was not angry at Estelle. Her fury belonged to the power that granted her these blasted visions, that moved lives around like pieces on some grand chessboard, part of a game with an end that Lily was not made privy to.

It continued to taunt her with visions she could do nothing about. She was mad—desperate with rage—that whatever plan it was executing this time involved the woman behind the door at her back being brutally murdered.

*Not this time.*

It was an impulsive thought, one that defied rationality. Every shred of logic, all her years of hard experience, told her that this battle was unwinnable.

It didn't matter.

She had been skimming around the truth for days, telling herself that her efforts were aimed at justice for Lord Deveral or for the women already murdered. That had never been anything but a cover.

This was about saving Estelle—about winning a battle with fate.

She knew it was lunacy, a cause with as little chance of success as Icarus trying to fly to the sun.

It didn't matter. She was going to try, using every resource at her disposal.

A wave of frustration shook her. Those resources looked desperately thin. She had only one lead and its link to the threat she sought to avert was beyond tenuous. It lay in an absurd faith that her visions had, for once, done what she asked of them.

She would pursue it anyway, right to the bitter end.

That meant she had a favor to ask of someone who had little reason to help her, but first she needed to make sure she was properly equipped for the coming war. There was something she needed to collect.

Lily turned left, striding down the stairs and pushing out the front door.

# TWENTY-ONE

$\mathscr{T}$HE BLOND-HAIRED MAN STANDING across from her building looked every inch the respectable city clerk, the sort who slaved over books ten hours a day for a boss who made six times his salary. He was too well-dressed to be a punter, too respectable to pass for a loafer. So why had he been lingering on the pavement for the past forty minutes?

She had never seen the fellow before. It didn't matter. When she spotted him outside her window after returning from her errand in Highgate, Lily's instincts asserted that he was there to watch her.

Having beaten a would-be assailant with her walking stick that morning made her less inclined to second-guess her paranoia.

It seemed impossible that she could have been followed that morning, particularly traveling by crowded omnibus—a ride she had barely caught, hopping on board just as it pulled away from the stop. So it was unlikely this surveillance related to her trip to the hospital in Southwark.

Whatever their reason for watching her, she had no intention of allowing herself to be tracked for the rest of this evening's activities. In fact, her success at what she had planned fairly depended on it.

Thankfully, that wouldn't be a problem.

⁓

The Triumph rested between the rusty pitchforks and underused rakes in her elderly neighbor's garden shed. It was a more humble accommodation for the machine than the bay she rented in Highgate.

She had retrieved the motorcycle that morning, taking a crowded tram to the edge of the heath. It sported a brand new chain, with little more than a few scratches on the green paint left to indicate what it had suffered.

The ride back into the city had been significantly faster than the trudge out.

Lily wheeled the Triumph out of the shed into the narrow alley that separated the buildings. She leaned over to tickle the carbs, then swung a trouser-clad leg over the side, put her feet to the pedals, and spun the engine to life.

She tore out onto March Place, feeling an inexpressibly deep sense of satisfaction at the shocked look on the face of the out-of-place clerk as she flew past him toward Gower Street.

It was almost too soon when she arrived at Bedford Square.

She stopped just shy of the square itself, turning into the mews that ran behind the elegant townhouses. She slid to a stop, propped the Triumph on its kickstand, then strode over and knocked firmly on the carriage house door.

"Sam?" she called.

There was no answer.

She tried the knob. It gave beneath her hand and she stepped inside.

The bay beside her was entirely taken up with the long, gleaming length of an enormous motorcar, shining like a silver ghost in the dim light of the carriage house. It was the Rolls Royce Sam had mentioned before. It appeared that the chauffeur had completed whatever maintenance had disabled it the night of Annalise Boyden's death.

She rolled the motorcycle inside, leaning it against the wall, then made her way past the silent length of the motorcar to the far door.

It opened onto an elegant garden that extended for the length of both of the townhouses that comprised The Refuge.

A path to her left led her to a set of steps that descended to a narrow wooden door set on the ground floor of the house. The window beside it was fogged, but Lily could see figures moving on the far side.

She hesitated. She had no notion what part of the house she

had come to. By all rights, she ought to hike back down the mews, around the corner, and up to the front door on Bedford Square, like any proper guest would.

Then again, she wasn't really a proper guest. She hadn't come to call on the master of the house.

She knocked.

The door swung open, revealing Cairncross in his shirtsleeves, a handkerchief tied over his nose and mouth, a jeweler's glass pushed up on his forehead.

"Miss Albright! What a delightful surprise. Do come in," he said, as though ladies he was acquainted with frequently showed up at the kitchen door wearing trousers.

An apothecary cabinet sat on the kitchen table. It looked scarred and battered. Many of the small jars and vials inside of it were cracked or completely broken.

Cairncross sat down in front of it, picked up a pair of tweezers and lowered the jeweler's glass. He continued picking what appeared to be tiny shards of broken glass out of a pile of pale tan powder on a tin baking sheet.

Mrs. Liu cast him a wicked look from where she stood at the stove. She rattled off a string of words. The language was unfamiliar, but the tone was clearly a scold.

"We have a guest, Mrs. Liu," Cairncross noted gently. "Our illustrious housekeeper is upset that I am playing with poison where she needs to roll noodles," he explained to Lily. "Some of these compounds were acquired from regions of the world that cannot be reached without taking a very long camel ride through the Hindu Kush," he continued, directing his tone to the older woman behind him as he evenly, slowly removed another splinter of glass from the powder. "I would prefer to salvage as much of them as possible and there is more light here than down in the vaults."

He sifted the tan substance with a razor, spreading it to a fine mist across the surface of the baking sheet as he studied it again with the jeweler's glass. Satisfied, he tapped it carefully onto a clean piece of paper. He then used that to funnel the stuff, which amounted to little more than a gram, into a new vial.

"There we are," he announced, popping the cork into place. He pulled the handkerchief down to his throat. "The blasted shelves rotted out in the cellar. There was a slow leak. The whole thing collapsed. I've no one to blame but myself, of course. It is my responsibility to see to the condition of all the archives."

"You have archives in the cellar?" Lily asked.

"There are parts of Mr. Ash's collection that are best not left on display," Cairncross replied seriously.

"Like that *Book of Days*," Mrs. Liu contributed, casting a glance at Lily and clearly attempting that less comfortable language out of courtesy to her. "Nasty thing." She added a further thought in Mandarin.

"If it comes in here again uninvited, you may call me to remove it. But there would likely be uncomfortable consequences should you go so far as to chuck it into the fire."

"The *Book of Days*?" Lily asked.

"Never you mind about that. And you needn't be concerned, Mrs. Liu. I can assure you it is thoroughly restrained."

"Hmph," the housekeeper replied with less than total satisfaction.

Lily wondered only vaguely of what sort of book had to be restrained in the cellar lest it find its own way into the kitchen, where it would be considered threatening enough to be burned. Her attention had been captured by one of the intact vials in Cairncross's apothecary case. It was a small, narrow tube of glass filled with a dull green liquid. The contents were identified in a thin, spidery hand, scrawled across a yellowed label in age-dulled brown ink.

*Wine of Jurema*

Lily knew that name. Ash had mentioned it on their walk to Tottenham Court Road.

*A shortcut to a greater sense of their potential power.*

Cairncross rose, carrying the tin baking sheet to the sink. He dampened a piece of newspaper and used it to carefully wipe clean the tray.

Before she could think twice about it, Lily's hand flashed out, closed around the vial, and dropped it into her jacket pocket.

"You had better just dispose of the spotted water hemlock, Mr. Cairncross."

The voice from the doorway startled her.

Lily turned to see Ash and felt a quick start of guilty fear. How

288

long had he been standing there? Long enough to see her snatch the bottle?

If he had, he gave no indication.

He was dressed in a tángzhuāng, the long robe cut of unornamented gray silka. He looked pale and tired.

"Well, how would you suggest I dispose of it? Burn it in the fire and hope the vapor doesn't murder the odd passer-by? Flush it into the Thames? No. We will not dispose of the spotted water hemlock. We have already popped it back into a vial and will return it to the vaults where it will be far less likely to send anyone into fatal convulsions."

"I defer to your expertise on the matter," Ash replied evenly. "Miss Albright, would you care to join me for a moment? There is something I wish to show you."

The vial in her pocket seemed to grow in weight. Was this just his polite way of calling her aside to confront her about what she'd just done?

"Of course," she replied and followed him up into the hallway.

He spoke as he lead her toward the grand stair.

"I apologize for the informality of my attire," he said. "I am not feeling very well today."

Lily contemplated her own attire, which currently consisted of a pair of canvas trousers, riding boots, and a fleece-lined driving jacket. She made no comment.

At the top of the stairs, she was momentarily arrested by the sight of a room opening onto the landing. It was light, the bright windows stripped of any curtains or hangings. The space was utterly empty of any furnishings, but the sun streaming through the glass illuminated a series of weapons mounted on the wall. They were not antiques but a modern and apparently well-used assortment of staffs, swords, and other implements she did not recognize.

"Ah. You have not seen the studio."

"What is it for?"

"It is where we practice our tàijíquán," he replied. "I believe I have mentioned something of that art before and its potential application for charismatics?"

She thought of the crashing impact of bodies hitting the floor she had heard the first day she arrived, and of how Strangford had appeared on the landing that now stood behind her, his dark hair damp with the sweat of his exertion.

"Is this what you wanted to show me?"

"No," Ash replied. "This way."

They passed more rooms—some bedrooms and an intimate, informal parlor—then came to a narrower set of stairs that led up to the attic.

At the top lay a plain wooden door.

"Through here," Ash said and pushed it open.

The space was vast. It extended for the entirety of both of the buildings that made up The Refuge. The air was still and cold, smelling of dust and old wood.

The walls were completely covered in long lengths of black curtain. Small windows set into the gables illuminated the space remarkably well, the light dancing with motes of dust suspended in the air.

Then she noticed the ceiling and gasped.

It was painted.

The entire, enormous expanse of it was covered in an elaborate mural, done in rich tones of blue and gold.

The style was Egyptian. It consisted of hundreds of figures. Some were immense, stretching for ten feet or more across the plaster. Others were minuscule, forming armies of tiny bodies. There were figures ruling from elaborate thrones, or plowing the earth, or poling featherlight boats down blue rivers.

Animals marched side-by-side with gods, their skin hued ivory or earth-toned or vibrant lapis blue. Scorpions danced with snakes and jackals. A baboon held an slender pen delicately in his hand, poised above the white surface of a scroll. A woman with a profile marked by strength and determination held a winged scarab over her head, surrounded by both the living and the dead.

Woven through all of it were the stars—hundreds upon hundreds of shining silver stars.

It was Egyptian, but not, the renderings both more abstract and more alive than what Lily had seen of Egyptian art in journals or encyclopedias, or in the halls of the British Museum.

"The ceiling of the Temple of Hathor at Dendara," Ash said quietly from beside her. "Scholars believe it is most likely some kind of astrological chart. A depiction of the influence of the stars over the destiny of gods and men. Not an exact replica, of course. She took some liberties with it."

"Your wife painted this?"

"Yes."

There must have been thousands of figures, each with its own distinct personality and character. Creating them would have been an immense undertaking, all while bent over half-backwards or suspended like Michelangelo under the Sistine Chapel.

But this masterpiece wasn't appreciated by endless crowds of worshipers. It was locked away in an attic where only the dust and forgotten things gazed upon its wonder.

"Why?" Lily demanded. "Why would she do this here?"

"I don't know," he admitted softly.

There was a tired sadness in his words that struck at her viscerally.

It was the woman he had loved who had made this, a woman who had been lost to him for thirty years.

"There is more," he added, before she could think of the right way to respond.

Her attention shifted to the black curtains that covered the walls, yard upon yard of dark fabric hanging still and quiet around the periphery of the room. It gave the space a funeral feeling, like the viewing chamber at a wake.

Her skin crawled. As much as she was still awed by the starscape on the ceiling, Lily began to wonder if perhaps she should never have climbed the attic stairs. The space around her felt like a sarcophagus should be resting in the center of it. It was a tomb.

"Under the curtains?" she asked.

"Her last work," Ash replied.

The silver stars twinkled over her head as Lily absorbed the enormity of it . . . and realized why she was here.

Ash had hinted at this before, the first day they met in the quiet gray light of the reflection room. He had told her then that he recognized Lily from his wife's last painting—a piece that had been completed years before Lily was born.

But this was no simple canvas in a frame. Under those curtains lay a painting the length and breadth of two enormous townhouses.

What did all that dark, shadowy fabric conceal?

Lily was not entirely sure she wanted to find out.

"Why is it covered up?"

Ash approached the wall. He brushed his fingers over the black cloth, which danced in response.

"Because it is not easy to see. When she painted this . . . her art and her power had reached their greatest intimacy. It represents what she was at her most complete, and that makes it . . . challenging."

"Her power. What was it?"

"I have told you about the force I believe drives your visions."

"You mean fate."

"Evangeline could sense it."

The room seemed to grow bigger around her and more cold, like the space between the stars.

"I don't understand," Lily replied.

"Your eyes are organs that translate light into image. Your ears turn waves of sound into song. My wife possessed an organ that was tuned to the relationships of meaning between all things. The manner in which people and objects and events are connected not by the laws of physics, but by significance. That is what her art was, Miss Albright," he explained, his voice patient but heavy with old pain. "Her attempt to translate that sense into something the rest of us could perceive."

The black curtains seemed to grow heavier, more substantial. The notion of what they hid felt something like a threat, even as nebulous as it was in Lily's mind . . . or like a very dangerous promise.

"So whose fate is this?" she asked, taking in the whole of the enormous, empty room.

"Mine, perhaps. Yours. Maybe all of ours."

The cold of the space was beginning to sink through the fleece of her coat, finding its way into her bones. It was also far too still in the attic, that tomb-like atmosphere taking on an oppressive weight.

"I want to show you part of this work. Are you willing to see it?" Ash asked.

She was afraid. It made her turn defensive, scrabbling for nonchalance in the face of something that was so clearly and undeniably extraordinary.

"Why wouldn't I be?" she tossed back.

Even Lily could feel how hollow the words sounded in the face of those yards of black curtain with the secrets of the entire sky spilled out over her head.

He crossed the room to the center of a long stretch of unbroken wall, moving unerringly to a seam in the fabric.

He pushed it apart, exposing the work underneath.

Lily gasped.

The colors were stunning, bolder than life. Red and green danced with purple on a background of the darkest midnight blue, all threaded through with gold. The figure of a woman was depicted there, with flames in place of her hair and eyes of cold silver. She held a staff in her hand. It sprouted branches covered in sharp green needles and crimson berries, marking it as a yew. It looked dangerous and alive, full of potential.

The shadow of an older man fell behind her, his face turned away, making him unrecognizable. It was lined with shame and grief. A tarnished crown sat on his head.

Behind that were the doors.

There were hundreds of them, of every imaginable shape, style and size, layered over each other to form a maddeningly complex puzzle.

Each one was cracked open, letting a thread of gleaming light spill through.

On the woman's gown, in crimson and gold, the rippling silk was marked with the forms of a thousand golden keys.

At her right, just visible beyond the edge of the black curtain Ash held in his hand, Lily glimpsed part of another figure.

It was only a hand, encased in a gauntlet of shining black steel. It extended toward the woman with the flaming hair, almost close enough to touch—but not quite.

Something about it compelled her, dared her to see more—a dare she felt a desperate desire to fight.

There was a banner under the woman's feet, just like the one Evangeline Ash had held in her hand in the portrait in the Carfax Gallery.

*The Prophetess*

No, she thought instinctively, fear washing over her. This wasn't her. It couldn't be her.

The figure on the wall was powerful, a veritable goddess. She was the center of a universe of significance.

Lily was a creature of the periphery. She had always been a half-step to the outside.

Her mother's relationship with Lord Torrington. The finishing school. The world of Drury Lane, where she had been accepted thanks to her pedigree but always viewed as something slightly other, something that did not entirely belong.

Ash had made a mistake.

And yet . . . the yew in the figure's hand, like the wood that made up Lily's walking stick. The sawdust that covered the floor under her feet, which weren't clad in delicate slippers, but in sturdy brown leather boots, much like the ones on her feet right now, which she wore for riding her Triumph.

And there in the corner, almost lost in the shadows under the crowned figure at her back . . . a pool of blood and jewels glittering in the darkness.

Like the paste gems that had scattered across the pavement when her mother had fallen to the knife of a thief.

The stars overhead were spinning, the gods and kings waiting for her answer to some unspoken question.

"What does this mean?" she managed to say, her voice like dust in her throat.

"That you have a vital part to play in what is coming."

"And what is coming?"

"I believe you are better situated to answer that than I am," he replied.

She looked to the rest of that enormous space, to the endless expanse of night-black curtain, hanging still as death over who-knew-what secrets.

"What else is here?" she demanded.

"A great many things."

With a reverent air, he slowly pulled the curtain closed over the image of The Prophetess.

With the painting was once more hidden from view, Lily's anger found room to rise.

She hadn't asked for this.

What purpose did it serve? All it had done was pose a thousand questions, none of which she was capable of answering. She was left feeling as though she carried an even greater burden than before.

How could she be so important and yet so useless? So powerful and so completely out of control?

"What do you want from me?" she demanded.

"I do not want anything from you, Miss Albright."

"Then why did you show this to me?"

"Because she would have wanted you to see it."

"It isn't me."

It was a weak denial, however forcefully she made it. Ash did not bother to refute it.

She turned and stalked toward the stair, the need to leave becoming overwhelming.

She stopped at the top, turning to face him again.

"What I can do—it is an accident. Nothing but happenstance. It's no use to anybody."

"Perhaps, Miss Albright. And perhaps you are far more than you have ever suspected."

Her temper flashed, threatening violence. She remembered herself before it lashed free. This place was sacred. It was the heart of a grief even she couldn't claim to understand, a grief that belonged to the man who stood before her. However shaken she was by what she had seen here, she had to respect that.

She needed to leave.

"I'm sorry. I have to go."

She did not wait for an answer. She ran down the stairs, leaving Ash standing in the center of that tomb-like gallery like an ancient monk in his dark robes, acolyte of some isolated and unwelcoming temple.

# TWENTY-TWO

$\mathscr{S}$HE WANTED TO HURT something.

It was a mindless violence, wrapped up in the instinct to run from what she had been confronted with in Robert Ash's attic.

She contained it as she stalked down empty halls and grand staircases until she came to the familiar entryway with its marble Newton and battle-blazoned shield.

Rattled as she was, even the grand scale of that space felt oppressively close. She needed air.

She moved to the door at the far end of the hall and pushed through it into the garden.

It was enclosed by high brick walls. Twisted branches and dry stalks indicated dormant shrubs and blossoms, still bedded down and sleeping.

She breathed in the crisp, cold air, waiting for the pounding in her head to pass.

It was nothing but the madness of a brilliant but disturbed artist. The woman's husband, in his lingering grief, filled it with undue significance. The figure in the attic was not a representation of her destiny. It was oil and pigment on plaster. That it had felt for a moment like something more was due to the artist's undeniable talent and the unnaturally still atmosphere of the room.

She shouldn't have come here.

She kicked at the gravel of the path, then followed it toward the carriage house.

She pushed through the door and stopped at the sight of a tall, thin figure crouching next to her motorcycle.

"This is yours?" Sam Wu asked without taking his eyes off the bike.

"I'm sorry for parking it here. I didn't want to leave it in the mews."

"The 500 cc Roadster."

"It is," she confirmed.

Sam took a rag from his back pocket and wiped a line of dust off the engine cover.

"They've got a 550 cc out now. It'll run over 50 without an ounce of bother."

"I can imagine."

He stood, tucking the rag back in his pocket and adjusting his cap.

"Still. Nice motor."

"Thank you."

"Need help getting it back outside?"

Part of her wanted nothing more than to grab the Triumph and roar out of the mews away from The Refuge, but she had come here for a reason and now, unexpectedly, she found herself with the opportunity to pursue it.

She wondered how what she planned to ask would be received. She had every reason to suspect the young man in front of her viewed her with nothing but suspicion and hostility. She wasn't entirely sure she could blame him.

He was also her best hope of executing the next part of her plan—a step that had to be taken for her to settle, once and for all, whether the hospital was a clue that might save Estelle or another damned distraction.

"Actually . . ." she began. She was cut off by the creak of the door opening behind her, the light it admitted flashing off the chrome of the Rolls Royce.

"Sam, have you seen . . ." Strangford stopped as his eyes fell on Lily.

He was framed in the light pouring in through the doorway. There was something just a touch more disheveled than usual about his hair. He must have been riding, she surmised, then realized that the sight of him was triggering an unusually potent reaction somewhere inside her chest.

She fought it.

"Good afternoon, my lord," she replied.

From the corner of her eye, she saw Sam raise an eyebrow at the strict formality of her tone.

Strangford noticed it to. She could see the question it raised in his eyes, but it was not one he would ask aloud in front of the chauffeur who stood beside her.

"I called on you earlier," he said.

"Yes. I got your card. I planned to return your call as soon as I was able."

The response felt lame.

"Are you alright? Is there anything—"

"No," Lily cut in. "No, it's all very well, thank you."

The dust motes danced in the still air of the garage, sparkling in the glow that spilled in behind him from the garden.

Silence stretched, patently awkward, across the space where some other conversation should have happened.

Sam cleared his throat, scratching at his hair under his flat cap.

"I should go," Strangford said. "The session opens at four."

The session at the House of Lords. Her thoughts flew back to the news she had learned from Roger the paperboy—that Lord Deveral's arraignment had been scheduled for little more than a week away.

Strangford was a peer. As such, he held a seat in Parliament and would be among those who heard it.

"But if you need me—" he began.

"If I have need of you I will be sure to let you know," she cut in smoothly.

She was exquisitely aware of the awkwardness of her words, of how inadequate they were to what had already passed between her and the man who stood in the doorway. They were a hand against his chest, pushing him back. She told herself the distance should make him feel safer as well.

Her effort did not go unnoticed. She could read the surprise and confusion clearly in his face, along with something else—hurt. He covered it up, wrapping himself in courtesy like a cloak.

"Then I shall wait to hear from you." He turned to Sam. "I came to ask if you had seen Cairncross."

"He's in the kitchen with my gram," the younger man replied promptly.

"The one place I didn't think to look. If you'll excuse me, then."

Lily realized he was actually waiting for her to do so.

She nodded, not quite trusting herself to reply.

He turned to go.

"Strangford," Lily called after him, the name tumbling out of her lips.

He stopped, looking back.

She caught herself, reining in whatever impulse had prompted that outburst.

"Nothing. Good afternoon."

His gaze lingered on her for a moment. Then he was gone.

She found herself looking longer than was strictly necessary at the open square of the doorway.

Distance, she reminded herself firmly.

"Did you need a hand, then?"

"Sorry?"

"With the motorbike," Sam clarified.

Lily snapped back to herself. There was work to be done.

"No. But I was hoping I might speak with you for a moment."

Sam's expression shifted, a touch of wariness coming back into it. He walked over and closed the door through which Strangford had left, cutting off the spill of light.

"I'm supposed to be seeing to the horses."

"I can talk while you work."

"Suit yourself."

He strode across the bay, passing the quiet silver shadow of the big Rolls and the black, looming presence of the carriage, its lacquer polished to a dark shine. A door on the far side opened into a narrow row of stalls.

The air smelled of fresh hay and manure. The space glowed with a warm, comfortable, animal heat. Two spacious stalls held the chestnut and the bay Lily remembered from their trip to Abney Park.

They whickered as Sam came in, tails twitching. He plucked a brush from a rack on the wall and opened the first stall. He moved inside and began working the bristles through the bay's coat.

"I need your help," Lily said, stepping up to the door of the stall.

"Didn't his lordship just offer that?"

Lily felt the quick jab of that, but refused to let it provoke her.

"This isn't something he can do," she asserted.

"What is it?"

"Trespassing."

There was a hitch in the rhythm of his strokes. The bay snorted. After only a moment, Sam picked up the regular motion again.

"What makes you think I'd help you with that?"

"Nothing," Lily admitted frankly. "But you're the one I know can do it. And I need to get inside."

He didn't answer. He continued to brush, moving to the far side of the horse.

"This about your friend?" he asked at last. "The one who's in trouble?"

"Yes."

Sam set the brush aside. The bay nudged at him with its nose.

"Don't you start," he chided the animal. "Go eat your supper."

The bay snorted once more, then clomped over to the bucket that hung from the wall. It pressed its nose inside and began to munch.

Sam stepped back into the aisle, gently closing the door to the stall. He leaned against the weathered planks, his arms crossed over his chest.

"What building?"

"A charity hospital in the Borough, near the old Mint. But it's been closed for months. There was a fire."

"Not a nice place to be wandering about late at night. And there'd be other risks, even if we do manage to get in."

"Such as?"

"Might not be the first ones to get the idea. Could be others knocking about, likely not the nicest sort. And if it burned, then there's the structure to worry about. Stairs giving way, floors falling out from beneath you."

The bay came over. It pressed its nose against his shoulder. Sam reached back to stroke it absentmindedly.

"When?"

"Tonight," Lily replied.

He opened the door to the other stall, where the chestnut waited patiently. He took up the brush again and began to repeat the ritual, long strokes smoothing the rich, dark coat.

"I'll collect you at eleven," he said without looking up.

She felt her heart skip.

"Actually, it would be better if I met you."

"Why?"

"I think I'm being watched."

He glanced up at her over the back of the horse. Then he shrugged.

"Here, then."

"I won't be late."

She turned to go. His voice stopped her.

"That stick of yours. The one you're always carrying about."

"What about it?"

"You don't have a limp."

"No," Lily confirmed.

"So I take it you use it for something other than walking."

She didn't answer.

"Bring it along," he ordered and continued to brush.

&#126;

The mews behind Bedford Square looked different at night, the long shadows warping the profiles of the elegant houses.

It was cold. When Lily coughed, fog burst from between her lips, lingering in the still winter air.

Any day now, that recalcitrant chill could turn to snow. Yet here she was on what could very likely be a fool's errand.

The clatter of carriage wheels broke the silence of the night. Lily stepped back, concealing herself in the shadows that lined the narrow way.

The vehicle that turned into the mews wasn't the polished, well-kept carriage of one of the denizens of the tonnish square. It was a hackney, one that had seen better days, likely when Queen Victoria had been in the fresh blossom of youth. The paint was chipped where it wasn't obscured by mud and one of the wheels was clearly out of alignment. The driver was as ancient as the carriage, a wizened old stick of a man with a dirty white beard, perched like a gull in the seat, a fraying cap set on his head.

It rolled to a stop beside her.

Lily had a moment of fear. She had been careful when she left March Place, slipping past Mrs. Bramble's bedroom to the kitchen, where she'd used the service entrance to make her way out. She had circled around the block before finding her way back on course for Bedford Square, checking all the while for followers.

Perhaps she hadn't checked well enough.

She shifted her grip on her walking stick as the door of the hackney swung open.

Sam poked his head out.

"Come on, then," he urged impatiently.

Lily hopped onto the step and swung through to the narrow interior.

"Alright, George," Sam called up through the opposite window.

The carriage jolted into motion, swaying with the uneven movement of the wheels.

Her companion for the evening slouched in the seat beside her, crossing his arms over his chest. After giving her a quick look over, he turned his face toward the open window as though daring her to object to the rush of cold air that poured inside.

"George said he'll hold for us if you pay him a double fare."

"That's fine," Lily replied.

It made sense, of course. Sam couldn't have taken his employer's carriage into the verge of one of London's most notorious slums and left it there with no one to mind it while they went scavenging through someone else's property. The hackney seemed carefully chosen to deflect any unwanted attention from the denizens of the Mint.

The lanky young man beside her knew far better than she did what they were getting into that night, including all the attendant risks.

"Do we have everything we need?" she asked.

"Like what?"

"I didn't know if there was equipment required for this sort of thing."

"The more you carry, the harder it is to run."

"Do you expect we'll be running?"

Sam shrugged.

They rode in silence, the seat bouncing with the uneven motion of the hackney.

"Thank you for agreeing to help me," Lily said at last.

"We ain't done it yet," he retorted without looking at her.

They stopped near the Borough Market. It looked very different from the bustling, crowded place Lily had passed through that afternoon. The market hall itself was closed and dark, the neighboring stores and stalls all shuttered. Lights still shone from the nearby brewery. Lily could hear the calls of the night shift workers and the clatter of machinery.

Sam leaned out the window.

"Over there," he ordered.

The driver turned the hackney into a narrow bay beside a second-hand furniture store.

Sam hopped down, neglecting to hold the door or offer her a hand. Lily made her own way out without trouble. She was still clad in her riding gear. It had seemed a sensible choice. As Sam had pointed out, they had no way of knowing the condition of the interior of the building. She also thought that her coat and trousers would be less likely to draw attention on the shadowy streets that surrounded the hospital.

"Take care of George," Sam ordered.

Lily took a generous pile of coins from her pocket.

"We might be a while," she warned the driver as she handed the money over.

George tipped his cap and flashed her a gap-toothed smile.

"Where is it?" Sam asked when she rejoined him.

"This way."

Lily lead them down the high street. It was far from deserted. A couple enjoyed an embrace in the shadows of a shop door. A few boys, too young to rightly be out, dashed down the road, kicking a ball ahead of them. Like Drury Lane, where she had once lived, this neighborhood was never entirely asleep. It couldn't be. Many people here needed to work during the time when the quiet, middle-class residents of Bloomsbury were all tucked into their beds.

They turned to pass the Golden Fleece. There was a raucous burst of laughter from inside the pub, which was hosting a lively crowd. Lily was aware of the glances of a pair of men who lingered at the door, measuring her and Sam as they passed on the far side of the road. The looks didn't last, Lily's ensemble and the relative darkness of the night keeping her from attracting more than a precursory notice.

They stopped in front of the clinic. It looked grander in the darkness than it had during the day. The burnt roof timbers rose like a scaffold against the night sky and the limestone shone paler in the darkness, the stains of soot and coal-smoke less apparent.

Sam put a toothpick between his lips and considered the prospect, hands in his pockets.

"Likely there's a service door out back," he concluded. "That'll be our way in."

The alley smelled of rotting cabbage and dog waste. Rats dodged across the way in front of them, then paused, raising their heads as though taking notice. Their eyes followed Sam for a moment. He ignored them. Lily saw the creatures move on and wondered if perhaps she was simply imagining the shift in their attention.

The door at the back of the clinic was unassuming. It had been boarded up, as had the windows along the ground floor.

"Keep a lively eye, eh?" Sam said as they approached.

He took a knife from his pocket and used it to pry free a few of the boards. Then he took out a slender tin cigarette case, which opened to reveal a row of metal picks topped with variously crooked and pointed ends.

He knelt at the lock and Lily turned her attention to the alley. It remained deserted as he worked. After a moment she heard a click as the lock gave way.

He pushed at the door. It opened only a foot or so.

"It's blocked from the inside. Give us a hand."

Lily tucked her walking stick into the back of her belt, then lent her weight to the effort, wedging the heel of her boot against the paving stones and shoving. The door slowly gave way, accompanied by the scraping shift of some unseen obstacle.

Sam glanced around, then motioned her through.

"Go on, then. Look sharp."

She tossed her stick inside, then followed it, squeezing through the gap in the boards.

It was impossible to tell what this room had once been, as most of the one above had collapsed and fallen into it. A spill of bright moonlight revealed plaster and shattered tile covering the floor along with the burnt and twisted wreckage of a half-dozen metal cots. The source of that illumination became apparent as Lily retrieved her staff and looked up. Above them, a great hole in the ceiling opened to the upper floors and, beyond that, to the night sky where a full winter moon gazed down at them between the jagged remains of the rafters.

Water dripped down from somewhere, landing with a musical ping on an overturned basin. On the far side of the space, a staircase had half-crumbled into dust. One wall had been completely torn away, leaving the steps hanging in the air like a row of broken teeth.

Sam crawled in beside her. He straightened, taking in the wreckage.

"That don't look good. If part of the floor's caved in, there's no telling how stable the rest of it is. Sure you want to do this?"

"I'm sure."

"Could also be we ain't the first ones in here. And some of those others might still be lurking about."

"You're welcome to wait here, if you'd rather," Lily replied coolly.

"I can handle myself. Just making certain the lady knows what she's getting into."

"Duly noted, Mr. Wu."

Sam grinned. He popped the toothpick back into his pocket.

"Right, then. Let's get to it."

They clambered over the wreckage, boots slipping on slick tile or raising little clouds of plaster dust. Lily used her walking stick to brace herself and keep from skating down the debris.

The door at the far end of the room opened onto a wide, dark hallway.

The boarded windows obscured all but a few filtered rays of soft blue light. Lily's eyes took a few moments to adjust, but accustomed themselves as she and Sam moved slowly and quietly along.

The fire had not made so much of a mark here, but signs of other intruders were visible. A few sandwich wrappers littered the floor along with an empty bottle of bitters. In one of the rooms they passed, which looked as though it had once been some kind of laboratory, Lily glimpsed the remnants of a campfire next to a singed mattress.

There were offices and storerooms, largely cleared out of whatever might have been left in them after the blaze. Here and there between the shadows, piles of linens sat gathering mildew, or jars lay smashed on the floor.

The fire had taken place only a few months before, if Berta was to be believed. Walking through the shadowy corridor, Lily felt like she was inside something that had been rotting for years.

In another lab, she pulled open cabinets, rifling quietly through the few intact pieces of glassware within.

"What are we looking for, anyway?" Sam asked.

"I'll know when I see it. Help me with this?"

Sam came to the other side of a toppled trolley. Together, they hefted it upright. As they lifted, a door in the cart fell open, a pile of tin chamber pots spilling out and clattering brashly against the floor.

Lily held her breath, meeting Sam's eyes across the metal table.

He lifted a single finger to his lips, then raised it.

Lily could read the signal.

*Quiet. Wait.*

He inched toward the door, keeping his body close to the wall. He waited there, listening.

Lily moved herself back into a deeper well of shadow, holding her breath.

The silence stretched, tense as a bowstring.

Then Sam stood. He kicked an empty tin across the floor. It pinged neatly off the leg of a table.

"Nobody here," he concluded.

"Clearly someone was at some point," Lily countered, relaxing her grip on her stick and nodding toward the tin.

Sam shrugged. "Like as not they found someplace better to hole up. Or they might've been moved along."

"Moved along? By whom?"

"Ain't you got more cabinets to check?" He nodded toward the line of doors.

Lily wavered for only a moment before moving to the low metal bays.

She opened them one after the other, her eyes adjusted enough to the darkness now to make out their general contents after a moment or two.

"So who taught you how to pick locks?" she asked as she nudged aside a mound of rubber tubing.

"Bloke named Cannon."

"You worked for him?"

"It was employment of a sort."

"How old were you?"

Sam shrugged. "Old enough."

"But small enough to get into places a grown man couldn't reach," Lily hypothesized. She had heard stories of how some of the less scrupulous denizens of the East End made use of desperate young boys to do their dirty work for them, climbing into places—often dangerous places—an adult couldn't access.

Of course, when someone got caught, it was far more likely to be the boy, not the man who put him up to the job.

"My father couldn't find work. No one would hire him. Năinai, she got a job in a laundry. Came home every night with her hands boiled, all for a few pennies."

"Năinai?" Lily asked.

"My grandmother. My father sold everything we had to pay for passage here. Somebody had to keep us all from starving."

"He let you do that?"

"He knew I'd got work. He didn't need to know what sort."

Lily closed the last cabinet and stood.

"There's nothing here," she announced. "Is there another stair?"

"End of the hallway."

"Let's try it."

They stepped over a barricade of toppled chairs, continuing down the darkened hall.

"Why did your father leave China if it meant coming here with nothing?"

When Sam didn't answer, Lily realized her questions had become presumptuous. He had agreed to help her break into this place, not share his life story with her.

"I'm sorry. You don't have to answer that."

"Course I don't," he retorted.

He kicked a tin bedpan aside. It clanged off the tiles.

He entered the darkened stairwell and began to climb, Lily following.

"It was my fault," he said at last.

"But you must have been fairly young when you left China."

"I was ten."

"What could a ten year-old possibly do to drive his whole family out of their country?"

"Fell in with a bad crowd."

"Worse than a bunch of East End housebreakers?"

"Aye. Worse."

Lily knew there must be much more to the story. She opened her mouth to ask but was overwhelmed by a sudden instinct.

It was as clear as it was sharp, sudden and undeniable.

*Move.*

"Go!" she shouted. She pushed Sam forward, scrambling after him. They tumbled onto the landing just as the stairs beneath them broke from the wall and crumbled, collapsing in a cloud of dust.

Sam glanced over at her from where he slouched against the wall.

"Your talent raise that alarm?"

"I . . . don't know what it was," Lily admitted. "It's not usually like this." She touched her hands to her temples, feeling dizzy.

Had she just picked up on some subtle cue in the atmosphere? Perhaps a minute shifting of the stone under her feet, or some sort of sound that indicated the steps were about to crumble?

That wasn't what it had felt like. It had felt like the knowledge that Frank the Spiv was about to turn the corner earlier that morning. Like one of her visions but clearer and carrying with it an urgency to act.

It had been like this before.

She had forgotten until her father mentioned it during his unexpected visit. The awareness of what was approaching had been natural. The postman would arrive shortly. It was going to rain. Her father would drop by that afternoon.

She had taken delight in it, in knowing what no one else seemed aware of.

That had been gone for years. Why had it resurfaced now?

Perhaps because the day before, she had deliberately provoked a vision.

In front of that scrying glass, Lily had kicked open doors she spent the last fourteen years trying furiously to shut. They might not have simply closed back up once she was done.

The idea frightened her. That wasn't how this was supposed to work. She was doing what she must to try to save Estelle but when that proved futile, she would go back to her old life, to the way things had been before.

Nothing was supposed to change.

"Are you coming?"

"Sorry," Lily replied to Sam's call. She climbed carefully up the remaining steps. They seemed solid enough under her feet. Could she trust this instinct of hers to warn them before another part of the building collapsed?

Sam waited for her on the first floor. It was brighter here, as the windows still opened to the pale light of the moon. They moved slowly past wards furnished with neat rows of narrow beds. There were shadowy storerooms and what looked like it might have been some kind of parlor. Lily saw a plush sofa and a coffee table, though the coziness of the space was compromised by the slashes cut into the upholstery and the foul-smelling liquids staining the walls where jars had been thrown and shattered.

The damage from the fire was more apparent as they neared the end of the hall. Soot stains flared out from around the door that closed off the other half of the building, the smell of damp, charred wood becoming stronger.

"It'll be chancier, the further we head that way," Sam warned.

"I need to check in there," she said, pointing to a room a few steps further down the hall.

It was a generously-sized office dominated by a large oak desk. The fire had kissed this space, coming close enough for the heat to blister the paint on one of the walls. A glass-fronted cabinet of pharmaceuticals had been ravaged, the lock broken off. Only a few empty bottles were left behind. An articulated skeleton in the corner was missing its head and someone had driven a scalpel, viciously, through the back of the posh leather office chair at the desk.

It was the file cabinets that caught Lily's attention and made her risk coming this close to the more heavily damaged part of the building.

They were an expensive variety, made of steel with a lock on each drawer. Painted black, they looked like heavy monoliths at the back of the room. These were clearly designed to hold records that not just anyone was to have access to—records that might tell her the truth behind the rumors and speculations she'd been following.

"We might need those picks of yours . . ." Lily began, but trailed off as she tried the first drawer and it slid open under her hand.

Empty.

She pulled open another, and a third.

All empty.

Sam peered over her shoulder.

"There aren't any ashes in those drawers. If what's in there had burnt, there'd be ashes. So either they were empty to begin with . . ."

"Or someone has come and emptied them," Lily concluded. She slammed the drawer shut, fighting against rising frustration.

She needed answers, not empty drawers.

"Could there be more records upstairs? Some sort of archive?" she demanded.

"I'm game if you are," Sam replied.

# TWENTY-THREE

$\mathcal{T}$HE ATTIC WAS ENORMOUS, stretching the full length and width of the building. The rafters made Lily feel like she was inside the roof of a cathedral, all flying buttresses and Gothic elegance. The elegant curves were formed by sections of the roof that had been gutted by flames, leaving them bare to the wild moonlit night above.

Under the open wound of that damage, the space was packed with rows of metal cots and chairs stacked into unsteady towers, crates with mysterious contents jammed in between.

She and Sam picked their way through, stepping over pieces of tumbled struts, boots splashing in puddles lingering on the wood floor. Light, soft feathers dusted the boards. Lily could hear the gentle rustling and cooing of doves tucked up into the remaining rafters.

She stopped a few yards shy of where the floor gave way. The opening was jagged, edged in black, spilling down into the darkness of the levels below.

"I don't see any files," Sam pointed out.

Frustration welled up inside of her. There was nothing here but broken glass and ashes. She had come for answers. The building refused to give any away.

She turned from the empty maw of the broken floor.

"Maybe we missed something. I'm going to look around."

"Suit yourself," Sam replied.

He made himself comfortable on the edge of one of the narrow gabled windows. A pair of doves fluttered down from the rafters. They settled onto the windowsill beside him. One hopped onto his knee while the other pushed against his hand, cooing softly.

He scratched the bird's neck as Lily set down her stick and started wrangling with a row of cots jammed together like cards in a deck. They came loose with a scream of protesting metal, jangling like Jacob Marley's chains as she dragged them across the floor.

"So you and Lord Strangford, then. What's all that about?" Sam asked casually.

Lily kicked a mound of dusty linens aside.

"I have no idea what you're talking about."

"Come on. I could've run a saw through the tension between the two of you back in the garage."

The image of Strangford standing in the doorway came back to her, hurt flashing through his dark eyes.

"You must have misread the situation."

"So you don't fancy him?"

Lily turned back, glaring at Sam.

"Why are you asking me this?"

"Just passing the time."

More doves had joined the scouts on Sam's knee. They fluttered down to the ground below his window, prancing like soldiers on parade.

Lily moved to the other side of the attic. She wrenched aside an old door, revealing a pile of stained mattresses.

"Can I usher your wedding?" Sam asked. "A Chinese man for an usher at a grand toff wedding. That'd be something, eh?"

"There isn't going to be any wedding," Lily snapped in reply, shoving a rolling trolley out of her way. The wheel caught on some uneven shoal of floorboard and the boxy steel contraption tipped over, crashing to the floor in a cascade of breaking glass.

She fought back the curse that wanted to burst from her lips and turned instead, calmly, to the stack of mattresses.

"No light matter, then," Sam remarked. "But where's the trouble? Seems simple enough to me."

"I'm not his type."

"He don't have a type. Never seen him more than half interested in a lady before you."

"He is not—"

"Oh, he is."

Lily pushed aside the surging conflict of emotion this assertion sparked in her.

"I mean that I'm not the type a peer of the realm marries."

"How's that? You look like the type. Sound like the type. You telling me you didn't have some high-class governess teaching you how to talk like that?"

"I went to school."

"One of them high-class ladies' schools, no doubt."

"I told you. I'm not what I sound like."

"So—what? You're not a toff? What's it, then—your people in trade? That's nothing, these days. More money in trades than titles. All them nobles are broke. Death duties, you know," he clarified, putting on a perfect aristocratic drawl.

Lily moved a precariously stacked chair out of her way, tossing it aside. The impact rattled another pair of beds together, the metal clanging.

"I'm a bastard. That make it clear enough?"

The doves fluttered up to nearby rafters, a few light gray feathers drifting down behind them.

Sam considered her from his perch in the window.

"Bastard who got sent to finishing school. Not some back alley swive, then. But if the money was on your dame's side she'd have been shipped off to one of those convent hospitals in Switzerland. You'd have been adopted out and raised yapping German. So it must be your old man. What's he—a Russian count? Scottish baronet?"

"English earl, actually," Lily snapped, wrenching up the lid of a crate.

"That's not a joke, is it? Your old man's an earl? What're you sulking for? If your old man's an earl, it don't matter what side of the blanket you were born on. No one'd look down on his lordship for making that kind of a connection."

"There is no connection. I'm not acknowledged."

"So get acknowledged."

Lily scoffed, slamming the lid back into place.

"Why are you so determined on this?"

Sam shrugged, posture turning a touch defensive. "He's just a decent bloke, is all."

Lily opened her mouth to retort but held back as the more subtle cues in Sam's words and posture finally broke through her own too-ready defenses.

He cared. Though he'd likely deny it if she asked outright, he thought of Strangford as a friend. Lily expected Sam didn't put very many people in this world into that category.

"I'm sure there is a perfect mate for Lord Strangford out there somewhere," she said, gentling her tone. "But I'm not her."

"I haven't met many daughters of earls, but I suspect most of them are all frills and furbelows. Doubt there are many who'd toss burnt buildings in trousers on a long-shot chance to save a friend."

Lily paused with her hands on the lid of the next crate. The compliment caught her off guard, striking with more force than she'd anticipated.

She looked over at the tough Limehouse lad in the window. He was slouched against the glass, arms crossed defensively over his chest.

"Just saying it ain't so far-fetched. But no worries. I know how it is. You're scared, is all."

"Excuse me?"

"It's alright. I've been there myself. It was this flower girl back in Limehouse. I couldn't get three words out to her. Just 'D-d-daisy, please.'"

Lily finished rifling a the crate, replacing the lid and pushing it aside. Another stack of mattresses lay before her. She began yanking them out of the way, one by one.

"This story have a happy ending?"

"Nah. She got knocked up by the butcher." Sam scratched his nose. "Think it'd go better for you two, though. If you'd chance it."

Lily pulled the last of the mattresses aside. The sight of what lay beneath them made her pause.

"What's that?" Sam asked, rising. The movement disturbed a few birds who had returned to cluster around him in the window. They warbled in protest, hopping out of the way.

"Suitcases," Lily replied.

There were perhaps two dozen of them tucked under the eaves of the roof. They were humble things, battered and scratched. A few were held together with an old belt or a bit of twine. Some weren't suitcases at all, but a mere canvas sack.

The collection felt out of place next to the rest of the contents of the attic, which had so clearly fallen under the umbrella of surplus hospital supplies.

What did a hospital need with a bunch of third-hand baggage?

"Who'd you think those belong to?" Sam asked, giving voice to the question ringing through Lily's mind.

"I would assume the patients."

"There ain't any patients left, if you hadn't noticed. How come these are still here?"

"Perhaps they're the property of the ones who never made it home."

This had been a charity hospital. Would those employed here have gone to the trouble of seeking out the next of kin of the patients who died in their care? Unless someone came to claim the deceased's property, it would simply have been taking up space. She supposed it should be seen as a sign of compassion that they hadn't simply thrown it on the rubbish heap.

Still, something about the sight of those poor, battered cases hidden in the dust of the attic made her skin crawl.

Sam pulled off his cap, scratching at his hair. The doves trilled softly in the rafters.

"Should we look in 'em?" he asked.

She found herself thinking of Abney Park and the moment before Dr. Gardner thrust his crowbar into the lid of Sylvia Durst's coffin.

Something about what she was contemplating felt just as profane, but Lily had come here for answers.

She pulled the first of the cases toward her and tossed back the lid.

What lay inside was as humble as the exterior of the bag would suggest—a threadbare nightgown, a pair of old handkerchiefs. A woven belt and a scrap of crimson ribbon. They were the few possessions an impoverished woman had thought might offer her comfort in this place—a place she had come to for healing. Instead, she had found death.

The others were similar. Sam joined her after Lily had made it through three of the bags. He knelt beside her in the dust, tugging another suitcase free and examining its contents with a solemn reverence.

Lily closed one case and moved on to the next. It was made of cardboard thinly covered in black twill. She tugged loose the knotted twine that held it together and opened the lid.

She moved aside a pair of stockings and a little sachet that still smelled faintly of lavender. Next came a ruffled blouse, the seams showing signs of having been carefully re-sewn.

As she lifted it, something slipped from a pocket, landing on the floor with a knock.

She put down the blouse and reached for what had fallen.

"What was that?" Sam asked, glancing over at her.

It was a small silver charm.

Lily rubbed at the tarnish that darkened its surface. The metal had been shaped into the form of a human hand, thumb extended. Its surface was covered in tiny characters in a language Lily had never seen. The minuscule, blocky letters ran up and down each finger, crisscrossing the palm.

"That's Jewish." Sam had come to crouch behind her shoulder. "I've seen those letters on the signs in their shops over in Whitechapel."

Lily flipped the charm over, examining both sides of the piece once more, running her hand along the plain leather strap that would have been used to hang it around someone's neck.

She stood, slipping the charm in her pocket.

"It ain't worth much," Sam pointed out.

"I'm not taking it for money."

Why had she taken it? She didn't have an answer. It was an impulse, just simple instinct, but there was little more than that guiding this whole mission.

She closed the suitcase lid, tucking it back into place among the others.

"I think we've found everything we're going to here," she announced, retrieving her walking stick. "Let's go."

On the floor below, Sam glanced down the shadowy hallway.

"Can't go back the way we came."

"We'll have to find another stair. There's likely one at the opposite end of the building," she suggested.

"There's more damage from the fire that way. I can't speak to the sureness of the floor."

"Let's at least take a look."

Lily led the way. The smell of char and wet ash grew stronger as they passed the ransacked offices, moving closer to the heart of the now-extinct blaze.

They stopped at a set of doors. Narrow windows set into them were criss-crossed with wire and warped with long-ago heat. A cot was jammed into the opening, the mildewing mattress and blanket stained with soot.

Lily climbed over it and slipped inside.

The room was vast and black. Smoke stains climbed the walls like angry fingers reaching towards the jagged hole the fire had cut into the ceiling. Above them, a few scattered stars and the ghost of the moon shone through the frail covering of thin clouds.

Beds lined the walls, scraps of mattress and blanket, charred to ash, clinging to the coils of the springs. Beyond them, the glass of the windows was cracked and glazed behind sets of sturdy iron bars.

The floor ended a few yards in, the boards turned to blackened stumps extended over a deep void.

"This must've been where it started," Lily noted.

"Looks more like a prison than a hospital," Sam noted.

Lily felt cold, looking at the wisps of burnt linen clinging to the beds. "What direction is this?"

Sam considered. "East."

The East Wing. The place Berta had said was kept locked, the women within cut off from communication with those on the other side.

Her imagination took over, envisioning what this space would have looked like packed with sick and crippled women, windows barred, the flames chewing hungrily up the walls as the inmates clawed at the door, desperate to escape. It was a scene out of Dante, a slice of hell in Southwark.

Sam turned his attention to the door, examining the chipped and blistered paint. "This was locked. Looks like they used this cot as a battering ram. No easy thing, given the door had a deadbolt. Would have to have been some muscle behind it."

"Or a lot of them, working together."

The pieces fell together in Lily's mind.

No one had come for them. The building had been burning and the doctors, nurses and orderlies had fled, leaving the women of this room to die.

The notion filled her with a rage quick and hot as the blaze that had once engulfed the room.

"There's our stair," Sam said, pointing to a doorway in the far wall, across the open chasm where the floor had been. "Looks like we ain't getting out that way."

In the end, they returned to a closet in the hall for a load of mold-stained sheets. Sam neatly knotted them into a rope, then dropped it through the hole in the floor.

He went first, then caught her stick as she tossed it down to him. She followed, her arms aching as she worked her way down the twisted lengths of linen to where he waited, balanced on the collapsed remains of the East Wing.

"Something odd about this fire," he commented as she descended.

"Oh?" she grunted in response.

He peered up at the hole in the floor, tilting back his cap.

"Didn't start at the hearth."

Lily's feet reached the ground. She shook out her arms, then looked up.

"See the floor by the fireplace?" he noted. "There's three, four feet of it wasn't burnt. If the fire'd started in the hearth, that would've been the first bit to go up." Sam studied the great, charred opening. "It's almost like it sparked up in the middle of the floor."

Something about the notion sent a chill up and down her aching arms.

She thought of the most outlandish part of Berta's tale.

*I heard it was a witch that done it. That they tried to lock her in, so she turned herself into a witch-fire and burned the whole place up with her.*

"Don't suppose it really matters now, though, do it? Home, then?" he asked, handing her back her stick.

Lily glanced at their exit, the door leading back into the alley. Then her gaze was drawn in the opposite direction, to where a rectangle of deeper darkness indicated another opening in the far wall.

Lily could almost feel what it would be like to crawl into her bed, letting the weariness seep out of her bones.

Without any of the answers she had come for.

"One more place to look," she said and picked her way to the dark doorway.

It opened onto a stairwell. On one side, the steps rose to what remained of the East Wing. On the other, it descended into utter darkness.

He pulled the stub of a candle and a book of matches from his pocket.

"I thought you said you didn't carry gear."

"Hard to toss a place if you can't see where anything is. You sure you want to go down there?" Sam asked.

"I need to see it."

He shrugged, readying a match. Lily reached out, grasping his hand to stop him.

"The gas," she noted.

Sam looked up at the hole in the ceiling. Broken pipes jetted out from between the charred floorboards.

"They'd have turned it off by now. The works wouldn't want the stuff floating out into the ether, particularly if no one's paying the bill. Still, if you'd rather not chance it . . ."

Lily studied the stairwell. The way before her was pitch, devoured by the dark.

"Light it."

Sam met her eyes, raising a brow.

"Here's to our luck."

He struck. The match flared—then burned, small and steady, a single spark in the darkness.

He mated it to the wick of the candle and the light grew brighter.

The stairs to the basement lay clear before them.

"Ladies first," Sam offered.

The ceiling was lower here than on the floors above. The whole of the space was enclosed in sterile white tile. There was no sign of the raging blaze, no ash on the floors or smoke staining the walls. It was as though the space had been stopped up in a jar and preserved.

The whole of it was sunk below the level of the street. There were no windows, not so much as a sliver of glass to break up the monotony of the tile. Lily's footsteps echoed as they moved down the hall.

The first room they passed was the boiler. The walls here were unfinished concrete, the space dominated by an enormous black furnace. It was still and cold now, but must have put off a monstrous heat and roar when fired up. There were several iron doors set into it—more, Lily realized, than were necessary merely for adding coal or regulating the fire.

"What're all those for?" Sam asked.

"I think they must have used it to dispose of waste," Lily replied, keeping her voice even.

Sam made no further comment.

They made their way down the hall past more empty labs and storerooms. Their contents seemed largely intact and untouched, as if even the thieves and scavengers had hesitated to invade the sanctity of this dark space.

The light of Sam's candle flickered off the polished tiles, casting dancing shadows along their way.

At the end of the hall lay the operating theatre.

It was a large space, though the low ceilings still gave it a claustrophobic feel. Cabinets lined one wall, stocked with jars labeled *alcohol, witch hazel, iodine*. There were boxes of cotton wool and sterile bandages with mildew slowly crawling up the labels. On the other side, a polished steel trolley was laid out with syringes, rubber tubing, and a gleaming set of surgical instruments.

A human skull, most likely liberated from the skeleton in the office upstairs, rested on top.

In the center of the room were a pair of tables, set side-by-side. Each was equipped with a row of sturdy leather straps.

"I don't know much about doctors, but isn't it a bit odd that there's two of them?" Sam pointed out. "What, were they operating on two patients at once?"

"It doesn't make much sense," Lily admitted.

She unfolded a strange metal leg from the foot of the table. There were two of them, articulated to extend both up and out from the base. At the ends were metal hoops that reminded her of the stirrups on a horse.

"What're those for?"

"I'm not sure you'd want to hear my guess," Lily said, thinking of the trouble that had brought Berta and her colleagues to this clinic in the first place.

Sam picked up one of the solid metal buckles that lay across the center of the table.

"This the usual sort of thing? Tying people down before you operate on them?"

"No. I don't believe it is." Fingers of unease crawled up her arms.

"Something ain't right about this place," Sam concluded, dropping the buckle back onto the table.

"Let's go."

The wrecked hall above felt welcoming after the cold horror of the basement. Lily picked her way over the debris to the door, using her stick to keep from sliding on the shifting mass of charred wood and cracked tile.

"Did you find what you were after, then?" Sam asked.

"No," Lily replied shortly, frustration burning through her.

"Maybe you brought the wrong escort. Seems to me his lordship might've been more help to you than I was."

It had occurred to Lily as well. Strangford might have run his sensitive hands over those tables in the basement and teased out the full extent of their secrets.

He could do it now, if Lily went to him and asked . . . subjecting him to who-knew-what horror along the way.

How could she demand that of him when she couldn't be sure this place had anything to do with the killer they sought?

Ash had told her that was a dead end. Lily couldn't control her power. That she had seen this place in a vision provoked to reveal Estelle's killer meant nothing.

She couldn't go to Strangford until she had a better reason for thinking this place was worth his trouble.

Where did that leave her?

She thought of the broken lock on the door to the East Wing.

There had been women in that room when it burned. Some of them must have succeeded in fighting their way out.

Any one of those women would certainly be able to tell her more about what happened inside this nightmarish place. What had become of them? If Berta's impression held true, they would all have been terribly ill or otherwise damaged when they escaped. Could they have survived long outside a hospital? Lily didn't know enough to say.

Unless some of them hadn't stayed out for long. As their illness continued to progress, they might have sought help. There were certainly other places in the city where they might have found it—other charity hospitals.

Like St. Bart's, where Dr. Gardner worked.

Lily followed Sam through the gap in the boarded-up door to the alley. She was still so engrossed in her own thoughts, she bumped right into him.

He stood still and tense only a step from the door, staring at the six men who faced them across the alley.

"Bit of warning about this one would've been nice," he muttered under his breath.

"Up to a bit of late night shopping, are we?"

The man who spoke stood near the center of the group. He was older than the others, silver showing through in his mustache. His face was concealed by the shadow from the brim of his bowler hat.

Something about him seemed familiar, the tone of his voice sending prickles across Lily's skin.

"Just having a look," Sam replied.

"Any luck?"

"Nothing much. Place is well picked over, unless you're in the market for rusty cots and wet bandages."

Sam's manner was easy, but Lily noted that his hand had gone to his pocket, where she knew he had secured the knife he had used earlier to pry the boards off the door. Quietly, she adjusted her grip on her walking stick.

Then the clouds shifted. Moonlight spilled down into the alley. It glinted off a bit of brass pinned to the lapel of the man who stood beside the thugs' leader. He was dark haired and clean-shaven, both better and more soberly dressed than the toughs who stood around him.

"Look sharp, Art. That's her, from before."

Lily had no trouble recognizing the man who pointed at her from the end of the row. It was Frank the Spiv, his nose purple and twisted from their encounter earlier that day.

"So it is, Frank," the leader of the thugs agreed. He stepped forward and the moonlight illuminated his own features.

It was the publican of the Golden Fleece, the one who had eyed Lily and Berta as he passed while the whore shared her story.

"Not just shopping, then, are we?" Art mused. "We are not over-fond of strangers nosing around our old Liberty, are we, gents?"

"We are not," Frank the Spiv replied.

"I assume you gave the lady fair warning to mind herself, when you encountered her previously?"

"I did, but she weren't much for hearing it." Frank spat at the pavement.

"Seems a firmer hand is needed."

"How firm?" asked a hulking brute at the other end of the row.

"She was asking names," Frank replied.

"Pity," Art noted. He checked his pocket watch. "Right, then. Best get on with it. Vince, take the lady. Towers, Frank, you should be able to handle the lad."

Sam stepped out from the wall of the hospital. Lily instinctively turned her back to his. Quickly glancing down, she saw him slip the blade from his pocket, the shining length of it just concealed behind his leg.

She lifted her walking staff, taking hold of it with both hands.

"Watch for the stick, Vince," Frank called.

Vince, the hulking brute, lumbered closer. Lily went low, swinging into the vulnerable spot just above the outside of his knee.

His leg buckled and he fell back, grabbing it and cursing.

"Bitch broke my leg!"

"I said, watch the stick," Frank countered.

"It's a boy and a woman," Art snapped. "Quit mucking about."

Lily felt Sam move behind her. She risked a glance, watching as he burst into action.

He fought like a Limehouse tough, handling blade and fists like someone who had been forced to do so before. He took a blow to the jaw, head snapping back, but quickly retaliated with a sharp swipe of the knife. The man named Towers screamed, pulling back his wounded arm.

Art turned to the man who remained standing beside him—the one who wore the brass lapel pin. "It appears the matter requires further assistance, Mr. Gibbs. Are you willing?"

"It's a disappointment, Mr. Bennington, but what needs must be done."

"Mickey, help Mr. Gibbs with the lady. I'll assist Frank with the chink."

The last of the publican's thugs, the one he called Mickey, ran toward her, Gibbs following more sedately behind him.

As he moved closer, the full moonlight revealed the detail of his pin. It was shaped into two interlocked carats—the sigil of Joseph Hartwell's eugenics club. The shock of seeing it there nearly cost her, delaying her reaction by a critical second.

She recovered just in time to strike the first of them in the gut with her stick, winding him as she shifted her body to the side.

Gibbs pulled a cudgel from his sleeve. Lily had only a moment to raise her yew to block the blow. The force of it rattled her arms. She made a quick jab for his face, but he skipped back, avoiding it.

Behind her, Sam had lost his knife. He ran at Frank the Spiv, jamming his shoulder into his midsection and driving both of them over a dustbin. He landed on top, striking three quick, brutal blows to Frank's already wounded nose.

The dandy screamed with pain, clutching at his face.

Bennington grabbed the back of Sam's shirt, yanking him away.

Lily blocked another blow from the cudgel, then stumbled, her heel catching on an uneven paving stone. Gibbs dove at her, knocking her to the ground.

Lily clasped her hands together, then drove her elbows down into the soft place where his neck met his shoulder.

He howled in rage and pain, rolling off of her. She scrambled to her feet, backing up to the door, where Sam met her.

Frank the Spiv remained sprawled over the dustbin, clutching his nose and moaning. The one named Towers, that Sam had sliced with his blade, was busy wrapping a strip of his shirt around the wound.

The others were still in the game.

Art Bennington stepped back and lit a cigarette, dropping the spent match into a puddle. He had taken measure of the situation—one she suspected was informed by a great deal of experience—and apparently determined his assistance would not be needed to finish this job now that Lily and Sam had been disarmed.

Vince stood, testing his leg. He stalked toward her, displaying only a hint of a limp. The other tough, Mickey, had recovered from his winding. He plucked Sam's knife from the pavement and tested the heft of it in his hand.

It was clear he had handled one before.

Gibbs collected his cudgel from the ground, moving in behind them. Since the blows Lily had struck to his neck, the light in his eye had changed from a sort of resigned determination to something quick, cold and murderous.

Lily considered her options.

They weren't promising.

Her eyes flickered to her walking stick, which lay a few yards away on the pavement. She leapt toward it, a desperate move, but Vince was not as crippled as she hoped. He grabbed her by the arm, throwing her toward the wall of the hospital.

Beside her, Sam closed his eyes and whistled. The note was clear and musical, dancing through the night air.

Lily's back hit the stone as Vince's hands closed around her throat. She kicked him ferociously, scratching at his hands with her nails, but it felt like her limbs were moving through mud.

Sam whistled again, the sound cut off abruptly as he blocked a blow from the cudgel, leaving his cheek open to a vicious strike from Gibbs's other hand.

As she fought for breath, pain blazing across her throat, Lily heard a strange noise from above.

It was a rustling, thick and soft, as hundreds of wings battered against the night air.

Through the jagged opening in the roof of the hospital, doves streamed out into the night. They whirled down into the alley and swarmed at the men.

Wings beat at their faces, knocking hats askew. Sharp beaks scratched and bit at exposed skin, driving cuts into cheeks and hands. It was like being inside a tornado of living things, of talons and soft brown wings.

Lily's throat was released as her attacker swatted desperately at the birds, whirling to escape. She staggered away, gasping for air, stumbling into Sam. He stood still and calm, blood streaming from the split skin of his cheek, watching as hundreds of doves tore and beat at their attackers.

The birds were nearly silent, just the rush of moving air and flapping wings, while the men screamed. Here and there, soft gray bodies fell to the ground, limping or lying still.

A pair of birds fluttered toward them and Lily cringed back instinctively. They landed on Sam's arm and shoulder, cooing and nudging at him. He stroked them, then lifted one to his face, whispering to it. He raised his arm and the bird flew away.

"Let's go," he said, wiping the blood from his cheek and flicking it onto the pavement.

He walked away.

Lily followed, snatching her walking stick from the paving stones.

"You did that. You made them come."

"Doves are very protective," Sam commented.

She heard another scream from behind and glanced back to see a stream of birds rise up into the night above the low buildings.

# TWENTY-FOUR

$\mathscr{T}$HERE WERE TOOTHACHES. LEGS tied to wooden splints with rags torn from some third-hand petticoat. Sores, wounds, a plethora of pleurisy. Lily heard the rattle of the coughs from around the corner before she turned to see the line of patients queued up to seek admission to The Royal Hospital of St. Bartholomew—or St. Bart's, as it was more familiarly known by most Londoners.

For three-score men, women and children suffering from some of the worst that life could inflict on them, they were a remarkably orderly group. The line was maintained with civility from the late-comers taking up their place in the back to a silent shuffling that made way for a patient carried in on a stretcher by grave-faced men—a slater who had fallen from a roof, Lily heard whispered.

She felt odd walking past the group to the door itself, as though someone were bound to rebuke her for not waiting her turn. But perhaps the fact that she was walking and not covered in blood or oozing pus or hacking the life from her lungs made it clear enough to those waiting that she was not a threat to their particular order.

Not to say that she was uninjured.

The high neck of her blue wool gown concealed the vicious purple bruises that covered her throat. Her nails had been trimmed down to the quick, an attempt to conceal how thoroughly she had torn them when scratching at the man that attacked her. More bruises marked her back and discolored her legs.

At least she had been able to pull the stitches out of her thigh that morning.

The admissions desk was a quiet whir of activity, a trio of nurses triaging patients with stern efficiency. This took place in a wide hall with high ceilings and tall windows. The murmur of low voices echoed off the walls in a manner that reminded Lily of a cathedral just before the start of service.

"Excuse me," she said, cutting in as one of the nurses finished turning away a gentleman whom he had determined was only suffering from eczema, not leprosy. "Where might I find Dr. Gardner?" She lifted the bag in her hand, from which arose the unmistakable odor of sausage and chips. "I've brought his lunch."

"He's on the Matthew Ward today," the nurse snapped in reply and turned to the broken arms and gout-swollen toes that awaited him.

Lily found her own way into the core of the hospital. It was like a great, stunningly engineered machine built of bodies and bleach instead of grease and metal. Men and women buzzed up and down the halls with quick efficiency, bees in a well-ordered hive. Trolleys zipped to and fro across well-scrubbed tiles. Brass plates by the doors to well-appointed offices gleamed with the identity of their prestigious occupants, names accented by the addition of "Sir" or a row of illustrious initials. The potted palms that punctuated the hallways were a glossy, well-watered green.

Only the smell broke the spell of precision the place cast—an odor of harsh cleansers overlaying that pervasive funk of age and death that no place of healing could ever really escape.

She had to catch an orderly by the sleeve to get directions to the Matthew Ward.

It was a bright space with pale blue walls and beds full of patients suffering from pneumonia and rheumatism.

Lily spotted Dr. Gardner at once. The big Ulsterman was perched on the edge of a cot holding a very small, very pale child.

"It is rotten," he said, his voice a soft, gruff rumble from his chest. "It tastes absolutely vile. Don't let her tell you any different." He glanced toward the nurse who stood frowning behind him, holding a small vial in her hand. "But you need it to make you better, lad. You want to get better, don't you? And get back out to setting firecrackers in postboxes?"

"Have you done that? How's that work?" the boy demanded, rising with sudden interest.

"Toss that down like a good soldier and perhaps I'll tell you."

Lily waited by the door until the boy had finished the vial, face pinched with distaste. As the physician rose, she stepped forward.

"Doctor Gardner?"

"Miss Albright. I should not have expected to see you here."

"I brought you lunch." She raised the bag, now well spotted with grease.

"I see you have. Come, let's go into my office."

Dr. Gardner's domain was something different than the plush seats of power Lily had passed on the lower floor of the hospital. Instead of gleaming oak and soft leather, his space was crammed with file cabinets and a chipped pine table in dire need of refinishing. The room looked as though it had been converted from a closet, though Lily could discern that there was a clear order to the seeming clutter.

He tore the bag open carefully, picking out a chip and pushing the sausage roll to Lily.

"You can have this if you like. I haven't been much for eating flesh since seeing what Mr. Wu can do with animals. I also suspect it blocks up the heart."

"I'm not actually hungry."

"So to what do I owe the pleasure of this visit? I presume it was not simply to play lunch-maid."

"I'm hoping you can help me find a patient."

"I can try. Who are you looking for?"

"I don't actually have a name," Lily admitted.

"That makes it more of a puzzle. If you haven't a name, what do you have?"

"I know it's a female. Someone suffering from both syphilis and the after-effects of having been in a fire."

"We don't treat many syphilis patients here. They mostly end up at Lock Hospital. What makes you think she's at St. Bart's?"

"Frankly, I'm not even sure the person I'm looking for exists, but you're the only one I could think of who'd indulge me even this far, so I had to try."

"Well." He popped another chip in his mouth, then rose heavily from his chair. "Let's try, then. Shall we?"

~

The Records Desk was located at the other end of the hospital, another long walk along hallways buzzing with quietly urgent activity. It was a dark room that smelled of ink and glue.

"Mr. Gleeson," Dr. Gardner said in greeting as he entered.

"Oh. It's you," the thin man behind the desk replied flatly, blinking at them through his spectacles.

"Have we any syphilitic females on the wards at the moment?"

"Five, I believe," Mr. Gleeson replied shortly.

"Are any of them burn victims?"

Mr. Gleeson moved unerringly to one of the tall steel cabinets that lined the back of the room. He pulled open a drawer, flipping expertly through the files. He pulled one, glanced at it, then returned it to the drawer, slamming it shut with a clang.

"No," he replied shortly.

"Thank you. You've been most helpful," Dr. Gardener replied without a hint of irony.

Lily felt panic at the thought of this lead, however tenuous, being so easily cut off. She pushed her mind back to the corridors and charred ruins of the clinic—to the horror of the cold-tiled basement.

Her thoughts latched onto the image of the operating tables with those antennae-like stirrups attached to their bases.

"What about complications from abortion?" she cut in.

Mr. Gleeson raised his eyes, frowning at her.

"If you would please answer the lady, Mr. Gleeson," Dr. Gardner cut in gently.

Gleeson returned to his files, snapping open another drawer. His thin fingers skipped to another folder, which he plucked loose with a snap. He glanced over it, then closed it again.

"One of the syphilitic patients has had a hysterectomy."

"Any other complications?"

"She is reportedly suffering from the aftereffects of smoke inhalation."

"You didn't think that worth mentioning before?" Lily cut in, irritated. "When we asked about a burn victim?"

Mr. Gleeson snapped open the file, scanning it once more before closing it again.

"She hasn't got any burns," he declared flatly.

"Thank you, Mr. Gleeson," Gardner said patiently. "That sounds like our girl. Can you tell me where she is?"

"Sitwell Ward. Under Dr. Burton."

Dr. Gardner stepped back out into the hall, Lily following.

"It would have to be Burton's ward," he said under his breath.

"Is that a problem?"

Dr. Gardner began to walk, Lily falling into step beside him.

"The hospital is not a whole body, Miss Albright. Our wards are little fiefdoms and the resident lord is often quite jealous of his territory. Our Dr. Burton happens to be, as he will happily remind you, the great-grandson of the tenth Duke of Argyle. And he does not believe that the son of a Belfast tailor should be considered an equal to his Eton-and-Oxford-educated self, regardless of my years of study and practice."

"I see."

"Which is only to say that this could turn a mite uncomfortable."

"How uncomfortable?" Lily asked, taking his arm and pulling him to a stop. "I don't want you taking any risks for me."

Dr. Gardner stepped neatly out of the way of a rattling gurney.

"I was under the impression that the endeavor you are engaged in had rather high stakes. Or were we digging up graves in Abney Park for the fun of it?"

"It wasn't my idea to bring you into that."

"You'd have had Lord Strangford manage it on his own?"

"I tried to talk his lordship out of the whole notion," Lily countered.

"So the aim of all this must not be so significant, then."

"No," Lily admitted. "It is significant. But the chances I will succeed in it are . . . low. I will not see anyone else put themselves at risk for the sake of it, personally or professionally."

Her thoughts flew back to the night before, to Sam's head snapping under the force of a blow. To the birds that had fallen, the pale bodies littering the dark ground.

The doctor gently took her arm, guiding her to the side to avoid a nurse spinning out a door with a load of clean towels in her arms. He was a large man, towering over Lily, but moved with the thoughtless grace of a dancer.

"I'm not sure you understand how this works, Miss Albright."

"How what works?"

"The Refuge."

Lily felt her defenses snap up, readying her for battle.

"What does any of this have to do with The Refuge?"

"Those of us who are part of that place—when we are asked for aid, we give it. No matter how much we remain in the dark as to why. We do it because we're the only ones who understand what it's like to know the impossible things. Things nobody ought to know."

"I'm not part of that."

"Ah. I see."

His tone set her teeth on edge.

"What do you see, exactly?"

He stepped her out of the way of a trolley full of rattling sample jars.

"Perhaps that's a conversation for another time. Come along. I've only twenty minutes left of my lunch."

Lily stopped, holding back. A pair of nurses nearly bumped into her from behind, stepping around her with a glare of irritation.

"I told you I won't have you taking any risks for my sake."

"I am not taking them for your sake. I am taking them for the sake of whomever you are trying to protect."

"How do you know I'm trying to protect anyone?"

"Because you've made it quite clear this afternoon you have no interest in being under obligation to me or anyone else. And yet you already are. I do not believe you would have overcome your distaste of that for your own sake. Ergo, someone else's well-being must be on the line."

"I think your logic is flawed."

"Well, I never did have much of a head for it. But I'm right. So stop balking and come along. We haven't got all day."

~

The Sitwell Ward was located on the next floor down. Like Dr. Gardner's ward, it sported rows of tall, spotlessly clean windows through which the afternoon sun poured down onto the rows of beds. Dr. Gardner lead the way, walking with an easy pace down the central aisle. It looked as though he were merely stretching his legs, but Lily saw the way his eyes scanned across the charts that hung on clipboards at the end of each bed.

They were only halfway down the row when a nurse in a starched gray dress and white apron marched over.

"Dr. Gardner. Is there something we can do for you?"

"Just accompanying a friend of mine on a visit to one of your patients, Matron Roberge."

"I see. Which patient would that be?"

Lily could hear the sharp disapproval in the woman's tone. Clearly, her loyalties lay firmly with Dr. Burton, and not the Belfast tailor's son who had just strolled into her ward.

Lily moved a few steps past them, making her own quick scan of the clipboards.

"Miss MacAlister," she cut in, stopping at one of the beds. "I'm her cousin."

The matron turned an unwelcoming gaze on her.

"I was under the impression it was Mrs. MacAlister."

She placed a subtle but unmistakable emphasis on the title.

"Yes. Well," Lily paused meaningfully, glancing to the woman on the bed, who was watching the exchange with dull disinterest.

The matron took in the unimpeachably respectable cut of Lily's walking dress. She glanced at the brass watch that hung from a sturdy cord around her neck.

"You may have fifteen minutes. Then we must begin changing the linens."

"Thank you, Matron," Dr. Gardner said.

Lily moved closer to the patient. She was pale, thin as a famine victim, her dull brown hair falling lankly around her face. Vivid lesions stood out against the pale flesh around her mouth. The rest of her skin was covered with a fine mist of sweat. She breathed quick and shallow. Her eyes slid over to Lily as she lowered herself into the chair beside the bed.

"You're not my cousin," the woman rasped.

Behind Lily, Dr. Gardner moved to the window, his hands clasped at his back, gazing down at the courtyard.

"I had to say that so they would let me talk to you."

"Bernadette's man died in the mines. She left the baby with Gran and tumbled down the well."

"Who's Bernadette?" Lily asked.

"My cousin."

"Mrs. MacAlister . . . I need to know if you were ever in another hospital. Before this one."

"I don't like hospitals."

"What about a hospital over in Southwark?"

The woman seemed to shrink into the bed.

"Don't know anything about that."

Lily felt her pulse jump.

"You mustn't worry. No one will know. It'll be our secret, sacred as confession." She moved closer. "It was the one off Borough High Street, wasn't it?"

"They were supposed to help me with the baby."

"But they did more than that, didn't they?"

She looked away.

"He said it was best I let them take her out of me. That she'd only have been born with the pox herself and died in miserable pain."

"Your little girl," Lily offered.

It felt wrong. She was playing a part—the quiet, sympathetic listener, like a priest in his dark box. But every sense was sharp, her attention as avid as a gull at a picnic. The woman in the bed was raw, exposed like a nerve and just as vulnerable. She was also confused, half-lost in some dark wood of the soul. This was an exploitation, but Lily didn't have time for guilt. She had to know.

"Once it was done, why didn't you go?"

"He said they'd treat me, with a warm bed and three meals the meanwhile."

"And did they treat you?"

She shook her head. Her eyes fastened onto Lily's, sharpening with rage.

"He poisoned us. Put his devil poison into our veins."

"What do you mean?" Lily demanded.

"Syphilis is treated with mercury," Dr. Gardner cut in quietly from behind her, still looking out the window. "It is not a pleasant course. And it is largely ineffective."

Mrs. McAllister struggled to sit up, looking around, her breath rasping in her chest. "Where's Gran? Must tell her about the baby . . ." Her hand fluttered to her flat abdomen. "Always said it would come to that. But she'll not turn us away. Not . . ." Her wandering gaze fell on Lily and her brow furrowed with confusion. "Who are you, then?"

"Something isn't right here." Dr. Gardner turned from the window.

"What do you mean?"

"Those sores around her mouth are indicative of the secondary stage of the disease. But this mental confusion . . . I wouldn't expect to see that until later. Much later."

The doctor glanced over at the nurse's desk. The matron scribbled in a logbook, pausing to give some sharp order to a waiting underling.

He moved to the end of the bed, picking up Mrs. MacAlister's chart. He flipped through it, eyes quickly scanning the pages.

"Secondary syphilis. Distress of the lungs due to smoke inhalation. Well, that much is rather obvious."

He let the pages fall back into place. Lily glanced over to see the matron glaring in their direction, eyes locked onto Dr. Gardner. He set the clipboard down on the hook, moving back to the window.

"She's showing jaundice," he said. "That's the yellowing in her eyes. Syphilis doesn't cause jaundice, either. Can you touch her?"

"What's the big man saying?" the woman demanded, frowning at Dr. Gardner.

"Nothing you need mind," Lily smiled. She took her hand, patting it gently.

"Is she warm?" Dr. Gardner asked.

"Yes," Lily replied. The frail fingers in her palm burned like brands.

There was a clatter. Lily looked over at the nurse's desk to see the matron rise from her chair, turning on an elderly orderly who stood quaking by the remains of a shattered chamber pot. The acrid smell of it floated to her from across the room.

She glanced back to Dr. Gardner. She could see him fight a quick inner war. With a final glance at the distracted matron, he sat on the edge of the bed, the springs sagging under his weight.

"Mrs. MacAlister. I'm Dr. Gardner. Would you mind terribly if I checked your pulse?"

The woman didn't answer, just slid her hand from Lily's and extended it halfheartedly toward him.

The doctor took her small, thin wrist, holding it delicately in his massive hands.

His eyes closed.

Lily's senses flared to attention, her skin tingling. She was aware of every detail of the room—the sharp smell of ammonia, the scrape of the broken pieces of stoneware being picked up from the floor.

She was suddenly and entirely certain that Gardner was not counting the beats of this woman's heart.

He was doing something else.

His body was still, his breath deep and even. The moment stretched, slow and quiet, seeming to last forever though the hands barely twitched on the clock over the door.

Then it was done.

He opened his eyes and gently set the patient's arm back down onto the bed.

He looked over at Lily.

"This woman has malaria."

The pronouncement was so unexpected, it took Lily a moment to be certain she had heard it properly.

"But she's from Southwark. Who gets malaria in Southwark?"

"Mrs. MacAlister, have you ever traveled out of the country?" he asked.

The woman shook her head dreamily.

"Haven't been back to Ireland since I was a girl. My da said he'd whip me raw if I showed my face there again."

"Anywhere else?"

*"An' if they'd only shift the 'ackney Road and plant it over there— I'd like to live in Paris all the time."*

She sang tunelessly, her voice a hollow reed, but Lily still knew the tune. It struck her like a blow, drowning her in the perfect recollection of another voice lilting through those words.

A woman sitting at a vanity table, running a silver brush through a mane of glorious red hair. Her mother's bell-like tones dancing through the bawdy lyrics of an old music hall number.

Lily pushed the memory back, forcing herself to focus on the matter at hand.

"You're certain it's malaria. It couldn't be something else?"

"I know it as well as I know you've a ring of bruises on your neck under the collar of that dress," the doctor replied quietly. "Best loosen that if it starts to feel tight, by the way. Swelling after strangulation can be delayed and you don't want it to constrict your airway."

Lily's mind flew back to Abney Park, to his hand on her elbow as he helped her from the carriage—followed by his casual reference to the wound on her leg, an injury he couldn't possibly have seen.

*That itch isn't anything to worry about. Just the wound healing.*

The same hand had taken her arm in the hall a few minutes before, steering her out of the way of the whirling activity of the hospital.

"Are you like Strangford?" she demanded softly.

"No," he replied in the same low tone. "I'm not like his lordship. I just have a way of knowing how a body has gone wrong."

Her thoughts tumbled, a cacophony of questions fighting to be first to her lips. All the while the truth rang through her.

She had found another charismatic.

Just as the first query was about to spill from her lips, he cut in. "Another time and place, Miss Albright."

She looked to the nurse's desk where the orderly was hurrying from the room, the matron snapping her fingers at a young nurse with a mop in her hands.

She forced her focus to return to the matter at hand.

Malaria was a disease of tropical climates, carried in the bite of the mosquito. The disease might linger after its first appearance, going quiet for years only to emerge again with a vengeance. Those who had it were usually veterans of colonial wars or adventurers who found more than fortune and glory on their endeavors.

Not Borough whores.

"The malaria. If she didn't travel, could she have . . . caught it from someone?"

"It isn't sexually transmitted. The only way to get it is from the bite of an infected mosquito or some other form of blood-to-blood contact."

"It was that lying devil's blood."

The voice of the woman in the bed startled her.

"What lying devil, Mrs. MacAlister?"

"The one what took my baby girl." The whore's face crumpled, a still-raw grief distorting it for a moment. "*Can't you think of any other name but 'Baby' . . .*" she sang weakly. "It was his bad blood made us sick. Them it didn't kill dead. Florrie. Beth. Rita. The butcher's widow. That wee slip of a thing from Croydon, who run off after her father did worse than belt her. All dead. I was lucky. *It's up and down in life, boys, in and out of luck. Too-ral-lay . . .*"

The tune cut off with a cough, the sound tearing up from inside of her, racking her hollow frame.

"How did his blood make you sick?" Lily asked.

The whore slumped back on the bed, her frame seeming to sink deeper into the thin mattress.

"They run it into us with tubes and pins. Tied you to the table so you couldn't get away. Worse than an alley swive, that. There's no washing it out. Can't soap under your skin."

Lily's thoughts flashed back to the operating tables in the basement of the clinic, accented with thick leather straps and buckles.

"Are you saying that someone put human blood into your body?"

Gardner's voice rumbled from behind her shoulder, where he had come to stand.

"Some got it. Some lost it. He stole it out of them to run it into the lying devil. The blood ran out, the blood ran in—and he stayed hale through all of it while we women died or got the fever. But that's always the way of it, innit? They live high while we rot."

Lily rose to stand beside the doctor.

"Do you understand what she's describing?"

"It doesn't resemble any medical procedure that I know," he replied. "But she is not in the clearest state of mind. She needs to be treated for the malaria—she needs quinine."

Lily could see the tension in his posture, the frustration under the surface of his expression.

She understood. She knew how much easier it would be simply . . . not to know.

How likely was it that Dr. Burton, great-grandson of the Duke of Argyle, would allow his diagnosis to be corrected by the upstart son of a Belfast tailor? And yet how could Gardner not try to get the woman the treatment she needed?

Knowledge required action, action that entailed risk and difficulty and would most likely lead to naught.

*When we are asked for aid, we give it . . . because we're the only ones who understand what it's like to know the impossible things.*

"Go," Lily said. "Tell them."

He turned, then paused. "This may mean that your interview will be cut short. I would get to the meat of it now, if you can."

He crossed the ward, reaching the desk just as the matron returned to the room. Gardner's voice was a low, gentle rumble, words indiscernible from this distance, but the matron's reply rang out clear as a siren across the rows of beds.

"You must realize this is highly irregular."

Lily tried to ignore the confrontation at the front of the ward, turning her full attention to the woman in the hospital bed.

"Mrs. MacAlister, can you tell me more about the doctor who treated you?"

"Which doctor?" she replied dreamily. "The officer or the toff?"

The toff . . . the prestigious man who had his name in brass by the door. Lily didn't need the woman in the hospital bed to tell her who that had been.

"The officer," she replied. "Tell me about him."

At the front of the ward, Gardner spoke to the matron in urgent tones. The woman's face was growing harder.

"He fought the Boers in Africa. The toff said he was special, but we knew better. Just a lying devil with poison in his blood. He'd have poisoned every one of us if the Jew hadn't come."

Jew? Lily could feel the weight of the charm had found in the attic in her pocket, where she had slipped it that morning—the strange pendant marked with Hebrew characters.

"We were all fulfilling a great purpose," the whore said vaguely. "To cure man's ills and better the human race."

The voice, the tone, were not her own, like a phonograph scraping out an old recording. They were an echo of something else, something she had heard.

From a distinguished physician, perhaps, justifying the horrors he inflicted on a group of patients powerless to protest.

"Tell me more about the Jew."

"They kept coming back for her, again and again, taking her blood and giving it to the lying devil."

"They gave the officer her blood? What did he do with it?"

"Put it in his arm," the woman replied, as though Lily's question bordered on nonsensical. "But she weren't having none of their purpose. Said she'd put a stop to it. And she did. Poured the lamp oil over her hair, lit the match and burned up bright and pretty."

The horror ran through her, rippling down her arms. She remembered Sam looking up at the charred gap in the floor, frowning.

*Something odd about that fire . . . Didn't start in the hearth.*

Berta's story came back to her, a fairy tale of burning witches.

Mrs. MacAlister was singing again.

*"I dreamed last night that my true love came in . . ."*

"I want you out of this ward." The strident tones of the matron cut through the blur of Lily's thoughts.

"Just tell him to examine her blood," Gardner barked in response, his voice uncharacteristically sharp.

"Leanan sidhe," the woman murmured. "That's what Gran calls them. The blood-drinkers. You watch out for them. They'll drain you till there ain't nothing left."

Gardner came to Lily's side.

"We have to go."

She hesitated. There were too many questions she still needed to ask, too many things unknown.

"What else can you tell me about the officer? What did he look like?"

"Everybody. No one."

"What about his name?"

"Waddington," she replied, her voice and look as clear, in that moment, as they had been since Lily came in. "His name was Waddington."

"Miss Albright . . ." Gardner cautioned.

Lily paused only to squeeze the dying woman's hand.

"I'm sorry," she whispered, though she wasn't certain why she was apologizing. Was it for what Hartwell and his officer had done to her? Or for what Lily herself was powerless to change?

She rose, following the doctor out of the room.

She let him guide her back to the ground floor. He stopped at a small door set in the rear of the building, far from the busy admissions entrance.

He paused before opening it.

"When you asked if I understood what that patient was describing . . . I told you it did not sound like any legitimate medical procedure."

Lily caught the nuance in his tone.

"But it did sound like something."

"Do you remember in the carriage on the way back from Abney Park, you asked me what someone might do with human blood?"

She recalled vividly Gardner's description of the dangers and challenges of trying to transfuse blood from a human donor to a recipient. How even experimenting with the procedure had been abandoned by the medical community, since those experiments so often ended in death.

*Florrie. Beth. Rita . . .*

"You think they were experimenting with transfusion."

"I do not know what to think, Miss Albright. There are challenges to relying on the word of a delusional witness. But were I to hazard a guess, I might conclude that whatever you have gotten yourself into, it speaks of men of my profession who ought to be dragged through the streets and hung for what they've done."

Lily thought of the horror of that cold tiled operating room—and of the black holes by the door where an illustrious name had once hung, emblazoned in brass.

343

"If you could put blood from one person into another . . . it would make a great deal of difference in many medical situations. Wouldn't it?" she asked.

"It would be of earth-shattering consequence," he confirmed quietly.

"So how likely do you think it is that these men of your profession would be brought to account for trading the lives of a few whores to advance such an achievement?"

"There is more than one power that calls us to account," he replied. He bowed. "Good afternoon, Miss Albright. Please remember what I said about your collar. And The Refuge."

He turned, his big, heavy feet treading silently across the tiles.

—

It was cold outside.

The sky had turned a pale, uniform gray overhead, the air carrying the sharp promise of snow.

She was running out of time.

Much of the story of what had happened in Southwark was beginning to take shape in her mind. If Hartwell had been experimenting with blood transfusion, using an army doctor with dormant malaria in his veins, it explained how a Borough whore had managed to contract a tropical disease. It also explained why his followers still monitored the burned-out shell of that building, watching for anyone expressing undue interest in what had taken place there.

What it did not do was tell her why the illustrious physician might then move on to stealing the blood of sleeping mediums.

Something was still missing, the piece of this puzzle that would give her a clear image of how Hartwell's activities were connected to the murders. Until she had it, she could not hope to move against him. She could not even be sure he was the source of the threat to Estelle or a distraction that would let the real enemy slip past her.

It was all gossamer, threads of guesswork and intuition.

She needed certainty and she had no more time to waste in finding it.

Which left her only one place to go.

# TWENTY-FIVE

$\mathcal{B}$AYSWATER WAS QUIET, HUDDLED into itself in preparation for the promised storm. Carriages slid down the icy streets. Pairs of women or lone gentlemen, wrapped in wool, moved purposefully by, hurrying to complete their calls before the skies opened.

Lily hesitated at the foot of Strangford's steps.

The vision forced itself back into her mind—not the burnt shell of the clinic, but the foresight that had preceded it of bare hands sliding over her skin.

She did not want to go inside. It was dangerous here in a way that ran deeper than the threat posed by Hartwell's thugs, but she had pursued this thread of inquiry as far as she could. This was her last option for answering the questions that plagued her about Hartwell, the clinic, and a possible connection to Estelle. Too much depended on this for Lily to walk away without answers and only the man on the other side of that door could provide them.

Her ruminations were brought to an abrupt end as the door in front of her opened.

A woman glided out. She was small and elegant, wrapped in a froth of very tasteful emerald silk. Her dark hair was spun into an airy coiffure, topped by a gravity-defying green hat. A fat, elderly pug tumbled out of the doorway behind her, lumping down the first three steps before stopping, presumably to take a rest.

"I'll be by again next week. Don't forget to restock the sherry. Your economical ways are admirable and all that, but there are limits. Oh!" Her dark eyes lit on Lily, then moved thoughtfully to Strangford, who had appeared behind her on the threshold.

Who was she? Not a wife. He could not have hidden a wife from her through all this. A fiancée? She wore a wedding ring on her finger. A lover? Lily felt stabbed with ice. It was an entirely useless reaction. She forced it down mercilessly.

The pug snorted, round eyes blinking lazily. It had positioned itself directly above the sculpted iron dog Lily had previously noted decorating Strangford's steps.

The two were nearly identical.

"Are you here for a charity?" the woman asked.

"No, she is not," Strangford replied.

The emerald woman considered this. "How very intriguing."

"Virginia, this is Miss Albright. Miss Albright, allow me to introduce my sister, Mrs. Eversleigh."

Yes, the pugs matched. So did the two pairs of dark eyes that looked down at her from the top of the steps. He had mentioned a sister before, the one who gave his horse that ridiculous name Strangford had never seen fit to alter.

"Do you need me to stay and play chaperon, Anthony?" she asked Strangford, not entirely under her breath.

"That won't be necessary."

Mrs. Eversleigh smiled. "Even more interesting. Well. I do have that hair appointment to keep, else I would certainly turn right back around and impose myself for a bit longer. Alas, one does not keep Jorge waiting, and it took me over a month to book him. But I do look forward to encountering you again, Miss Albright. Strangford," she said, nodding to her brother. "Come, Horatio," she ordered as she descended the steps, followed by a cloud of perfume and the waddling pug.

Her departure left a wake of silence that stretched just long enough to be awkward. Lily finally broke it.

"Can I speak with you?"

"Of course. Should we go in?"

There was just a hair of hesitation before he made the offer. Combined with the appearance of his fashionable, *tonnish* sister on the steps a moment before, it brought home to Lily the potential impropriety of the situation.

When she had been alone with him in his home before, the urgency of the circumstances had required it. She had no such excuse now.

"Perhaps we could walk."

"I'll get my coat," he replied.

~

They went to the park.

Strangford did not offer to take her arm, nor did Lily ask. They moved in parallel silence down the path. The normally busy way was all but empty, their only company a few harried-looking travelers who rushed along, their scarves wrapped tightly around their faces.

Even those passers-by were still more company than Lily felt comfortable with. When a narrow trail broke off from the paved way, Lily took it. Strangford followed her until they reached a quiet grove.

The lime trees that encircled them were bare, branches forming a crown that framed the pewter gray of the sky.

"What can I do for you, Miss Albright?"

His tone was formal. It was an unfamiliar sound. She realized what it implied—that she had succeeded in her attempt to push him away from her. She supposed she ought to be happy.

"I wondered if I might impose upon you to use your talents for me once again."

"Certainly," he replied, as though the last time she had asked that of him, he had not ended up enveloped in walking death for near fourteen hours.

That grated her.

"Aren't you even going to ask what it is?"

"Does it matter?"

"I should think it would, to you."

There was a quick flash of irritation in his dark gaze.

"Where have you been?" he demanded, a gust of wind unsettling the dark curls of hair.

"Conducting a few inquiries."

"Sam Wu took a beating last night. Were you with him?"

"I don't see how that—"

"Damn you, Lily." The formal mask was gone now, his anger quick and apparent. "Where?"

"Following a very thin lead at an old hospital in Southwark."

"Southwark?"

"Near the old Mint," she clarified purposefully. There was little point in evading that she had been in the vicinity of one of London's most notorious old slums. After all, he would likely discern it in a few moments when she handed him the object in her pocket.

"Why didn't you come to me for help?"

"I didn't think your help would be necessary."

"But Sam Wu's was."

"He can pick locks."

Strangford absorbed this with an unsettling stillness.

"Were you hurt?"

"No," she lied, feeling the soreness of the bruises around her throat. She straightened her back. "I rather think I have imposed on you enough in this matter."

He looked down, his hands thrust into the pockets of his black wool overcoat. Dry leaves skittered across the grass at his feet.

"Imposed upon me. Is that what you think this is?"

"Coming to you for help with something that isn't your battle? Yes. I should call that imposing."

"Not my battle?" He raised his head, his eyes flashing. "Do you forget that I know who he's killed? I know them far better than you."

The words were edged, and they cut. Lily thought of Annalise Boyden with her clear, church bell laugh. Sylvia Durst, whose last moments the man before her had inhabited both body and soul, an intimacy she couldn't possibly imagine.

He stepped closer as the wind tugged her skirts. His anger was as clear as it was uncharacteristic. It startled her, sparking a reaction that felt uncomfortably like guilt.

"Do you truly think I don't know who's next? That I can't discern the pattern here and connect it to a motive for your own interest in the matter? How much of a fool do you think I am?"

There was no answer she could give him. She should have known all of this and been sensitive to it, but she had been too wrapped up in the discomfort of her own attraction to the man. She had been looking for any excuse she could find to escape him and those she had chosen—that this wasn't his responsibility, that it was for his own protection—were as false as the painted backdrop on a stage in the face of his truth.

Silence lingered, becoming more uncomfortable. Should she apologize? How could she? It would mean admitting the reason for what she had done.

It was Strangford who finally broke it.

"What did you bring me?"

She took the pendant from her pocket.

"I should warn you . . ." she began as he pulled off his gloves.

". . . that this could be difficult?" He tucked the gloves back in his pocket and extended one of those pale, elegant hands. "I'm aware."

She hesitated.

"Strangford . . ."

"Just give it to me, Lily."

She placed the pendant in his palm.

He moved away from her, closing his eyes.

She waited as the skeletal branches danced against the pale sky.

"There is a forest. Mountains, wolves in the wood. Not England. Far too wild for England. A burning forge. Voices. Chanting, like an incantation."

"Too far back," Lily cut in. "We need London. Something more recent."

He shifted, tilting his head. Sharp emotion flashed across his features, anger mingling with fear.

"Someone had his hands around your throat." He opened his eyes, broken out of the reading, and the fury in his dark glare made her mouth dry.

"Not that recent," she replied, voice a touch hoarse.

He tore the glare away from her with obvious effort and closed his eyes, pushing himself back into the object in his hand.

"I smell soot. The stink of the river. Something else . . . brewer's yeast. A woman was wearing this someplace foreign and dangerous. Dirty. Things worse than wolves roaming about."

"Someplace foreign? Not London?"

"It's London."

"She was foreign," Lily filled in.

"Yes."

"Can you see a hospital? How did she get there?"

"There was a baby. It was . . . she was frightened. The community would force her out and alone in this place she would die. She's so certain of that. She doesn't have any choice. She has to get rid of it. God, it hurts her . . ."

The muscles of his face convulsed, grief shuddering through the lines of his jaw, the twist of his mouth.

"They told her not to go. She should have listened to them. They warned her."

"Who warned her?"

"The dead," Strangford replied.

The world stopped. Time stretched across a heartbeat, her focus complete.

"How did the dead warn her?" she asked, forcing her tone to remain even, neutral.

Strangford opened his eyes. His tone shifted, emptying of all the pain and confusion of the moment before, though Lily's careful gaze could still see the vestiges of it in the slope of his shoulders, the tension around his eyes.

"She could see them. Hear them. Had been able to ever since she was a girl."

"The woman who wore this was a medium," Lily clarified. She had to be certain.

"Yes. She was," he replied. His tone was hard.

He extended the hand with the pendant.

Lily retrieved it, slipping it back into her pocket.

"Thank you. That was most helpful."

Her voice didn't shake. It was a small miracle, given the tumult quaking through her.

The Jewish woman in the clinic had been able to see the dead. The woman that Hartwell had become obsessed with, whose blood he had stolen over and over again until she finally burned herself alive to be free of him.

Another medium with her essence ripped from her body. Her life forfeit.

The connection. The link she had been waiting for. This was it.

What the mirror had shown her had been no accident. It was not just the latest in the parade of horrors she had been subjected to all her life. She had asked something of her power and it had delivered.

It was Hartwell.

But why? Why was he doing it? Was it just some sort of madness? She thought of the man she had met in the gallery. He had not seemed at all mad. He was lucid, clear and sharp as glass. So what could he possibly hope to gain by stealing the blood of women who saw the dead?

Strangford stepped away from her, tugging back on his gloves. His gaze was directed across the clearing, every line of him rigid.

"You're angry."

"Yes. I am angry." He turned to face her. His voice was even but his eyes flashed. The tension in him was taut as a bowstring. "You come when you have use for me. You make me part of this and then you shut me out of it to go barreling into another victim—to end up assaulted by thugs in the street with only a boy for protection."

"Sam isn't a child."

"That is not the point."

"Must I run every decision I make in this matter past you?"

"No," he countered. "You'll not deflect this into some other argument. I want to know why. Why do you insist on shutting me out of this, on shouldering all of it alone even though there are other people's lives on the line?"

Lily raised her chin, meeting his glare evenly.

"I have always taken care of myself and my own matters, and I will continue to do so. I will not be anyone's burden."

"Who ever gave you the impression that you were?"

"Then who do you do this for? Mrs. Boyden? You'd barely spoken to her in years."

"She didn't deserve to die like that."

"So justice, then? Some abstract ideal?"

"It is hardly abstract to the women who have died."

"Women die every day in this city. I did not think you made a habit of prowling the streets in search of rapists and murderers and heavy-handed husbands."

"What do you want from me?" he snapped, coming closer. She could feel the heat coming off of him, the force of the emotion raging through him.

She refused to step back.

"I merely needed some help with a necklace. Nothing more," she replied, channeling all her strength into holding up that thin facade of calm and control, making herself as placid as a lake in winter.

"That is not what I asked you."

"It's still the answer."

"And I know it is a lie," he replied.

He was close, the fight pulling him nearer until only a breath separated them. She remembered when they had stood like this before, when his hands had grazed the surface of her skin, his mind delving into the innermost secrets of her soul.

It took a mountain of effort to remain steady in both voice and body.

"This is not a level playing field."

It was meant to be a blow, to force him away, and it succeeded. The anger in him cracked like a mirror. He dropped back, pulling his hands through his hair, disheveling it.

"A level playing field isn't possible with me. It never will be. No matter how I bared my soul to you, it would be nothing compared to what I could pull from yours with a single touch." He held up his black-clad hands like weapons that had to be sheathed. "Do you understand what that would mean for any intimacy I ever shared with someone?"

"I never asked for intimacy."

"There's no point in equivocating. I know—"

"—that I wanted to take you to bed?" Lily cut in baldly. "I feel desire for you, Strangford. That is hardly worth denying, as those hands of yours undoubtedly learned it from me. But there is a vast distance between desire and action. I never had any intent to try the latter. You may rest assured on that."

It was as though she had struck him, a quick slap to the face. He drew back.

"I see."

She should have left it there. It would have been the wiser thing to do, to simply allow him to believe that her feeling for him had a mere impulse of the body, as fleeting as it was shallow.

But it was wrong. Safer, perhaps. But wrong. She owed him more than that and to ignore it meant she was, at the heart of it, nothing but a coward.

She forced the truth out, coughing it up as though something were still strangling her.

"I will not be any man's secret. I have seen what it does to the souls of all parties involved and I want no part in it."

"You thought I would make you my mistress?"

His voice was dry with shock, rasping from his throat.

"As I am the daughter of a woman who made the better part of her living on her back, there is hardly another option for 'intimacy' between the likes of you and I."

"Ah," he said. "Because I am a peer of the realm. And I must have a respectable wife."

"To pretend otherwise would be foolishness."

"And we mustn't be foolish," he concluded.

There was something off in his tone, something that rang of sarcasm. The possible implication of that rattled her, unsettling her presumption that this man who put glorious scribbles on his walls and saw unthinkable truths with every touch would give a fig what society thought of his mate.

That was a door she must never open. She should not even know it existed. It would only make this harder, make the inevitable fall all the more crushing.

She wouldn't give anyone the power to do that to her again.

The wind gusted through the clearing. A spill of dead leaves danced across the ground that separated them.

"Well," she said. "That's settled, then." She stepped back. "I'll not take up any more of your afternoon."

Across the clearing, he raised his head, dark eyes locking onto her own.

"May I make one final request?"

"Of course," she replied, though every fiber of her body screamed for escape. This conversation was twisting her into knots, no matter how well she pretended otherwise.

"I have told you that I am committed to this. There is nothing you could ask of me to further it that I would consider an imposition. So I must beg, Miss Albright, that you ask. Before you are throttled again."

The leaden sky twisted overhead, roiling between the naked branches of the lime trees.

"Your request is noted, my lord."

"Then I wish you a good evening," he replied stiffly.

He turned and walked away.

She watched him go, waiting for her knees to steady enough to make her own escape, her energy focused on holding together the fault inside of her that threatened to split into a chasm.

She could not be a chasm. Not now. There was a murderer out there and she could think of only one way to stop him—a path that led her straight into the den of the most dangerous lion she knew.

# TWENTY-SIX

$\mathcal{T}$HE PALACE OF WESTMINSTER rose in Gothic spires and imposing towers on the banks of the Thames. Around the looming statue
of Richard the Lionheart, his crusader's sword held aloft over the
restless hooves of a war horse, a snarl of gleaming carriages slowly
unfurled, delivering Britain's noblest to the gates of the House
of Lords.

"Stop here," Lily ordered her driver. She paid her fare and alighted
from the hackney at the entrance to the courtyard, making her way
along the jam of polished and painted vehicles to the palace itself.

The cold air bit at her cheeks. The leaden sky hung heavy over the
ornate elegance of the building. From the clock tower, the bells of
Big Ben peeled out, the hands of the great clock showing Lily it was
half-past three.

The Lords was set to enter session at four o'clock. The stream of
bodies clad in well-tailored overcoats and silk top hats were all making their way to the prominent entrance set into the center of the
wing. The gaslights that accented it were already lit, glowing against
the encroaching gloom of an early twilight.

Lily steered away from it to an unobtrusive door set at the base of
the great Victoria Tower.

This was the public entrance to the building. A pair of guards at
the door were carefully scrutinizing everyone who walked through.

One of them gave a long, skeptical look at Lily's walking stick but finally waved her on.

The stream of bodies pushed her along a twisting corridor, then out into a wide, elegant hall. It was crowded with peers, a river of men moving in and out of the cloakroom, eddying into little clusters of conversation punctuated by raucous laughter.

The women stood out like exotic birds, the bright hues of their gowns startling against all that black and gray and tweed. Lily was uncomfortably and unavoidably conspicuous here, but there was nothing to be done about it.

She had a greater challenge to consider—how she was going to find the Earl of Torrington in the midst of all this aristocratic chaos.

She wove her way out of the flow of bodies, taking up a position by the wall between a pair of marble busts that allowed her to make a quick scan down the length of the hall. There was no sign of him, though she did catch herself on the receiving end of a few puzzled looks, as though the sight of a lingering woman were something slightly untoward in here.

"You heard, of course." The nobleman beside her was whispering to a colleague. Lily could smell the sherry on his breath from where she stood.

"Of the arraignment?"

The word drew her attention—*arraignment*.

"Torrington hasn't said a word about it, that I've heard." The sherry-scented one's voice had grown bolder and drew a few glances from other men in the hall.

His companion stepped back, his own tone lowering.

"I'd not assume the father will fall with the son. That man is clever as a cat and twice as resilient. Best watch your words," he added in a whisper, then moved away.

The House of Lords hadn't brought one of their own to trial in half a century. It was apparently the talk of the halls that Lord Deveral was set to break that record.

Well, that would make Lily's errand a bit easier. If she wanted to find her father, she need only watch the gossip move through the crowd.

She stepped out from her niche and joined the flow of bodies. It carried her around a bend and down another corridor. Some of the lords moved along while others pressed directly into the chamber of the House of Lords using the doorway that lay directly in front of her.

As men passed the entrance, she saw them pause, heads peering round into the great room. Whispers were exchanged.

Lily knew that sort of whisper.

She moved to the side, studying the doorway. The chamber beyond was huge, with plush red leather benches and walls of ancient, elegantly carved wood. A great golden throne, just visible from where she stood, gleamed untouched on a dais.

There were several men already inside. She caught glimpses of them moving back and forth, calling out to an acquaintance or shuffling to a seat.

Lily's gaze lit on the tall, straight-backed figure of her father.

She crossed the hall to the door.

"No ladies on the floor."

The voice was strident, the words as practiced as a mass. The speaker was a plump, elderly man in a gray suit decorated with several prominent brass pins and seals. A docent of some sort, Lily surmised.

She didn't have time for this. She needed to get inside.

She pulled herself up straight, fixing him with her most haughty glare.

"I'm Lord Torrington's daughter. I need to speak to him before the session starts."

The docent was unmoved. He merely puffed up his chest, like a pigeon intimidating a rival, and repeated his line.

"No ladies on the floor."

She was contemplating the value of simply creating a scene and hoping it garnered her father's attention before she was tossed out into the street when she noted a few brightly-colored figures glittering in the gallery that overhung the Lords' chamber floor. The handful of women clustered there looked like butterflies lost in a dark wood.

"Can I view the session from there?" she asked, indicating the gallery.

"Visitors' stair is through the Peers' Lobby." The docent pointed a stiff arm down the hall.

The lobby felt like it belonged inside a cathedral. The richly tiled floor was barely visible under the press of polished black leather shoes. A massive chandelier was suspended overhead, its light glittering across the gilded archways and the shining surface of the great brass gate, which currently sat open to admit a continuous flow of noblemen. Stained glass panels set into the high walls bore the crests of some high-ranking family or another.

A dark, narrow doorway on the far side indicated the promised visitors' stair. Lily started to make her way toward it, threading through the press of men.

A pair of peers stopped in front of her, blocking her way, as unconscious of her presence as if she were merely another piece of the decor.

"Did you lunch well?"

"Just a sandwich. Her ladyship's insistence—she claims I am outgrowing my waistcoats."

"Pity that. I've heard it's to be a long night."

They moved on, the tight-waistcoated baron grumbling about knicking an apple from the dining room.

"Strangford!" someone shouted nearby. She turned.

He was there, just a few feet away from her. His eyes were on a sheaf of papers in his hand. He looked tired, a darkness she hadn't seen an hour before noticeable under his eyes.

She slipped behind a corpulent marquess. The man who had called found his way to Strangford. As she risked a glimpse over the marquess's shoulder, she noted that the gentleman had to take Strangford by the arm before he noticed him.

They were moving slowly toward the door to the chamber.

No—not that, she begged silently. He couldn't enter yet.

A peer at the door exclaimed at the sight of Strangford's companion. Vigorous handshakes ensued and to Lily's relief Strangford was pulled into a niche for some further exchange.

She moved quickly. Abandoning the cover of the marquess, she wove over to the stairs and climbed up the dark, twisting way.

The gallery wound around the entirety of the room. It was narrow, making her wonder how the women of fifty years before, with their hoop skirts and crinolines, would have managed to navigate it. But then, perhaps it had never been intended that women should invade the sacred precincts of the Lords, even as remote observers.

The handful who had braved their way to perch here eyed her thoughtfully as she came in, the quick chatter of their voices lowering as she made her way along the length of the chamber.

She ignored the looks and stopped as she reached the part of the gallery closest to where Lord Torrington stood on the chamber floor, not far from the gilded throne.

She waited.

The men below paid her no heed. It was as though the gallery, and the women upon it, existed on some other plane.

She tried a loud cough. It earned her a few more looks from the ladies but no notice from the peers.

Somewhere over her head, a very large clock was ticking.

She took the brass head of her walking stick and rapped it sharply against the rail of the gallery.

Heads turned. Her father's was late in joining them, but his eyes locked onto her directly with clear and instant recognition.

He nodded toward the stair.

As she moved back along the gallery, she wondered if the gesture hadn't meant simply "get out of here." At any rate, she could hardly do anything else, unless she planned to start shouting and have herself carried out of the room.

As she neared the end of the gallery, Strangford stepped into the chamber.

For a moment, she was frozen, startled into paralysis, but he did not look up. She pulled herself out of it and quickly left for the safety of the dark stairwell.

Her father was waiting in the lobby. He offered his arm as she emerged. She accepted it and he guided her out of the cacophonous chatter of that high space and into the relative quiet of the hall.

They left behind the splendor of the official rooms, passing tiny offices where clerks shuffled mountains of paper, a startlingly mundane sight between all the paintings and marble statues.

At the end of the hall, he opened a plain wooden door and motioned her inside.

It was a room of more regular proportions, though the view was extraordinary. Gothic windows framed the Thames in a manner that made Lily feel as though she must be floating over the dull, gray river.

The walls were papered in crimson and gold, richly contrasting with the dark, carved wood of the wainscoting. The space was simply furnished with long wooden tables, chairs, and a few leather benches.

"Committee room," Lord Torrington explained, shutting the door. "We won't be disturbed here. Though I haven't much time. I must be back in the chamber before the session commences."

"I only need a minute. It's about Lord Deveral."

"I'm listening."

He was. She could see that. The full force of his attention was on her. He was a man whose attention carried weight.

Against her will, her mind fluttered back to that night in Deveral's house, to the words he threw at her like a weapon.

*Father wanted to foist you off on us like some lost puppy . . .*

He had wanted to acknowledge her. To make her part of his family.

But he hadn't, she reminded herself forcefully.

"I know who killed Annalise Boyden." She paused, then played her card. "It was Dr. Joseph Hartwell."

"Dr. Joseph Hartwell was with me the night of Mrs. Boyden's death," her father countered evenly.

"What?" Lily was unable to hide her shock.

"His society is advocating for amendments to a marriage bill we're debating. Some . . . restrictions on matrimonial unions. He managed to get an appointment with the prime minister. Loreburn begged off so I went to represent—unofficially—the position of the Lords in the matter. He was closeted up with Asquith, Lloyd George, and myself for most of the night."

"Till when?"

"Three in the morning."

The revelation shook her, shifting the landscape of the case she had begun to build from under her feet. She struggled to catch up, moving other pieces into place.

"He didn't do it himself. He has an accomplice—I believe it to be former army doctor by the name of Waddington. But it was done under his orders."

Her father crossed to the window. He was quiet, but Lily could see his powerful mind working behind that haughty facade.

"This is not a man to be lightly accused."

"You think I do this lightly?" she retorted.

"What evidence do you have?"

"There is a clinic in Southwark. Burned now, but he was conducting experiments there on charity patients. Attempting human blood transfusion. One of the women he had locked in there was a medium."

"What has any of that to do with Mrs. Boyden?"

She was going too fast. She caught herself, forced herself to slow, despite the urgency firing through her.

"He's been killing mediums. Draining them of their blood. There are at least three other victims that I've identified. Mrs. Boyden was holding séances. Privately, but Hartwell must have learned about it."

"I was under the impression the lady's throat was cut."

"There was less blood than there ought to have been. I'm sure you have managed by now to get your hands on the medical examiner's report."

"I have seen it," he admitted.

She moved closer, pressing her case.

"Your son's arraignment is in a week. Give them the real killer and save him from that ordeal."

"I would gladly do so. But Dr. Hartwell is one of the most respected intellectuals in Britain."

"Respected men have been guilty of foul deeds before."

He was silent. Time was slipping away from her. She had to convince him to act. Feeling desperation rise, she played another card, this one with a more trembling hand.

"He will do it again," she said quietly. "I swear to you, a woman will die if something is not done to stop him."

"How do you know that?"

She lifted her chin, forced out the answer.

"You know how."

He crossed the room to a painting of some long-dead king leading a troop of men and wild-eyed horses.

He was not a man who showed his agitation, but Lily could see it in the tap of his finger against his leg. She waited, biting back further arguments, knowing that he must have his time to think.

He shook his head.

"I cannot accuse such a man on nothing but hearsay."

It was as though he had struck her.

"What?" she said quietly, stepping back.

"There is nothing you have given me that directly connects him to Mrs. Boyden or any of these other victims."

"It is there. But it must be looked for to be found."

"You think the powers of the law leap simply because I point my finger?"

"Wouldn't they?" Lily demanded.

"It is not so simple. There are other concerns at play."

"More important than the life of your child? Or do you find all of us expendable?"

It was a low blow. She knew it and half expected him to lash out at her for it.

He did not. He was all the earl once again, cold and imposing, immobile as stone.

"He was the last man to be seen with her alive. It is established that they argued. The murder weapon belonged to him. Did I not know him so well I could easily credit the accusation."

"But you do know him."

He looked tired.

"Yes. I do. And that is why I cannot speak on this matter. It is well known that the case against him is strong. Any action on my part to shift the blame to another would only be viewed as a father's desperate appeal to save his heir."

"You won't do it."

"I am telling you it would have no impact if I did."

"You don't know that."

"You have no evidence."

It should not feel like betrayal, she told herself. She had no right to expect anything from him. He had never given her any reason to think otherwise. She had come here out of desperation, and it had proved as futile as most desperate moves were.

She stepped back, mustering her own front of cold indifference.

"I see. I am sorry to have troubled you, my lord."

"Lilith . . ."

"I believe your session is about to start. You needn't worry, I can find my own way out."

She left.

She had to fight her way through the lobby, which was thick with the last rush of peers making their way into the chamber. She collected her coat and hurried out into the street, where the cold cut at her in welcome.

She strode down the building to the Commons entrance and waved to a hackney that had just deposited a late-arriving MP.

"March Place, Bloomsbury," she ordered.

The sky overhead weighed dark and heavy as the cab lurched along Whitehall. A few spiraling flakes fell, dying against the glass of the window.

It tore at her, the desperation, the feeling of complete powerlessness. Torrington had been her last card. She had played it out and failed.

She should have known how that would go. She should never have allowed herself to expect anything more from him. It had been a mistake, hoping that he might surprise her—that perhaps Deveral's revelation about his attempt to bring her into his family had meant something.

This was a futile line of thought. She needed to act, not stew over old wounds.

What could she do?

She could warn Estelle. It was another desperate move, one that failed her time and again in the past. But this time she had names, descriptions. She could make Estelle understand the seriousness of the threat. Perhaps she and Miss Bard could go away, leave the city tonight for someplace no one would expect to find them. Scotland. Bermuda. Lily would convince them it was necessary, that there was simply no other way.

At March Place, she paid the fare and hurried inside. She knocked at Estelle's door.

No answer.

She knocked again, more forcefully.

"They've gone out," Mrs. Bramble barked from the hall floor below.

"Where?" Lily demanded.

"How should I know? Miss Bard departed earlier this morning. Miss Deneuve left a few hours ago. She just said she'd not be back for dinner and to go ahead and lock the door as she'd bring her key."

That meant she would be late, Lily thought as she slumped down to sit on the steps outside Estelle's door. There was no telling how late. She could wait here, of course, and catch her as soon as she returned.

No. There had to be more she could do than wait. There was no time to sit here in the dark.

Her father's voice resounded through her mind.

*You have no evidence.*

He was right. It was all as thin as a spiderweb, connections drawn of inference and intuition. True, of course. Lily believed that now with her entire being. But without some concrete proof she could show to the world, no one would risk acting on it.

She needed something real. Something even the most skeptical person could not possibly deny.

There was one place she might stand a chance of acquiring that.

The audacity of what she was considering shook her—but her encounter with her father had proved to her that she could not depend on his assistance.

She didn't need it. She didn't need anyone. The risk was her own, along with the fight, and she would see it through.

# TWENTY-SEVEN

$\mathscr{I}$T WAS DARK. TWILIGHT had come prematurely, hurried by the cloak of thick clouds that obscured the sky over the city.

The cold bit at her cheeks above the scarf she had wrapped around her neck and mouth. The Triumph bounced over the uneven paving stones.

A few snowflakes spun past her, isolated, vanishing as soon as they struck the ground.

Lily opened the throttle, racing along the dark expanse of Hyde Park. She turned the heads of the few travelers she passed. The city was quieter than usual, most of its residents reading the promise of the sky and opting to stay home, close to the warmth of the coal fire.

The wide streets of Kensington, which lay to the southwest of the park, were even quieter. The buildings were tall and elegant, marble and limestone gleaming in the light of the gas lamps as though immune to the soot that pervaded the rest of the city. Everything here was new, bigger than it felt like it ought to be. The district was full of squares and gardens, undoubtedly lush and peaceful in the light of a summer day but dark and secret now, marked by the twisted branches of trees laid bare by winter.

Lily slowed the Triumph to a stop. She hopped off and jogged beside the bike for a few streets, ducking into an alley when a lone carriage rolled past.

She turned into one of the shadowy parks that lay between the rows of sprawling townhouses.

Children were playing somewhere nearby, their shouts echoing through the garden. She caught glimpses of life through the lit windows of the surrounding houses—servants hurrying back and forth in kitchens, elegantly dressed women gliding through well-appointed dining rooms.

The house she was looking for was in the middle of the row. It was easily three times the size of her own, all glittering windows and gables.

Even for a physician, Dr. Joseph Hartwell was clearly doing quite well for himself.

She concealed the Triumph behind a yew hedge on the far side of the park. Grabbing the low-hanging branch of an oak next to Hartwell's home, she pulled herself up.

Perched in the tree, shadowed by its branches, Lily watched the house.

The bright windows on the ground floor revealed the location of the kitchen, where Hartwell's staff were busy preparing his supper. Above, slivers of light gleaming at the edges of the windows indicated life behind thick curtains, drawn against the winter chill.

The same chill crept through her trousers and the jacket she pulled tight over the layers of wool she'd donned beneath.

She got as comfortable as she could and waited.

The clock of some nearby church had tolled nine when her chance came.

The back door opened and a kitchen boy jogged out, carrying a bucket of scraps. He turned around the corner of the house, toward the alley with its dustbins.

He had not locked up behind him.

Lily swung down, dropping silently to the ground, the cold in her bones protesting at the movement. She ignored the ache, running on light feet up to the house.

She felt naked without her walking stick, vulnerable. But it would only be a liability on tonight's errand.

She put her hand on the knob and it turned.

Without giving herself a chance to question the madness of this endeavor, she stepped inside.

366

A blast of warm air enveloped her, emanating from the kitchen, which lay at the end of the dark hall to her right. She could smell baked apples, cinnamon and ginger.

To her left was a narrow staircase, likely the servants' way up to the family rooms on the floor above.

*Move.*

The instinct was clear. Lily heeded it, yanking open the nearest door and ducking inside. She found herself crammed into a tightly-packed pantry.

She held herself still and silent as a footman hurried past, carrying a massive roast on a silver platter. The scent of it made her stomach rumble. When was the last time she had eaten? She couldn't remember.

Someone shouted from the kitchen.

"You'd better have brought that bucket all the way out, Thomas, not left it in the garden like last time."

The boy. He would be back any moment.

If she was caught in here, an obvious house-breaker . . . but there was no time to indulge the fear.

She stepped out of the pantry and climbed the stair.

It was narrow and twisting, as though added to the house as an afterthought. She knew she must be only a turn behind the footman with the roast, but he would also be clearing the way ahead of her, giving her warning of anyone trying to make their way back down.

She reached the top.

At the end of the hallway, light spilled from the dining room as the footman opened the door to go inside. Lily glimpsed the full table, glittering with crystal and fine china. Elegantly clad women circled it, bright with jewels, alongside a younger man in evening dress— an adult son, perhaps? A burst of cheerful laughter echoed down the hall. It was a warm scene, a glimpse of comfortable family life— the sort of life Lily had never known. In the midst of it, just beyond where she could see, sat a murderer.

Well, he would not be so comfortable for much longer.

As more footsteps echoed up the stairs behind her, she slipped across the hall, ducking into the first dark doorway.

It was a water closet, smelling of bleach and lavender.

Over her head, the ceiling shook with the pounding of young feet.

A high squeal of delight filtered down to where she stood beside the great claw-foot tub. She must be beneath a nursery.

She stepped back from the cracked door as the footman returned, carrying a load of dirty plates.

Something rubbed against her boot and Lily jumped, nearly knocking the door closed.

A cat blinked up at her. It mewed loudly, then nudged her leg again.

The footman glanced over at the door. She knew a moment of heightened fear until he turned and hurried on his way.

Once he was gone, she slipped back into the hall. She moved to the back of the house, farther from the warmth of the dining room, and opened another door.

It was dark. The wide French-style windows overlooked the garden. It must be stunning in the summer when they could be thrown open to let in the warmth and the fresh air.

Her eyes, adjusted to the gloom, picked out the shape of a great oak desk, walls lined with bookshelves . . . and a row of file cabinets.

Hartwell's study.

She stepped inside.

The fire in the hearth had burned down to embers, left to die for the evening, but the room still retained some warmth. Her toes and fingers had thawed since she came inside and were starting to hurt, a tingling pain that she ignored.

She moved to the desk. It was meticulously tidy. Not so much as a drop of ink marred the blotter. A few papers sat in a neat pile on the surface. She scanned them quickly. They were assessments for a property on Hampstead Heath, a mortgage signed in Hartwell's sprawling hand.

The square footage of the property was enormous. What did Hartwell intend to do with such a space? Was it intended to be a lavish new country home?

There was nothing else on the surface of the desk except for the unusual luxury of a telephone. That it was here and not in a hall where others in the family might have access was telling. The expense of the device was clearly incurred for Hartwell's use alone.

She tried the drawers. All locked.

She moved to the file cabinets.

There were no locks here. The drawers were packed with files. She opened the curtains, letting a bit more light into the room. She could barely make out the names on the folders. Lily pulled a few at random, bringing them closer to the window and flipping through them. Everything was in pristine order, alphabetized, dated, and cross-referenced.

She felt her pulse jump. There must be something here, but there had to be hundreds of files. Where should she begin?

Boyden, she thought.

She flipped through the B's.

Nothing.

Heller. McKenney. Durst. Lily looked for the names of all the murdered mediums. The meticulous organization of the rest of the files made it clear that they would not merely have been mislaid. There was simply nothing there.

She fought the urge to slam shut the drawer.

There was one more name to try.

She opened the last cabinet, flipped to the W's—and finally found what she was looking for.

According to his file, Lieutenant Jeremy Waddington was a veteran of the Royal Army Medical Corps, active during the Boer conflict.

*Discharged for medical reasons: malaria*

Beneath the typed diagnosis was an additional note written in Hartwell's hand.

*Patient is asymptomatic carrier.*

Carrier. She thought back to Mrs. MacAlister, wasting to nothing in a bed in St. Bart's.

*Just a lying devil with poison in his blood.*

Lily turned the page.

There was a photograph. It was a black and white image of the face of a man she realized she had seen before.

It had been the night of Estelle's last séance, when Lily had been coerced into opening the door for an early guest—an ordinary man with pale brown hair and a neatly trimmed mustache, the kind of face you felt certain you had seen a dozen times before.

He had been inside her house.

The instinct to run, to drop the file and race back to March Place, was overwhelming. But what good would it do? Estelle wasn't there to be warned and no authority would believe Lily's word about the danger she faced. She needed evidence. It had to be here.

She flipped through the rest of Waddington's file, scanning the pages of notes. One section was underlined emphatically, Hartwell clearly deeming it of exceptional importance.

*Patient's blood exhibits unusual characteristics. Resistant to clotting when mixed. Have yet to find incompatible donor. Possible advanced human characteristic?*

The man in the photograph stared out at her, dark brown eyes like shallow pools.

Dr. Gardner had told her that the obstacle to successful human-to-human transfusion was the unpredictable reaction one patient's blood had to that of another. If Hartwell's note was accurate, then Waddington was indeed exceptional—someone who could receive blood from any donor without the ill effects that took the lives of others.

She flipped hurriedly through the rest of his chart as a door closed down the hall, a child's bright tones echoing from upstairs.

She stopped, staring down at a page labeled *Record of Procedures*. It was a list of names, dates. A line or two of description.

*Mary Ellen Smith. April 4 1909. Donor compatibility test. Successful.*

*Anna Faucett. April 6 1909. Donor compatibility test. Successful.*

*Mary Ellen Smith. May 12 1909. Partial transfusion, 1 pint. Successful.*

She scanned down the list of similar entries, then stopped at a name that caught her eye.

*Mariah Reznik. July 7 1909. Partial transfusion, 1 pint. Successful. Addt. Note:*

*Transfer of desired donor characteristic observed. Effect duration roughly 3 hours.*

Reznik. She searched for the woman's file, pulling it from the drawer as the sound of clinking dishes from down the hall indicated the end of dinner.

The folder was thick. On the first page, a photograph of the woman had been pasted into place. She was dark-haired, glaring at the camera with such force, Lily felt chilled just looking at her in the dim light from the window.

*Race: Jewish*

*Place of origin: Belz, Galicia*

The intake form used as the cover for the file had a field specifically for syphilis, which for this patient was marked *None*.

The following pages were covered with extensive notes of treatments and procedures inflicted upon the woman in Hartwell's elegant, unhurried hand.

*July 29, 1909. Partial transfusion 1 pint, Lt. J Waddington. Donor characteristic transfer, effect temporary.*

*August 12, 1909. Partial transfusion 1 pint 8 oz, Lt. J Waddington. Donor characteristic transfer, effect temporary.*

*August 19, 1909 . . .*

The list went on. August 30, September 10 . . . effect temporary.

*Subject grows recalcitrant*, Hartwell noted.

Mrs. MacAlister's words echoed through Lily's skull.

*They kept coming back for her . . . she weren't having none of their purpose.*

Near the end of the file, a more elaborate comment, scrawled as though in a moment's inspiration.

*Indications are that partial transfusion yields only partial transfer of the desired characteristic regardless of methodology. Could complete transfer yield permanence?*

Lily stared down at the words on the page as the pieces started to fall into place in her mind.

The Society for the Betterment of the British Race, Hartwell's eugenics club—an organization devoted to harnessing the powers of heredity to direct the future evolution of humankind.

Heredity was slow. Human generations took a long time to grow to maturity. Even if he was successful at Parliament with his marriage bill, Hartwell's vision would take centuries to come to fruition.

The Carfax Gallery. The crowd of admirers surrounding Hartwell, gushing about his research—about the revolutionary potential of discovering that human blood could be classified into types.

Dr. Gardner's voice, rumbling across the confines of a darkened carriage.

*If there was a safe way to transfer blood from one person into another, a great many lives we currently lose could potentially be saved.*

The portly toothpick maker on Bury Street outside the warm glow of the gallery, a rune gleaming on his lapel.

*And that is exactly what our future promises if we are bold enough to grasp it—a race of noble heroes.*

What if there was a shortcut?

If Hartwell could discover a means of transferring desirable traits from one body into another that did not require breeding . . . he could reshape the world in his image in no time at all.

The audacity of his goal was shattering, rocketing through her with all the horror it implied.

Hartwell's interest in blood wasn't about saving lives. It was about controlling the future of the human race.

Lily fought to close the circle, to complete the nightmarish picture forming in her brain. According to Mrs. MacAlister, Hartwell had become obsessed with Mariah Reznik. Waddington's file showed that once she arrived at the hospital, the other transfusions stopped. What desirable characteristic had a poor Jewish woman possessed that made her the singular focus of Hartwell's interest?

The ability to see and hear the dead.

Her khárisma.

Hartwell was searching for a way to steal it from the woman gifted with it and bestow it on another.

But it hadn't worked.

*Partial transfer yields only partial transference . . . could complete transfer yield permanence?*

Complete transfer.

She snatched up Waddington's file again, flipping to the list of procedures at the end. She scanned to the bottom of the list.

The last entries were dated from within the past month, long after the destruction of the Southwark hospital.

*D. Stokes. Feb 19 1909. Complete transfusion. Addt. Note: Transfer of desired donor characteristic duration 2 days.*

D. Stokes. Sylvia Durst had lived in Stoke Newington.

A complete transfusion, draining a woman of her entire stock of blood and pouring it into the veins of another.

They had done it because she had something they wanted, a power they thought someone more worthy should carry.

The person herself—all her memories, her dreams, her wholeness—was discarded, left behind like refuse. What was one woman's life weighed against the potential to exalt the human race into a higher state of evolution?

Dora Heller, Agnes McKenney, Sylvia Durst, Annalise Boyden, Mariah Reznik . . . they had all been deemed expendable in the name of a greater purpose—their power harvested and granted to someone Joseph Hartwell deemed more worthy.

And he'd recorded it here in black ink.

*B. Belgrave. Feb 22 1909. Complete transfusion.*

B. Belgrave. Annalise Boyden, Belgravia. The date of her death was marked down on the page. He'd merely disguised the name.

It was proof. Evidence.

And it changed nothing.

He would deny it. Claim the records were related to other patients, that the dates were coincidence. Lily checked for files on Stokes or Belgrave. There were none. The lines that offered such damning proof to her would easily be brushed aside by others less inclined to doubt the integrity of one of Britain's foremost men of medicine.

She looked to the desk, looming in the darkness, hiding its secrets behind locked drawers.

Before she could second-guess the decision, she stalked over to the fireplace and pulled the poker from the rack of tools.

She moved to the first drawer, wedged the tip into the crack at the top of it, and broke it open.

A sharp crack echoed off the high walls.

She froze, listening with heart-thudding intensity.

Feet pounded across the floor upstairs, the sound of children racing down a hall. Lily could hear the strident tones of a nurse calling after them, trying to round up recalcitrant charges.

There was a distant clink of silver dinnerware.

She pulled the drawer open.

It contained only a single page, which she lifted to the pale light that spilled in through the window.

The paper felt thin in her hand. At the top was an address.

*War Office, Whitehall, S. W.*

The message was brief.

*We thank you for bringing this research to our attention. The Secretary agrees that this line of inquiry is potentially of profound value. Your continued work is encouraged. Please notify us of any progress.*

The signature at the bottom was smudged, unrecognizable.

A line of type at the bottom of the page, however, was perfectly clear. The neat black letters struck like knives.

*Copied: P.M., Ld. Torrington*

Lord Torrington. Her father.

*We thank you . . .*

The telephone rang.

Lily froze.

The jangle of the bell sounded wildly and unnaturally loud in the stillness of the room.

Should she answer it? Was there some other way to silence it?

Footsteps clipped down the hall. No time.

She shoved the memorandum in her pocket, snatching up the fireplace poker along with Waddington and Reznik's files. She closed the desk drawer as much as she could, the bent lock preventing it from shutting completely. She ducked behind an armchair on the far side of the study, tucking herself into a ball and going as quiet and still as she could.

Hartwell wore his evening clothes. He touched a switch at the door and an electric light flared to life. The glare was blinding after the time she'd spent reading in the near darkness.

He sat down at the desk and picked up the receiver. The bell silenced. In the quiet that followed, every noise seemed larger than it should, from the creak of Hartwell's weight in the chair to the regular thud of her heart in her chest.

"This is Kensington 603," he said. "From the Borough exchange? Yes, I'll take it. You can reverse the charges."

There was a pause as the call was connected. Lily glanced past Hartwell to where the desk drawer still hung slightly ajar.

"You have her? Good. What's her status? That's unfortunate but I did foresee the likely necessity. What did you inject her with? I would wait until after five to ensure that she's fully metabolized it. Stabilize her with chloroform until then. Yes, we're moving forward as discussed. You know where to set up? No, the new property isn't ready yet. The warehouse will do. You may run the initial protocols. I'll be over at dawn."

He hung up the receiver.

"You may as well come out," he said evenly.

Lily stood. There was little point in continuing to crouch behind the chair.

Besides, it was easier to run or fight on her feet.

"Was that Waddington?"

"Lieutenant Waddington, please. He is an officer and deserves the according term of address. Whom have you collected?" He glanced toward the files she held in her hand.

"Mariah Reznik. And a file on Lt. Waddington that includes references to several murders."

"You must be mistaken."

"You disguised the names but not the dates. It's clear enough."

"Is it, though? Clear enough."

He seemed unperturbed by Lily's possession of the files.

Because he was right. There was nothing clear about her evidence, nothing he couldn't refute should she try to bring it to the attention of the law.

"What is clear is that you have broken into my home. Which makes you a thief, Miss Albright. I am afraid my patience for your antics has run rather thin, so I am not inclined to overlook this latest violation. Alastair!"

He barked the name at the opened doorway and a footman came running. His eyes widened at the sight of Lily, in her scarf and trousers, standing in the study.

"Go to the station and speak to the inspector on duty. Tell him we have caught a burglar in the house. Now."

The footman cast her another surprised look before dashing off to follow Hartwell's instructions.

"The police? Aren't you going to turn me over to your thugs in the Mint?"

"That was you? I suppose I should have guessed as much. You're lucky you weren't killed."

"Luck had nothing to do with it." She felt the anger rise in her. "You will be called to account for this."

"There is nothing to account for. I am a scientist engaged in research with profound implications for the future of our empire. Of the entire human race."

"And what are the lives of a few women weighed against that grand aim?" she snapped in reply.

"The presumption that every life is of equal value will do little to advance our species. Quite the opposite. We may fail to recognize that, but you can be assured that other nations will. We cannot afford to be left behind. Do you wish to sit down? The station is only a short walk away. The inspector will be along momentarily."

He examined the broken lock on his desk, making a brief huff of disapproval. Lily waited, tense and still, the poker and the files clutched in her hands.

"You paid a visit to Westminster today. I presume his lordship must have been less than convinced to aid you or you wouldn't have been so desperate as to attempt this foolishness. He is rather consumed with legal troubles related to his legitimate child at the moment. It is unsurprising he has little time to spare for a bastard."

She looked to the desk, to the other locked drawers. Had she chosen the wrong one? Perhaps another had the incriminating evidence that might bring Hartwell down.

No. There would be no proof. Hartwell was too clever for that. She accepted it now, the truth settling over her.

This was a mistake.

She recalled the carbolic scent of the hall of St. Bart's, Dr. Gardner's quiet assurance.

*When we are asked for aid, we give it.*

She thought of Strangford standing among the bare lime trees.

*There is nothing you could ask of me that I would consider an imposition.*

She hadn't asked—not Strangford, or Gardner, or Sam or Robert Ash. She had plunged forward alone, unwilling to let anyone else put themselves at risk . . . though was that the truth? Had she been trying to protect them? Or had she been driven by her own fear of emotional entanglement and the potential for pain, betrayal and disappointment that letting herself care for someone entailed?

There was no point answering that question. It was done. She had blown her chance to get the evidence she needed and in doing so, had given Hartwell an incontrovertible power over her. He could remove her from the game. And he would.

His next moves were mapped. Lily felt the claustrophobic weight of his checkmate. There was no avoiding it. She could not win.

What was she going to do about it?

She set the files down.

"Thank you for returning my property, Miss Albright. But I'm afraid this has progressed rather beyond my forgiving the trespass."

Lily adjusted her grip on the iron poker, weighing it in her hand.

The calm of his expression shifted, replaced, for a moment, by a real fear.

The sight of it fired a quick satisfaction through her veins. For all his cold confidence, he recognized that she could be dangerous.

"Strike me with that and you'll hang."

"Don't tempt me," Lily replied.

She moved toward him. He stepped back, circling toward the door, putting the desk between them. She let him do it. As much as part of her wanted to fight, it wasn't a battle she was going to win.

She stopped with her back to the wide, elegant French windows.

Hartwell shouted over his shoulder.

"Edward! Mr. Kendall! To me!"

Lily turned to the glass panes. She flipped the latch and yanked them open. Cold air blasted into the room, tossing the curtains. It was snowing, the white flakes spilling down onto the plush green carpet.

She stepped onto the sill, looking down.

The garden was too far away, at least twenty feet from where she stood to a cold flagstone patio.

"You'll break a leg, at the very least, if you attempt to jump," Hartwell said behind her. "You may trust my word on it. I am a physician."

He was right. To jump would be madness.

Lily looked up.

A footman and Hartwell's butler arrived in the doorway.

"Restrain her, please," he ordered.

They moved toward her.

She swung the poker out before her. The hooked end caught the telephone wire bolted to the side of the house. Lily adjusted her grip on the handle, then, as Hartwell's men reached for her, she fell.

The wire bowed under her weight. She slid along the length of it, flying out over the shrubs and pathways of the garden. She reached the low point in the wire's arc and stopped with roughly ten feet between her dangling boots and the soft grass below.

There were shouts from the house and the shrill peel of a police whistle.

Lily let go.

She fell, twisting to take the impact on her side, rather than her ankles. She rolled across the snow-dusted lawn, then stumbled to her feet and ran.

Behind her, there was a crack as a door flung open, followed by the sound of pounding feet. She risked a backwards glance and saw Hartwell's men racing after her across the lawn.

She sprinted for the yew hedge, grabbing the Triumph from its hiding place. She engaged the ignition, then hopped on and pedaled furiously. The engine caught, roaring to life, and she flew forward, leaving her pursuers behind.

She rode blind, the snow stinging at her face. She tugged her goggles from her saddle bag and strapped them on. The road slipped under her tires but she refused to slow, keeping her breakneck speed until she had left Kensington behind her and wove her way through the familiar dirt and clutter of the city.

She reached Piccadilly Circus. The marquees were dark, the broad thoroughfares, usually jammed with traffic, all but deserted. Black pavement vanished under a drifting fall of snow. Roads radiated out from the still, empty fountain like the spokes of a wheel.

Which way to go?

Hartwell's men were lost a solid mile behind her. The constable who hurried past, his collar turned up against the storm, spared her barely a glance.

That wouldn't last. They would come. She had gone beyond the pale, handing Hartwell the power to silence her. He would see her thrown into Newgate, tried and convicted as a housebreaker. And who would stop him?

Ash and The Refuge? She had shut them out, refused their help.

Her father? He had turned her away. Why would he put his position, all the power he had spent his life carefully accumulating, on the line for the sake of a daughter he didn't even claim as his own?

If there wasn't an even deeper reason for his refusal to go after Hartwell, she thought, aware of the crumpled memo in her pocket.

As for Strangford . . .

The thought of him brought with it an unexpected ache.

There was no point denying it now, pretending it was anything else. It had been fear, plain and simple, that had driven her decisions—fear of how much he was coming to mean to her. Fear of how deeply she wanted him. Fear of how vulnerable that would make her to being hurt again, being abandoned. She had shut him out and now she had run out of time.

Hartwell would come for her. Among the many paths that sprawled out from where she stood, straddling the idling Triumph, it seemed there were only two ways this could go. She could wait and allow herself to fall under his power. Or she could run, abandoning the life she had built, the people she had come to care for, and disappear.

Lily came to a decision.

She revved the engine, then turned the motorcycle and skidded into gear, blasting up past the shuttered theatres of Shaftsbury Avenue—towards home.

# TWENTY-EIGHT

$\mathcal{L}$ILY STEPPED INSIDE.

The warmth enveloped her, wrapping her up like a blanket after the bitter cold of her ride. Her hands ached inside her leather gloves.

The hallway of 702 March Place looked as it always did, from the rust-hued wall-paper to the worn oriental carpet on the floor. The space smelled of boiled greens and suet, Mrs. Bramble's infamous nettle pudding.

But something was off.

The sad pilchards still glistened in the horrid still-life on the wall, next to the stuffed kittens frozen into their scene of cozy domestic bliss. Yet in the air was something other than the scent of steamed nettles, an energy of tension that radiated down the stairs.

Estelle's door was open. There was nothing unusual in that, but there was in the low voices that drifted to where Lily stood, their murmuring quick and agitated. The mat under her feet was soaked, marked with still-melting bits of snow. Mrs. Bramble should be there, scolding her about neglecting to clean her boots. The house felt as though it were waiting, hushed and uncomfortable.

She climbed the stairs. They were silent under her boots, no creak singing out her arrival as she reached the open door and looked into Estelle's flat.

The signs were subtle, easy to overlook. The room appeared as it always did, save for the full glass of vermouth sitting on the table. The dreadful Chinese urn was toppled from its stand onto the rug. The dog-shaped lid had come off and cracked in two. No ancient emperor's ashes lay inside, just a cobweb and the delicate remains of a moth.

Lily didn't call. She walked inside, heart pounding against her ribs, and followed the sound of the voices through the drawing room and down the hallway to Estelle's bedroom.

"Are you sure she isn't still out?"

"The lecture should have ended two hours ago. Even with the storm, she should have been home by now."

"Perhaps she met a beau, went out for a drink. Or she might have run off with the gasworks man."

"Honestly, Agatha!"

Lily stepped up to the door. Miss Bard and Mrs. Bramble turned to look at her. Miss Bard's face was pale, making her eyes look wide and dark like some frightened animal.

"What's going on?" Lily asked.

Before they could answer, her gaze fell on the mirror behind them, the glass over Estelle's vanity table. It was cracked, a spiderweb of fractures radiating out from a point of impact.

The images of the vision played out, vivid and clear as a set of photographs. Estelle at her glass. The shadow behind her, moving from the open door of the closet. The glint of silver in its hand, a weapon thin and sharp as a rapier.

No, she realized. Not a rapier.

The dream had been imperfect, as they always were, her mind filling in for the unfamiliar, the things it lacked the experience to grasp.

The dog split in two on the floor in a pile of ashes—it was how she had interpreted the breaking of a Chinese urn she'd never seen before.

The shadow stood in for the form and face of a man she hadn't met. She could fill them in now, knew who it was that had made his way into the house, probably hours before, when the comings and goings of the inhabitants would've masked the sound of one more door opening. Who waited, concealed inside Estelle's closet, until she was there, alone, at her table.

*You have her?*

Those were Hartwell's words into the telephone an hour before. He hadn't been discussing the transfer of another poor prostitute unlucky enough to fall into his care. It had been Waddington reporting the success of his mission to retrieve Estelle.

*That silver weapon in his hand?*

It was a needle.

*What did you inject her with?*

He had come for her, driving the needle into her arm, drugging her with some sort of sedative. She had fought him, the mirror breaking during their struggle.

Lily could imagine it, fill in the spaces the vision had left empty or jumbled with symbols—how he must have dragged her into the drawing room, Estelle reaching out weakly, just managing to strike the urn off its pedestal as they passed.

And then . . . ?

She recalled the rest of what she had foreseen—an unfamiliar space, shadows shifting in the flickering of a single flame against a backdrop of walls of dark glass. They resolved themselves now, took a firmer form as she melded them to Hartwell's words over the telephone.

*Yes, the warehouse will do.*

It was one of the thousands of warehouses that crowded the city's wharves. That's where he had taken her, where he would prepare her for the next phase of Hartwell's experiment.

Draining the blood into bottles, stealing it from victims while they slept, hadn't worked. He would try something different this time, a *new protocol*. Something that required not just the blood to be stolen but the woman herself.

A procedure that would see Estelle's blood taken from her veins and poured directly into Joseph Waddington, a change Hartwell hoped would make the transfer of her power permanent.

Lily could see her as vividly as if she were in the room. Estelle, sitting up, pale as a ghost. The blood seeping through the hand clasped to her throat, her eyes wide and vacant.

*Thief. Murderer. Alukah.*

*Alukah.* Blood-drinker.

The full horror of the truth settled in.

They had been watching her.

Hartwell had set his men to follow her after she had provoked him in the gallery. She had noticed them outside the house, dismissed them as a case of paranoia.

One of them must have seen the guests streaming in and out through the door and become curious. All it would've taken was a casual question and he would learn that a medium lived here.

That's how Waddington had known where to find her. Estelle didn't advertise her services. Lily thought that would keep her safe. Meanwhile, she had led a killer directly to her front door.

She remembered Estelle's story the morning after the séance— after Lily had let Waddington inside the house—of a client at the séance she believed was a competitor, a man who could see the dead.

It was Waddington, using a power he had stolen from Annalise Boyden, his grasp on it fading as he searched for a new victim.

It was her fault. Lily had made this happen, brought all of it about through her foolish attempts to change what was to come.

Just like she had before.

The horror of it hit like a blow, roaring in her ears, pushing her back from the doorway.

"You alright? You've gone over a bit queer," Mrs. Bramble noted, frowning at Lily.

Miss Bard looked over as though just noticing she was there.

"Do you know what this is?" she demanded. "Do you know what's happened to her?" She stepped forward as Lily backed away.

"I'm sorry. I'm . . . not well."

She ran, bolting down the stairs, tearing open the door. She staggered out into the street, the cold snapping at her, snow-covered stones slipping under her feet. She fell, tumbling to her knees in the middle of the road, the rows of respectable brick houses standing stoically back to observe through their darkened windows.

She was alone. No carriage tracks or hoof prints desecrated the unbroken perfection of the snow, even her own trail quickly swallowed up in the thick, hushed fall of it.

The cold seeped up through her trousers, sinking into her bones.

Estelle was going to die.

And she had made it happen . . . just like she did fourteen years ago.

The world shifted to another night on another street, one far less respectable than March Place. A Covent Garden alley, papered with fading playbills, stinking of stale beer and urine. The sound of drunken laughter rang in the distance alongside the hoarse calls of prostitutes.

She had agreed not to wear red. To leave her jewels at home. Not to go alone. She had done it, kept all the promises Lily had wheedled from her, begged and cried for her to adhere to.

Lily's intercession had led directly to her mother lying on the ground, blood spilling from the stab wounds in her chest, turning a pale blue gown to crimson. Paste jewels sparkled, scattered across the paving stones. A dead man lay beside her, another casualty of Lily's attempt to thwart what some greater force had already ordained.

Her fault. All her fault.

In the emptiness of March Place, the snow melted to ice against her knees, dusting her back, the storm whirling around her with the ferocity of a wild animal.

It would always be like this. She would be battered with knowledge that meant nothing. Any action she took would rebound back upon her, destroying the lives of the people she loved most. There could be no purpose in that, no hope—just an unending torment of grief and powerlessness.

Despair rose up, choking her as she stood in a vortex of spinning snow.

She had failed. She was always going to fail.

The full implication of that knowledge came at her like a shadow rushing out of darkness. She held her breath, braced for it, for accepting everything it would mean . . .

The wind changed. It fell back. Instead of twisting and consuming her, the snow hung suspended in the air. The world went quiet, the thick and pregnant silence of a room full of people anticipating some great announcement.

The snow-covered ground beneath her wasn't a respectable city street any longer. It had become something else—a crossroads with the darkness of the unknown waiting at either end of it.

There was still a choice.

She could acknowledge that her power was the embodiment of futility and go back to desperately ignoring it, abandoning any hope of something more. Of a purpose.

Or . . .

She remembered Hartwell's voice, the words ghosting into the black receiver of the telephone.

*I'll be there at dawn.*

It wasn't dawn yet.

It was next to hopeless, a gamble with almost no chance of success. There had to be a thousand warehouses in this labyrinth of a city and Lily had no logical way of narrowing her search to discover which one Estelle was being held in.

She would be giving up her chance to flee. Hartwell would already be positioning his forces, preparing to exercise the control he knew he had gained over her. Any hope of gathering what scraps of her life she could and running would be gone.

But she could still choose to fight.

She thought of The Refuge's attic, of the figure from Evangeline Ash's painting—a goddess out of myth, a force to be reckoned with.

She hesitated.

Against all her own logic, she knew she was looking for a sign. For something like Robert Ash's Parliament of Stars to tell her which way to go.

The wind turned again. The ebb of the storm had passed and it redoubled in intensity, blowing into a howl. Ice battered at her cheek, stinging in its ferocity.

She stood, her bones aching, muscles battered.

There was one weapon she still possessed, one course that presented her best hope of turning this slimmest of chances into something real.

The idea of using it filled her with fear.

She would do it anyway . . . but not alone.

# TWENTY-NINE

THE TRIUMPH SKIDDED TO a stop, tires sliding across the snow-covered Bayswater street. She shifted her weight, fighting for balance, barely saving herself from wiping out.

Lily had been taking the roads slower than her racing heart would have liked, but it didn't matter. The storm was thick enough now that the motorcycle was a liability. She would need other means of transportation for the rest of the evening.

She killed the engine, pulled off her goggles, and looked up at Strangford's front steps.

They were covered in an unblemished blanket of white. A little cone of snow rested on the head of the iron pug. The flakes continued to drift down around her, glittering in the glow of the gaslights. At the end of the road, the park was a wilderness unmarked by so much as a single hoof print.

It was past midnight. The windows of the fine houses lining the road reflected the storm like dark mirrors. Everyone in this respectable quarter of the city was certainly asleep. It would be hours yet before even the cooks and chambermaids rose from their beds.

It was an abysmally poor time for a call.

She looked up at Strangford's dark windows and felt a quick jolt of fear. The thought of being turned away cut as surely as the cold in the air.

No, she admitted. This door would open for her, no matter how inappropriate the hour. She knew that with a bone-deep certainty.

She set the Triumph against the iron rails of the fence and jogged up the steps. There was only a moment of hesitation before she grasped the brass knocker and rapped it, loudly and repeatedly, a demand no one could mistake for anything else.

Then she waited.

There was no answer.

The trepidation crept back. She forcefully ignored it, took the knocker, and swung it again.

*Rap-rap-rap-rap-rap-rap-rap*

The door flew open. Strangford's country footman, Roderick, stood there, his livery jacket buttoned askew over his nightshirt. He blinked out at her blearily, holding a lamp in his hand. Then his eyes cleared enough for him to recognize who was standing on the step.

"Is Lord Strangford in? I promise you that it's terribly urgent."

The boy's gaze moved quickly from her trousers to the snow dusting her hair, stopping at her face.

He stepped aside, opening the door wider to invite her in.

"I'll wake him," he said.

"He's awake."

Strangford's voice floated down from the top of the stairs, where he stood wrapped in a gray dressing gown. His hair was mussed, looking longer and wilder than usual as a result.

Lily's mind flew back to the vision of his hand on her shoulder, his lips moving to her neck, setting fire to her skin.

By coming here like this, imposing on him in the middle of the night, she was claiming an intimacy she could not take back. It opened the door to a future she had tried desperately to avoid, with all the heartbreak it surely promised.

It didn't matter. She was done running from it. The truth of what he was to her was undeniable now.

"I need you."

The words came easier than she had thought they would.

He didn't question, answering without taking his dark eyes from the place where she stood.

"Roderick, show Miss Albright to the study. Put some coal on the fire. I'll be down in a moment."

"This way, miss." Roderick clung to some semblance of his footman's habit as he gestured her down the hallway.

He led her to the study, turning on a pair of electric lamps. They cast a warm, even glow over the room.

The fire had died to red embers in the hearth. Roderick crouched before it, adding a few scoops of fuel. One lump jumped back, rolling past him across the carpet. He caught it, tossing it back in and then brushing off his hands.

"Can I get you anything, miss?" he asked as he rose. "Tea or . . . something?"

"That won't be necessary. Thank you, Roderick."

He gave a quick bow and showed himself out, leaving Lily alone in the quiet sanctuary of Strangford's study.

Her pulse continued to race. It had been pounding since she left March Place, every fiber of her screaming for action, movement. She had chosen a path and it brought her here, where for a moment there was nothing to do but wait.

She had been here before, but then her impression of the space had been limited to quick surprise at the bright and furious panoply of the paintings that adorned the walls, works that would not be at all considered proper for the home of a respectable member of the ton. Any temptation to give them greater attention had been blown away in the immediacy of Strangford's obvious distress.

They were universally startling, executed in vivid colors and bold, primitive lines, like the crayon strokes of a joyful child.

There were forests of white trees, woven through with dancing figures in exotic gowns. The haunted gaze of a beautiful but hollow-cheeked woman, holding a tawny cat in her lap. Elsewhere, a pair of skulls cloaked in brightly patterned robes moved together as though for a kiss. Other canvases exploded with light and color representing no natural view she had ever seen.

Every piece was unique, united only by an energy and intensity that made them feel more alive than any expert mimicking of the forms and hues of the real world.

She moved closer, drinking them in.

"What do you think?"

Strangford stood in the doorway. He had quickly dressed in his usual plain black suit, but had forgone a tie. His hair remained untamed.

"They are wonderful."

He stepped into the room.

"I don't show it very often."

"You selected each of them personally?"

"I chose everything here."

"Even the inkwell?" she asked, trying to break the tension she could feel mounting inside of her at the sight of him surrounded by this art, at the whispering notion of what the gallery revealed about the curator—that something wild lived beneath that quiet exterior, something so passionately full of life it might hurt you to look at it.

He moved to the desk, running a gloved finger along the dent in the pewter.

"The inkwell belonged to William Blake. It was an excessive indulgence. But his mind is such a remarkable place to share, even in echo." He dropped his hand, turning serious. "What's happened?"

The moment of peace, of letting herself forget why she was there, passed. Lily felt the weight of her intent settle back onto her.

"What I've been trying to stop."

"Estelle?"

"He's taken her." Her voice hitched on the words.

"Who?" Strangford demanded.

"Hartwell."

She felt a moment of fear, part of her waiting for Strangford to push back, to demand evidence or argue that a man like Dr. Joseph Hartwell couldn't possibly do such a thing.

Instead, he headed for the door.

"Let's go."

He believed her, without question. The impact of that shook her.

"Where?" she demanded.

"There's a police kiosk at Paddington Station."

"We can't go to the police," she cut back quickly. The knowledge that her description could well have been circulated to the stations scattered about the city came home to her again. "Even if we could convince them to act against one of the most prestigious men in Britain on our word, they'd find nothing at his home. She isn't there."

"Then where is she?"

"That is what I came here to find out."

"You have something for me?"

The assumption came so easily—that she had woken him in the night simply to make use of his hands again. She felt a stab of shame that her treatment of him justified it.

"No. I have something for myself."

His dark eyes were intent, focused on her entirely.

"You mean to use your gift."

"I don't think you'll approve of the method." She met his gaze.

"And the method is?"

She took the little blue bottle containing the Wine of Jurema from her pocket and handed it to him.

He studied the label.

"Mr. Ash said it would act as a shortcut to unlocking greater potential in my . . . ability."

"He gave you this?"

"No. He did not."

She read the disapproval in his look.

"You should have gone to him, not come here. You know he would help with anything you asked."

"I don't want Ash for this. I need someone I trust."

*Trust.* The word hung in the air between them, heavy with significance.

Emotion strangled her, stripping her voice raw.

"I have treated you abominably. And I would understand if you turned me out."

"I would never do that," he replied quietly.

She felt both the pain and the relief of that wash over her.

He returned his gaze to the Wine of Jurema.

"Do you know how it works?"

"No," she admitted.

"Have you any idea how much you can safely take?"

"I'll work it out."

He was tense. She could read the disapproval in every line of his body. He held the bottle up.

"This could be poison."

"Hartwell will tie her to a table and drain the blood from her body," she retorted, feeling brittle. "There is no one else—no one—who can get to her in time. I will not stand here and debate. I am doing this. Will you stay with me?"

"Yes," he replied.

At the sound of that single syllable—*yes*—falling into the stillness of the room, some last shred of resistance inside of her shattered.

There had never been someone she could depend upon—not her mother, certainly not her father. Yet here stood a man who offered her what she asked of him without question or condition.

There was no time to contemplate what it meant or to react against the terrifying vulnerability it entailed. She needed to act.

She scanned the room, her eye stopping on the deep green chairs by the fire.

"No. Not there," Strangford cut in, reading her intent.

He shrugged out of his coat, folding it into a neat bundle and setting it down in the center of the rug.

"Here."

"On the floor?" she asked, surprised.

"Neither of us has any idea what the contents of that bottle will do to you. And one cannot fall off of the floor."

She considered it for a moment, then acknowledged the wisdom of the suggestion. She sat down.

"There are a few rules I must insist upon before you proceed."

"Name them," she said. It felt odd to speak up at him from the ground.

"First. I must have your consent to physically restrain you should it prove necessary."

The notion was unsettling, a potential implication she had not considered.

"Yes. Of course."

"Second. If at any point in these proceedings I detect a serious threat to your own well-being, you agree that I may call for assistance. I am to be given complete discretion on that point."

She had sidestepped Strangford's concern about the contents of the bottle, but this concession brought it firmly back. She had no idea what the substance inside it was or what it would do to her. He was right, of course. She should have gone to The Refuge and begged Ash to assist her. But if Ash's assertion about the powers of the Wine of Jurema was correct, she was about to blast the doors off of a part of herself she had fought desperately for most of her life to shut out.

She had not been lying when she told Strangford why she came here instead of Bedford Square. She needed him, far more than she needed to know the proper way to go about doing what she was about to do.

"You have my permission to take whatever action you deem necessary."

There was a pause the length of a breath as he stood over her in his shirtsleeves.

"I don't like this, Lily."

"I am done waiting in the wings while the people I love are taken from me." The words shook with more grief than she would have cared to admit. "If there's something inside me that stands even a chance of saving them and this helps me find it, then it is worth it. Whatever the risk."

He pulled the stopper from the bottle and offered it to her. It passed from his gloved hand to hers, their fingers brushing.

The scent of it was woody, honeyed and acrid, both alluring and terrible.

She contemplated the level of liquid inside. It was filled to the brim. How much should she take?

A few drops, perhaps? Then wait for some effect, carefully assessing whether it were having any ill impact on her body?

She looked to the clock on Strangford's desk. It was one thirty. There was no time.

She put the bottle to her lips, tipped back her head, and drained it. The taste was terrible, like off wine soaked in sawdust.

"Damn it, you might have started slow."

"In for a penny."

She laid back on the ground, resting her head on Strangford's folded coat. The rug was soft and the fire had flared up in the hearth, wrapping her in warmth. She was far less uncomfortable than she had thought she would be.

Strangford paced. The clock ticked.

"Tell me how you're feeling."

"Perfectly, entirely—"

The next word was to have been "ordinary". It failed to leave her lips as she was distracted by the realization that the room had become brighter.

Had Strangford turned up the lamp? No, it was something more than that. The colors themselves had changed, becoming vivid, more saturated. The green upholstery of the chairs glowed, the pale gray wallpaper shimmering like the inside of an oyster shell.

It was as though the room was turning into one of the paintings it housed.

The paintings had changed as well. Or rather, they were as they had always been, but Lily saw them more clearly now. She understood how they had never been confined within their frames. The wild colors, the mad lines, spilled out across the wall, enveloping everything they touched. The desk, the bookcase, the darkened windows, all rippled as though moved by the brush of a hyperactive artist.

Her ears roared. It was merely the crackling of the fire but amplified almost to the point of pain. A rich hum joined it, slow and substantial as the crashing of waves on the strand—the sound of Strangford's voice.

She couldn't make out the words, but she could see his concern. He had come closer, kneeling beside her. She had just arrived at the conclusion that she should reassure him when all the lines in the room fell apart.

She fell from impression to abstraction, enveloped in a stunning nonsense of shape and color that meant nothing and everything. It was a language she had forgotten, but if she could learn to read it—this painting that was life—she would understand everything. The answer to every question she had ever struggled with.

Electricity surged through her. Circuits mated that had previously been severed. Connections arced and fired, and abruptly, shatteringly, the lights came on.

She went somewhere else.

Sprawled across an enormous four-poster bed, the light of a fire dancing over the sheets. Soft, sensitive hands roam over her body. Skin brushes against skin, setting off sparks of precise and wildly intense connection. She clasps Strangford's face in her palms, tastes him, feels the silk of his lips against her own. Pleasure rises, crests like a wave . . .

. . . then breaks with the roar of artillery shells. Crouching in a hole in the ground built of mud and barbed wire, she is wet, bone-drenched, rattling with cold as the earth shakes under the assault. Strangford, his uniform covered in mud, shouts at her, voice hoarse, roaring for her to *go go go go*. Gloved hands shove her. She tumbles back as the wall explodes, mud and wire and splintering wood blowing past her . . .

. . . landing on her back in a field, the seed-heads of the greenest grass in the world dancing over her head. A fat bee buzzes from wildflower to wildflower. She sits up, climbs to her feet. The field goes on forever, perfect in its silence, lined with row after endless row of plain white crosses marching in stillness to eternity, a field of a million unmarked dead . . .

. . . back in London, the rain sleeting down. Sam Wu glaring at her with unspeakable grief in his eyes. The ravens pour down from the sky, surround him like a whirlwind, a maelstrom of black beaks, feathers, alien intelligence gleaming from dark pebble eyes . . .

. . . shining from the face of a photograph cradled in the big hands of Dr. Gardner, slumped in an iron chair in the ward at St. Bart's. An empty bed beside him, sheets stained, his heavy shoulders wracked with sobs . . .

. . . rain streaking down Cairncross's face as he stands outside The Refuge, a great brass key in his hand. The iron set to his face as he turns it, flipping the tumblers and locking the door . . .

. . . inside the attic, spinning dust catching the golden light of the late afternoon sun. The curtains gone, the mural shining out at her from every angle, the bright colors an assault. Truth leaps at her from every detail—the boy with the rats worshiping at his feet. The healer with a wounded soul. A warrior crowned with the golden light of a saint, black gauntlets on his hands . . . because they need protecting and because they are dangerous. A thin woman laughs, delighted, in the bony arms of the dancing dead.

The artist wears a paint-stained apron, jars and brushes scattered at her feet. She sets another key into the robe of the flame-haired woman on the wall, working on a painting she completed thirty years ago.

"This can't be right. I'm not capable of seeing the past."

"You have no idea what you are capable of," Evangeline Ash replies.

"This isn't what I came here for," Lily protests. "I have to find Estelle."

"Then stop fighting and ask for what you want."

She moves to the figure in the circle of skeletons, the laughing woman robed in peacock blue.

*Stop fighting. Ask for what you want.*

It is impossible. Even in the midst of this barrage of things-to-come, the fight coils tightly around her. It is what keeps her from falling in to the abyss, from losing herself to despair or something worse. How can she stop? What will be left of her if she does? The pain roars back in with a few notes of an old music hall jingle, with the glitter of jewels in a pool of blood. If she is not in control then how can she possibly protect herself?

She can't.

She stops inside the stillness—the dust floating in the air, the light suspended around her.

The truth of it settles in. Lily acknowledges it and the coil releases, leaving her defenseless.

She shapes the words inside herself, carefully and deliberately, then speaks them aloud.

"Show me where I will find her."

. . . and she is there.

It is the dark space she has seen before. Towering walls made of dark glass, glittering in the flickering flame of a single lantern. This time, she is aware of the smell in the air—rotting wood, Thames mud, mice. A warehouse, set somewhere on the river.

But where on the river? There are a hundred such places, a hundred possibilities.

Estelle lies on a table. It has arms, elegant limbs of articulated metal. One embraces Estelle, wrapped across her chest, holding her down. Another extends up from the surface, fingers pressing a wrinkled ball of white fabric against her nose and mouth.

A man steps into view. He pulls a dropper from a brown vial and measures a dose onto the bunched cloth, then moves away again. She hears the clatter of glass as Waddington shifts bottles aside, pulling up a tray of equipment. There are clamps, fat needles. A rubber tube wriggles like the body of a snake.

This doesn't tell her what she needs to know. She must find another perspective.

Dark glass glints over the lieutenant's shoulder. It is a window, just visible between the stacks of crates.

*There. Go there*, Lily thinks . . . and she does.

Waddington is next to her, close enough that she can smell the damp linen of his coat. It is too intimate, this nearness, her whole being aware of the horror of what this ordinary man has done.

He must sense her presence. But he does not, because she is not really there. He is not really there—not yet. This is the future, something that has not been, perhaps by as little as a moment or two. It is Lily's power answering her demand, taking her as close as it can to what she seeks.

Waddington moves away and Lily returns to her purpose. She focuses on the glass, on seeing through the darkness to what lies beyond.

Narrow water, black and still, where otherwise a road might have been. Across the open space is another row of warehouses. They are bland, anonymous—a view one might see a hundred places in London, were it not for the steel dragon clinging to the facade.

The beast is long, its tail submerged in the dark water. The metal head extends out from the roof while thin folds of skeletal iron wings arch back against the skyline.

Lily knows her mind is filling in gaps in the details, substituting for the things here she does not yet know like a child finding monsters in the clouds. She needs more to reliably orient herself, something unmistakably familiar.

She looks to the broad expanses of the Thames. Two dark pinnacles, barely visible against the dull glow of the clouded sky, rise above the water. They form a silhouette no Londoner could possibly fail to recognize.

Tower Bridge.

But from what angle?

She is on some kind of inlet. There are two inlets this close to the bridge—St. Katherine's Docks beside the Tower and St. Saviour's Dock on the Southwark side, otherwise known as Shad Thames, where the now-demolished rookery of Jacob's Island once reigned terror.

St. Katherine's is a short waterway, one that gives quickly onto two great basins.

She moves closer to the window, peering down the length of the inlet. It narrows, disappearing into the darkness between the close-set buildings.

Her heart thuds noisily against her ribs.

She knows where she is.

Behind her, Waddington lifts a syringe. The needle glints in the lamplight. Estelle groans.

The room shifts beneath her and she falls, tipping backwards past the crates through a dark hole in the floor. She crashes into ice-cold water, then fights for the surface, choking . . .

. . . but something holds her down. She is submerged in the frozen darkness, lungs screaming for release, pushed to the edge of their resistance. Then she is free. She surfaces, gasping.

She is not in the warehouse. It is a tiled bathroom and Lily sits in a tub full of water and floating chunks of ice. A narrow window looks out over a broad stretch of open ground—familiar ground. Some-place she has been before.

Two men in white uniforms grasp her by the arms and drag her from the tub. She is pulled down a long hallway, past rows of closed and locked doors.

It is a prison. No . . . it is someplace worse. She thinks of the horror of the burnt-out hospital, the tiled underground hallway lined with quiet nightmares, a place where no one would answer your screams.

Panic chokes her, fear buzzing in her brain.

She wants to escape. She wants to go home, to hide from all the knowledge she doesn't want to have. She wants to be free of this terrible gift, free of its limits and its dreadful responsibilities. She wants . . .

*Stop fighting. Ask.*

It is impossible. She always fights. It is how she has survived despite the pain, the constant weight of failure. She battles for control either by shutting the thing out or by trying to wrestle it into submission—grants it the narrowest crack of entry, directed toward her own dire purpose.

But perhaps . . . just perhaps . . . there is another purpose at play.

Perhaps there always has been.

Her arms ache under the grip of the uniformed men. Her knees drag against the tiled floor, the doors sliding past her. She knows what waits for her at the end of this hallway. It is horrible.

She closes her eyes. For the first time, she lets go.

"Show me what you want me to see," she speaks aloud.

The men are gone.

She stands alone in the hallway lined with doors. It has grown longer, stretching infinitely before and behind her—thousands upon countless thousands of doors.

She holds her walking stick in one hand. It has grown taller, magnificent, sprouting green leaves and red berries.

In the other hand, she holds a key.

It shifts and shimmers in her grasp, changing shape with every movement of her wrist.

The doors whisper to her. They are infinite and they are powerful, every one opening to an as-yet-unthought future . . .

To endless possibility.

And she holds the key.

For a moment, it dawns. She comprehends it, understands the unimaginable potential that lies before her and her astonishing place in it.

*You have no idea what you are capable of.*

The power and the responsibility is greater than she had ever dared to suspect. It is as wonderful as it is terrifying.

She wants to run. She wants to wish herself back to ignorance. She wants to laugh.

Should she choose? Does she dare?

The door waits before her, one of millions. The key shifts in her hand. She fits it to the lock, turns it . . .

Light spills through, impossibly bright. Something moves on the far side—something familiar, something utterly new, coming toward her . . .

. . . and then she returned.

The floor of Strangford's study did not feel comfortable any longer. There was a crick in her neck and her mouth was dry, suffused with a terrible taste.

"For god's sake, Lily, wake up."

Fear had stripped Strangford's voice raw.

She opened her eyes.

He knelt beside her, hair askew, as worried as she had ever seen him. His eyes closed in relief and he moved back as she slowly sat up.

The paintings had returned to their frames. The fire crackled softly in the hearth, the darkness still lingering outside the tall panes of the windows.

It flooded back to her, the impact of everything she had seen, running over her like a freight train. Strangford's hands on her body, the sight of him obliterated in an explosion of mud and wire. The endless sea of graves. Sam and Gardner shattered, The Refuge locked and abandoned . . .

All the doors. The key she held in her hand.

She had touched something, come close to an understanding that would change everything. It was slipping away from her even now, fading like the wisdom of a dream.

One certainty remained: there would be no walking away from this. Not again. Not ever. No matter how hard it got.

There was no time to worry at it any further. They had to get to Estelle. While she'd been dreaming, Hartwell had been making his preparations. How much had all those detours cost her?

"How long as it been?"

The words were thick in her mouth. She felt a quick panic cut through the lingering fog of the vision. How narrow had their window become? Or had they used it up entirely?

"Twenty-three minutes," Strangford replied.

She winced. Her head was pounding.

"That's not possible."

"I can assure you I was quite aware of the time."

She risked a look at him.

"You were worried."

"You drank what looked like a bottle of poison and then fell into a stupor. Of course I was worried. Can you stand?"

"I think so."

He put a hand under her arm, another at her back, and helped her rise. She was aware of the pressure of his fingers against her skin, her senses sharp, still tingling from the after-effects of the drug.

He kept his hold on her as she reached her feet, as though afraid she would fall over if he let go. It put him close to her.

He was not happy.

"You're lucky I didn't drag you out into a carriage and drive you straight to St. Bart's."

"A carriage . . ." she muttered.

The rest of the pieces fell into place. She grabbed Strangford's arm, hard. "We need a carriage. Now." She met his dark eyes, her own intent sharpening, becoming clear. "I know where to find Estelle."

# THIRTY

HE STORM RATTLED THE windows of the carriage, a gust of wind making it sway. Snow blew past in violent swirls. Lily felt a pang of guilt at the thought of the driver bundled in layers of scarves, hunched over the reins.

Their progress was much slower than she would have liked, but then, they had been lucky to find this hackney at all. Even at Paddington Station, there had been only a handful of carriages waiting at a curb usually lined with dozens. Roderick, who had been sent running the half-mile to the station from Strangford's home, had sent this one back to them, taking another himself in the opposite direction. He would make his way north through the storm to wake The Refuge and summon help.

Strangford had seemed poised for resistance when he demanded that they alert Ash and the others. Lily hadn't fought him. Whatever reticence she might once have had about imposing in such a manner on people who owed nothing to her was gone, obliterated in the need of the hour.

She had quickly vetoed Strangford's suggestion that she be the one to head to Bedford Square, letting Roderick join him to proceed directly to the warehouse. She was the one best positioned to recognize the right place and besides, she doubted Roderick would be any use in a fight.

And she was expecting a fight.

She shifted her grip on the walking stick she had plucked from the stand at Strangford's door. It was ironwood, heavier and less flexible than the yew she was accustomed to carrying. It would do.

The carriage skidded around a turn and the driver slackened his pace, making their progress through the deserted, snow-covered streets of the city even slower. Lily glimpsed the dark silhouette of Tower Bridge through a gap in the buildings. They were getting closer, but the state of the roads left her with no illusion about how quickly Roderick would be able to reach Bloomsbury. She and Strangford could not afford to wait for the others to arrive. They were in this on their own.

Inside the carriage, silence carried weight. Lily knew it should be broken, but each means she grasped to do so dissolved from beneath her, seeming paltry and insubstantial in the face of all that had passed between her and the man beside her.

It was Strangford who broke the impasse.

"There is something I must make clear, in case tonight's errand proves . . . well." The pause after the word spoke volumes.

"I'm sure that's not necessary," Lily countered.

"Are you?"

She could feel his eyes on her. The question carried more weight when posed to a woman who could see the future.

She looked away.

He continued to speak, quietly, across the darkness of the carriage.

"I let something stand yesterday in the park. Something you said that I should have addressed. I would like to correct that."

She realized that he was waiting—that he was asking for her permission to continue.

She hesitated. The fear roared up by sheer habit, demanding that she stop him, that she open the door and leap from this carriage before something was said that changed things in a way that could not be ignored or undone.

She held firm against the onslaught. She was not running anymore.

"Go ahead."

The carriage rocked under another blast of wind.

"There is no time to be anything but blunt in this, so I beg you'll excuse my being less circumspect than I would prefer. In the park yesterday, you argued that because your mother was an actress—"

"A whore," Lily cut in. She turned to look at him, defenses prickling. "My mother sold her body in exchange for the financial support of a protector. She was a whore."

"You argued," Strangford continued, relentless, "that because of your parentage, you could never be anything but a mistress to a man of standing."

The words bit even though Lily knew they were nothing more than the bald truth, plainly spoken.

"I need you to know that you are wrong."

"My lord . . ." Lily began, but he cut her off, uncharacteristically quick.

"No. I am a man of standing and you are already something other than that to me. You are a colleague. You are the only woman I have met who knows what it is like to be burdened with this terrible knowing. And you are my friend." He spoke the word fiercely, as though prepared to battle for it. "I know your character—I have seen it, more intimately anyone else possibly could. Your bravery, your strength—such ferocious loyalty. I will not have you continue to live under the abominable notion that your worth begins and ends with the circumstances of your birth. You are more than that." He swallowed thickly, his voice fracturing but pressing on. "You are so much more than that."

Something broke inside of her, crumbling under the impact of his words. For a moment, she wondered if the rest of her would fall apart with it.

She answered him quietly but firmly.

"You can't just bat away the mores of an entire society."

"Says the woman in trousers."

She could hear the wryness in his tone and felt an answering tug at the corner of her own mouth.

"I should have said that to you yesterday. I didn't because I was afraid it would seem like an invitation." He stopped, catching himself. "No. That isn't what I mean. It's . . . me, Lily," he finished, as something in him seemed to give way. "It's me. For anyone to be close to me is unavoidably . . . They would lose everything—every secret, every scrap of privacy. That . . . place inside yourself where you keep the things that are only yours. It would be an inordinate sacrifice, one that could not possibly be comprehended until after it was already made." He took a deep breath. "I just . . ."

"I know," Lily cut in softly.

In the shadows of the carriage, Lily felt the distance between them grow closer, filled with something like fire. It licked at her, both drawing her in and threatening to consume her.

"If I were only a little less—"

"Don't you dare," she snapped. "Don't you dare wish yourself other than what you are."

The silence extended, the carriage rattling over the bridge.

"Well," Strangford said at last, rubbing his gloved hands across his knees. "I am glad we have clarified things."

Lily burst out with a laugh.

She felt him smile back at her through the dark and the tension built again, setting her aflame with awareness. Her resistance to it had weakened, inviting all manner of complicated possibilities.

The carriage lurched. Lily grabbed the strap as they slid to a stop.

Strangford glanced out the glass.

"We're here."

Lily climbed down into the whirling storm.

The carriage had reached the end of Shad Thames, where Jamaica Road swallowed the last narrow sliver of the old River Neckinger. The dark water of St. Saviour's Dock wove out before them, visible through the veil of drifting white.

Strangford joined her, his boots crunching against the frozen ground.

"Where is it?"

"Somewhere on the east bank, near where it meets the Thames," Lily replied.

"Should we keep the carriage?"

She glanced back at the hackney, the driver a round pile of snow-dusted rags.

"We don't know how long it will take."

Or whether they would be back at all.

He moved to the driver. Lily knew the man would be compensated generously for delivering them here to the heart of this old haven of thieves. The slum had long since been leveled into the ground, the mills and warehouses lining the dock springing up in its place.

The carriage rolled slowly away behind them. Lily tried not to feel as though some lifeline were being severed.

Strangford came beside her.

"Would you take my arm?"

Surprise made her hesitate.

"It is rather slippery," he added quietly.

She answered by setting her hand around his sleeve.

They walked up Mill Street, leaning against the blowing snow. At the end of the lane, a low arch opened onto a glimpse of the darkly glimmering Thames and the shadowy length of a wharf.

Beside them, another entry opened into a narrow yard set before a long brick building. The windows of the ground floor were blocked up with only a slim iron vent at the top. The warehouse was old, stained with decades of soot, but the doors were not. They were sturdy oak, set with new locks.

On the upper floors, the glass of the windows was dark, reflecting only the faint light of the gas lamps that lined the distant road.

It looked silent, still, and deserted.

She tried to match it to the place from her vision. She couldn't. The window she had peered from must have been near the Thames, but how near?

Assuming there was a real place to be found at all—that her vision wasn't just some drug-addled nightmare.

No, she thought, clear and certain. It had not been a dream. She couldn't doubt that anymore, no matter how much safer it might make her feel.

"Where's Sam when you need him?" Strangford muttered, eyeing the brass locks.

"We're looking at this from the wrong angle. I need to see it from the river to know where we are." She glanced back at the lane. "We need a boat."

They ducked into the narrow arch that opened onto the wharf.

Rows of fishing boats and barges that plied the waters of the river during daylight hours rocked quietly against the piers, sails bundled against their booms.

Lily's eyes lit on a rowboat tied to the far end.

Then her instinct flared.

She moved her grip to Strangford's hand, tugging him forward. They reached a ladder mounted against the side of the wharf.

"Down," she hissed.

He descended quickly and quietly, Lily following nimbly after him. Strangford made room for her on the ladder, hanging from the side of it. They went still, boots suspended a few inches from the cold, lapping water of the Thames.

Footsteps echoed across the boards, accompanied by a low, tuneless whistle. Lily clung to the ladder, willing herself to complete silence, close enough to Strangford to feel the warmth of his body through his coat.

The footsteps passed. She waited, the instinct still prickling. After an eternity, she heard them return, the regular thud of some night watchman making his rounds.

She waited until he had receded through the narrow arch, then slowly allowed herself to breathe.

It had been stronger this time. The little pricks of awareness she had felt in the Southwark hospital and in Hartwell's stairwell had blossomed into something more, a clear and undeniable knowing.

The drug had provoked something more in her than just the vision on Strangford's floor.

It was possible it was merely some lingering fragment of the stuff in her system. She clung to that explanation. The alternative was far less comforting.

Her father's voice came back to her, the story he had told in her parlor.

*I remember your hunches.*

"We can move," she said, keeping her voice even, not wanting Strangford to see how shaken she was.

They climbed back onto the wharf, making their way quickly and quietly to the rowboat. Lily jumped in, settling the walking stick on the floor. Strangford untied the rope and tossed it down, then stepped in himself and took up the oars.

He rowed quietly, dipping them expertly into the water and gliding the little craft along the dark river.

They turned into the mouth of the dock.

He stopped once they had passed into the protected waters with their milder current. The boat floated before the water side of the warehouse.

Lily studied the buildings lining the opposite side of the dock.

The perspective was different. She was lower, at the water level, not perched near the roof of the building. From this angle, there was no way to see the familiar silhouette of Tower Bridge. Nor was there anything distinct about the buildings themselves. They looked like any other riverside block in the city, save for the distinct shape of a hoist suspended from one of the warehouses that bordered the water. The steel crown of it thrust out over the dock while a counterweight of elegant girders arched back over the roof. She felt a familiar pattern in it, could imagine steel jaws and dark wings.

"We're here," she confirmed.

She looked back at the warehouse, studying the facade. The brick walls extended down into the water where perhaps at a lower tide, the pilings that supported the building might be visible. It was solid save for a set of massive doors at the far end.

"Look. Up there."

Lily followed the direction of Strangford's gaze. Behind one of the dark windows of the top floor of the building, something flickered—a brief flash of lamplight, there and then gone again.

There was someone inside.

"We need a way in," Strangford noted.

Lily's gaze returned to those enormous doors. There were similar openings facing the city's canals on buildings that had been set over some arm of the water. They were used to allow barges to carry goods directly inside to unload without having to be ported by hand onto to the shore and then transferred.

She looked more closely at the shadowy space between the bottom of the door and the water.

"There's a gap." She kept her voice low and pointed across the water. "Under the door."

Strangford eyed it dubiously.

"It's too narrow for me to row us in."

"Not if we're sitting up."

He considered the gap, frowning.

"It's still rather close."

"I don't see an alternative."

"We could wait for the others. Sam could—"

"There isn't any time," Lily cut in.

She saw him weigh it, two undesirable options. He picked up the oars, rowed them to the far bank of the dock, then turned the boat around, pointing the bow at the doors.

"Guide me," he ordered.

Lily nodded.

He began to pull, setting aside silence for long, sure strokes of the oars. The boat picked up momentum, slicing across the narrow water.

"More to the left. There's still a current."

He adjusted course, the doors rapidly approaching. Lily eyed them uncomfortably, the slender black space beneath looking far less generous than it had from a distance.

They drew closer, the boat moving faster.

"Now," she whispered, sliding herself down to the floor.

Strangford pulled up the oars, then dove down beside her.

They were tucked into an awkward intimacy, pressed against each other on the angled planks. The boat continued to glide forward, propelled by the remaining momentum of Strangford's strokes.

Looking up, Lily watched the bottom of the thick, water-stained doors approach, then pass smoothly over her head. The boat scraped lightly against the wood, bumped up by a low ripple in the water.

They were inside.

She stayed low, pressed against Strangford's body as they continued to drift forward. She could feel his breath on her hair.

They stopped abruptly, bumping up against an unseen obstacle. The hollow sound of it echoed through a broad, open space.

Lily felt her pulse jump. She remained still in the bottom of the boat, listening intently for some sign that their intrusion had been detected.

Beyond the gentle lapping of water against wood, the space around them was silent.

Finally she rose.

They were bobbing against the side of a square pool set into the heart of the warehouse. It was open above them to a dizzying height, the rafters just visible overhead.

Around her, the massive space was largely deserted. A few sacks of rotting flour were piled against one of the walls, a ghostly bulk in the near darkness. With the windows bricked up, the interior was lost in gloom. It smelled of Thames mud and mice.

She thought of the sturdy new doors set into the street-side of the building. No one would go to the expense of all that oak and brass to protect an empty room.

Nearby, the steel beam of a hoist rose from the water, towering up to the roof of the building. Lily could see the hydraulic engine that powered it resting on the warehouse floor. It looked well-oiled, free of rust. The hook that would haul pallets of goods to the upper floors dangled from its cable.

The place might look deserted, but it wasn't. Someone had a use for it. Something was being kept here they were motivated to protect.

Strangford grabbed the side of the pool and pulled himself out onto the warehouse floor. He held the boat steady as Lily did the same.

Then he turned the craft and gave it a strong push toward the doors.

It drifted forward, bobbing its way back out of the building.

She knew why he had done it. The presence of a rowboat in the pool would be a clear indicator that there were intruders in the building. With it gone, there was less chance that Waddington would guess his hiding place was discovered.

They could hardly fit three bodies into the floor of it to affect their escape, not with the tide rising. Still, the sight of it gliding away clenched at her, taking with it their only sure means of getting free of this place.

A wooden ladder was mounted beside the steel beam of the hoist, extending up to the floor above. Strangford indicated it and Lily nodded. She tucked the walking stick into the back of her belt as he started to climb, then followed him.

Their progress was silent save for the rush of her breath—until one of the wooden rungs snapped under the weight of Strangford's boot.

The sound cracked across the space, echoing like a thunderclap.

Lily froze.

Perhaps he hadn't heard it.

No—it would have been impossible to miss in the heavy silence around them.

Would he dismiss it as the building settling? Or the machinery of some nearby factory clanging into gear for the morning shift? Perhaps he wasn't even there anymore. He might have gone . . .

There was nowhere he would go. Not at this hour. Not with a kidnapped woman in his care.

Waddington was here and he had heard them.

Strangford appeared to know it as well. He climbed quickly but quietly up the rest of the ladder, then ducked behind the bulk of a massive wooden crate, motioning urgently for Lily to join him.

She tucked herself in beside him, pulling the stick from her belt, and waited.

Like the level below, the space around her sprawled across one enormous room, but it was not empty. The rows of windows let in a soft, ambient light from the street below.

The floor was a jumble of furniture. Rows of hospital beds stood upright, pressed together like dominoes. Chairs were bound together with rope into tower-like stacks. Islands of rolling carts and tables turned the place into a maze of narrow aisles, lined with things that would move and clang with the slightest bump.

At the far end of the maze, another set of double doors opened onto a stairwell.

She put her lips to Strangford's ear and whispered.

"Were we heard?"

"We must assume so." He considered the shadowy landscape. "If he's waiting, he'll do it at the top of the ladder."

"And if he isn't waiting?"

"It's easier to fight on stairs."

He slipped out of their hiding place and wove his way silently across the floor. Lily followed, keeping her steps light, carefully bending out of the way of the jutting angles of the stacks of furniture. One bump could send some tower toppling, setting off a racket that revealed to Waddington exactly where they were.

Everything here was new. The wood veneers were free of chips and stains. The metal coils of the beds showed no rust. None of this had been here for very long. It had been purchased and brought here fairly recently, a thought that left her feeling even more uneasy.

It came to her what united the assortment of furnishings and supplies that surrounded her. This was the equipment one would need in any hospital.

She had never questioned why Waddington might have come here. She had naively assumed that he was simply a squatter, making the space available to himself. Of course Waddington would never do that. He was far too careful, too deliberate. He would have had to know this location was secure before he would bring another victim here. And he had. He had known it because this was Hartwell's warehouse, packed with Hartwell's goods, the furniture and supplies he needed to open up another hospital.

Her mind flew back to the burnt shell of the clinic, to the horror of the tiled basement and the monstrous operating room. He was going to do it again in some other place to a new batch of women. The evidence of it was all around her.

Hampstead Heath, she thought, remembering the mortgage papers on his desk.

Strangford extended a hand. Lily took it, letting him help her over a mattress that had slid out of its pile, blocking their path. Through his black glove, his grip was strong and steady.

*You are so much more than that.*

She set the thought firmly aside. Then they were at the door.

# THIRTY-ONE

THE STAIRS WERE BROAD, lined with a sturdy iron rail. Narrow windows cut into the brick provided some illumination.

It felt terribly exposed, that long expanse of metal and concrete extending before and behind her. There was nowhere to dodge for cover.

She listened for some sign that Waddington had anticipated their route and was waiting for them.

Her blasted power should be able to show her this. Was it only going to cough up a warning when it wanted to, then skip off when she needed it?

How long would the effect of the Wine of Jurema last?

The stairwell remained silent.

Strangford met her gaze, then tilted his head up. Lily nodded.

She climbed carefully, keeping her footfalls soft, her body close to the wall. As they rounded the last bend, they saw another open doorway leading into the top floor of the building.

It was dark.

She shifted her grip on the walking stick. Strangford glanced back at her and frowned. She knew he was fighting the instinct to tell her to stay behind. Instead of voicing it, he turned and moved to the doorway.

They slipped inside and immediately pressed themselves against the wall.

A slight rattle fell across the silence that filled the hall, Lily's back brushing up against a shelf loaded with ceramic basins.

The sound was small, but she still stiffened against it, feeling terribly exposed.

This level was different from the ones below. Where those had been vast and open, this was a warren made up of tall shelving units and stacks of wooden crates. The shelves and stacked boxes extended far above her head, creating tight alleys and small rooms that made it impossible to see more than a few yards ahead. The place was a labyrinth.

A narrow hallway stretched before them. The contents of the boxes on either side of it were scrawled on labels. *Linens*, Lily read on the nearest one. *Doz flat sheets, doz pillow cases, quilts (5).*

Strangford led the way. Lily wanted to pull him back. After all, she was the one with a weapon, though the narrow confines of this space severely limited her ability to wield it properly.

They moved past a shelf stacked twelve feet high with chamber pots, bundles of mops and brooms, crates of gauze and plaster. Their path twisted, turned into dead ends, doubled back on itself. All the while, she listened for some sign of Waddington. There was nothing, the silence broken only by the thump of her heart against her ribs, the rasp of her own breath.

It didn't matter. She knew he was somewhere in the darkness, stalking them. A man who could slip into homes undetected, linger there in some shadow, then emerge to steal the blood of a sleeping occupant—he would be careful. He would wait until he had a full grasp of the situation before he acted. He would get the measure of the obstacle he faced and proceed thoughtfully, deliberately to thwart it.

Hartwell's superhuman was gifted with the both the caution and the ruthlessness of a snake.

They passed another alcove, a narrow space lined with jars. They were full and Lily could make out some of the names on the labels. *Iodine, mineral spirits, rubbing alcohol . . .*

*Carbolic.*

*Ammonia.*

Something glimmered in the glass of the arrayed rows of jars—a sliver of lamplight.

Strangford put out his arm, warning her back. He eased forward, Lily following. They turned the corner and she found herself looking down a narrow hall formed by stacks of crates, ending in a wider space illuminated by the glow of a paraffin lantern.

They stopped short of entering it, backs pressed against the crates, keeping to the last bit of shadow as they peered into the room.

Lily had seen it before.

Shelves lined the space, glittering with glass vials and jars, racks of tubes and pipettes. In the center of the room lay a table, a prone figure arranged on its surface.

Estelle.

A fall of white gauze obscured the lower half of her face, suspended over her nose and mouth by a metal rigging clamped to the side of the table. A canvas strap crossed her chest, holding her in place.

She was very pale and very still. A needle protruded from her neck, attached to a rubber tube pinched shut by a metal clamp.

Waddington had made everything ready for the next stage of Hartwell's research—for draining Estelle's blood from her body, using her own living heart to pump it into Waddington's veins.

There was no sign of the doctor.

Strangford pushed forward. He moved to Estelle and sniffed at the gauze.

"Chloroform," he said softly, meeting Lily's eyes across the table. The gauze was the mechanism Waddington was using to keep Estelle anesthetized.

Strangford plucked it from the rigging and tossed it aside. He worked at the straps that secured Estelle to the table.

Lily's instincts prickled.

She looked around. The room was still empty, still silent, but something would soon be here. Something dangerous.

She adjusted her grip on the walking stick—not too tight, staying loose and flexible, just as she'd been taught.

Strangford paused with his hand over the needle in Estelle's throat, then backed away, joining Lily by the shelves.

"I can't take the needle out," he whispered. "I don't know what would happen if I did."

Lily couldn't answer. For all she knew, it would leave an open wound in Estelle's neck, sending her blood pouring onto the floor. She wasn't a doctor. The only doctor here was a killer.

She glanced back at the table. Estelle looked pale and terribly still. She seemed older than she ever had to Lily before, the lines on her face deeper and more harsh.

Then the sense of threat abruptly peaked.

The awareness was sharp, screaming through her. She grabbed Strangford by the arm and hauled him into a run just as the shelves behind them lurched forward and came crashing to the ground.

Glass exploded. Lily felt it pelt against her back. She heard Strangford curse and looked over to see him put a hand to a bright red gash in the flesh of his cheek.

She looked over at the table. Estelle had been spared the brunt of the impact, though her caftan glittered here and there with tiny fragments of broken vials.

Strangford rose, the broken glass sliding from his back and tinkling against the floor as it fell.

She turned. Where the wall of shelves had once been, Waddington stood looking at them.

His brown eyes were cold. They quickened with recognition when he looked at Lily.

He reached into his lapel pocket and pulled out the shining silver blade of a scalpel.

"Get Estelle," Strangford ordered. He stepped forward, his boots crunching on the glass.

Lily felt a quick burst of fury. She was the one with a weapon in her hands and therefore far better equipped to deal with a man with a knife—though the thought of avoiding that sharp, shining blade turned her stomach. But there was no time to protest. Waddington had hopped onto the shattered remains of the shelf, crossing it quickly and surely. Then the two men were upon each other.

Lily's grip on the staff tensed, her body ready to leap into the fight.

The blade flashed in Waddington's hand, swinging low toward Strangford's gut.

Strangford moved. The gesture was simple, light as the step of a dancer. His body twisted aside, one arm pressing into Waddington's, forcing the blade down. His other hand snapped up, striking a quick, sharp blow to the man's jaw.

The doctor staggered back, then bulled forward again. He swung the blade. Strangford met him with another strange movement of his arms, made with the brutal grace of instinct. This time, the doctor landed on the ground.

The tàijíquán, Lily realized. The art Ash had been teaching Strangford to increase his focus and control. He had told her it was also a school of self-defense. Strangford was applying it as such, whether intentionally or as a matter of reflex.

From the floor, Waddington grabbed the heavy, broken remnant of a glass jar and whipped it at Strangford, forcing him to duck back. Then he was on his feet again.

Behind her, Estelle groaned, her hand fluttering to the needle in her neck. Lily raced over, catching the woman's wandering fingers and forcing them back to her side.

Waddington and Strangford came together again, but the doctor was prepared now, recognizing that Strangford's lack of a weapon didn't mean he was defenseless. He feinted with the blade, then surprised Strangford with a blow to the side.

The force of it pushed him into another tall block of shelves. It wobbled, then tilted, crashing into the one behind it. Lily threw her body across Estelle's as more glass shattered onto the floor, knocking over the small table that held the kerosene lamp.

It smashed. Flame rushed across the oil spilling over the dry wood of the floorboards.

The two men, locked in a ferocious embrace, lurched out of the half-demolished room.

Lily looked to Estelle, who lay on the table, eyes closed, fingers twitching. She could hear the crashing sounds of the fight, smashing soup bowls and splintering wood.

She dropped her stick, grabbed the table, and hauled it across the floor, as far from the flames as she could get before running into the debris of the fallen shelves.

Then she picked her weapon up again and ran toward the sounds of battle.

Another crash, the quick bark of a curse—Lily rounded a corner to see the two men squared off at the edge of the hole in the floor that opened down to the pool below.

There was a new slit in the arm of Strangford's coat, a place where Waddington's blade had found a mark. Lily couldn't tell how deep it went.

Strangford's cheek was bleeding, his jaw smeared with red. Waddington had him pinned, the dark abyss of the gap opening behind him.

"Stay back," he barked.

She didn't listen.

Lily ran forward. She snapped the ironwood at Waddington's side, but Strangford's protest had alerted him. The doctor turned as she approached, taking the blow at an angle and catching the stick in his hands. He wrenched it and it slid from Lily's grasp, flying out over the hole in the floor. She heard it splash as it landed in the dark water below.

He swung at her with the scalpel. Lily fell back to avoid it, landing on the rough floor. Waddington lunged to come at her again but Strangford hit him from the side. The impact took them both to the edge and then over it.

She heard the water break as he hit it.

She scrambled to the edge, looking down into the abyss, waiting.

Waiting.

The gasp of his surfacing echoed up from below. She could barely make out the pale oval of his face against the dark water.

"Get out of there, Lily!"

She glanced along the opening. Waddington hung from the floor a few yards away. As she watched, he swung his leg on to the surface, pulling himself up. His hand flashed out, grasping the silver glimmer of the scalpel.

Lily ran.

The firelight was dancing across the roof. The blaze was spreading. She had to get Estelle.

She plunged back into the maze. The twists and turns felt like they were intent on tricking her, forcing her to double back. The air was thick with smoke, her lungs burning. She wanted to cough but fought the urge, instead crouching, moving lower to the ground, waiting all the time for some sign of Waddington behind her.

At last, she rounded another corner and found herself back in the room of glass.

Estelle was still on the table, but she was sitting up, her eyes open. The room around her danced with flame. The needle rested in her palm. Blood streamed from her neck, staining the side of her caftan.

Lily hurried to her and pressed Estelle's hand to the wound.

"We have to go," she said, trying to keep her voice calm.

It was as though Estelle didn't hear her. Her gaze was distant, unaware of the building turning into an inferno around her.

She muttered something. Lily couldn't understand the words. They were nonsense or some language she had never learned.

"Estelle, please. I need you to stand up."

The medium's eyes drifted to Lily, then kept going, coming to gaze at some unknown distance over her shoulder.

"Thief," she said, the blood oozing from between her fingers. The word was thick, heavy with an accent that was not Estelle's. "Murderer. Alukah."

*Alukah.*

Blood-drinker. Hebrew, the language of Mariah Reznik, a woman driven to self-destruction by Waddington's use of her body, her blood. The words of a dead woman coming from the mouth of a woman who could hear the dead.

Estelle wasn't gazing into the distance. She was channeling the voice of a victim who was looking into the eyes of her killer.

Right over Lily's left shoulder.

She dropped.

Instead of driving into her neck, the scalpel screamed over the top of her head. Lily scrambled around the table, lurching back to her feet. She grabbed a piece of shelving as she rose, whipping it back at Waddington, who paused to take the blow against his shoulder.

She skidded around the corner, taking the broken board with her. Splinters dug into her palm. At the far end of the wood, the pointed end of a wrenched nail protruded.

Waddington leapt at her.

He caught her around the waist, his breath hot against her neck, his grip like an iron coil around her body.

Instinct sang and she threw the board up in front of her. The scalpel that sliced toward her throat instead collided with the wood.

She kicked out at the solid brick wall in front of her, driving Waddington back into the shelf behind. He loosened his grip on her to protect himself from a fall of glass spilling down from above, giving Lily time to put an arm's length of distance between them.

He shifted his grip on the blade and moved toward her.

He would kill her. She knew he would do it without a moment's thought or hesitation.

Her lungs spasmed, her eyes burning.

She made a desperate swing with the board. He dodged it, then retaliated. The blade flashed toward her ribs. She deflected the blow with the plank, pulling together some shred of control.

He would come for her again, just as he had before. She needed to be ready.

He charged. Lily threw herself to the side.

She swung as she moved, driving the board at him from behind as he passed her.

She aimed for his head and connected. The wood hit Waddington with a sharp crack, then stuck.

He lurched forward, the movement pulling the weapon from her hands. It was lodged in his head, the nail driven deep into his skull.

He crumbled to his knees, looking back at her with quiet surprise. Then he fell.

Lily stared down. Blood trickled from the place where the iron had driven through his brain. His eyes were open, sightless. He did not move.

The horror of that began to creep in, paralyzing her. Then another crash resounded through the warehouse, the smoke growing thicker.

She needed to get out of here.

Back in the operating room, Estelle was on her feet, wavering and unsteady.

"Lily, someone's set the room on fire."

Lily pulled Estelle's arm over her shoulder, bracing her own around the woman's waist. She propelled her forward.

They skirted the inferno, plunging back into the dark maze of hallways. She passed the alcove of chemicals, now lying in shattered puddles on the floor, the stench choking her as thickly as the smoke. Lily tried desperately to pull together the memory of the way they had come. Had it been right or left after that stack of crates? Straight or turn after the jumble of IV stands?

Then she saw it—the door to the stairs, lying at the end of the long, narrow hallway.

Behind her came another crash of crumbling, burning wood. Something in the air shifted. The atmosphere seemed to pull away from her then rapidly expand again. There was a whoosh, low and substantial, followed by the thunder of flames igniting several gallons of volatile chemicals.

She was thrown with Estelle into the shelf beside them. Chamber pots crashed to the ground, throwing up splinters of porcelain. The floor creaked, aching under the suddenly unbearable weight of Hartwell's next endeavor.

Lily hauled Estelle upright, then dragged her forward, her boots skidding on the floorboards. She heard more crashing behind her, shelves collapsing as the floor beneath them gave way. The blaze roared like a hungry beast, the air unbreathable.

She gasped as they spilled out into the stairwell. She pulled Estelle along, half-stumbling their way down. As they passed the floor of furniture, Lily glanced through the doorway just long enough to see that it, too, was now ablaze.

Strangford.

Had he tried to climb back up into the warehouse to find them? Was he somewhere in that burning nightmare?

The thought sent a panic screaming through her, threatening to cloud her thoughts more thickly than the smoke.

Estelle's arm pulled against her shoulder, the smoke choking her. Lily had to get her out of the building.

She ripped herself away from the burning maze, forcing them the rest of the way down the stairs.

At the bottom, they fell against the massive door. Lily let Estelle sink to the ground, freeing her arms to wrestle with deadbolt.

She pushed the door open, clean air spilling over them. Lily hauled up Estelle and staggered with her out into the snow-covered yard. The slap of cold winter brought home how hellishly hot the interior of the building had become. The clarity of the air invading her lungs burned worse than the smoke. She collapsed into coughing, gasping for oxygen.

She fell to her knees in the snow, Estelle drifting more slowly down beside her.

Where was Strangford?

The storm had passed. The air was still. Further up the Thames, the sky turned the soft pink of early dawn.

Carriage wheels crunched across the yard. The horses that pulled the vehicle were matched, a pair of perfect bays. The black lacquer of the body of it was polished as shiny as a hearse.

It stopped just before where she crouched in the snow. The door opened and a familiar figure stepped out—the long, elegant form of one of the empire's most distinguished physicians.

"You," Hartwell noted, considering Lily as she gasped and choked on the ground. "I suppose I should have expected as much when I saw the smoke."

More boots crunched against the snow.

"Any sign of Lt. Waddington?" he asked as two new sets of feet moved into Lily's view.

"He's dead," she wheezed.

"That is unfortunate." He sighed. "Let's salvage what we can from this." He lifted his gaze to the blazing warehouse. "At least it's insured."

He turned to the trunk strapped to the rear of the vehicle, tossing it open. He pulled a narrow case from inside.

"Put them both in the carriage, please."

Rough hands grabbed Lily's arms, hauling her upright. She recognized the face of the man who held her. It was Gibbs, the one who had made the bruises that still ringed her throat under the wool of her scarf.

She was too breathless to fight him, still winded by the impact of the clear, cold air.

As he dragged her to the carriage, her heels leaving twin tracks in the snow, she watched the roof of the warehouse dip, then collapse. The fire roared hungrily in response. The whole building was ablaze, every window shining with firelight.

The import of it hit her with the force of a train.

If Strangford was inside that building, he was dead.

Agony shot through her, a pain so sharp and complete it overwhelmed all thought.

Hartwell plunged a needle through the cork of a vial of clear liquid. He lifted the syringe.

"Bring her over by the carriage light, please. I need a vein."

Lily was thrust against the front of the carriage, her head knocking against the lacquered wood. The glare of the kerosene headlamp hurt her eyes.

Two men held her body pinned in place. Hartwell took a handful of her hair, yanking back her head.

"There we are," he announced. The needle slipped into her neck.

The world went gray. The fire seemed to rage in the distance like the memory of something that had happened a very long time ago.

*Strangford.*

The thought carried a last, desperate resistance. Then the darkness slipped over her.

# THIRTY-TWO

$\mathscr{L}$ILY WOKE ON THE floor of a bare, narrow room.

The walls were white, the acrid smell of fresh paint still thick in the air. The space was illuminated by the harsh glare of an electric bulb mounted on the wall and encased in a steel grid.

She crawled to her feet. Her mouth felt as though it had been stuffed with cotton, her head equally thick. Her clothes reeked of smoke. It was cold.

The room was completely bare, empty of any furnishings. It measured little more than a prison cell.

A single window was set into the wall opposite the door. It was covered by another steel grid hung on hinges bolted to the frame and secured with a weighty padlock.

She peered past it through the glass.

This certainly wasn't London. The landscape outside was pristine countryside, snow-covered fields and little tufts of woodlands. It was also vaguely familiar. She studied the low stone walls, the gorse hedges lining the gentle curve of the road.

Hampstead Heath.

Of course it looked familiar. She had taken her Triumph up and down these roads dozens of times, though never before in the snow. The curve she could see below her was the same one she had crashed on a few short weeks before.

But where was she seeing it from?

She forced her mind back to the day her chain had broken and flashed to the image of a great, sprawling old manor, sitting derelict on a low rise over the road. It had been enveloped in an air of desertion and neglect, despite the scaffolding covering one of the wings, causing Strangford to lead her to the farmhouse further down the lane for assistance.

Strangford.

Her mind shot back to a more recent memory, her last before she woke in this place—the glow of burning embers shooting up into the sky as the warehouse roof collapsed.

Had he been inside? Had he climbed up out of the dark pool in the building's core to try to find her?

If he had, he was dead. Nothing could have survived that blaze. Nothing.

Grief stabbed through her. She had pushed him away, done everything she could to drive him off. And why? Because she was so determined not to become any man's mistress?

No. She could see it all so clearly now. It had never been about a refusal to follow in her mother's footsteps. It was fear, pure and simple. Fear of caring about someone. Fear of letting that need make her vulnerable, open to the possibility of being abandoned again . . . just like her father had abandoned her.

Because of that fear, she had refused to acknowledge how much Strangford had come to mean to her.

Now he was almost certainly gone.

The pain of that tore, threatening to swallow her. She had to refuse it. She couldn't fall apart, not now, not yet. She needed to gather every resource she had to determine where she was and how she was going to get out of here.

From the angle of the road, she must be inside the great, abandoned house she had seen after she crashed. But how had she come here?

Hartwell. Her last memory was of ashes dancing around his polished boots as he stood in the snow of the warehouse yard and a needle pierced her neck.

He had drugged both her and Estelle, and now she was here.

She remembered the papers she had seen on his desk, a mortgage for a property on Hampstead Heath. This was it—Hartwell's next project. But why had he brought her here?

It had been just dawn when the warehouse had collapsed. The sun was still low on the horizon, but . . . it was the wrong horizon. Lily was looking west, not east. It was sunset. The same day? Or had she been unconscious even longer?

She felt a hum of alarm, an undeniable knowledge that someone was coming.

A moment later footsteps sounded in the hall. They stopped at the door to her room, which opened to reveal the solid figure of Mr. Gibbs.

"The doctor wants to see you in his office."

His tone was bland, but he watched her with a wary hostility. What she would give for her walking stick . . . She considered the likelihood of talking him into helping her. There were still scabs on his hands and face, the marks of vicious little wounds inflicted on him by Sam's army of doves.

No. She wouldn't get any assistance from that quarter.

She followed him out into the hall.

It was long and sterile, brightly lit by more steel-caged electric lamps. Doors marched into the distance in either direction, all identical save for the numbers neatly mounted to the left of each one. Lily had emerged from 109. She counted off the others as she passed them—111, 113, 115 . . . There was something vaguely familiar about the scene, but her mind refused to place it, instead thrumming with nervous energy.

They reached a set of stairs, climbing a single flight and then turning into another identical hallway. More close-set, regular doors marched by, numbers proceeding in rigid order—201, 203, 205 . . . Lily stopped at the door to room 207. It hung open, revealing a windowless tiled room dominated by an enormous iron tub.

She remembered cold, the icy water closing over her head, lungs screaming for air as hands held her pinned beneath the surface—a fragment of the vision sparked by the Wine of Jurema.

"What is that for?" she demanded.

"Best hope you don't find out," Gibbs replied before shoving her on.

The way branched at the end of the hall. One side was blocked by a tacked-up fall of painter's canvas. The space beyond it was dark, and a cold draft crept in around the gaps. A box of tools sat beside it—a carpenter's saw, hammer and crowbar peeking out. Whatever renovation this place was undergoing was very much a work in progress.

Gibbs turned her away from the curtain, leading her to the other end of the short hallway, where she stopped at the threshold of Hartwell's office.

It had once been some gentleman's study, but the room was now in a mixed state of decay. Strips of paper had been torn from the walls, which were roughly sanded in some spots. The floorboards were bare, showing the small holes where rows of carpet nails once pierced them. An electric lamp, run on a cord that extended out into the hall, illuminated a heavy oak desk.

There were a pair of windows, both tall and lacking the grille that covered the one in her room.

Hartwell stood behind the desk. He finished inscribing a note on a medical file. He turned and dropped it into the open drawer of a filing cabinet behind him. The steel cabinet was clearly new and obviously fireproof. Hartwell closed and locked the door, putting the key back in his jacket pocket.

"Miss Albright, Doctor," Gibbs announced.

"Thank you, Mr. Gibbs." Hartwell dismissed him. Gibbs closed the office door and Lily faced her enemy alone.

"I have been considering my options regarding you," he said, his tone expressing a mild irritation. "Turning you over to the legal authorities is, of course, one possibility, but I am forced to admit I do not find it as appealing now as I did earlier this evening. You have cost me a very great deal since then."

A gust of wind rattled the smeared, filthy glass of the windowpanes. Beyond them, the sun was sinking lower, light fading behind a dark stretch of forest.

"The goods in the warehouse can be replaced, of course. I would not be so foolish as to leave myself exposed to such a loss. It will, however, delay matters, a delay that should not have been necessary. Yet all of that pales in comparison to the matter of Lt. Waddington."

"It was him, wasn't it? Dora Heller. Agnes McKenney. Sylvia Durst. Annalise Boyden. He was the one who did it."

"The lieutenant was a very resourceful man."

"How?" she demanded. "How did he get in without anyone knowing?"

"Through the front door, I imagine," Hartwell replied, as though the matter should have been obvious. "Except perhaps at Mrs. Boyden's. She would certainly have had a service entrance."

"He posed as a servant?"

"A technician from the gasworks," Hartwell replied shortly. "That was his idea and a very clever one. It explained the need for a case full of equipment."

The pieces fell into place. She remembered Sam's stories of the best way for a thief to break into a house—by being invited in and simply failing to leave. There were enough tales of horrible accidents that resulted from faults in gas lines that no one would turn away a technician who claimed he was investigating a problem. All Waddington had to do was get inside and then disappear. In a busy household, everyone would assume that someone else had seen him out.

He simply found himself a place to wait, then emerged when the time was right to go about his work.

She remembered the vision that had started all of this. In it, a shadow wielding a silver needle had swept out of the closet in Estelle's bedroom.

That was where he must have hidden.

*She might have run off with the gasworks man.*

Mrs. Bramble's comment to Miss Bard, overheard as Lily stood in the hallway, the horror of realizing that what she'd foreseen had come to pass washing over her.

There had been other signs as well. In her vision of Annalise Boyden's death, the gas lamps in the room rose and fell, flickering like beacons.

She had even been told it all but directly, she realized with a sick lurch in her gut.

*Every time I ask her about it—who was it that did you in, Agnes?— she just shows me a lamp . . . a built-in gas fixture.*

The ghost of Agnes McKenney, communicating with Estelle. Sending her a precise and perfect warning that identified exactly who it was that killed her.

The man who'd come about the lamps.

Hartwell glared at her.

"Lt. Waddington was a unique resource. His hematological characteristics were extremely rare and to find that combined with a very competent and discreet medical assistant . . . well. The rub of it is that you are proving yourself an unusual menace. Which is why I have decided the most responsible course of action is to simply admit you."

"Admit me where?"

"Here."

"An empty house?"

"This is—or will be—the Greater Hampstead Ladies' Hospital. A private lunatics' asylum." He flipped through the remaining papers on his desk, making a quick notation. "It's a far more appropriate solution to the problem you pose. After all, I would not find it at all surprising that your outrageous behavior is, in fact, motivated by some mental disease. Sane women do not routinely go about London dressed as tanner's boys, breaking into private property."

It was also the quieter solution. The involvement of law enforcement meant a trial and trials gathered reporters like flies. Though Lily had little faith that the justice system would be willing to listen to her accusations against Hartwell, the tabloid reporters would certainly lick them up, causing him the inconvenience of a scandal. By shutting her up in his asylum, he ensured that any truth she tried to speak would be dismissed as the raving of a lunatic.

"Someone will find you out."

"Find me out for what? Practicing as a physician?"

"Physicians don't murder people."

His eyes narrowed.

"It is research, Miss Albright. Research with the potential to shape the course of the future of the human race. There can be no more meritorious purpose."

Connections continued to fall into place, triggered by his nearness, by the urgency of her situation.

She thought of a portrait on a gallery wall, a pointed warning from an artist thirty years dead. Mordecai Roth's story of a suitor spurned by a woman he had no logical reason to court.

She recalled words spoken in the dim silence of Robert Ash's reflection room.

*My wife was a charismatic.*

"Evangeline Ash," she said abruptly.

At the sound of that name, Hartwell's attention sharpened.

"Careful, Miss Albright."

"Did you know?" She pushed on, refusing to let him intimidate her into silence. "Did you know what she was?"

"I'm not sure I know what you mean."

"I think perhaps you do," Lily countered. "This was never about research. It was about her. You couldn't have her then, so you set about taking some echo of what she was from anyone who fell under your power. There is nothing noble about that, Dr. Hartwell. It is simply greed."

There was a pause, as though the room itself were holding its breath.

He set his pen down on the table, hard enough to send a splatter of ink across the blotter.

"Do not pretend to see into my soul. You think you stand on such firm moral ground? I am a doctor. I spent the first twenty years of my career in a charity hospital. I have seen the misery and degradation a human life can sink to, every imaginable form of it. You pass judgment on me without a thought for the countless thousands whose future suffering will be alleviated because of what I empower our race to become." He caught himself, reigning control back in. "I forget myself. One doesn't reason with lunatics."

He took up the pen again, made a few more quick notes in his careful hand. "I will take the precaution of altering your name on the admission papers. Though there isn't really anyone to come looking for you, is there? Nonetheless." He blotted the page, lifted it. "Mrs. Amanda Church. Suffering from nervous mania. Treatment regimen . . . water . . . therapy . . ." he spoke as he wrote.

Lily thought of the horror of the great metal tub, of icy water and the battle for air.

He frowned, considering. "I should really have you on laudanum. We can start with a full dose and reduce it based on your response. You may quite like it. It has a very calming effect."

"What about Estelle?"

"The sapphist? She won't be here long. I just need to find another research partner with a compatible blood type."

Fear crept in. It moved quickly, wrapping cold tentacles around her heart.

He could do it. He could do all of it. He could lock her back in that room under another woman's name. Even were she lucky enough to gain access to someone from outside, would they believe the ravings of a certified lunatic over the word of a respected physician?

No one would hear her. No one would question her presence. Hartwell would gain complete control over her for as long as she lived, secreted away in hell. And Estelle?

He would tear her apart as soon as he had the means.

How could she stop him? She had nothing. There was no threat she could levy, nothing she could put on the table to try to bargain with him . . .

Except there was. She had one asset that would almost certainly capture Hartwell's interest. But could she turn it into an appropriately powerful bargaining chip?

"What if I could provide you with a more desirable research subject?" she asked.

"How would you possibly do that?"

Lily ignored his dismissive tone, pressing on. "Assuming that I could, would you let Miss Deneuve go? You must have kept her drugged, as you did me. If she remembers anything of the warehouse or of Waddington, it will only be confused fragments. When she wakes here, you can tell her she was brought for medical attention and that you have no idea what happened to her. She'll believe you. She'd have no reason not to. I never told her anything about any of this."

"It's a plausible scenario but I fail to see—"

She cut in before he could finish.

"If I can give you something better, will you swear to me—on your honor as a physician and a gentleman—" The words nearly choked her, but Lily forced them out. "Will you swear that you will release her unharmed?"

"You've stood there judging my actions and now you're offering to sacrifice some other life to protect one you value higher. I do hope you are aware of the hypocrisy of that."

"Just tell me whether you agree to my terms."

"I reserve the right to judge whether the substitute you offer is truly a better subject. And I am not going to release the medium until this person, whomever she is, is securely under my care. Even then, the matter would have to be handled delicately . . ."

"Do we have a bargain or not?"

"If you can truly provide what you have promised, then yes. I can spare the woman. Though I fail to see how you can possibly do so, seeing as you have just been admitted to an asylum." He shook his head. "Gibbs!"

There was no mirror here, no convenient basin full of water for her to gaze in, but she had to find something. Hartwell would never take her at her word on this. Like the guests at Estelle's séance, he needed a show—a demonstration.

Her eyes moved to the shining black steel of the file cabinet, to the place where the light of the electric lamp was reflected on the surface of the dark metal.

She took a breath, forcing back her awareness of Hartwell's thug returning to the door. She made herself ignore the words they spoke, honing her attention desperately on the glow in that false glass.

This had to work. It *had to.*

The fear nipped at her, trying to pull her attention away. She refused to give in to it.

The light flickered, dancing like the flame of a candle across the black steel. The room narrowed, the far corners shifting into darkness . . . and then only the light was left.

*Ask for what you want.*

Something now, she thought fiercely. Something quick and now.

The vision presented itself to her, as clear as it was absurd.

Then it was gone and she was back in the moldering study once again.

She opened her mouth, the words falling quickly from her lips.

"A lorry is about to pass down the road. White. Headlamps on. It . . ." She paused at the absurdity of it, then plowed forward. She couldn't question it, not now. She had to trust this. "It's being driven by a dog," she finished.

Hartwell stared at her in dumb surprise, as though he were shocked to discover that she was, in fact, a lunatic after all.

"What's she going on about?" Gibbs demanded crossly.

Then the rumble of an engine crept through the thin glass of the window-panes.

It grew louder, drawing closer. Hartwell continued to stare at Lily, but his expression shifted, narrowing with intense interest.

He stepped over to the window, opening the sash to see better than the dirt smearing the panes would allow. Cold air spilled into the room.

A white lorry bounced down the lane. The rumble of the engine disturbed a murder of ravens scattered across the field. They startled up into the air, painted shadows flapping against the darkening sky. A few settled in the branches of the massive oak that dominated the yard.

The driver's window of the truck was open. The head of a beagle protruded from it. The dog panted delightedly into the breeze, perched on the lap of his master, who let up the throttle as he slowed the vehicle and turned it into the drive.

There was a crunch of gravel. Then the engine shuddered to a halt.

Hartwell turned to Lily.

"How? How did you know?"

She didn't answer, holding fiercely to an ongoing thread of knowing deep inside of her.

This was more than another bit of scrying. It was something else, something stranger and yet utterly familiar, like an old friend come back to her doorstep.

"You have a caller," she told him. She reached, feeling for more, sensing it was there. "Something about the temperature."

There was a sharp knock on the door below, a quick exchange of voices. A few moments later, footsteps sounded in the hall.

Lily recognized the man who arrived as the one who had been driving Hartwell's carriage the night before. He was tall and thin, good-looking in a dull sort of way. His chauffeur's cap was tucked into his trouser pocket.

"What is it, Mr. Northcote?" Hartwell demanded.

"Sorry to bother you, sir, but there's a gentleman below. Says he's come about the boiler."

Hartwell didn't answer. He just turned his gaze slowly back to Lily.

"Should I let him in, sir?" Northcote pressed.

"This isn't a convenient time," Hartwell finally answered.

"See, I told him that. He said it'd be a fortnight before he was back out this way again, and I'm knowing the paint won't dry in this weather without any heat. That's a fortnight with no work being done about the place, and you've said you were on a schedule—"

Hartwell's irritation was written clearly on his face. Northcote seemed immune to it.

The doctor snapped at Gibbs.

"Watch her. See she doesn't try anything foolish."

He stalked out, Northcote following behind him.

Lily let go. The tension of maintaining her deliberate connection with her power had been rising to a shrieking pitch. It broke, falling softly back, and she let out a long, shuddering breath.

How had she done it?

It had to be the drug. Though the vision had ended, some other effect still lingered. It had charged her like the battery in Estelle's magic lantern.

There was no time now to consider what that meant or worry about how long it might last. She needed to assess her options, quickly.

She made a quick study of the room. Her eye lit on a narrow line in the wall. It was a door, no bigger than that of a cupboard. It had been papered over in the same pattern as the wall. Had the paper not been half stripped it would have been nearly invisible. She judged her chances of exploring it while Gibbs watched from the doorway.

She moved to the window.

It was uncaged. Lily pushed up the sash. At least thirty feet extended between her and the hard, frozen ground. There was no way she could scale the smooth facade of the building. The great oak tree in the yard would be climbable, but the nearest branch was beyond her reach, even if she took the chance of leaping for it.

An enormous raven perched on the bare limb, staring blandly out over the heath.

"Try that and you'll break your neck," Gibbs barked from within.

The bird turned. Eyes like black pebbles locked onto Lily's, measuring her with dark intelligence.

*What's the cleverest animal?*

*Ravens.*

*What do you have to pay them?*

*More than you'd want to give.*

Sam's words came back to her, spoken in the drawing room of The Refuge while the portrait of Saint Francis preaching to finches looked blandly on.

Desperation choked her.

She couldn't get out of this on her own.

Strangford was gone. The grief of that hovered at the periphery, waiting for its time to consume her.

But there were others.

The bird outside the window ruffled its feathers, black eyes shining in the last of the evening light.

The action that suggested itself to her was utterly ludicrous, the act of a woman who probably deserved to be locked up in an asylum.

She did it anyway.

"There is a boy in Bloomsbury who talks to birds," Lily said.

The black bird on the oak turned, fixing her in its dark, unblinking stare.

Lily refused to flinch from that penetrating, alien gaze.

"Tell him that I am here. That I need help. Please. Whatever your price is, I will pay it. Just tell him . . ." Her voice caught. She swallowed thickly, pressed on. "Tell him that we are here."

"Oy, enough of that, now. Get out of the bloody window," Gibbs snapped from within.

"The boy in Bloomsbury who talks to birds," Lily repeated urgently as the raven continued to gaze at her. "Please."

Rough hands grabbed her arms, pulling her inside. The glass slammed shut, hard enough to rattle the panes in their frames. Outside the window, startled black birds flapped into the air again, circling over the yard.

All except for one, who continued to stare through the window, dark eyes glittering.

Hartwell returned. With a glance, he swept in Lily's position on the floor where Gibbs had tossed her.

"Put her back in her room."

Gibbs grabbed her arm, yanking her to her feet. Lily pulled against him, resisting, turning to Hartwell.

"Do we have a bargain?"

Gibbs tugged.

"Come on, you stupid bint."

She dug her heels in, compelling Hartwell to answer her.

"Do we have a bargain?"

"I am considering it," he snapped in reply.

Gibbs tucked his shoulder into her stomach and lifted her. He hauled her down the hallway, his bones digging into her with every step back to room 109, where he tossed her unceremoniously on the floor.

The door slammed shut. It was heavy, closing with a solid clang. The lock thudded into place.

Lily went to the window. The sun was nearly gone, the shadows thickening outside the steel-grated glass. She could barely see the dark form of the oak tree sprawling across the grand front lawn of the derelict estate.

Its branches were empty.

—

Gloom settled over the heath, the sun all but vanished behind the trees. Lily sat on the cold, bare floor, trying not to let the fear tear her to pieces.

She had exposed herself, shared her most intimate secret with a monster, hoping to wrest a promise from him to release Estelle.

It was a promise he would certainly break. Her best hope was that she had sparked enough interest in him to divert his attention from Estelle for a little while, perhaps long enough for some form of help to arrive.

Who was she fooling? Help wasn't arriving. Her only chance of that lay in a conversation with a bird, which had been decidedly one-sided.

Hartwell would take Estelle's blood as soon as he found a compatible and trustworthy recipient. The delay of securing that might buy her a few days, but nothing more.

Lily had been committed. As Mrs. Amanda Church, Hartwell could use her over and over again for as long as he liked, just as he had Mariah Reznik.

And there were no oil lamps here.

The despair threatened to choke her, thick enough to make her dizzy.

Her skin hummed, arms tingling with a low warning.

They were coming. She knew it, yet the knowledge meant nothing because there was nowhere she could run. Nowhere to hide.

A moment later, the door opened. Northcote and Gibbs came in.

"I'll need her coat removed."

Hartwell's voice floated casually from the hall.

The men grabbed her. Rough hands forced her onto her stomach on the floor. They tugged off her coat, her face grinding against the rough boards.

She saw Hartwell's boots as he walked into the room. He set a black medical case down on the floor beside her, flipping the latches and opening it to reveal two rows of tidy glass jars and the long needle of a syringe.

"Hold her securely and give me her left arm."

Northcote pinned her legs. Gibbs tugged her right hand up against her back, then knelt on it, the pressure threatening to crack her ribs. He wrenched her left arm up, twisting it until her shoulder screamed. He held it steadily.

Hartwell plucked one of the jars from his case. He screwed it onto the syringe.

She felt his fingers on her arm. They were light, gentle. He unbuttoned and rolled back the sleeve of her shirt, pushing it up past her elbow.

He took a rubber strap from the case and tied it around her triceps, snugly, then tapped at the sensitive skin inside her elbow.

"You may feel a slight prick," he said, his tone as even and detached as it would be during some routine exam.

The needle pierced her. The pain was small compared to the blazing tension in her shoulder, but it was constant. She felt the tip of the needle wiggle as Hartwell turned some lever on the syringe. He turned it back a moment later, and after another uncomfortable jiggle, he set the little vial down on the floor by her face.

It was full of blood.

He took a clean vial from the case, screwing it into place. Another twist of the lever.

Her body screamed. Gibbs's knee crushed her fingers, her ribs aching. Her cheek scraped against the cold floor.

Another vial joined the first. A third left the case.

Northcote shifted his weight on her legs and her knee twisted, sending pain shooting up her thigh.

The needle wiggled in her arm.

Finally, a third jar joined the others on the floor.

"That should be enough for testing," Hartwell announced as though to some unseen audience hovering at the edge of the room.

He tugged the needle neatly from her arm. She felt the pressure of his hand on the place where it had been.

Hartwell neatly, carefully wrapped a length of gauze around her arm. He secured it with a pin. Then he screwed lids onto each of the three vials, tightening them securely.

They were labeled *A. Church, Room 109.*

He set them neatly in their places in the medical case, then snapped it shut and stood.

At some unseen sign, the men let go. Lily rolled onto her side, then to her knees, hugging her aching arms to her chest. She didn't trust herself to stand, her legs tingling as the blood flowed back into them.

"See that she has something to eat. I don't want her weakened," Hartwell ordered. Then he left, taking the case with him.

Northcote tipped his cap to her as though apologizing for a mild inconvenience. Gibbs simply looked away, slamming the door shut behind him.

She braced one foot against the floor, pushed, and staggered painfully to her feet.

She was shaking, but not with terror, though threads of that still lingered, wrapping cold fibers around her heart.

It was rage. Pure, explosive rage.

*He would not get away with this.*

It didn't matter that she was locked away—alone, unarmed, with no hope of a rescue.

She was unarmed, but she was not powerless. She had never been powerless.

She reached inside, stretched herself fully and intentionally toward that strange instinct, the one that warned her when stairs were about to collapse or that danger was coming to the door. The same instinct that, years before, had always known when the housekeeper was going to knock a vase from the table, or that the tall, dashing earl who was her father was about to pay a call.

The part of herself she had spent so much of her life trying to run from.

The cold receded, and the pain, the walls of the room growing wider until they simply crumbled, dissolving into a space of unimaginable vastness.

Lily stood in the heart of it.

Knowledge hummed around her. Inside of her.

For decades, when she had felt that knowing, she had flinched away from it, tried to bury it as deep and far as possible. Knowing meant pain, meant a sense of responsibility she didn't feel capable of living up to.

In the middle of the flowing crowd on Tottenham Court Road, Robert Ash had told her that there was more than one role she might play—that success and failure weren't always so black and white. That sometimes to simply stand up and fight was enough, no matter the outcome of the battle.

She felt her power buzzing with life. This time, instead of running from it, she extended her mind to touch it . . .

. . . and it answered.

# THIRTY-THREE

$\mathcal{L}$ILY SAT IN THE center of the floor of the narrow room and waited.

She held her connection to her power, focusing her mind and the stillness of her body on maintaining it. It was less than perfectly steady. She could feel it flicker as though the lingering effect of the Wine of Jurema was already beginning to fade.

She would worry about that later. It was strong enough, now, for what she needed.

*There.*

Awareness hummed. Someone was coming.

Lily rose. She stepped behind the door, pushing her back against the wall. Her timing needed to be perfect. A moment too soon or too late and she would fail.

She held herself silent and ready.

Footsteps thudded down the hall. They stopped at her door. There was a heavy clang as the lock turned.

The door began to open.

Lily waited for a precise moment. Then, pressing her shoulders back against the wall, she lifted both of her legs and kicked with all her strength at the solid oak panel of the door.

It slammed into Northcote, catching him on the shoulder and throwing him into the far side of the frame. The bowl he was carrying crashed to the floor and shattered.

Lily didn't hesitate. If he had even a moment to recover, her chance would be lost. As soon as her feet returned to the floor, she grabbed him by the coat, extended her leg, and yanked him over it.

He tripped, falling into the room. Lily kicked him swiftly in the gut. Northcote groaned, pulling his legs up to protect his middle from another blow.

It didn't come. The reaction was enough to get him fully clear of the door. Lily leapt past him, grabbed the knob and slammed it shut behind her.

She threw the lock.

The hallway was empty. Numbered doors marched in either direction, illuminated by the harsh electric light.

She knew now why they seemed familiar. They reminded her of another hall, extending to an impossible distance, lined with infinite doors resonating with unimaginable potential.

In her hand she held the key, the power to choose from infinite possibilities of what might be . . .

The lingering hum of the vision shattered as Northcote began pounding violently on the door.

She ran for the staircase.

Halfway down the hall, the hum of awareness sang at her again. Someone was coming.

She grabbed a knob and ducked through the nearest door, closing it carefully and quietly behind her.

Footsteps pounded up the stairs. They hurried down the hallway, echoing past her hiding place.

She waited until they had just begun to slow, then darted into the hall.

Gibbs stood in front of the open door to Room 109. Both he and Northcote turned as she appeared and bolted for the stairs.

She heard them come after her as she entered the landing.

Every ounce of logic screamed to go down, a ground floor door or window offering her best chance of escape. She hesitated. This wing was renovated and was intended to be part of an asylum. Though she wasn't sure how far along the repairs to the ground floor had gone, if it was anywhere near complete, there would be no way out down there.

She thought back to the office Hartwell had claimed for himself. It had lain at the edges of the renovated wing of the building. Beyond it was the part of the old manor that faced the road, which she remembered looking entirely abandoned when she passed it on her ride a few weeks before.

If she had a chance of escaping this place, that was where she would find it.

She tore herself away from the desperate desire to descend and instead bolted up the staircase.

She reached the top and raced past another procession of horribly regular doors.

The painter's cloth still hung at the far end of the hall, as she remembered it.

She could hear Gibbs and Northcote hit the hallway behind her, their feet thundering on the floorboards.

She blasted past the cloth and found herself at the edge of a ballroom shrouded in gloom and decay.

There were no electric lights here. The high ceiling was hung with cobwebs and shadows. Mouse-eaten curtains trailed over the windows, pale squares on the wallpaper showing where paintings had once been displayed. It smelled of pigeon droppings and earth, the space bare save for a pile of smashed wooden chairs in a corner.

She didn't hesitate, sprinting into the room as the last rays of the setting sun faded against the filthy glass of the tall windows.

On the far side, she slid into the mouth of a midnight-dark hall.

Doors lined it, leading into rooms of furniture shrouded in rotting dust cloths, wallpaper peeling like flayed skin, plaster bubbling and splitting along the ceilings. The hallway twisted and turned, branching unpredictably. Lily dodged along it blindly, making random turns, throwing herself deeper into the bowels of the ruin.

She dashed down a once-grand staircase, now draped with rotting shreds of an old carpet runner.

Footsteps thundered behind her, coming closer.

Knowing she was running out of hallway, she picked a room at random and dodged inside.

Once, it must have been elegant. Now, only the crooked frame of a four-poster bed remained, stripped of mattress and hangings. The closet door was ajar, windows shuttered, save for one that hung pre-cariously from its hinges.

Nothing else. Nowhere she could hide—save for that closet itself, which was as good as a trap if anyone came to look. And they would certainly look.

She heard the steps slow, voices drifting to her down the short length of hallway that separated her from her pursuers.

"Which way did she go?" Gibbs demanded.

"I don't know. I can't bloody see."

"Weren't you listening for her?"

"I couldn't hear her over your blasted racket."

"She's in one of the rooms. Check them."

Her heart pounded against her chest as she surveyed the room once more, panic growing. Where could she hide?

The answer came to her. It was mad. It was also her only option.

Taking a deep breath, willing herself to calm, she reached for her power once again.

It was less steady than it had been back in Room 109. Perhaps what she had done already had drained it. It felt more distant and ephemeral.

Fear quickened. She forced it back. She could do this—she would do this.

The connection settled, grew stronger . . . and she *knew*.

What would come in a few moments was clearer to her than what had just passed, more real and substantial, complete to the last detail.

She put her back to the wall beside the door, maintaining that awareness steadily. Then, as she had known he would, Gibbs entered the room.

*Now.*

Instinct prompted her. She glided neatly, silently into place behind him, then took another half-step to the right as he turned and looked at the place where she had been.

*Left.*

She moved. Gibbs swung around to pull back the door, peering into that darker corner of the room, as Lily watched calmly, quietly from behind him.

*Right again. Forward.*

She was a shadow dancing behind him, the knowledge of where

he would go coming just a moment before he moved. That brief space was all the time she needed to choose her own reaction, time it perfectly—a quick step to the side as he turned to examine the closet, ducking inside. Slipping behind him as he reversed and made his way back into the center of the room.

She knew when he would stop. Knew that he would rub his hand along the back of his neck as though sensing her eyes there. He would turn, abruptly, but she was already ahead of him, already moving to keep her body just out of his line of sight so that all he saw, as he whirled, was the empty room.

He studied it suspiciously, then muttered under his breath.

"Bloody ghosts."

As Lily watched him from the center of the room he had just thoroughly searched, he walked away.

The knowing flickered, sputtered. She felt the connection thin, then snap, worn through by the effort she had just demanded of it.

She reached for it again, desperately. What answered her was only a fragment, an echo of what she had felt before.

The sense of loss, sharp and painful, surprised her.

Whatever shortcut she had taken to find that place inside herself was broken. To return there again, she would have to take the long road—the road Ash had described, made up of practice and training and discipline.

But if she did choose that road . . . she had a hint, now, of what might be waiting for her at the end of it.

Evangeline Ash's voice echoed through her mind.

*You have no idea what you are capable of.*

Discovering what she meant would have to wait. Right now, Lily needed to determine how she was going to get out of this place alive.

She moved to the window and peered out the opening made by the half-fallen shutter.

She had descended to the first floor. An ancient, twisted wisteria vine climbed up the exterior of this side of the manor. She could reach the trunk of it from the window. It would offer easy means of scaling her way down to the leaf-strewn, cracked stones of the patio.

From there, she could head for the road in hopes of flagging a passing car or carriage. There was also the farmhouse where she'd had her leg stitched up a few weeks before. She could run there and tell them to send for help, help that could come barreling through the doors to save Estelle.

Except Estelle wouldn't be there anymore. If Hartwell knew Lily had escaped, he would move his other research subject or simply dispose of her before the authorities could arrive. They would find only a renowned physician in a half-renovated building, inconvenienced by a raving woman in trousers who was at best a housebreaker and at worst, an escaped lunatic to be remanded back to Hartwell's care.

No. She couldn't run. Not without Estelle.

She thought back to the long, glaring hallways of doors. Estelle might be behind any one of them. She could hardly hope that Gibbs and Northcote would stay distracted in the ruined part of the manor long enough for her to try them all, and there was still Hartwell himself to consider.

She didn't have time to guess where Estelle had been hidden. She needed to know. Her power wouldn't help her, even if she could manage to force a reconnection to it. There weren't any answers there. It couldn't tell her what was happening now, only what was coming.

How could she know?

The files.

She thought back to the ones she'd rifled in Hartwell's study—all detailed, painstakingly organized.

There had been a file cabinet in the office he'd commandeered here in the manor. It was far too new to be some relic of the old estate. Hartwell had brought it there before he'd moved so much as a stick of other furniture or supplies.

Somewhere in that cabinet was a file on Estelle. It wouldn't list her true name, of course. But the rest of it would be perfectly accurate— including the number of the room where she was being held.

Urgent footsteps echoed down through the ceiling as Lily made her way back to the ballroom. She slipped past the painter's cloth, returning to the glaring white hall of Hartwell's asylum.

She paused to pluck a crowbar from the toolbox on the floor.

The weight of it felt good in her hands, familiar like an old friend.

She crept up to the office door.

It was empty.

The electric lamp on the desk still lit the space, though outside the windows night had fully descended. The light felt harsh, exposing her to anyone who walked by.

Her pulse pounding, she strode to the big steel file cabinet, wedging the crowbar into the edge of the first drawer and throwing all her weight against it.

The drawer cracked open with a squeal of twisting metal.

It was empty.

She slammed it shut, knowing speed was what counted now, and jammed the crowbar into the next drawer.

It popped open, then caught. Lily stomped on the crowbar and the drawer wrenched free. A handful of files rested inside.

She grabbed them and tossed them onto the desk, quickly flipping through the contents.

First was a 75-year-old female from Islington, diagnosed with dementia. Next was a 20-year-old with melancholia. There were no room numbers on either file, making these most likely patients that Hartwell had already arranged to take up residence in this sterile hell once it was ready to open.

She tossed them aside, knowing it could not possibly be long before she was discovered.

She opened the file of a female, age unknown but described as "middling", approximately 5' 10" in height. Diagnosed with chronic delusions. *Sapphic*, Hartwell had neatly penned on one of the lines.

*Sapphist.* The slur he had used to refer to Estelle.

On the opening line of the chart was a room number.

204.

"There!"

The shout came from the hall. Lily looked up to see Hartwell and Northcote striding toward her.

She snatched up the crowbar.

Could she fight them both?

The narrow door in the wall caught her eye. She ran to it and wrenched it open. A narrow stair lay behind, leading up.

As Hartwell entered the room, she bolted through that dark opening.

Shouts echoed up at her as she climbed. The stairwell was tight, twisting and turning dizzily. Cobwebs brushed her face as she ran, her feet slipping in the dust. She didn't allow herself to wonder what could possibly be at the end of it. She simply ran until a solid wall stopped her.

She felt at it frantically in the darkness. Cold air seeped through cracks in the wood. Her hand brushed a knob. She rattled it but it refused to turn.

Footsteps from below shook the boards under her feet.

The wall behind her was rough, not wood but brick. She braced herself against it, then kicked—once, twice. The third time, something shattered and the door swung open.

Lily ran through it out onto a narrow path that stretched across the apex of the roof.

The sky overhead exploded with stars, dizzying in their abundance. The cold air slapped her, fogging her breath.

She could see the road and beyond it, the broad expanse of the heath, the familiar landscape made strange by a shroud of winter. Around her, the peaks and gables of the house were a treacherous mountain range blanketed with snow. She could see the two great wings of the building, but there was no sign of another door like the one behind her or any promise of a way down that didn't involve tumbling to her death.

Voices sounded from the stairwell behind her. Out of alternatives, she ran out along the narrow, frosted path. It ended at the solid brick wall of another chimney. She turned, letting the crowbar hang at her side.

Hartwell stepped out onto the roof.

"If you will wait a moment, Mr. Northcote," he spoke into the darkness behind him. Then he turned to Lily.

"Miss Albright."

"Doctor Hartwell."

His face looked cadaverous in the pale light of the stars, the hollows of his cheeks cast into sunken shadows. His tone was casual, as though he had simply happened across her here on the peak of the roof.

"You have noted, I am sure, that there is no other means of egress from here."

Lily didn't answer, adjusting her grip on the crowbar. Her fingers were cold, the metal sucking the warmth from her hand.

"Mr. Northcote is fairly cross with you. I gather Mr. Gibbs is as well. But I have made both of them promise not to exact any retribution for the trouble you caused them this evening if you agree to return quietly to your room. I'm sure you must see this is the only sensible course of action."

There was nothing sensible about it. To return to the room was to put herself back under Hartwell's control. He would take what he wanted from her—quickly or slowly—and then he would kill her.

The snow-covered roof offered nothing, no scaffolding she could scale back to the ground, no convenient tree she could climb. There was only a steep, slippery pitch to either side of her and beyond that, a long drop to the dirt.

The silence where her answer should have been stretched, grew undeniable.

"I see," Hartwell replied shortly. "That is unfortunate." He called back to the darkened door. "Mr. Northcote? I am afraid Miss Albright will need to be retrieved."

Hartwell moved a step to the side and Northcote slipped past him onto the path.

"Can you handle it?" she heard Hartwell ask, voice low.

"She's just a girl," Northcote retorted.

He approached, moving cautiously down the narrow walk.

As he came, Lily heard a thick fluttering overhead. She looked up to see a wave of black wings pass across the sky, dark bodies obscuring the thick veil of stars.

The ravens circled, a few breaking away from the others and coming to rest on the cracked pots crowning the chimney behind her. They stared down at her and Northcote, black eyes indifferent.

The driver continued to stalk toward her. He was a large man. She had no illusions about her chances of resisting him if he managed to get his hands on her. At the moment, she had only one advantage.

She took a step out from the bricks, the crowbar hanging in the shadow of her leg.

As Northcote reached the place where she waited for him, the silence of the night broke, interrupted by the distant rumble of an engine.

Beyond Northcote's shoulder, a pair of headlights pierced the darkness of the heath, moving far faster than they ought to be up the snow-covered road.

He turned toward the sound, surprised.

Lily seized her chance and swung.

She aimed the crowbar for the driver's back, his broadest target. The impact sent him lurching forward, but he turned as he fell and clutched at the sleeve of Lily's jacket.

Northcote's weight pulled her off balance. Her feet slid on the snow-covered path and she tumbled after him, sliding down the icy slates of the roof.

She swung the crowbar up over her head, wildly. The hook of it slammed into the path and held, wedged in place. She dangled from the end, feet hanging halfway down the roof, as Northcote slid past her.

He stopped at the copper gutter, clinging to it. The metal creaked.

"Doctor!" he shouted.

The rumble of the approaching engine grew louder. The headlights were drawing closer to the drive, their glow illuminating the shadowy forms of another handful of ravens settling on the hedge that lined the road.

"Miss Albright?"

Lily looked up to see Hartwell standing over her. He knelt down in the snow, extending his arm.

"Take my hand, please."

Behind her, a louder wrench signaled another shift in the gutter. Northcote screamed.

Lily glanced down at him. He had managed to wrap one of his legs around the metal, but the copper pulled away from the roof, revealing a few inches of open air.

"We can fetch a rope for Mr. Northcote once you're somewhere safe."

Hartwell's voice was calm, placidly reassuring. His pale hand remained suspended in the darkness above her as the cold iron of the crowbar grew slick under her sweating palms.

She was under no illusion as to why he offered her his help. He wanted her body. He wanted to rip it open and find the source of its power. He would tear it out of her and make it his, acting out some dark dream of possession cloaked in altruistic glitter.

Below her, metal screamed and twisted as the gutter tore away from the roof. Northcote's voice rose to join it, a howl of animal fear as he slid down the remaining length of it and then tumbled from view.

The howl ended abruptly with a dull crunch in the snow of the yard.

Hartwell's hand hovered in the darkness above.

She felt the tension between two terrible options—to fall, or to let Hartwell save her and be placed fully under his power for whatever remained of her life.

Her hands slid against the cold iron of the crowbar and her mind flashed back to a hallway of infinite doors, to the cold weight of a key in her hand. The connection to that space became present, firing through her. With perfect clarity, she knew exactly what it was.

The future spilled forward from the moment in which she hung. She felt it splinter, multiplying like a kaleidoscope in which every facet revealed something subtly different. Possibilities unfurled behind countless doors. Lily knew them all, saw the myriad ways they could unfold, based on the pivot of this moment.

In many—nearly all—Hartwell continued his work. More women died in the name of his research, research with the potential of proving that desirable talents could be harvested with the blood of those who bore them, then granted to others deemed more worthy.

It was a discovery that would justify unspeakable horrors.

And yet there were other doors—slimmer, less tangible—which lead to a very different outcome.

She was suffused with the knowledge that, at this precise minute, she held the key to one such future in her hand . . . a third option that lay between letting go and giving in.

One where she took Hartwell down with her.

She could become a murderer herself and in doing so, prevent a thousand untold murders from ever being thought.

It was a choice that chilled her with horror.

Lily pulled against the crowbar. She walked her feet up the icy slope of the roof, bracing them against the slates. She pulled her right hand from the iron and lifted it. Felt Hartwell's cold palm clasp her own, his grip sure, and prepared to use that leverage to push both herself and the man who thought he was going to save her off into the open air.

At the top of the drive, the headlights swung towards the great ruined house. Tires skidded across the snow, caught, and spun a gleaming silver Rolls Royce into the yard.

The light from below washed over Hartwell, chasing the shadows from his face, leaving him exposed and thoroughly surprised.

On the chimney pot, a raven ruffled its wings and croaked.

Impossible.

It was impossible . . . but impossible things had been happening all night.

They'd been happening all her life.

Hartwell turned his gaze from the car in the drive to Lily's face, surprise shifting to suspicion, run through with veins of something else—a reluctant respect.

His hand in hers, her legs still braced against the roof, Lily met his eyes. She felt the perfect balance of the moment. The decision was hers to make, but only for another breath.

Down the drive, car doors slammed, the engine rumbling to a stop.

She let out her breath and then, shifting the angle of her feet against the roof, allowed Hartwell to haul her back to the path.

Voices called out below, sharp and urgent. Lily singled out a familiar Ulster brogue as Dr. Gardner's tones floated up to where she stood on the peak of the roof.

"There's a man on the ground over here!"

Hartwell still held her arm, keeping her as close as a lover as he looked down at the activity below. Figures moved across the headlights of the Rolls, their forms thrown into silhouette. Lily could see Gardner's broad shoulders as he pulled a case from the car, then jogged over to where something lay beyond her line of sight.

Sam grabbed a lantern and ran to the end of the drive, where he waved it at three more sets of approaching headlights making their way across the heath at a more measured pace.

Someone else remained in front of the vehicle, his gaze directed up at the roof. Though he was cast into shadow by the headlamps, Lily knew him. She knew his shape—the set of his shoulders, the unfashionable fall of his hair.

Strangford.

Alive. Here.

The relief shattered over her, bursting into a thousand pieces, releasing her from a grief so deep she hadn't allowed herself to feel it.

She felt his eyes on her and knew he had made her out on the peak of the roof—along with the silhouette of the man who gripped her.

He ran, sprinting toward the house.

"How did you do it?" Hartwell demanded. "How did you tell them where to find you?"

"I had help," Lily replied.

The other cars had reached the drive. They turned, carefully negotiating the snow-covered corner to enter the estate. Lily could see the decals of the Metropolitan Police painted onto the sides. They stopped and uniformed men spilled out, heading for the house or to the place where Northcote had fallen.

Beside her, Hartwell watched them come.

"I think . . . this can be salvaged," he said thoughtfully, slowly.

There was a thin current of fear in his tone, a flicker of uncertainty. It shocked Lily. He had always seemed sure, certain of himself and the rightness of his actions.

She felt her pulse quicken, her senses sharpening.

"The Sapphist has been drugged. She won't recall anything of substance. There is nothing in the building that should not be here given its intended purpose. Gibbs will validate any case I make. There is only Northcote who must be accounted for."

"I think you're forgetting something," Lily snapped.

"No. I am merely envisioning the picture that will be made if the most troublesome piece of the puzzle is eliminated."

Her heart pounded. She did not need any power to understand what was coming next.

It would be a neat enough story. The good doctor would simply be trying to do what was right for the lunatic who had been witnessed breaking into his house—a lunatic who was now on the roof from which his loyal servant had fallen.

Even if Strangford and the others tried to speak the truth, it would look groundless without the key witness in all of this.

Without Lily.

On the chimney, the raven called again, another harsh, demanding croak, a restless flap of dark wings.

She felt the pressure on her arm shift.

There was no time to think, no time to weigh outcomes. Lily acted on instinct, countering him with the only resource she had available.

She grabbed his arms in return and when she felt him push, threw the weight of her body toward the yard.

They toppled together from the path.

She hit the snow-covered slates, sliding. She pushed Hartwell away and reached out wildly.

Her fingers clasped cold iron.

She grabbed, the metal scraping against her palm. Her momentum jerked to a stop, her shoulder screaming in protest.

Beside her, Hartwell glided across the icy slates. He reached the bottom of the roof where the gutter had torn away and without so much as a gasp, tipped over the edge and vanished.

Lily dangled from the far end of the crowbar, her hand burning, and watched him go.

There was no scream, only silence, then the thick crunch of impact.

The raven rose from the chimney, flapping lazy black wings. It circled over her, then swooped down to the place where Hartwell had fallen.

Cold metal slipped under her palm.

"Lily."

She looked up.

Strangford knelt on the path. There were cobwebs in his dark hair, his pale cheek marred by the scar of his struggle with Waddington. He tugged at the black gloves on his hands, shoved them into his pocket. He reached across the roof to her.

"Hold on to me."

She felt her precarious grasp on the crowbar slip. She kicked her feet against the snow covering the slates, searching for purchase, and found it—hardly anything, just the toe of her motorcycle boot catching against a chip in the stone—but she used it, wedged in as far as she could, and pushed.

She swung her hand up, met Strangford's bare fingers, and clutched.

He brought his other hand down to catch her, his grip warm and sure. He pulled. Lily scrambled and a few slippery, precarious steps later, he hauled her back onto the path.

His arms came around her, solid and real. She let herself fall into his embrace, all the tension and fear crumbling, leaving her raw, vulnerable to the horror of how close she had come to losing herself.

"Strangford," she said, her voice as hoarse as the raven.

"I know," he whispered, his breath warm against her hair, his bare hands cradling her. "I know."

# THIRTY-FOUR

*One week later*
*East Sussex*

$\mathcal{T}$HE AIR WAS WARM, a balmy spring breeze sharp with the scent of the sea. Lily stepped down from the express train, crossing the platform at the quaint coastal town of Hastings.

The steam whistle blew. She wove her way through a light, busy crowd, stopping at the baggage car. She handed over her ticket. The boy who took it paused only a moment to gape at her driving coat and trousers before he disappeared into the darkness of the car. He emerged a moment later, wheeling her Triumph.

Lily grabbed the handlebars, helping him bounce it down the steps onto the platform.

A few waiting passengers stared as she pushed it down the ramp.

The road before the station was busy, bustling with shoppers or couples walking arm-in-arm through the warm spring afternoon. Ladies clad in soft pastel gowns showed off their straw bonnets. Crocuses bloomed in the window boxes and the air smelled of the fresh salt of the shore.

She swung her leg over the motorcycle, hopped onto the pedals and spun. The engine caught, roaring to life. A few startled gazes turned her way as she opened the throttle and shot up the road.

Out in the country of West Sussex, the grass was turning a verdant spring green in the fields, the few remaining patches of snow quickly melting. Sheep grazed contentedly while hens pecked at the side of the road. Between the budding hedgerows, Lily caught glimpses of the broad, blue sea to the south.

The landscape grew wilder as she turned inland toward the weald. Stretches of forest intermingled with the fields, hills rising around her. As the Triumph rattled over a wooden bridge, she caught a glimpse of a torrid little waterfall spilling white water down into a narrow stream.

She turned at an ancient gatehouse.

The drive was long, covered in neatly combed gravel and sheltered by a row of massive lime trees. Their regular trunks marched by as she flew along, slowing only when she had reached the yard.

She turned to stop in front of a rambling but elegant Jacobean manor, an assortment of gray wings and towers nestled at the edge of a wood.

Brede Abbey, the Torrington family seat.

A still, shining pond reflected the ivy-covered walls. The green lawn was scattered with ancient trees, their roots circled with white and purple blossoms. She could see sheep grazing, a pair of gardeners raking a path. An ancient church sat just beyond the house, a relic of the monastery from which the place took its name.

She killed the engine, and quiet settled back over the landscape. It was beautiful—her father's home, this place that she had never seen before.

She kicked down the stand of the motorbike and dismounted, tugging off her goggles. At the front door, she hesitated only a moment before lifting her hand and knocking, firmly.

It opened.

A butler, dressed in a pristine black suit, stood in the entry. He was quite old, at least seventy. His frame had likely once been impressive but was starting to bow with age, though his carriage was still straight. Clear eyed, he took in her appearance with only the briefest glance, eyes flickering over her fitted trousers, wind-tossed hair, and the Triumph parked on the drive behind her. Then, with perfect courtesy, he greeted her.

"Good afternoon."

"Miss Lily Albright, to see his lordship," Lily announced, handing him her card.

"Very good, miss," the butler replied, accepting it without missing a beat. "I shall see if he is in."

He opened the door, motioning Lily into the entry. She felt her own unexpected note of surprise, some part of her anticipating that she would be left waiting on the step. Obviously, the staff of Brede Abbey had been trained to offer courtesy no matter who called at the front door.

"If you'll wait here."

Lily nodded and the butler made his way down the hall. He walked slowly, favoring one of his knees.

She waited in the entry. The ceiling was high, paneled in rich, dark wood, as were the walls, carved in elegant patterns glowing with years of polish. The furnishings were a mix of old and new, an ancient tapestry on the walls hanging dangerously close to a propped-up cricket bat and a pair of extraordinarily muddy shoes. A grand Tudor chair, embroidered upholstery faded with years, held a woman's feathered hat and veil alongside a set of pale lavender gloves. Someone had left a copy of Herodotus on the table next to the silver salver for calling cards.

It was one of her younger brothers, most likely—the brothers she had never met. The hat was a relic of their mother, the countess. Her father's wife.

At the end of the room, an enormous clock ticked steadily, then struck a rich, resonant one.

The butler returned.

"Apologies for the delay. His lordship is in the study. May I take your coat?"

"That won't be necessary. I won't be staying very long."

She followed him down the hall past large, elegant rooms that spoke of generations of history and the influence of a woman's particular eye. The combination could have been jarring, but wasn't. Instead, the house felt lived in, real. She could too easily imagine reading a book while curled into the brown armchair next to the drawing room fireplace, or racing a set of unruly boys down the grand central staircase.

She forced the images away, locking them out.

The butler turned into an open door.

"Miss Albright, my lord," he announced as she followed him in.

"Thank you, Mr. Manning," her father replied, his voice as rich and resonant as the toll of a great clock.

Mr. Manning bowed and showed himself out, leaving her alone with the earl.

The study was large. A row of tall windows looked across the east lawn. She could imagine the room must be exceptionally bright and warm in the mornings, an inference confirmed by the empty fireplace at her back.

The walls were covered in more rich wood, lined with bookshelves. The volumes that filled them were obviously there for reference, not for show. There were well-thumbed books on law, history, agriculture and finance beside tomes on philosophy and a complete collection of the works of Shakespeare.

A grand old desk held court in the center of the room. It was comfortably cluttered with stacks of papers, a half-finished cup of tea and a scattering of photographs in elegant little brass frames. She glimpsed the faces of a pair of mischievous young boys beside a pale-haired woman in an elegant gown.

Lord Torrington stood at the desk, clad in a tweed jacket with patches on the elbows, his feet tucked into a pair of loafers that looked well broken-in. The light from the windows brightened the thick silver of his hair.

"Would you like tea?" he asked.

"No, thank you."

A silence stretched across the room.

"How is Lord Deveral?" Lily asked.

"Cleared of all charges. Thanks to you."

"That was Mr. Ash's doing, not mine."

After Lily had told Strangford and the others the whole of how Hartwell and Waddington had managed their crimes, Ash had said simply that he would see to the details.

The details had turned out to be coordinating with law enforcement to confirm that a man matching Waddington's description had been admitted to the location of each of the murders, claiming to have come from the gasworks.

Of course, the gasworks had no record of any leak or of dispatching an inspector. When a search of Waddington's flat revealed a case of syringes and rubber tubing, any lingering doubt about the matter had been put firmly to rest—in time for Deveral's arraignment to be quietly canceled.

As for Hartwell, the world believed he had leapt from the roof of his asylum out of the shame of discovering he had been unwittingly harboring a murderer among his staff. His true part in the affair remained known to only a few.

It didn't matter. He was dead.

"You undervalue your role," Lord Torrington countered. He moved from behind the desk and paced to the window. He seemed uncomfortable, an emotion Lily suspected was rather rare for him. "You should not have had to come here," he said, looking out over the lawn.

The words stung. They shouldn't have. It was hardly a surprise that he thought that way. Lily shrugged, refusing to let it show. "I knew it would be safe."

"Safe?"

"That your wife would be out."

He stared at her as though shocked by her words. Lily pressed on, forcing a casual tone.

"You always came to us on Wednesdays. To my mother. Because that was when the countess made her social calls."

"You misunderstand . . ." He stopped, looking down. When he raised his head again, the lines on his face seemed deeper, as if he had grown older in that moment. "What I meant is that this visit should not have been necessary because I should have come to you. To thank you for what you did. And to apologize."

His words left her feeling even more unsettled, as though the ground were threatening to shift beneath her feet.

"There's no need for that." She looked away, hiding herself in a study of the Arcadian landscape beyond the glass.

"You came to me for help and I did not give it to you. That choice put you in the path of a great deal of harm."

"No," Lily snapped in reply. "It was my own choice that did that. Not yours."

He moved to the chair, dropped into it.

"I am arguing with myself," he muttered.

Something lurched in her chest. She ignored it. Turning to him, she cut to the core of the reason she had come.

"I know about the memo. The one Hartwell wrote to the War Office. The one you were copied on."

She waited for the impact of her revelation, of the accusation it implied.

"You read it?" he asked quietly.

"I read the reply acknowledging receipt. Saying how very interested the office was in the outcome of Hartwell's research."

The questions burned against her lips, demanding to be asked. How much had he known? How much had he condoned?

She kept them close. She would wait and see how he rose to the challenge she had thrown at him.

He stood and joined her by the window.

"A war is coming," he said from beside her.

The light shifted, a cloud momentarily obscuring the clear spring sunlight, casting its shadow across the idyllic landscape beyond the glass.

"Perhaps with Germany, though it might just as easily be Russia or even the Ottomans. It will be great, unlike anything we have fought before. More brutal. More terrible. There is no avoiding it, not by any possible scenario I have reckoned." He glanced over at her. "But perhaps you already knew that."

Lily remembered what she had seen. The vision of crouching in a hole cut into the cold, muddy ground braced with wood and barbed wire. The shaking, ear-splitting impact of artillery shells. How the world had exploded, Strangford torn from her in a blast of dirt and splinters.

A war.

"England will need every advantage she can muster to come out of it intact," he said, his voice low but steady. "We cannot afford to turn our backs on any option, no matter how far-fetched it might seem."

"No matter what it costs?" Lily countered.

"No," he countered clearly, firmly. "Cost must considered. That is what keeps us from becoming monsters."

"And what Hartwell's research would have cost? The lives of a few women?"

He looked at her, his gray eyes—so very like her own—shot through with regret.

"I didn't know. None of us knew. God help me, I thought he was a gentleman."

"Oh, he was a gentleman," Lily retorted.

She felt the blow hit, as it had been intended to. He went quiet beside her, the stillness stretching between them, tense as a bowstring.

"It would seem that I am perpetually failing you," he said.

Her throat caught. She looked away. Outside, the clouds shifted once more, light dancing across the spring-green fields.

The question that had been burning inside of her finally forced its way to her lips, spilled out into the room.

"Did you want me here?" she asked. "After my mother died."

"Yes," he replied simply. "I wanted that very much."

She felt the impact of the words. They hit with all the force of an artillery shell, shattering something inside of her.

"But you sent me away."

"I had a duty to my family."

"To your family," Lily echoed numbly. "Of course."

When he spoke again, his voice was rougher than it had been, more uneven.

"How could this have ever been your home, if they would not welcome you? If I'd brought you here in spite of them, you would always have been an outsider."

"Sending me away didn't change that."

He pressed his hand to the glass, his shoulders bowing.

"God help me, but I have made a mess of things. I wronged you, Lilith. I wronged my wife, my children. And yet I cannot regret it. Not for a moment."

She felt exposed, her senses sparking, sensitive to the point of pain. Part of her wanted to stop right here, walk away before the conversation could go any further, reveal more of what she both wanted and was desperately afraid to know.

Her own voice had grown rough.

"Because you loved her."

He looked at her, the grief written on his face.

"Because I loved both of you."

A spring shower burst over the great green lawn. The raindrops pelted against the small spring leaves, rattled against the window-panes. It was the sort of storm that would pass quickly, leaving newness in its wake.

He cleared his throat, moving over to his desk, rearranging some of the papers.

"I am returning to London next week, Tuesday at the latest. Perhaps we could . . ." His voice caught, halted.

She felt the space left by those unspoken words, that sudden, aching vulnerability reaching across the room.

She burst out, the words spilling from her, sounding as raw as they felt.

"I won't be anyone's secret."

The quick downpour rattled against the glass, tapping impatient fingers as he looked at her from across the desk.

"No," he said firmly at last. "Never be that."

The rain passed, fading into a spare few drops dancing on the wet blades of grass.

Her answer to the question he had not quite asked should have been harder to give. It should have involved more of a struggle within herself. But something had changed.

"Then perhaps we could," she replied quietly.

~

The coachman was wheeling the Triumph up from the garage as she stepped out the front door, the full freshness of spring after rain enveloping her. He stopped at the foot of the stairs and held the motorbike ready with a posture she suspected was nearly identical to the one he used to help dowagers into their Daimlers.

She climbed on, ignited the engine, and roared down the lime-lined drive of the estate. The air smelled of new mud, forest and the sea, the wind tossing the loose tendrils of her hair. She flew across the weald knowing that something fundamental had shifted, like a curtain thrown open on a view she had not known existed.

She throttled the Triumph up to speed and laughed.

# THIRTY-FIVE

$\mathscr{T}$HE LIGHT WAS TURNING golden over Bedford Square, casting a warm glow over the residents who strolled along the pavement or stood chatting on the bright green grass of the park.

Lily stopped the Triumph next to the wrought iron fence that lined the narrow front garden of her destination.

She should have come sooner. She knew that. She also knew that the inhabitants of the building before her were better equipped than anyone to understand why she hadn't.

No one here would judge her for needing time and space to come to terms with all that she had learned.

All that she had done.

She leaned the motorcycle against the rails and climbed the steps.

Automatically, she lifted her hand to rap on the rich blue paint of the door—then hesitated. Her eyes drifted to the small brass plaque mounted by the entrance, engraved with a series of Chinese characters.

She couldn't read them. She didn't have to. She knew what they said.

Instead of knocking, she lowered her hand to the knob. She turned it and the door swung open.

Lily stepped into the hall.

It was empty and quiet. The Ming vase stood on the narrow table in the entry, the bright orange goldfish swimming busily among a field of blue lotus blossoms. Beside it, the bust of Sir Isaac Newton watched her impassively.

A burst of bright, familiar laughter rang from the door to her right. Drawn toward it, Lily stepped into the library.

Estelle reclined in one of the armchairs. She was draped in her peacock blue caftan, a light gauze bandage wrapped around her throat. The rich hues of her turban stood out boldly against the subdued colors of the books that surrounded her.

She held a cup and saucer in her hands. As Lily entered, she took a break from laughing to sip her tea.

"It is not the least bit funny," Cairncross countered from the chair across from her.

"Of course it is," Estelle retorted.

"You mustn't mind her, Mr. Cairncross," Miss Bard cut in. She stood on the far side of the room, plucking a volume on Polynesian religions from the shelf. "She gets a bit giddy after her third cup of Darjeeling."

"This has nothing to do with tea and everything to do with envisioning James in his knickers, facing down an angry hippopotamus."

"They are extremely dangerous animals," Cairncross protested. "Especially when one's rifle is back on the beach with one's trousers."

Estelle snorted from behind her teacup. It struck Lily how impossible this moment should have been. Only a few weeks before, she would have believed—known beyond doubt—that this woman would be dead, lying cold in her grave.

Instead, she sat here in the warmth of the library, mercilessly teasing Cairncross and eliciting a wry little twitch of Miss Bard's lips.

It was not that Lily had been mistaken from the start about the import of her vision. That foresight of Estelle bleeding, pointing an accusing hand at some unseen threat, had meant her death. She knew that with a certainty that went beyond logic to someplace bone-deep and undeniable.

Between the vision and the moment the events it foretold came to pass in the world, something had changed. The context had shifted, turning a nightmarish end into the slimmest possibility of hope.

Because of Lily.

Because of the choice she made and the chances she took to achieve it.

*What if changing the future was never the point?*

It was the question Robert Ash had posed to her in the middle of Tottenham Court Road.

She thought of the painting upstairs, the powerful images drawn through the gift of a woman who had died years before she was born—of doors and keys and infinite possibilities.

Lily didn't know what her purpose was meant to be, but perhaps—just possibly—she was starting to guess.

"Miss Albright!" Cairncross called, spying her in the doorway. "I see you have been riding. And a lovely afternoon for it."

"Hello, Mr. Cairncross. Is Mr. Ash in?"

"He's off humming to himself," Estelle said, waving her hand dismissively.

"Meditating. In the sanctuary," Cairncross corrected. "You may wait here with us, if you like, though I'm sure he would not mind if you joined him."

"Thank you."

She left, another burst of cheerful laughter following her out.

At the end of the hall, she paused to pull off her boots, setting them down next to a pair of worn but well-polished brogues on the mat by the door. Then she slipped through the dark curtain into the quiet stillness of the sanctuary.

Silence blanketed the dimly-lit space. The air was cool, smelling of old wood and fresh water.

Ash, clad in a dark suit, sat in the center of the floor, legs crossed, his hands resting gracefully on his knees.

Lily lowered herself to the ground beside him, folding her body into a similar position.

She waited.

Her pulse was pounding. It was hard to remain still, to simply sit there while Ash continued to meditate.

She resisted the urge to twitch or tap her finger, ordering her body to submit to the notion of staying quiet for a few minutes.

The stillness settled around her. Her breath deepened, instinctively trying to take in more of that fresh, cool air. Something inside

of her shifted, the racing of both her thoughts and her heart beginning to settle.

The cause of her restlessness rose to the surface, revealed itself.

She was afraid.

She had no rational reason to be. Ash had already answered the
question she wanted to ask him, weeks ago. Yet so much had changed
since then. So much more was riding on what he said—the shape her
life would take from this moment on.

Exposed, the fear lost some of its edge. It became another facet of
the room, no more threatening than the wooden beams or the water
running through the channel in the floor.

Her leg tingled, starting to cramp. She resisted for a few moments,
then finally grimaced and, as slowly as possible, unfolded it and
stretched it out in front of her.

"How have you been, Miss Albright?" Ash asked.

From anyone else, it would have been just a common courtesy,
demanding a rote response. Not with Ash. Lily knew the inquiry was
genuine and invited the truth in response.

"I'm fine. Really."

"Do not be surprised if it comes back to you, in bad dreams or a feeling of panic that comes over you when you have no reason to expect
it. You have been through an extraordinary trial. It takes time for both
your body and your mind to recover from such an experience."

He spoke with a clear, simple certainty, and Lily found herself wondering if he'd won that knowledge himself, the hard way.

Her thoughts fell back to the vision, to the conversation she'd had
with Evangeline Ash as she stood, painting, in the attic of this house.

That exchange had not been a vision of the future, nor an echo of
the past, but something else—something she suspected had nothing
to do with her own power, but had been born instead in something
she didn't understand and perhaps never would.

Should she tell him? She considered it, aware of Ash's presence
beside her.

No. She suspected that wound was still raw, no matter that it was
thirty years old. He didn't need her reopening it. Besides, the message
had been for her and it had been received.

That was why she was here.

"May I ask you something?"

"Please," Ash invited calmly.

"When I came here before, you made an offer. You said you would help me learn more about what I am. What I can do. What that means. Does that offer still stand?"

"Yes, Miss Albright," he replied. "It stands."

She took a deep breath, an attempt to let the calming atmosphere of the room settle the rapid fluttering of her nerves.

"Then I accept."

The words were ordinary, but she felt their weight, the significance of the commitment they entailed.

Once, that had seemed impossible, even terrifying. Now it was as clear as anything in her life had ever been. She would learn. It would be hard, full of challenges and frustrations—but she would do it, because do to otherwise would be to deny who she was. She was done with that, forever.

She thought of everything she had done in those last weeks—the visions, the powers that had manifested in the house on the heath. They were faded now, only the faintest echo of what they had been. It didn't matter. Lily knew there was more where that came from, things she couldn't even guess at yet. It would take work to get there—a great deal of work, but she would come to know all of it eventually. The thought was both terrifying and exhilarating.

"When do we start?"

Ash considered. "Tomorrow morning. Six o'clock."

Lily laughed.

"Six o'clock? Do I need to be presentable?"

"Not in the least."

She hesitated, trying to think of the right thing to say. All that came to mind was the most obvious phrase. She just hoped he understood quite how much it meant.

"Thank you."

"You are very welcome, Miss Albright," he replied.

~

Outside the sanctuary, she tugged on her boots, then stopped, letting out a long breath.

She had done it, taken the first step. It felt far bigger than a few words exchanged in a dark, quiet room. Her senses tingled with excitement, her adrenaline flowing. She felt like she should be running or shouting something from a rooftop.

A clatter sounded from the far end of the hall, followed by the mingling of quick voices. Lily followed the sound down the stairs to the kitchen and stepped inside.

It was warm, the windows fogged with steam from the stove. The air smelled sweet and savory, of steamed rice and ginger.

Mrs. Liu clanged pans in the sink, running the tap. A man with graying hair sat at the table, a pouch of gardener's tools tied to his waist. He sipped a cup of tea, a plate of biscuits and a newspaper covered in foreign characters resting in front of him.

Sam approached the stove, plucking the lid from one of the pots simmering there. The housekeeper snapped at him in Chinese, tapping his hand with a wooden spoon.

The man at the table cut in with a quiet remark in the same tongue and Sam looked over to see Lily standing in the doorway.

He nodded toward the pot.

"She's got lotus seed buns in there. I can take one out without losing all the steam, Nǎinai," he promised Mrs. Liu.

"Three more minutes," Mrs. Liu retorted.

"Have you met my father?" Sam said, moving to the table. "Bà, this is Miss Albright."

"Very pleased to meet you," the gardener said in slow, even English, turning the page of his newspaper.

"Come on, this way." Sam pulled Lily through a narrow door into the pantry.

He hopped onto a stool and pulled a package wrapped in waxed paper from the top shelf. He unfolded the paper to reveal a box neatly-packed with some strange confection.

He plucked one from inside and tossed it into his mouth, then offered the box to Lily.

"Sugar melon. They're delicious."

"I'm sure they are." She paused, then pushed forward. "Sam . . . there's something I want to ask you."

"You're wondering about the ravens?"

He asked it as casually as he had offered the candy, sucking a stray bit of sugar from his finger.

She felt as though the shadow of a dark wing passed over the room.

"So it's true. That's how you knew where to find me."

He popped another treat into his mouth, then shuffled the neat rows in the box to hide the missing pieces. He re-wrapped it and tucked it back onto the shelf.

"I'd just nipped out for a smoke when that big blighter came up on me—he waited till I had the match in my hand to start croaking. Near burned myself. Can't say how it might've gone had he turned up any later. His lordship was ready to take down Hartwell's door, pull off the gloves and start reading everything in the house, with me and Cairncross set to beat off the peelers when they came to carry him off. Which would've gone swimmingly, I'm sure." He crossed his legs, leaning back against a shelf packed with jars of pickles, and looked away. "To be fair, I wasn't that far behind him."

His admission of concern tugged at something deep in her chest, as did his revelation about Strangford's state while she was missing.

"Thank you."

He shrugged.

"Anyway, you needn't worry about it. The ravens, I mean. You're all settled there."

She felt a chill.

"You mean they don't want me to pay?"

"Oh, no. Never that. But it's usually just one eye they ask for. You gave them four."

She thought of Northcote's scream as the gutter ripped away and he plunged to the ground.

The scrape of Hartwell's body against the snow as he slid across the slates . . . and before that, an officer sliding to the ground with a nail through his skull.

Three men sent to their deaths by her hand.

Each time, she had acted to save herself from the same fate or something even worse. She knew that to be true and yet the thought of those satisfied ravens set ice into her bones.

Sam pulled off his cap, scratching the back of his neck.

"They're happy enough with how it all came out. Said to let them know if you wanted to work with them again."

"I see." She reached out, setting her hand on his arm. "Thank you. For being there to hear them."

He shrugged.

"Weren't nothing."

"It was quite a bit more than that," she countered quietly.

She moved to the door. Sam's voice stopped her.

"He's out in the garden. If you were wondering."

Tension quickened inside of her, set her pulse fluttering. She looked back.

"Who would that be?" she asked, keeping her tone carefully even.

"Who'd you think?" he retorted, plucking an apple from a basket, tossing it into the air and neatly catching it.

~

She stopped in the hallway. To one side lay the front door and beyond it, her Triumph and the short ride back to March Place.

On the other side, set into the wall behind her, was the narrow wooden portal that opened into the garden.

She took a deep breath, then turned and opened the garden door.

It was late. The sun was beginning to sink, the garden painted with a mix of long shadows and splashes of deep, golden light. The shrubs and trees that had been blanked in winter stillness a few weeks before were now budding, sending up bright green tufts of new leaves. White and purple crocuses decorated the lawn, mingling with the verdant shoots of daffodils and red-tipped tulips.

There was a chill in the air, the last lingering bite of the season.

Strangford sat around the corner of a tall privet hedge. His hair looked longer, as though it had grown in the week since Lily had last seen him. It brushed at the collar of his dark wool coat.

His gloves were folded neatly beside him and his bare fingers brushed over the soft, barely-budded leaves of an elegant Japanese maple.

He spoke without looking up.

"Sometimes I just need to feel something other than the inside of my gloves."

"Something safe?" Lily offered, crossing the lawn to stand by the bench.

He paused, his hand going still.

"Nothing's entirely safe."

She sat down beside him.

"What do they feel like?"

He considered. A soft distance settled into his expression, the look she now recognized meant that his mind had gone somewhere else, running down his arm and through his fingertips into whatever he was touching.

"Fresh. A little surprised. As though they never expected to be here." His mouth twitched, a quick hint of a smile breaking through, and she was struck, deeply and undeniably, by how much she had come to love him.

There was so much she had yet to know about him. After only a few weeks, how could there not be? It didn't matter. She loved him—loved his kindness and his vulnerability, his loyalty and that remarkable sense of joy that stubbornly refused to give up, even in the face of unimaginable horror.

She had come so close to losing him. The pain of that was still sharp, tied up in the memory of what it had felt like to watch the roof of that burning warehouse come down. Even now, in the peace and calm of the garden, she could still see the raw red scar on his cheek, a visible reminder of how near he had come to death, and it set her pulse racing.

She didn't care anymore what the world thought, or of the artificial boundaries set by the vast difference in the circumstances of their birth. Running from her mother's history had only ever been an excuse, a way of keeping herself safe. But Strangford was right. Nothing was ever really safe. If she waited for safety before reaching out for the chance of joy, she would be waiting forever.

Yet so much had changed.

*It's usually just one eye they ask for. You gave them four.*

She stood, moving away, crossing to the budding branches of a dogwood tree.

"I'm sorry. That I didn't come sooner. I just . . ." The words failed her, leaving her throat dry.

"You don't have to explain."

She brushed her own fingers over the newly sprouting leaves. They were soft, kissed with the fading warmth of the sun.

"I never had a chance to tell you. When you fell back in the warehouse . . . how glad I am that you got out. That you left before . . ."

Behind her, he stood.

"Is that what you thought? That I left?"

She turned to face him.

"You must have. I saw that roof come down. Nothing could have survived inside that. Nothing."

He looked down at the bare skin of his hands.

"It was the oddest feeling. I'd taken the gloves off. They were wet. I was afraid they'd slip on the ladder as I was climbing. And there was this . . . humming. In the wood. The bones of the building crying out before they gave way. I felt it and I just . . . let go. Fell back down into the water and then swam as far as I could before I came back up for air. I made it all the way back out into the dock. Looked up and saw what had happened and . . . Damn it, Lily, I couldn't know if you had managed to get out, or if you were still inside, and there was nothing I could do but float out there and watch. Have you any idea what that feels like?"

"Yes."

He raised his head and met her gaze, only a brief stretch of green, rich garden separating them. Swallows fluttered through the branches overhead, the quick twitter of their calls dancing through the stillness of the falling afternoon. It was still and peaceful, and yet Lily felt the tension stretched between them so thick and real it seemed to vibrate in the air.

"Lily . . ." he began.

She cut him off.

"No. Please—let me say this before I get too frightened and bury it all again. I have made a great many mistakes over the last few weeks—over my life—but the ones tearing me apart are those I made with you. I am sorry that I pushed you away. That I locked you out of this and threw you all those pale excuses when you had the gall to ask why. Because the real answer is that I was terrified of how much you were coming to mean to me, and the only thing I have ever known to do when someone gets close to me is to run away. But I will not run from this any longer. Whatever it is—whatever it leads to—I am done running from it."

She stopped, letting the echo of those quickly-falling words fade. Her heart pounded as though it really were preparing her to turn and bolt out of the garden, just run out into the street and keep going.

But she didn't run. She stayed and let the fear pound through her, refusing to grant it control.

"It can't be easy," he warned, his own voice less than perfectly steady. "What kind of relationship can thrive with one side always knowing more than they should?"

"Not a level playing field," Lily said quietly, echoing the words he'd used back on that wind-swept clearing and feeling the quick pain of them strike through her.

He stepped forward, closing the distance between them.

"Not a level playing field," he confirmed. "But God help me, Lily, I want you anyway." He caught himself, reining in some powerful impulse. The tension simmered in him and Lily felt it echoed in her own body, a sparking, wild thing.

"It is damnably selfish of me," he continued, his voice hoarse, moving closer. "And if you choose to leave this garden right now, I will never think less of you for it."

"What I think . . ." Lily said slowly, meeting his gaze, "is that you should touch me."

The tension snapped. He raised a hand, fingers trembling, and—after drawing in a quick, full breath—brushed it across her cheek.

The sensation of it singed, electric, across her skin, setting her whole body tingling with awareness. His fingers slid into her hair, the fullness of his palm coming to rest against the bare skin of her neck.

"Oh . . ." he breathed, his pupils dilating, gaze shifting inward.

And then he laughed, an explosion of pure delight. Lily felt it echoing inside of her, spilling out into the light of the garden.

"May I kiss you now?" he asked, his eyes clear, present, locked onto her own.

"Yes," she replied.

And he did.

They came together and the colors became brighter, wilder, like to one of the canvases of his gallery, a place beyond past or future. A thousand undreamed possibilities opened before them—and Lily knew that she had come home.

# NOTES FROM THE AUTHOR

**See what's next for Lily and Strangford** in *The Shadow of Water*, book two of The Charismatics series, coming in Spring 2021 and available for pre-order now.

~

To **stay informed about other new releases**, sign up for Jacquelyn Benson's newsletter at <u>JacquelynBenson.com</u>. As a bonus for subscribing, you'll also get access to *The Stolen Apocalypse*, a free, exclusive novella featuring a young Lord Strangford.

~

**Please take a moment to rate or review** *The Fire in the Glass*. It's a simple thing that has a real and powerful impact for independent writers like myself.

# The Shadow of Water

COMING IN SPRING 2021

*The Charismatics continues with another historical fantasy
full of deadly mystery and arcane powers.*

Lilith Albright can see the future, and it looks like hell.

In an England at the brink of war, Lily is plagued by visions of a coming disaster—the cataclysmic destruction of the city she calls home.

An ancient prophecy is coming to fruition, presaged by the gruesome discovery of a corpse in London's sewers. The only hope of preventing Lily's nightmarish visions from coming to pass lies in uncovering the truth behind the murder.

To unravel a tangled web of conspiracy and violence, Lily will need the help of all of her fellow Charismatics—the men and women who know "the impossible things." That includes the enigmatic Lord Strangford, whose ability to see into the darkest corners of Lily's soul threatens to tear their relationship apart.

In a race from the gutters of the Limehouse and the champagne-soaked ballrooms of St. John's Wood, Lily exposes a plot that could bring the British empire to its knees. But changing fate and preventing an apocalypse will put Lily's charismatic powers to the ultimate test—and could cost her everything she holds dear.

*Get ready to return to the dark, mystical streets of Edwardian London once again by pre-ordering* The Shadow of Water *today at [Books2Read.com/TheShadowofWater](http://Books2Read.com/TheShadowofWater).*

# The Smoke Hunter

*Jacquelyn Benson's thrilling debut novel takes you on a race for the truth behind an ancient legend.*

Frustrated suffragette and would-be archaeologist Ellie Mallory stumbles across a map to a city that shouldn't exist, a jungle metropolis alive and flourishing centuries after the Mayan civilization mysteriously collapsed. Discovering it would make her career, but Ellie isn't the only one after the prize. A disgraced professor and his ruthless handler are hot on her heels, willing to go any extreme to acquire the map for themselves.

To race them through the uncharted jungle, Ellie needs a guide. The only one with the expertise is maverick surveyor Adam Bates. But with his determination to nose his way into Ellie's many secrets, Bates is a dangerous partner.

As Ellie gets closer to her goal, she realizes it's not just her ambitions at stake. A powerful secret lies hidden in the heart of the city—and if it falls into the wrong hands, it could shake the very fate of the world.

*Grab your copy now at Books2Read.com/TheSmokeHunter.*

# ACKNOWLEDGMENTS

There are many who need to be thanked for their part in this book. Howard Morhaim gave straight-talk and sage edits. Anna "Bruiser" Brown offered great advice on realistically getting your butt kicked—any remaining implausibilities in the fight scenes of this book are my own choice, not her lack of razor-sharp battle skills. My readers provided invaluable feedback on earlier drafts of this novel. This story is greater because of their contribution—so extend your gratitude to Chris Mornick, Sheri-Lynne Hinton, Mike Dunbar, Cathie Plante, Jasmin Hunter and Danica Carlson.

Cathie Plante gets additional props for her careful and elegant layout of the print and e-book editions of this work. With her brilliant eye and boundless creativity, Sara Argue is the only person I could imagine conceiving of the cover.

Of course, the greatest thanks goes to my wonderful Dan, whose patience with many late nights spent rattling a keyboard or talking his ear off over some tangle in the plot cannot be measured. Additional appreciation is extended to Tula and Henry for refraining from spilling juice on my laptop.

# ABOUT THE AUTHOR

 Jacquelyn Benson writes smart historical thrillers where strong women wrangle with bold men and confront the stranger things that occupy the borders of our world. She once lived in a museum, wrote a master's thesis on the cultural anthropology of paranormal investigation, and received a gold medal for being clever. She owes a great deal to her elementary school librarian for sagely choosing to acquire the entire Time-Life *Mysteries of the Unknown* series.

Her debut novel, *The Smoke Hunter*, was nominated for Best Historical Fiction by RT Times. When not writing, she enjoys the company of a tall, dark and handsome English teacher and practices unintentional magic.

If you'd like to be friends:

- **Join the email list on her website:** JacquelynBenson.com. You'll also get a free download of an exclusive novella, *The Stolen Apocalypse.*

- **Follow her on Bookbub:** BookBub.com/Authors/Jacquelyn-Benson and stay informed about deals and discounts

- **Follow her on Goodreads:** Goodreads.com/JacquelynBenson

- **Find her on social media:**
    **Instagram:** @jbensonink
    **Twitter:** Twitter.com/JBensonInk
    **Facebook:** Facebook.com/JBensonInk
    **Pinterest:** Pinterest.com/JBensonInk